THE NEXT TO DIE

The phone rang and Dayle grabbed the receiver. "Hello?"

"Dayle? It's Susan. I got your page. I'm on my way over. I'll be there in fifteen minutes if traffic allows. Is Estelle there with you now?"

"Yes. She's in the john," Dayle said, watching Sean wander toward the closed bathroom door.

"Fine. I'll see you soon." Susan hung up.

Sean turned to Dayle. "That dryer's been on for at least ten minutes...."

Dayle put down the phone. She rapped on the bathroom door. "Estelle?"

No answer. Dayle pounded on the door again. "Estelle? Can you hear me? Estelle!" She jiggled the doorknob. Locked. At the crack under the bathroom door, blood seeped past the threshold onto the beige shag carpet. "Oh, my God," she whispered.

Dayle threw her weight against the door. "Estelle!" Dayle kicked at the spot just below the doorknob until it finally gave. But the door didn't move more than a couple of inches. Something was blocking it—something heavy and lifeless.

Dayle peeked into the bathroom and gasped.

There was blood on the white tiled floor, leaking from a slice across Estelle's throat....

Books by Kevin O'Brien

ONLY SON
THE NEXT TO DIE

Published by Kensington Publishing Corporation

THE NEXT
TO DIE

Kevin O'Brien

PINNACLE BOOKS
KENSINGTON PUBLISHING CORP.

www.pinnaclebooks.com

PINNACLE BOOKS are published by

Kensington Publishing Corp.
850 Third Avenue
New York, NY 10022

All Kensington Titles, Imprints, and Distributed Lines are available at special quantity discounts for bulk purchases for sales promotion, premiums, fund-raising, and educational or institutional use. Special book excerpts or customized printings can also be created to fit specific needs. For details, write or phone the office of the Kensington special sales manager: Kensington Publishing Corp., 850 Third Avenue, New York, NY 10022, attn: Special Sales Department, Phone: 1-800-221-2647.

Pinnacle and the P logo Reg. U.S. Pat. & TM Off.

First Printing: May 2001
10 9 8 7 6 5 4 3 2

Printed in the United States of America

For my lifelong friends,
George and Sheila Kelly Stydahar

ACKNOWLEDGMENTS

Many people helped launch this book. I'm grateful to Mary Alice Kier and Anna Cottle—my agents, friends, and literary guardian angels. Another great big thank-you goes to John Scognamiglio, my editor at Kensington Books, who also happens to be a good buddy. And thanks to all my other pals at Kensington, especially Doug, Kate, and Amy.

Several friends and family members also helped me whip this novel into shape—either with feedback from reading early drafts or with ideas they allowed me to steal. My thanks and love go to Kate Kinsella, Dan Monda, George Stydahar, Doug Nathan, Wendy Orville, Dan Annear, David Buckner, and Bonny Becker.

For support and inspiration in my career, I want to thank Louise Vogelwede, Terry and Judine Brooks, John Saul and Michael Sack, and Julie Smart and all my friends from good old Adams News.

A special thank-you to my brother and four sisters, and my dear pal, Cate Goethals.

Prologue

Without having to wait, Jim Gelder secured a cozy window table in one of Portland's swankiest restaurants that Thursday night. If only the maître d' had sat Jim somewhere else, the thirty-two-year-old salesman from Seattle might not have met such a gruesome death.

Jim was good-looking, and he kept in great shape. He still weighed the same as he had in college: 170 pounds, perfect for his six-foot frame. His hair was usually slicked back with gel that made the straw color appear a shade darker. He had blue eyes, a strong jaw, and the kind of self-assured smile that drew people to him.

He felt lucky that Thursday night. His waitress was cute and friendly, a redhead in her early twenties. Amid the white tablecloths, candlelight, and polished silverware, she seemed like the only waitperson there without a snooty attitude. She even flirted a little when she delivered his tangueray and tonic. Jim had never been unfaithful to his wife, but he wasn't opposed to some innocent flirting—especially during lonely business trips like this one.

He poured on the charm every time the waitress returned to his table. After the meal, when she came by with his decaf, she brushed her hip against his shoulder. "You've been my favorite customer tonight—just thought you should know. Be right back with your check."

Smiling, Jim watched her retreat toward the kitchen, Just then, someone strode into the restaurant. Nearly everybody noticed him, but no one gawked; this was much too ritzy a place for the late dinner crowd to fuss over a movie star.

Tony Katz seemed smaller in person, not quite as brawny as he appeared on the screen, but every bit as handsome. Women just loved his wavy, chestnut-colored hair and those sleepy, sexy aquamarine eyes. Jim had heard that Tony Katz was in Portland, shooting a new movie.

He tried not to stare as the maître d' led Tony to a table next to his. Tony threw him a smile. Jim kept his cool and smiled back. Very nonchalant.

The maître d' left a menu at the place setting across from the film star. Jim hoped he'd get to see Tony's wife, Linda Zane, a model, whose appearance in a *Victoria's Secret* catalog last year was still etched in his brain. But Tony was joined by a balding, middle-aged man who must have been parking the car. He staggered up to the table, all out of breath, then plopped down in the chair. He wore a suit and tie. In contrast, Tony Katz had on a black turtleneck and jeans. He looked annoyed with the guy. "I'm having one drink with you, Benny, that's all," he grumbled.

"Okay, okay." The man took off his glasses and wiped them with the napkin. "Now, where were we?"

"I believe I was calling you a scum-sucking weasel," Tony Katz said.

Jim couldn't stifle a laugh, and this caught Tony's eye. The movie star smiled at him again. "Excuse me," he said to Jim. "Can I ask you something?"

Dumbstruck, Jim nodded. Tony Katz was actually talking to him.

"If you were a serious actor, what would you think of an agent who wanted you to star in a crappy movie sequel instead of a Tennessee Williams revival on Broadway?"

Jim shrugged. "I'd say he was a scum-sucking weasel."

"Benny, I think I love this guy." Tony gave Jim an appreciative grin.

Benny studiously ignored Jim and glanced at his menu. The waitress approached their table and told Tony how much she *absolutely adored* his latest movie. Tony politely thanked her and ordered a mineral water. His agent ordered scotch. For the next few minutes, the two of them argued quietly. Jim made it a point not to stare.

"Excuse me again, what's your name?"

Jim blinked at Tony Katz. "Who, me?"

"Tone, please," his agent whispered. "Listen to me for a sec—"

"I'm talking to my buddy here," Tony said. Then he smiled at Jim. "I didn't get your name."

"Um, I'm Jim Gelder."

"Mind if I join you, Jim?"

"Oh, now really, Tone," his agent was saying. "Don't be this way—"

But Tony Katz switched chairs and sat down across from Jim. He toasted him with his mineral water. "Thanks, Jim. I owe you."

Dazed, Jim laughed. "God, my wife isn't going to believe this."

Tony glanced over his shoulder at his agent friend. "Bye, Benny. I'm with my buddy Jim here. Take the car. I don't need it. Adios."

Benny pleaded, but Tony Katz ignored him. He was too busy

asking Jim where he was from, what he did for a living, and if he had any kids. To Jim's utter surprise, even after the agent defeatedly stomped out of the restaurant, Tony remained at the table. It was as if he genuinely cared. "No kids, huh?" Tony said, finishing his drink. "Me neither. Linda and I are thinking about adopting. But there's a lot to consider, y'know?"

Jim nodded emphatically.

"I mean, look at how everyone's staring at us. It's life in a fishbowl, and that's no way to raise a kid. Plus there are some real nutcases out there. Lately, I've been getting these strange phone calls—on my private line, no less. Death threats, real nasty stuff. Makes me think twice about bringing a kid into this world." He shrugged and sat back. "Anyway, it's nothing to dump on you. So—what are your plans for the night?"

"I don't really have any plans," Jim said.

"Great. Because I'd like to buy you a drink for being such a good sport. Only not here. It's too stuffy here. I know a place you might like."

The place was called Vogue Vertigo, at least that was where Tony told the driver to go once they climbed into the taxi. They settled back, and Tony slung his arm around Jim's shoulder—as though they were old pals. Jim was still in a stupor over this instant bond with the movie star. "I think you'll dig Vogue Vertigo," Tony said. "I hear this straight crowd is starting to take over. But that's mostly on weekends. I don't think we'll have to put up with them tonight. We'll see."

The driver studied them in the rearview mirror. Jim caught his stare, and he suddenly became aware of how the two of them must have looked together, huddled in the backseat, one guy with his arm around the other.

Chuckling, Jim grinned at those disapproving eyes in the rearview mirror. "Hey, bub, what are you staring at?" he asked. "Think we're queer or something? Do you know who you've got back here? This is Tony—"

"Shut the fuck up," Tony whispered.

Jim fell into a stunned silence. He recognized the cold, deadly tone. Tony spoke that way to characters in the movies seconds before blowing them away. He frowned at Jim, then slid over closer to the window.

They went on for three more blocks without saying a word. All the while, Jim tried to figure out what he'd done wrong. It seemed as if his instant friendship with the movie star had just as instantly expired.

"This is good right here, driver," Tony said, pulling out his wallet.

The taxi pulled up to the curb. Jim warily surveyed the neighborhood. He'd seen worse areas, but had never been dropped in the heart of one this bad—this late at night. Half of the stores looked as if they'd been shut down years ago, and the others didn't look long for this world. The cab stopped near a dark, cheesy little grocery store.

Climbing out of the taxi, Jim could barely make out the green neon VOGUE VERTIGO sign in the window of a squat brick building farther down the block. "Why didn't you let him take us right up to the place?" he asked as the taxi pulled away.

"Because you don't want to go in there," Tony replied. He pulled a cell phone from the pocket of his jacket. "Listen, Jim. I made a mistake. I'll get you a cab—*another* cab, and pay for your ride back. Our plans for tonight are kaput."

Tony switched on his phone, punched in some numbers, then cradled it to his ear. Apparently, he wasn't getting a dial tone. Frowning, he rattled the phone in his fist. "Damn it," he grumbled. "Battery's dead. You don't have a cell phone on you, do you?"

Jim shook his head. "Sorry. Listen, what's happening here? What's going on?"

"We'll have to use a pay phone in the bar," Tony said. "I didn't want to take you in there, because you'll probably freak out. It's a *gay* bar, Jim. I was wrong earlier. I don't think you'd like Vogue Vertigo after all."

"This place is a gay bar?"

"Bingo. Go to the head of the class." Tony started to walk toward the end of the block.

Jim grabbed his arm. "I don't get this. You're married to Linda Zane, for chrissakes, and you're gay? How could you be gay?"

"I'll tell you what James Dean said when someone asked him the same question. He said, 'I'm not about to go through life with one hand tied behind my back.' "

"What's *that* supposed to mean?" Jim stepped in front of him. "I still don't understand. What made you think I was gay?"

Tony sighed. "I thought you were good-looking. Seemed worth a shot. I was wrong. I'm sorry, okay?"

"But I told you, I'm married."

"There are lots of married gay guys, Jim," he replied. "I'm a movie star. Sounds callous, but married men are my safest bet. They don't talk. Now, I've already apologized, and I mean it, I'm sorry to have taken you out of your way." He gave Jim's arm a little punch. "So how about it? Do you think you can relax and be cool in this bar while I call you a cab? Or do you want to go on acting like an asshole?"

Jim stared at him for a moment, and realized he was arguing with *Tony Katz—who was gay.* His wife wasn't going to believe this. "I think I'll go on acting like an asshole," he replied, chuckling. "It's all right, I'll be cool. Still, can you blame me for being pissed? I mean, my one big chance to get it on with a movie star, and it's another guy. Just my luck."

Tony laughed, but suddenly he froze up and his smile disappeared. He stared at something beyond Jim's shoulder, and those famous aquamarine eyes filled with dread. The color left his face. "My God," he whispered. "Run. . . ."

"What?" Jim turned around. His heart stopped.

It happened so quickly. Jim hadn't even heard the minivan pull up behind him. Two men sprang out of the back. Both of them wore nylon stockings over their heads, the faces hideously distorted—like something out of a nightmare. One of the men had a gun.

Jim wanted to yell out, but he could barely breathe. As if paralyzed, he helplessly watched the two men descend on him. The one with the gun grabbed him by the scalp and jammed the .38 alongside his head. Jim felt the barrel scrape against his cheek, then dig into his ear. It hurt like hell, and he cried out with what little breath he had. Clenching a fistful of hair, the thug yanked his head back, until Jim thought his neck would snap. The guy ground the gun barrel into his ear. Jim felt blood drip down the side of his neck. He could barely hear his attacker barking at Tony: "Get in the van or I'll blow your boyfriend's brains out! Hurry!"

"Leave him alone!" Tony demanded. "If it's me you're after, I hardly know this guy. Let him go—"

The thug swung Jim around and threw him into the backseat of the van. Toppling onto the floor, Jim blindly reached for the door handle, then realized there was no door on the driver's side. No escape. Suddenly, Tony fell against him. He was unconscious.

Jim began to shake uncontrollably. He'd never been so scared.

Somebody climbed into the bench seat in back, then someone else jumped in front. Doors slammed, and the car started moving.

Wendy Lockett ran along the same trail through St. Helens Forest Preserve every morning before going to work at the bank. She had a Walkman blasting the Eurythmics' greatest hits and Cushman, her black Labrador retriever, keeping her company on that lonely path. It was a cold, drizzly Friday, and still quite dark in the heart of the forest.

Sweat rolled off her forehead, and Wendy's long brown

ponytail slapped against the windbreaker on her back. She approached the halfway point, a little clearing in the woods, where she usually turned around.

"Cushman, stick with me!" she called. The dog bolted ahead of her, then disappeared behind some bushes. "Cushman?" she called again, catching her breath. Annie Lennox still wailed in her ears. "Cush? Come here, buddy. . . ."

The Labrador was there for her protection. The thirty-three-year-old divorcee didn't go jogging in the forest at five-thirty in the morning without her dog—and a small canister of mace in the pocket of her track pants. Cushman had pulled this vanishing act a few times in the past—running after a squirrel or a deer—and Wendy hated it.

She slowed down to a trot, then pulled off the earphones. "Cush? Come here, boy!" she called. She felt so alone and vulnerable without her dog. She approached the clearing, then stopped suddenly. She thought she heard twigs snap, rustling noises. "Cushman?" she called in a shaky voice.

The dog answered with an odd, abbreviated bark.

"Where are you, boy?" As Wendy came into the clearing, she noticed several tire tracks in the mud. Then she realized why Cushman's response had been nothing more than a distracted grunt. He was too busy sniffing at something by the shrubs. From where she stood, it looked like a dead deer. "Cush, get away from there!" she called. "You heard me. . . ."

As Wendy stepped closer, she saw that bits of the animal's white flesh had been nibbled away by hungry forest creatures. Whimpering, Cushman repositioned himself to poke his snout at the poor thing from another vantage point. "Stop it, Cush! Stop that right now! Stop—"

Wendy choked on her words. The dead thing was a naked young man. He had flaxen blond hair, and his eyes were fixed open in a horrified grimace. Her dog lapped at the blood from a slash across his throat.

She couldn't scream, she couldn't even breathe.

Cushman backed away from the body. He let out a couple of barks. Something else had caught his interest. Wendy tried to call to him, but no words came out. She stood paralyzed in the forest clearing.

The dog trotted over to an oak tree and started sniffing. Tied to the trunk was another corpse, slouching against the ropes, now slack from hours of holding his deadweight. He'd been tortured and mutilated beyond recognition.

Wendy Lockett didn't know she was staring at someone she'd seen several times before—in the movies.

The Oregonian, Saturday, September 20

FILM STAR TONY KATZ MURDERED

The nude bodies of film actor Tony Katz, 35, and a male companion were discovered in a forest preserve in St. Helens, Oregon, on Friday morning. Both men had been beaten and repeatedly stabbed. St. Helens police are still searching for clues in the double murder that has been described by one witness as "ritualistic."

Katz's friend has been identified as James C. Gelder, 32, a salesman with Kingbee Diagnostics in Seattle. Katz and Gelder were last seen Thursday night outside a Portland gay bar, Vogue Vertigo. Katz had been shooting a film, "Gridlock Road," in Portland for the last three weeks.

The two bodies were discovered along a popular nature trail by Wendy Lockett of St. Helens, OR. Lockett, 33, said that the murders appeared to have been "some kind of cult killing.

"They were tied up," Lockett said. "It reminded me of pictures I've seen of lynchings of black people back in the thirties. These two were tortured. It was gruesome, an absolute nightmare."

> *Portland's Director of Citizens Against Hate Crimes, Vera Stutesman, announced her intentions to "thoroughly investigate if sexual orientation of the victims was a factor in these brutal murders."*
>
> *In the quiet community of St. Helens, citizens expressed shock and outrage over the double homicide.*
>
> *Katz's wife actress-model Linda Zane, 26, was unavailable for comment, but the couple's publicist, Shannon O'Conner, issued the following statement: "Tony Katz was one of our finest, most talented actors. He was a loving, devoted husband, and a thoughtful humanitarian, who gave his time and talent to several charities. His terrible murder is a shock to us all . . ."*

Linda Zane made only one public appearance in the wake of her husband's death. A bodyguard accompanied Linda to Tony's memorial service. Two hours later, she boarded a private jet to Greece, destined for the secluded villa of a millionaire friend.

Over two dozen "protesters" also showed up at the funeral. Picketing outside the church, they carried signs that declared TONY KATZ BURNS IN HELL, and GOD HATES FAGS. Some protesters bought their children along.

Jim Gelder's widow told reporters that her husband wasn't a homosexual. But everyone already had him labeled as the boyfriend of Tony Katz, so her claims fell on deaf ears. Tony's agent, Benny Gershon, insisted that the two men couldn't have been romantically involved, because they'd met for the first time just hours before the murders. No one believed him. After all, Benny also swore up and down that his famous client wasn't gay.

Several quickie paperback biographies of Tony Katz were thrown together in the wake of his death, and two networks announced different forthcoming TV movies about Tony and his "secret life."

Despite having earned two Academy Award nominations during his brief yet distinguished career, and despite his devotion to several charities, Tony would always be most remembered for the bizarre, shocking death that exposed him as a homosexual.

At 7:13 P.M., Saturday, September 27, the following Internet dialogue appeared on the Dog Lover's chat line:

COOKIE'S MOM: My 18 yr old schnauzer, Cookie, has bad arthritis & is now going blind. The vet sez I should think about putting her to sleep. Anyone else out there ever had to do that to their dog? Can't imagine killing Cookie.

PAT: It's for the best . . . keeping her alive would be cruel.

SPARKLE'S OWNER: i've had to say goodbye to 2 other doggies that way—it isn't easy—B brave.

RICK: Sorry about Cookie . . . Request Private Chat w/ Pat.

Dialogue from a private mailbox, between "Rick" and "Pat," at 7:15 P.M., Saturday, September 27:

PATRIOT: What's up?

AMERICKAN: Re: Portland job last week . . . Congratulations to you & your team . . . Updating you on plans for L.S., like old Cookie, that black bitch needs to be put to sleep . . . Will B another Portland job . . . Details to follow . . . God Bless U . . . SAAMO Lieut. signing off.

One

"Stay tuned for *Common Sense* with Elsie and Drew Marshall!"

The tiny portable television was propped up on the desktop of a young film executive. Dennis Walsh was thirty years old, chubby but handsome with dark blond hair, dimples, and a killer smile. Despite his girth, he wore clothes well and had an Ivy League look uncommon in southern California: oxford shirts, pleated pants, and penny loafers.

At the moment, Dennis paid little attention to the TV. Instead, he was updating his Franklin Planner and getting ready to see his boss. Helena, his assistant, wandered in and tossed a fax on his desk. "God, Dennis," she said, frowning at the TV. "How can you watch that garbage?"

"It's time for a little *Common Sense!*" the TV announcer boomed, over a swelling of patriotic music. "Ladies and Gentlemen, Mrs. Richard Marshall!"

He sighed. "Well, I don't have any passion in my life. So I have to settle for hating Elsie Marshall."

"We need to find you a girlfriend soon." Helena slipped out of his office.

"Hello, everybody!" chirped the woman on TV. Sixty-five years old, slim, blond, and rather pretty, she looked and dressed like a Republican First Lady. "God bless you!" she said, waving to her studio audience. Then she looked into the camera. "I'm Mrs. Richard Marshall, but you can call me Elsie."

"Hi, Elsie!" her studio subjects chanted.

She wandered back to the set: a desk in front of a bookcase, crammed with copies of *A Little More Common Sense*, the second best-seller by Mrs. Richard Marshall. All the covers were turned forward, of course. On her desk sat a framed photo of her late husband, also turned forward. There were two easy chairs, one reserved for her guest—usually a politician, washed-up film star, or retired sports figure. The other easy chair belonged to Elsie's son and cohost, Drew, the real force behind the show. Handsome and articulate, thirty-year-old Drew brought in younger viewers and seemed groomed for future presidency, a beacon for fundamentalism in the twenty-first century. Drew gave his mother the first ten minutes of every show, then strolled onto the set to claim his chair and the remainder of the program.

Presently, Elsie Marshall basked alone in the spotlight. "I almost didn't make it out of the house this morning," she said, sitting at her desk. "All my recycling bins are by my back door. I knocked over the cans, and, oh, what a mess! Cans everywhere! Am I the only housewife in America who's fed up with recycling? Those bleeding-heart ecologists make you feel like Attila the Hun if you so much as toss an old newspaper in the trash. Do our forests really need saving that badly?" She frowned. "Oh, and speaking of forests, isn't it a pity what happened to Tony Katz and that other young man?"

The studio audience murmured an affirmative.

Dennis glanced at the TV and sighed. "Oh, shit."

"But I'll tell you what's even more of a pity," Elsie went

on. "And I'm sure if my Ricky were alive today, he'd tell you the same thing. The real pity is that Mr. Katz and his—you know, *friend*—decided to carry on the way they did in the middle of a forest preserve. Can you imagine?

"Certain segments of the population gripe that they're victimized. But what do you expect when they're fornicating—if you'll pardon me—in parks, public rest rooms, and movie theaters? I think it's sad what happened to Tony Katz and his friend, but sometimes people bring these things on themselves. . . ."

"Christ on a crutch," Dennis grumbled, pulling away from his desk.

Clipboard in hand, he hurried out of his office, down the hallway, and out of the climate-controlled building. A gust of warm air hit him. Dennis put on his sunglasses. His boss was filming in a soundstage around the corner.

He'd be back in time to catch the end of Elsie's show. Watching the program was a true masochistic experience. For three years, Elsie and Ricky Marshall had had a syndicated half-hour talk show, expounding their ultraconservative values. They peppered their dialogue with cutesy, domestic chatter and good-natured bickering. Their popularity grew and grew. Then Ricky dropped dead of a heart attack. Elsie carried the banner, but the show's ratings sagged until Drew came aboard as cohost. The mother-son raillery became a crowd pleaser. America's Most Eligible Bachelor, Best-Dressed Man, Sexiest Hunk was smart enough to know his mother still held a big influence over their audience. The sweet old widow with "common sense" could get away with those cutting remarks about a murdered homosexual actor, but Drew might not fare as well. So at times, she was his mouthpiece. Elsie attacked anything and anyone who didn't fit in with The Marshalls' idea of American family values. She even made a list of celebrities whose films or TV programs "ought to be missed by decent people."

Dennis Walsh's boss was on that list.

The soundstage door's red light wasn't on, which meant they'd taken a break in filming. Dennis stepped into the vast hall, threading around all the sound equipment, cameras, cables, and lights. "Is Dayle in her trailer?" he asked one of the camera operators.

"Yep, working on her wardrobe," he said, between gulps from a Mountain Dew can.

Dennis thanked him and headed for the trailer in the corner of the soundstage. On the door was a plaque: — DAYLE SUTTON — ENTER AT YOUR OWN RISK. Dennis knocked and entered.

Inside the dressing room trailer, Dayle Sutton stood with her arms outstretched as if crucified. Two middle-aged women were sewing a white satin evening gown on her. She felt them pinch and tug the material around her ribs. "Can't be tight enough," Dayle cracked. "I'm still breathing."

She was filming a drama based on a best-seller, *Waiting for the Fall*. Today's scene involved a flashback sequence, in which the thirty-nine-year-old actress had to look twenty without the benefit of extra filters on the camera lens. Dayle was up for the task. Besides, she had good lighting men.

She also had a good man in Dennis Walsh. He was a production assistant with the studio, and had worked with Dayle on her last picture. He'd become indispensable. He talked to Dayle's agent more than she did, acted as liaison with every department in the studio, and even reviewed story ideas and screenplays for her. That was why Dennis had come to her studio trailer now. He sat on the couch by Dayle's dressing table, and unwrapped a Tootsie Roll. "Ready for the pitch?" he asked, glancing at the clipboard in his lap.

"Fire away," Dayle said, arms still spread out like a regal scarecrow. Along with the 1950s gown, she also wore a long blond wig.

"You're the First Lady, and you begin to suspect the president is really an imposter, because he starts acting different with you. And the things he does are more radical and dangerous until the world is on the brink of nuclear war.''

"Sounds like *Dave* meets *Suspicion* meets *Fail Safe*," Dayle said.

"Exactly. It's a thriller."

"I hate it."

"So do I," Dennis said. "But I figured you wouldn't mind playing a First Lady who defies her husband and saves the world from nuclear destruction."

"Next?"

"Okay, this one's a true story," Dennis said. "It's about a guy who gets attacked outside a gay bar. Four college frat boys try to beat him up—"

"Don't tell me," Dayle said, watching the seamstresses work on her sleeves. " 'Ripped from today's headlines,' shades of Tony Katz."

She'd met Tony only twice: first at a fund-raiser, and again when they'd been paired up as Oscar presenters last year. Dayle had found him charming and sexy. He was also extremely active in campaigns against discrimination and censorship. Everyone in Hollywood knew Tony was gay. His marriage to Linda Zane was a smoke screen. But he was so well liked, no one wanted to see his cover blown. His horrible death changed all that. Nobody talked about Tony Katz, the actor; they only talked about Tony Katz, the closet homosexual who was killed with his pants down.

Dennis snacked on his Tootsie Roll. "According to 'Just call me Elsie,' " he said, between chews, "Tony and his friend brought it all on themselves. How about that? God, I would love to punch that old gasbag's lights out."

"Yeah, well, take a number," Dayle said, lowering her arms a bit for circulation. "Anyway, about the movie, is there a part for me?"

"Yes, indeedee," he said. "See, the guy kills one of his

attackers—cuts a frat boy's throat with a broken beer bottle. So believe it or not, they put him on trial for murder. He hires this lesbian attorney to defend him, and after a lot of opposition in this small, affluent college town, she gets this guy acquitted. It's an old script that's been floating around, but Soren Eberhart wants to direct, and Avery Cooper's interested in playing the gay guy."

"*Philadelphia* meets *The Accused*," Dayle said. "And you want me to play a lesbian lawyer? Next, please."

"Why are you passing?"

"Two words," Dayle replied. "*Survival Instincts*."

That was the title of her ill-fated action-thriller. Dayle had played the leader of an environmentalist group, stalked in the wilderness by a team of crazed hunters. As the lean, mean, no-nonsense heroine, Dayle had given her sexually ambiguous character some lesbian undertones. She'd been a bit too convincing. It set people wondering about the lack of chemistry between Dayle Sutton and her last few leading men. Despite good reviews, the film came and went, but the wild rumors about Dayle's private life prevailed.

"*Survival Instincts* was a couple of years ago," Dennis said. "Middle America just wasn't ready for you as a butch-female action hero—"

"Huh, *Rambimbo*," Dayle muttered, rolling her eyes.

"Attitudes have changed. It's not so taboo to play a lesbian anymore. And this is a primo part for you—"

"Next, Dennis," she said, an edginess in her voice.

Dennis sighed, then tossed what was left of his Tootsie Roll in the wastebasket. "Okay. Not your cup of Liptons." He checked his clipboard. "Last but certainly least is a zany comedy. You and another star—Bette Midler, if somebody puts a gun to her head—are mothers, each with teenage daughters giving you loads of trouble. Turns out the gals were switched at birth."

"Imagine that," Dayle said.

"There's madcap high jinks galore as you adjust to your real daughter and some heart-tugging moments as you miss that little hellion you've come to love now that she isn't yours anymore."

"Stop before I throw up. It'll probably rake in a fortune. You may shoot me if I ever show interest in a project like that. Anything else?"

Dennis consulted his clipboard again. "Messages worth mentioning—you had a call from Leigh Simone this morning."

Dayle turned to glance at him. "Really?"

A call from Leigh Simone was pretty heady stuff. The vibrant, black rock artist was the kind of superstar even other stars admired. Already a legend, she'd been dubbed The High Priestess of Rock.

"We're almost done here, Ms. Sutton," one of the wardrobe women said. "You can lower your arms now."

"Thanks, Pam," Dayle let her tired arms drop to her sides. She gave Dennis a nonchalant look. "So—did the call come from Leigh herself?"

"No. From her personal assistant, Estelle. She wants to know if you're available next Thursday night. I checked, and you are. Leigh has a concert in Portland. She's donating the profits—speak of the devil—to one of Tony Katz's favorite charities. Leigh wants you to read a tribute to him."

Dayle frowned. "Why me? I met Tony only a couple of times. That hardly qualifies me to give his eulogy at some benefit."

"In Hollywood it does. Besides, this is a worthwhile cause, and publicitywise, it wouldn't hurt to share a stage with rock's high priestess."

"I'll have to think about it," Dayle said. "Listen, I could use some time alone here. Are we almost finished, Pam?"

"All done, Miss Sutton."

"Hallelujah." She smiled at the seamstresses, then turned

to Dennis. Her smile slipped away. "Knock when they need me on the set, okay?"

"Will do." He and the two wardrobe women headed out the trailer door.

"Damn," Dayle muttered, now alone. She felt as if she were suffocating. She wanted to strip off the tight gown and yank the blond wig from her head. Maybe then she'd breathe easier.

She hated feeling so afraid. It clashed with the image she'd built up for herself: Dayle Sutton, the strong, sexy, intelligent actress. Sixteen years ago, when she'd first started making movies, Dayle had fought against playing glamour girl roles. She had to prove that she was more than a pretty girl with a head of long, wavy auburn hair and the body of a centerfold. An Academy Award helped earn her respect—and superstardom. *Playboy* labeled her "The Thinking Man's Sex Symbol." Back in the late eighties, she'd refused an offer to appear on their cover in a skimpy bunny suit.

But a year ago, *Vanity Fair* seemed to fulfill Dayle's longtime wish by calling her "Down to Earth Actress, Dayle Sutton." The epithet was emblazoned at the bottom of an Annie Leibovitz cover photo of Dayle up to her shoulders in a mud bath. It was a provocative pose, sexy and smart.

That had been before the tepid box office of *Survival Instincts*—and all those rumors that she was gay. Not only had Dayle's career suffered, but she'd also incurred the wrath of several anti-gay groups. Plus the film's depiction of hunters had outraged the gun advocates. Dayle had received stacks of venomous hate mail—and dozens of death threats. She'd made a great show of nonchalance, but it had been a scary time.

In a way, the short life of *Survival Instincts* in the theaters and video stores was a blessing. The gun lovers and the gay haters quickly found other targets for their animosity, and Dayle was able to breathe easier.

She wasn't ready to set herself up as a target again by playing this lesbian lawyer character. Social conscience be damned.

What happened to Tony Katz was a startling reminder of how far some people could go with their intolerance. The same fate might have befallen her when *Survival Instincts* had opened. In an ironic way, old Elsie Marshall was right. Perhaps Tony had bought his death upon himself. Though married, he refused to change his lifestyle or avoid controversy. He wasn't afraid of pissing people off.

And he should have been. What was the old saying? *The braver the bird, the fatter the cat.* She had good reason to be scared.

Still, Dayle didn't like herself very much right now. She remembered back when she was a child, all those times making believe she was somebody else. It was one reason she became an actress—to escape from that scared, lonely little girl inside her.

There was a knock on her trailer door, followed by Dennis calling that she was due on the set.

"Thank you, Dennis!" she called, her eyes closed. Dayle emerged from the trailer. Stepping over cables, she strolled onto the set: a hotel veranda, overlooking a seascape—to be provided later with back projection. For now, Dayle's stand-in, Bonny McKenna, waited on the fake balcony in front of a blue screen. Dressed in a white gown and donning a blond wig, she drank a Diet Coke. She grinned at Dayle, and offered her the can of pop.

"You're a lifesaver." Dayle took a sip from Bonny's straw.

Four years younger, Bonny was Dayle's mirror image—only not quite as beautiful, like the kid sister who didn't quite match up to her gorgeous sibling. Bonny had been a policewoman for several years, and was married to a cop. The star and her stand-in were best friends on the set. Bonny stepped behind Dayle and massaged her shoulders. "God, you feel tense," she whispered. "You okay?"

"Just peachy." Dayle sighed, "Oh, that feels like heaven. Don't stop."

"Quiet on the set!" someone yelled. "Places!"

"So much for not stopping," Bonny said, pulling away.

Dayle handed her the Diet Coke. "Thanks anyway." Stepping on her mark, she took a deep breath. The man with the clapboard announced the scene and take. The cameras began to roll. Then Dayle Sutton became someone else.

Dayle chose her black silk pantsuit with the big rhinestone buttons for the Screen Legends Salute tomorrow night. She would be a presenter. *People* magazine ran a photo of her last year in this suit when they put her on their Best Dressed list. *Understated elegance.*

She hung the pantsuit, still in its dry cleaning bag, on her closet door for tomorrow morning. She'd change at the studio, have her hair and makeup done there, then go to the event. A long day ahead.

Dayle took another sip of Cabernet, finishing off the glass. "Let's go, Fred," she told the short-hair gray tabby lying at the foot of her bed. He was named after Federico Fellini. She didn't trust him alone around the silk suit. He'd start clawing at that plastic bag the minute her back was turned. "C'mon, babe," she called, strolling toward the kitchen with her empty glass.

Sometimes late at night when she couldn't sleep, she'd pour a verboten brandy, then wander around her beautiful penthouse and admire what she'd done with the place. The apartment had been featured in *Architectural Digest* a few years ago: her spacious living room had a fireplace and a panoramic view of Los Angeles; in the dining room, an ornate inlaid cherry-wood table seated twenty; her study held a large antique desk and volumes of books, which The Thinking Man's Sex Symbol had read. She'd carefully chosen the artwork for these rooms, including two original Hopper paintings, a small Monet, and a Jackson Pollock. The art piece that most fascinated the *Archi-*

tectural Digest people was a glass-top pedestal in her living room. It held her Academy Award. The base and stem of the pedestal had been forged from several pairs of broken and tattered high heels wired together to create a swirling funnel effect. Dayle had worn out all those shoes walking from auditions to agencies during her struggling starlet days. "I saved them, knowing I'd do something with them one day," she told the interviewer.

The magazine layout also included photos of her private exercise room and the modern kitchen. But they weren't allowed to take any pictures of the large, informal pantry and TV room area off the kitchen. This was where Dayle let herself relax, where she snuggled up with Fred in her lap to study a film script, or indulge in some low-fat microwave popcorn and a good video. Of the four fireplaces, the one in this room was used most. The best view came from this picture window: a sweeping vista of the Hollywood hills. The walls were decorated with framed photos of herself with other celebrities and a few of her better magazine covers. It was the only room in the place where she felt comfortable putting her feet up on the furniture. The other rooms were for entertaining. This one was for friends and family. But Dayle had spent the majority of her time in this cozy room alone with Fred. Thank God for the cat.

She poured a half glass of wine, sank back on the sofa, and let Fred curl up in her lap. Dayle reached for the remote and switched on the TV. The news came on. The anchorwoman was talking about a Fullerton couple who had died in a boating accident. Then the picture switched to what looked like a protest demonstration.

"Two weeks after the deaths of Tony Katz and James Gelder, a special memorial service was held in Seattle, Washington, for Gelder, the thirty-two-year-old 'other victim' in the still-unsolved double murder," the newscaster announced.

Dayle stared at the TV, and a line of demonstrators marching in front of a church. There were about a dozen of them, and they held anti-gay signs, the same FAGS BURN IN HELL slogans brandished for Tony Katz's funeral. In fact, according to the anchorwoman, this demonstration had been organized by the same minister who had masterminded the protest at Tony's memorial.

"Assholes," Dayle muttered, shaking her head at the TV.

"I'm grieving my brother's death right now, and I don't need to see this," James Gelder's older brother told a reporter outside the church. He was a handsome man in his mid-thirties, impeccably dressed in a dark suit. Behind him, the demonstrators waved their signs. "It's wrong," the surviving brother went on. "Jimmy was happily married. He wasn't gay. He doesn't deserve this."

"Oh, so if he was gay, he'd deserve it?" Dayle growled at the TV. She wasn't mad at him—really. All of it was so wrong. Frowning, she grabbed the remote, switched off the TV, and got ready for bed.

While brushing her teeth in front of the bathroom mirror, she glared at her reflection. "Gutless," she said to herself. Was she going to let malignant morons like that minister and those idiot protesters scare her? How could she allow them to influence her career choices? If anything, she wanted to defy them.

Dayle rinsed out her mouth, marched down the hall to her study, and switched on her computer. The film star was dressed for bed in a very unglamourous, extra-large man's T-shirt. She clicked on to e-mail and sent the following message to Dennis Walsh:

Hey, Dennis:
   I've been rethinking the Portland benefit. Tell Leigh Simone I'd be happy to participate.

Dayle bit her lip, and quickly typed the next part and sent it before she had time to change her mind:

Also, I might have been too hasty on that gay-bashing trial story. Tell Soren Eberhart that I'd like to see the script, especially if Avery Cooper is coming aboard. Keep your powder dry, kiddo. See you in 7 hours.
     —D.

Dayle Sutton didn't know that she'd just written her own death warrant.

Two

"I'm definitely interested if Dayle Sutton's interested," Avery Cooper grunted between push-ups on the floor of his trailer. He was talking on the speaker phone to his agent, Louise.

"The script's a little dog-eared, but they're rewriting it. With Soren Eberhart at the helm and Dayle Sutton starring, you're in great company." Louise paused. "By the way, what's with all the huffing and puffing? What are you doing? Or shouldn't I ask?"

"I'm doing my crunches," Avery said, sitting for a moment to catch his breath. The shirtless thirty-four-year-old actor worked hard on his taut physique. Yet fans considered Avery Cooper more "cute" than "hunky." The handsome, blue-eyed former TV star never made anyone's Sexiest Man Alive list. Still, he possessed a sweet, beguiling, nice-guy appeal that made him enormously popular during the five-year run of his hit TV sitcom. Those same qualities had landed him a role as the hapless hero who comes to the aid of a hooker in danger, played by America's new sweetheart superstar, Traci Haydn.

The film was called *Expiration Date,* and he had one more week shooting here in Vancouver, British Columbia (doubling for Seattle), before they returned to the Hollywood studios for interior shots. Avery couldn't wait to get home.

"Devil's advocate time," Louise announced. "You ought to consider the possible backlash to playing this gay man. You just had a controversial role. Maybe you should play it safe for a while."

"Do you mean that, Louise?"

"Not a syllable, but I had to say it for the record."

Avery smiled. He loved Louise. She'd been his agent for nine years. She understood him. "This is a good part, Avery," she said. "But you can make some enemies. The network says you're still receiving poison-pen letters for the TV movie last month."

The film, called *Intent to Kill,* tapped into Avery's nice-guy image. He played a doctor, paralyzed after being gunned down by protesters outside an abortion clinic. The controversial "network event" won him critical raves—along with piles of hate mail, even some death threats.

Avery got to his feet and grabbed a couple of thirty-pound dumbbell weights. "A lot of the letters were very supportive," he pointed out.

"And a lot of them were damn scary," Louise said.

Someone knocked on the trailer door. "C'mon in," Avery called.

Bob, a studio gofer, stepped into the trailer, and set a package on the sofa. "This arrived for you special delivery a little while ago, Avery. Looks kind of personal. I don't know."

Avery put down the weights. "Great. Thanks, Bob."

Bob ducked out of the trailer, not closing the door entirely.

"What did you get?" Louise asked over the speaker phone.

"I don't know yet," Avery said, reaching for the box. He tore off the brown wrapping. "There's no return address."

"Well, wait a minute!" Louise barked. "What if it's a letter bomb or something? You already have all these nuts wanting you dead. Wait—''

"Too late, Louise," Avery said. The box bore a Ralph Lauren polo insignia. He set the top aside, parted the folds of tissue paper, and found a card resting on a gray hand-knit sweater.

"What it is?" Louise asked.

"It's a sweater that must have cost a few hundred bucks." Frowning, Avery read the card insert. "Here's what the enclosure says: *I bet it's cold up there in Canada. Thought you'd need this. Love, Libby. P.S. Did you like the tie? Why haven't I heard from you?*"

"My Lord," Louise muttered. "She just won't give up, will she? You're too nice. You should let me or someone from the studio write and tell her in a polite way to piss off."

The sweater was the most recent in a long line of gifts Avery had received from an obsessive woman named Libby Stoddard, who claimed to be his biggest fan. She'd sent the first present a year ago, a book on Bob Hope, because Avery had said in an interview that he was a sucker for old Bob Hope movies. He thanked Libby in a letter and included an autographed glossy. She thanked him right back with a video of *Son of Paleface*. After that, her presents became more extravagant. Avery started sending them back. He stopped enclosing "No Thank You," notes with the return packages, figuring they fed something in her. Shortly before Avery had left for Vancouver, he got a call at home, and was stunned to hear a woman on the other end of the line say, "I can't believe I'm actually talking to you! This is Libby."

He probably should have hung up on her right away, but he was stupid enough to think he could talk sense to her. "Um, hello," he managed to say. "How did you get my home number?"

She laughed. "I hired someone to find out for me, that's all. I have a lot of money, you ought to know that from the presents I send. This is so neat! How are you, Avery?"

"Well, ah, Libby, I'm—not too happy about this call. I know you're probably a really nice person, but this is an invasion of my privacy. The gifts you've sent are very generous, but—"

"I thought for sure you'd keep the aviator jacket. It cost a lot."

"I'm sure it did. That's why I sent it back to you. This has to stop. I can't have you buying me all these clothes—"

"But I want to. . . ."

"Well, what you're doing borders on harassment. And I don't think that's your intention."

"What do you mean?" she asked, in a hurt little-girl voice. "Is your wife there? Is that why you're saying these things? Should I call back later?"

Avery took a deep breath. "I'm asking you not to call me or send me any more gifts. I'm sure your intentions are good, but—"

"I can't believe you'd be this ungrateful," she said. "I must have caught you at a bad time. Listen, it's okay. I'll call back later—"

"No—"

"Don't worry, I still love you, Avery." Then she hung up.

Avery had left for Vancouver two days later. There had been several hang-ups on his answering machine during those forty-eight hours. His caller ID showed seven of those calls were from "L. B. Stoddard: 555-1939."

Now she'd discovered the film location address here in Vancouver. Avery stared at the sweater. "Christ," he muttered. "Think she'll ever give up?"

"Highly doubtful," Louise said. "I told you last year when you left the show—you need someone to run fan interference. The network did it for you for five years. You can't be Mr. Nice Guy all the time, Avery. Let me handle this Libby character, okay? I'll have my assistant, Nola, send her a very officious letter telling her to knock it off."

"I guess you better." Avery set the Ralph Lauren box on the sofa.

At that moment, someone stepped into the trailer. "Hey, nice . . ."

Avery looked up and caught Traci Haydn leering at him. The twenty-seven-year-old ash blonde with an angel's face was smoking a cigarette. Her breasts stretched her blue T-shirt to its fiber limit. The shirt barely came down over her rib cage, exposing her toned belly and a gold ring piercing her navel.

"Traci, hi," was all Avery could say.

"Where have you been hiding that bod, Avery?"

She tossed her cigarette outside, then shut the door. "Is there a no-shirts policy in this trailer?" she asked. Then with a giggle, she shucked the tiny T-shirt over her head.

Avery backed into his dressing table. "Jesus, Traci . . ."

A bobby pin must have come out when she tossed off the shirt, because some of the blond hair fell over her eyes, and Traci looked damn sexy. But he loved his wife, and this woman was trouble.

"Traci, put your clothes back on. There are people outside—"

Sauntering toward him, Traci grinned. "If the trailer's rockin', they won't come knockin'."

"Lord, did I hear her right?" Louise asked over the speaker phone. "Did she really just say that?"

"What the fuck?" Traci's playful grin vanished.

"Traci, I'm on the speaker phone with my agent," Avery explained. He ran a hand through his wavy black hair. "Um, do you know Louise Farrell?"

"Hi, Traci," Louise piped up.

Traci Haydn rolled her eyes, then deliberately stepped up to Avery. Those firm, beautiful breasts rubbed against his sweaty chest. She stood on her tiptoes, and her nipples grazed his. "I'm going to get you, one way or another," she whispered.

Then she gave his ear a long, slow lick. Backing away, Traci smiled at him.

Avery tried in vain to camouflage the erection stirring inside his jeans. "Traci, how many times do I have to tell you no?" he whispered.

Ignoring his question, she put her T-shirt back on. "Bye, Laura or whatever your name is," she said. "Nice talking to you."

"Oh, you too, Traci, dear," Louise replied.

Avery watched her go; then he sank down on the sofa. He sighed. "You still there, Louise?"

"Honey, I wouldn't hang up for the world right now. How many passes does that make from your happily married costar?"

"That's the third one this week, and it was a lulu, about a five-point-five on the Richter scale. I tell you, she's worse than Libby."

"Sounded like she said something about 'no shirts.' Was she topless?"

"Yes. And my ear is still wet from her licking it."

"Well, Mr. Avery Cooper. Do you realize what you just experienced? Traci Haydn is the fantasy girl for millions of boys and men, the stuff wet dreams are made of. What do you have to say for yourself?"

"I miss my wife," Avery replied.

"Hi, sweetie. I erased all the other messages, because we maxed out on the machine. Aren't we popular?"

Avery smiled. He sat at the desk in his suite at the Vancouver Four Seasons. Simply hearing Joanne's voice on the answering machine at home soothed some of his loneliness.

Joanne Lane was a stage actress. Twice nominated for a Featured Actress Tony, she'd made a name for herself on Broadway. Elsewhere, she was Mrs. Avery Cooper. Her latest play hadn't fared well with critics. Unless business picked up, the production would close next week, and she'd return home to L.A. Under such gloomy circumstances, Avery tried not to celebrate their reunions too eagerly. Joanne had bouts with depression. She was on medication, but still required kid-glove handling at times. Things were always a little touch and go whenever one of her plays failed, but it also meant they could be together for a while.

They'd met four years ago, during a summer hiatus from his TV show, *Crazy to Work Here*. Avery had played a "nice guy" who has horrible luck with women. Quickly he'd become the star attraction among the ensemble cast of "wacky" characters employed at an ad agency. Comparisons to Jack Lemmon and Tom Hanks abounded for the former Northwestern drama major and Second City alumni. He was also a favorite guest on the talk show circuit. On Letterman, he stirred the studio audience into a sing-along frenzy with an impromptu rendition of "Wild Thing" on his harmonica. And to Rosie, when pressed, Avery humbly admitted, "I can count on one hand all my sex partners—including the hand."

That summer away from the show, Joanne Lane became the fifth woman in Avery's life. With lustrous shoulder-length light brown hair and blue eyes, Joanne had an undefinable star quality. Though no great beauty, she had a sultry voice and a toned, taut body. She oozed sex appeal. The Broadway actress had landed a role in Avery's first "starring" feature film, a forgettable romantic comedy called *Five Feet of Heaven*. She played his slutty sister, and outside of falling in love with her screen brother, she found film acting incredibly tedious. Joanne ran back to Broadway, and Avery reluctantly returned to Los Angeles and *Crazy to Work Here*. But they couldn't stay away from each other. Avery used his clout to get Joanne some guest shots on the show. He spent summers and holidays on the East Coast; she took breaks between plays to be with him in Hollywood. All the traveling and scheduling became quite complicated. So they kept the wedding simple. They were married in a small chapel in Avery's hometown of Fairfax, Virginia.

One advantage to Avery and Joanne's bicoastal marriage was that the relationship never had a chance to grow stale. After two years, they still acted like newlyweds. If anything had grown stale it was all the traveling and the time apart. Before this recent theatrical misfire had lured Joanne back to Broadway, they'd been trying to have a baby—without much luck.

"I made us another appointment with the fertility specialist on Wednesday, the eighth," Joanne told him on the answering machine. "Also I committed us to another public service announcement for handgun control. They won't film until late December, so we can put that on the back burner for now. I miss you, sweetie. I wish it were next week already so we could be together. It's midnight here. I'm hitting the sheets. Good night, love."

Joanne had left the message an hour ago. Avery decided not to call and possibly wake her. Instead, he went to his suitcase in the closet. He snapped open the locks, and took out a video— a sexually explicit video starring Mr. and Mrs. Avery Cooper.

Several months back, he'd been concerned about his first R-rated love scene—in this movie with Traci Hadyn. Joanne had playfully suggested they "rehearse" together. At her urging, he'd broken out the video camera and tripod to tape their lovemaking. After some initial shyness, they began to have fun, and eventually forgot the camera was there. The resulting video was more silly than sexy. Avery stashed the tape in his underwear drawer, and pretty much forgot about it.

But his first night on location here in Vancouver, he'd unpacked his bags, and found Joanne had taken their little sex epic out of mothballs. She'd hidden the video in his suitcase— along with a Post-It note: *Dear Husband, Keep Rehearsing! Your Loving Wife.* She'd left for New York that same day.

Now Avery popped the cassette in the VCR connected to

the hotel TV. He sat at the end of his bed and watched. He ignored his own video image: that dumb wiry guy with the erection and the birthmark on his butt. Instead, he focused on Joanne's lithe body, the way she smiled and giggled. He felt himself grow hard.

Someone knocked on the door. Avery stood up and tried to adjust his erection. His first thought was: *God, please don't let it be Traci Haydn.* He ejected the video and turned off the TV. There was another knock.

"Mr. Cooper? Turn down your bed?"

Stashing the video back in his suitcase, Avery went to the other room and checked the peephole. It was the old lady who pulled back the bedcovers every night. As far as Avery was concerned, her job was the most useless service a hotel could provide. But, hell, she was a sweet woman of sixty who walked with a limp, and he didn't want her put out of commission. Besides, slipping her a Canadian five for a tug at the bedsheets and a mint on his pillow made him feel good. He opened the door.

"Hello, Mr. Cooper!" she chirped. "Turn down the bed, aye?"

"Yes, thanks a lot," he said, stepping aside.

"I know you go to sleep late, aye, so I saved you for last," she said. With her basket of mints in tow, the uniformed woman hobbled into the bedroom. Then she let out a frail cry that escalated to a scream. It sounded as if she were having a seizure. Avery raced into the room. She was staggering away from his bed, her hand over her mouth. The basket of mints had spilled onto the floor.

"Are you okay?" Avery asked. Then he saw what the old woman had found beneath the quilted bedcover.

On his pillow, someone had left four dead mice, two of them cut in half. And there was a note—on hotel memo paper: *You played a monster who kills little babies that aren't even this big. He deserved to die, and so do you.*

* * *

The old woman was still a bit shaken when someone from hotel security led her out of Avery's suite. The manager on duty kept apologizing to Avery. He didn't understand how this could have happened—what with the high security and the professional staff. Could they move him to another suite?

Avery told them that would be nice. "And could you please make sure that lady gets a ride home tonight?"

Later he left a message at the house for Joanne, telling her that he'd switched hotel rooms. He didn't explain why. He said that if she woke up in the middle of the night, she could call him here. It didn't matter what time. He probably wouldn't sleep very well tonight anyway.

During a break in filming the next day, Avery retreated to his trailer, sat on the sofa, and telephoned Joanne. "Has anything kind of weird happened to you lately? Have you received any hate mail or strange phone calls?"

"Why do you ask, Avery? Did something kind of weird happen there?"

"Yeah, just a creepy note in my hotel room," Avery said. "It's these nuts who didn't like the TV movie. I'm concerned about you, that's all."

"Avery, I can take care of myself," Joanne calmly pointed out. "That said, okay, yes, something happened last week after the show. I came back to my dressing room, and on the vanity, someone had left a—well, it was a small Gerber's baby food jar, only they'd stuffed a dead mouse in it."

"Jesus," Avery murmured. "Why didn't you tell me about this?"

"Because you would have freaked out," Joanne said. "I know what a worrywart you are. Nothing has happened since. They've kept a lookout for me backstage, and I've been careful. So don't sweat about it. Okay?"

Avery got to his feet and started pacing around the trailer, the phone to his ear. "Listen, I'm hiring you a bodyguard. Let's not take any chances—"

"Sweetie, I reiterate, *nothing has happened since.* Someone didn't like your movie, and I had a little scare. End of story. I don't want a bodyguard."

"Joanne, we aren't seeing each other for another six days. Until then, I need to make sure you're safe."

So when Joanne Lane Cooper arrived at the theater that night, a bodyguard her husband hired introduced himself and showed his credentials. The man, whom Joanne would describe as "a pain in the ass," guaranteed her safety for the next six days.

Three

A number of bomb threats didn't keep fourteen thousand people from filling Portland's Colosseum for the benefit concert. Dayle Sutton read letters of remembrance from several of Tony Katz's friends and costars. Many of the letters were from AIDS patients he'd visited regularly, a few of them children.

Another actress might have manufactured some high emotion for the presentation, adding her own pregnant pauses and dramatic sighs, or allowing her voice to quiver. But Dayle chose a simple, dignified approach that focused on the letters, not on the celebrity reading them. When she finished, the audience stood and applauded. Dayle walked off stage left. The ovation continued, but she would not return for a bow. They were applauding the letters, not her.

On the other side of the stage, she glimpsed Leigh Simone, waiting in the wings. Dayle still hadn't met the force behind this benefit fighting discrimination against gays and lesbians. Two women hovered around Leigh, both of them rather chubby: one, a makeup girl, and the other, an older brunette who held a cellular phone and a clipboard. Dayle wondered if this was the assistant, Estelle Collier.

Leigh broke away from the two women, and waved to her. She was so charismatic, and full of energy. She wore a sleeveless, brown sequined dress with a scooped neck and a jagged hem serrating at her upper thighs. Her legs were long and tapered. The thirty-eight-year-old singer could have been an Olympic athlete with her taut, lean body. The cinnamon skin was flawless. She wore her hair pulled back in a long curly ponytail, which had become her trademark. Her smile could dazzle the recipient a hundred feet away.

Dayle waved back at her. Leigh blew her a kiss, then yelled something. But the applause had yet to die down. She took a pen from her assistant, then wrote something on the clipboard, and sent her off. Leigh waved to Dayle again, then shimmied and shook her way onto the stage. A thunderous applause greeted her, and The High Priestess of Rock began to turn her seductive powers on the audience. She sang an electrifying rendition of Elvis Presley's "Suspicious Minds." Mesmerized, Dayle watched her.

According to rumor, Leigh was a gay—or at least bisexual. Dayle didn't take much stock in the grapevine—after all, they were wrong about her. But Leigh never refuted the gossip, and the sexual energy she exuded seemed to spill beyond all boundaries—including gender.

Dayle felt a little silly for even wondering. But Leigh seemed to have been flirting with her from the other side of that stage.

"Pardon me, Ms. Sutton?"

Dayle turned and smiled at the assistant, who—close up—appeared about fifty years old. She was so professionally perky, she could have been an Avon saleswoman. The woman wore jeans and a violet pullover that didn't quite camouflage her weight problem. "Are you Estelle?" Dayle asked.

"Why, yes, hello. It's a pleasure to meet you. I have a

message from Leigh.'' She handed Dayle a sheet of paper. ''She's a huge fan of yours.''

Dayle stole another glance at Leigh, who was whipping the crowd into a fever. Then she read the note, hastily scribbled by Leigh herself:

> Dear Dayle,
>   What a wonderful tribute to Tony! Thank you so much. Can we get together tonight? Please say yes. I'm in room 1108—same hotel as you. 10:30? I love you, girl!

Dayle let out a little laugh. ''Sure,'' she said to Estelle Collier. ''Tell Leigh that I'd love to get together with her.''

Both Leigh and Dayle had been booked into the Imperial Hotel, the same place Tony Katz had stayed the week he was killed. The Imperial had received their share of bomb threats too, and they'd tightened security at the hotel this evening. Dayle's suite was on the twentieth floor.

For her date with Leigh, she'd changed her clothes several times, and finally decided on a pair of black stirrup pants and a dark green silk blouse. Like most women, she dressed for other women. In this case, she didn't want to be too alluring. Leigh's sexuality shouldn't have been an issue. But maybe Leigh was expecting more than a friendly chat tonight. Dayle hoped she wouldn't have to dodge a pass. She'd rejected enough sexual advances in her day, from both genders; that wasn't a problem. But she admired Leigh Simone, and didn't want to brave that kind of awkward situation with her.

Dayle was at the dresser mirror, brushing her hair when the phone rang. She grabbed the receiver. ''Hello?''

''Hello, Dayle?'' Leigh must have been at a party or in a bar, Dayle heard talking and laughter in the background.

''Yes, hi. Leigh? Where are you calling from?''

"My suite, believe it or not," Leigh said. "The only person I wanted to see tonight was you, and it's wall-to-wall people here. Don't ask me how, but this whole thing got out of control. Are you in a party mood?"

Dayle frowned. "Um, not really. But thank you anyway—"

"No, no, no. Don't thank me 'anyway' yet. I'm not in a party mood either. Could I come up? I figure I can sneak out of this circus in about a half hour. Is that okay? Do you mind meeting in your suite?"

"No, Leigh. I don't mind at all."

"Okay, I'll see you in a bit. I can't wait!" Leigh made a kissing sound, then hung up.

With Leigh arriving soon, Dayle began to straighten what little mess she'd made in her suite. She cleared some paperwork and clothes off the couch, then called room service and ordered champagne.

She'd just hung up the phone when someone knocked on her door. Dayle checked the peephole. Leigh Simone appeared nervous and tense. She rolled her eyes, took a deep breath, and started to knock again.

Dayle opened the door. "Well, hello, Ms. Simone! At last, we meet."

Leigh seemed taller in person. This close, Dayle couldn't help noticing the pale olive color of her eyes. Leigh wore black capri pants, fancy gold slippers, and a tuxedo blouse. She stood at the threshold for a moment, one hand on the door frame. "Before I come in," she announced, "I need to say this, Dayle. I'm really nervous about meeting you."

Dayle laughed. "Oh, stop. . . ."

"No, ma'am. You're my hero. My assistant, Estelle, can tell you, I was bowled over when you agreed to come to this benefit. I was shooting for the moon when I invited you. And then, tonight backstage, I kept asking Estelle, 'Do you think she'd like to get together? Should I ask?' "

"Well, I'm glad you did," Dayle said, feeling more at ease. "For the record, I was so jazzed up about meeting you, I changed my outfit four times. Now for God's sake, get in here."

With a hundred-watt grin, Leigh spread her arms and gave Dayle a fierce hug. "Dayle, this is a dream come true. You have no idea!" She unclinched, but continued to hold her hand. "You're my inspiration. You know, twelve years ago, when I first moved to New York—and I was waiting tables and living in this cheap hotel for women—I used to pattern myself after you in *Bending the Rules.*"

"That was one of my better ones," Dayle said.

"Oh, it was great. You were my role model in that. I saw the movie four times, bargain matinees. I used to daydream about being rich and famous. And get this, part of that dream was seeing my sassy little self lounging in a plush hotel room, having a heart-to-heart with my good buddy, Dayle Sutton. So I mean it when I tell you, this is a dream come true for me."

Dayle squeezed her hand. "Stop, you'll make me cry—and we haven't even sat down yet. C'mon. Champagne's on its way." She opened the minirefrigerator. "Meanwhile, what can I get you?"

Sitting on the couch, Leigh glanced toward the small refrigerator, then gave Dayle a wicked smile. "That chocolate bar in there. I'll split it with you. Shoots my diet to hell. But let's be decadent."

Dayle grinned. "It's a deal. Don't you want a drink?"

"No, but you go ahead. I already had a glass of wine at the party. I'm a lightweight—a total disgrace to the rock star profession. I don't do drugs or trash hotel rooms either. Half a glass of your champagne, and I'll be out like a light. I swear, I'll fall asleep right on this couch."

"Kind of like a slumber party," Dayle said, handing Leigh the candy bar and a glass of water.

"Oh, wouldn't that make the bees buzz?" Leigh unwrapped the Nestle's Crunch. " 'Leigh Simone Spends Night in Dayle Sutton's Hotel Room.' The tabloids would have a field day." She patted the sofa cushion. "C'mon, sit. I'm not wolfing this down alone."

Working up a smile, Dayle sat beside her. There was an awkward silence.

Leigh snapped off a corner of the candy bar, then put it up to Dayle's lips. Dayle hesitated, then took the chocolate in her mouth. Her lips brushed against Leigh's fingers. "Pretty sinful, isn't it?" Leigh whispered.

She nodded.

Leigh broke another piece off of the Nestle's Crunch bar and studied it. "Am I wrong?" she said. "Or is something happening here?"

Dayle shrugged. "Well, I'm picking up some signals—if that's what you mean. And it's very flattering. I really admire you, Leigh. You have—so much integrity. You've got the courage to say, 'This is me, I'm gay, and it's—' "

"Um, Dayle, I'm not gay," Leigh interrupted.

"You're not?"

"I know the rumors. If people want to think I'm a lesbian, that's fine. But you're not 'people,' Dayle, so I can tell you. I'm not gay." She took a deep breath. "In fact, I thought you were—"

"Gay?" Shaking her head, Dayle started to laugh. "No. God, we must be prey to the same warped rumor mill. I've been wondering all night what to do if you should make a pass."

"Ha, I was thinking the same thing!" Leigh gave her shoulder a playful push. Grinning, she nibbled at the candy bar again. "Want to know what else? I figured, if you tried any moves, I might just go along. After all, you're *Dayle Sutton,* for the love of God. Who—no matter what their persuasion—wouldn't want to give you a tumble?"

Dayle rolled her eyes. "Oh, please, cut me a break."

Leigh sighed. "Reminds me of those movies on late-night cable TV. They always have lesbian sex scenes. Only those girls are never lesbians, they're just experimenting."

Dayle laughed. "It's the guy myth that we females of the species are all one glass of wine away from becoming bisexual." She raised her glass in a toast. "So I gather you too have spent many a night on the road in a hotel room with only cable TV for company. That's me, filming on location."

"I'm on tour thirty weeks every year," Leigh said. "I can give you a list of the best hotels in every major city in the world—who has the best room service, the best on-call masseuse . . ."

"I've always been a bit leery of those hotel hands-on artists," Dayle admitted. "I figure, I'll have this great message in my room one night, and a week later, it'll be in the *National Enquirer* that I'm not a natural redhead."

"Folks like us, there aren't a lot of people we can trust." Leigh picked at the candy bar. "Not a lot of decent men who will put up with the crazy schedules we keep, the press and paparazzi, and all that excess baggage. Not a lot of friends either."

Dayle nudged her. "If you say, 'It's lonely at the top,' I'll smack you. Besides, much as I hate to admit it, my box-office clout has been slipping lately. I'm not so close to the top anymore."

"Then that makes the loneliness even worse, doesn't it?"

The quiet seriousness in Leigh's voice took Dayle by surprise. What she said hit close to home. Dayle tried to laugh and shrug it off. "My God, Leigh, how did we get so—*heavy* all of a sudden?"

Leigh sat back and smiled. "It's just part of that dream I was telling you about, Dayle. You know, the heart-to-heart talk? I know it sounds corny, but I'd like us to be friends."

Dayle took hold of her hand and squeezed it. "It is corny, but I'd like that too."

Living in Hollywood for the last sixteen years had made Dayle cautious. People she met always seemed to want something else from her. But all Leigh Simone wanted was her friendship.

They talked for fifteen more minutes. Leigh had snuck away from her party, and needed to rejoin her guests. She suggested meeting in the morning for a late breakfast. But Dayle had an early flight.

"Well, I'll be back in L.A. this week," Leigh said, standing in the doorway. "Let's do dinner. We'll really blow our diets, burgers and fries."

"It's a deal," Dayle said, grinning. "I'll call you tomorrow night."

Leigh nodded. "Okay, but you better be careful about seeing too much of me, Dayle. Don't forget, I have a reputation."

They laughed and hugged. Dayle felt a twinge of concern. Indeed it might add more fuel to those career-damaging rumors if she were seen with Leigh. She told herself it didn't matter—at least it shouldn't have mattered.

She squeezed Leigh a little tighter, and kissed her cheek. They said good-bye once more. Smiling, Dayle watched her saunter down the hall. Then she stepped back inside her suite, and closed the door.

Someone knocked on the door less than three minutes later. Dayle was at the honor bar, ready to pour herself a brandy. "Leigh? Is that you?"

She checked the peephole. It was a young man in a waiter's uniform. "Room service, Ms. Sutton!" he called.

Dayle opened the door. The hotel badge on his waiter's jacket showed the name, Brian. With dark hair and dimples, he was quite a handsome young guy. He carried a large tray with a champagne bottle on ice, two flute glasses, and a basket full of fruit, crackers, salami, and cheeses.

"You're a little late," Dayle said.

"Yes, I'm sorry, Ms. Sutton. The champagne and the food basket are compliments of the management. It's our way of apologizing for the delay."

She opened the door wider. "Tell management not to sweat it. C'mon in."

He set the tray on the desk. "May I open the champagne for you?"

"Yes, thanks." Dayle fished a few dollars out of her purse while he popped open the bottle. She started to hand him the money.

"Oh, that's not necessary," the young man said. Reaching inside his waiter's jacket, he pulled out a small black book and a pen. "In fact, I'd rather get your autograph—if that's okay. I kind of collect them."

Dayle took the little book—opened to a blank sheet. She turned back a page: *To Brian, A Very Special Guy, Sincerely, Tony Katz.* Dayle smiled. "I see you met my buddy, Tony Katz."

"His suite was below this one. He was a good friend of yours, huh?"

"Only in a show business way." She took the pen from him and scribbled in his autograph book, *To Brian, Many Thanks, Dayle Sutton.*

"I saw you on the news tonight," he said. "You were reading those letters about Tony. It got me thinking about him again. I delivered dinner to his room a couple of times. He—um, well, he made a pass at me."

"Well, consider it a compliment." Dayle handed the book back to him.

The young man blushed and glanced down at the carpet. "Y'know, I'm not gay. I—I have a girlfriend. I went to school in Texas, and all my friends—to them, queers are about as low as you can get."

Dayle frowned. "Why are you telling me this?"

"Because you were his friend. And I have to tell somebody or I'll go nuts. Tony knew he was going to die. These people threatened to kill him."

"Tony told you this? When?"

Brian hesitated. "After we—well, we messed around a little. I was explaining to Tony about my college buddies, and what they think of queers. Tony said that a bunch of 'good old boys' can take turns humping a heifer in a pasture and it's a bonding thing, but if two of those guys are caught kissing, then they're sick perverts. He was making fun, y'know, sarcastic?"

Dayle just nodded.

"Then he got serious, and he told me these people were calling him at home, saying they were gonna kill him and expose him as being gay. They said that the whole world would know he was a fag. And it's just what happened."

"What do you mean, 'they'? Was it more than one person?"

"That's the way it sounded." Brian's voice started to crack. "God, it could have been me who was murdered with him out there in that forest. . . ."

"You haven't talked to anyone else about this?"

He shook his head. "No, I can't. My girlfriend, my friends—"

"Didn't the police or FBI interview you? I'd think they would."

"They only talked to the people who were working that night. I didn't come in that Thursday."

"You should be talking to the police, not me," Dayle said.

"Couldn't you talk to them for me?" he asked. "You could say that Tony told *you* about the death threats. That way, I'd stay out of it. And people would believe you, because you were his friend and you're a movie star—"

"Wait a minute, honey—Brian." Dayle touched his arm. "I wasn't that close to Tony. Even if I was, I wouldn't wait two weeks after his murder to come forward with news about these 'death threats.' It doesn't make sense."

The young man looked so utterly lost. He kept shaking his head.

"I want to help," Dayle said. "But I can't go to the police for you, Brian. That won't work. If you want, I can have a lawyer talk with you—"

"Are you saying that I need a lawyer?" he asked warily.

"Only someone to give you legal advice when you go to the police—"

"No, I can't go to the police. I can't do that." Turning away, he opened the door. "I shouldn't have bothered you with this. I'm sorry—"

"Wait . . . wait a second. I want to help you, Brian—"

He ducked into the hallway and closed the door on her.

Jarnell Cleary had been a maid with the Imperial Hotel for five weeks, and she hated it. Scrubbing out toilets at the crack of dawn was not how she'd planned to spend her young life. But only twenty-nine more weeks of this crap, and she and her boyfriend could afford a trip to Europe together. She was thinking about Paris as she wedged opened the women's rest room door.

At the moment, there were only two other people on the mezzanine level, both of them janitors. Backing her cart through the doorway, Jarnell realized she had her work cut out for her. The place stunk, a rank odor. Someone had left a faucet on; she could hear the water trickling. The overhead lights had gone haywire and kept flickering on and off.

Jarnell almost tripped over the trash can, lying on its side. Garbage was strewn across the floor. She glanced over toward the sinks. Across the mirror, someone had scribbled in lipstick: LIES! LIES!

One of the sinks was stopped up with paper towels, and overflowing. Water dripped down to the tiled floor. Jarnell accidentally stepped in the puddle as she crept toward the first stall. By the toilet, something shiny on the floor caught her eye. Jarnell pushed the stall door open. She saw a fancy gold slipper on the floor. Beside it was a hypodermic syringe.

In the next stall, Jarnell glanced down at a purse lying on its side. Maybe it was because of the blinking lights, but she didn't notice anything else. She started into the next stall, expecting it to be empty.

Her shriek echoed off the tiled walls.

A woman sat on the toilet, her head tilted back and legs spread apart. Her black capri pants had been unzipped on the side, but not pulled down. The front of her tuxedo blouse was splattered with gray vomit.

At first, Jarnell thought the lady had passed out. But then the lights flickered bright again, and she could see it was Leigh Simone—with her tongue drooped over her lips, and a dead stare from those olive-green eyes.

Four

At 7:15 A.M., on Friday, October 10, the following Internet conversation appeared on Bullpen, a baseball historian's chat line:

FRANK: I still say The Babe was the greatest player ever.

JETT: But Hank Aaron broke Ruth's record with home run # 715 on 4/8/74.

PAT: Breaking records doesn't necessarily make a player great.

RICK: Request private chat with Pat.

Dialogue from a private mailbox, between "Rick" and "Pat," at 7:19 that Friday morning:

PATRIOT: Speaking of niggers and records ... there's a nigger singer who ain't making records any more ... no more rallies for queers either.

AMERICKAN: Watch what U say. Will there B enough humiliation 4 subject once L.S. is discovered?

PATRIOT: Yes ... went smoothly ... her assistant's cooperating.

AMERICKAN: Good ... you'll B coming to L.A. within week ... work begun on A.C ... details 2 follow ... SAAMO Lieut. signing off.

Avery Cooper shivered as he climbed out of the pool. He hiked up his dark blue trunks and threw a towel over his shoulders. As a little reward for finishing his morning laps, he gulped down a glass of orange juice.

Catching his breath on the pool deck, he glanced up at the back of his house, a beautiful two-story, Spanish white stucco. Avery reminded himself how lucky he was. The high-class hacienda had belonged to a big-name record producer, bankrupt after a misguided venture into filmmaking. Avery and Joanne had bought the place for a song. At least that was what his parents had said, and they were in the real estate business.

Married forty-two years, Rich and Loretta Cooper were still crazy about each other. Lo worked as a receptionist in Rich's office. Business was booming in Fairfax, Virginia. But they managed to have lunch together every day—sometimes later or earlier than they wanted, because a house needed to be shown; but they hadn't missed a lunch together in seventeen years.

It was a far cry from Avery's married life—with Joanne gone for months at a time. Sure, when they were together, the honeymoon went on and on. But he was lonely and miserable most of the time. And he had to keep reminding himself how goddamn lucky he was. After all, who wouldn't want his life? He was paid an obscene amount of money to work at something he loved. And he used his celebrity clout to advocate important causes. His gun-control commercials with Joanne made a difference.

Avery had a good friend in junior high school named Jimmy Fadden. Along with his sister and mother, Jimmy had stopped by for dinner one April night at an upscale burger joint called The Checkered Pantry, outside Fairfax. Avery had eaten there dozens of times—often with Jimmy. But he wasn't there that warm spring evening when a crazy man with a gun stepped into the restaurant and started shooting. He killed seven people and wounded six more before turning the gun on himself. Mrs. Fadden and nine-year-old Gina were among the seven fatalities. Jimmy took a bullet in the spine and spent the rest of his life a paraplegic. He told Avery that he'd been yelling at his kid sister for swiping fries from his plate when he'd heard the first shot.

Mr. Fadden remarried, and the family moved away when Avery was in high school. But he'd been thinking of Jimmy when he made *Intent to Kill,* about the doctor paralyzed by a gunman's bullet outside an abortion clinic. Amid all the hate mail, he also received a letter from Jim Fadden, complimenting him for his accurate portrayal of a paraplegic, and thanking him for his work advocating gun control.

The poison-pen letters had tapered off, and neither Joanne nor he had come across any more dead mice calling cards. They'd sent her bodyguard packing. Joanne had been home a week now. She wanted to stay awhile and work on having a baby. They'd been working on it all week.

Avery glanced up at the bedroom windows. The veranda doors opened, and Joanne stepped out on the balcony. She wore a long, teal silk robe. Her brown hair neatly fell down over her shoulders. Even from the distance, Avery could see she'd put on lipstick and mascara. She looked beautiful in the soft morning light. "Hey, sweetie, why are you up so early?" he called.

In reply, Joanne let the robe drop to the floor. She was naked.

Avery stared at her, mesmerized. She was a vision. After a moment, he threw off his towel, shucked down his swim trunks, and scurried over to the diving board. He was already semierect.

Joanne laughed, and covered her breasts from the cold. "Hurry up! I'm freezing!"

Avery thumped his chest like Tarzan, then dove into the water. He quickly swam the length of the pool, pulled himself out of the water, and ran naked into the house. He left a trail of water as he raced up the stairs, where Joanne waited for him at the landing, her arms open.

Lying with her legs up in the air after sex was supposed to increase her chances of conceiving. Joanne assumed this position at the foot of their bed. Avery's body had been wet and slick with pool water, so they'd made love on the floor.

Avery propped a pillow under Joanne's back, and tucked the silk robe around her. He knew other couples who had problems conceiving, and for the husbands, the sex-on-a-schedule became a tiresome ordeal. But Joanne worked to make it fun. The only thing Avery didn't like was having to produce on demand sperm samples for their fertility specialist.

They had nearly a dozen specimens stored at a lab, just the answer for a bicoastal couple trying to conceive. It was Joanne's idea—for when she was ovulating and out of town. His "little swimmers" were kept on ice, ready—if he wasn't—at a day's notice for shipment out to the East Coast. So far, she hadn't dipped into that reservoir yet.

Stepping into his undershorts, Avery figured he'd shower later in his trailer. He was due on the set in an hour. He kept picking up a bad odor in the room—someplace. "Do you smell something funny?" he asked.

Joanne adjusted the pillow beneath her back. "Yeah, now that you mention it. It's like spoiled food or something."

Avery went to the balcony doors and opened them again. Their bedroom had tall windows curved at the tops, mission-style furniture, and a thick, woven rug. Mexican tiles framed the small fireplace.

"I had a call from Saul yesterday," Joanne said. "That new play he sent, it's pretty good. He wants me to fly out there next week for a reading."

Avery turned from the doors and frowned at her. "But you just got back from New York six days ago—"

"Now, don't flip out. It's nothing definite. It's just a reading—"

"How can you expect us to make a baby when we're hardly ever together? Do you really want to have a baby?"

Joanne pointed to her legs in the air. "No, it's just an excuse to lie here like this. I find it very comfortable."

With a sigh, Avery pulled on a T-shirt. Starting a family had been his idea. He'd originally talked with Joanne about it a year ago, when she'd returned home depressed over a Broadway show that had gone down in flames. She'd said she was ready, but when they'd run into difficulties conceiving, she'd retreated back to The Great White Way and another play. That one had been a hit, and she'd been gone eleven months.

"I just wish we could be together—in the same place—for a while," Avery grunted, zipping up his trousers. "I'm tired of all the flying back and forth. You know, for every trip you've taken out here, I've seen you in New York five times. Check my frequent flier points. I could fly first class to Jupiter on the mileage I've accrued."

"I wish you wouldn't pick on me." Joanne lowered her feet. "You know, I'm off the antidepressants while we try for junior here. It hasn't been a picnic for me. How often have we had this argument anyway? I mean—"

The telephone rang.

Joanne sighed. "Ah, saved by the bell."

"It's probably the studio."

Avery grabbed the phone. "Hello?"

"Avery Cooper?" It sounded like a spaced-out teenage boy. "You're a fucking asshole and your wife's a pig."

Avery hung up, then glanced at Joanne, who started to sit up. "Don't answer if it rings again." He ran out of the room.

"What? Was it a crank? Watch the water on the stairs!"

Downstairs, Avery checked the caller ID box in his study. The number had been blocked. The phone rang again. Avery stood over the answering machine, waiting for it to click on. When it did, the caller hung up.

Libby—or someone she'd paid to do her dirty work. Avery's number-one fan had not taken graciously the officious letter from his agent telling her to cease and desist. She'd left a phone message the day he returned home from Vancouver two weeks back: *Hello, Avery. This is Libby. I got a mean note from your agent or whoever. You're really an asshole, y'know? I spent a lot of money on you, and this is the thanks I get. I should have realized what a shit you are when you did that awful pro-abortion movie on TV. Oh, and those gun-control commercials with you and your stupid wife. I own a gun and I'd like to use it on you, only I won't. You aren't worth being locked away in jail for. You can just go to hell.*

The calling number had been blocked.

In case he hadn't gotten the message, she'd dropped something in the mail to him—the autographed portrait he'd originally sent her. The photo had been torn in half and the eyes cut out.

After going to bed that first night back, Avery heard a noise outside—from the front of the house. He tossed aside the covers and crept into the guest room. From the window, he spied two teenage punks scurrying across the moonlit lawn toward the front gate. Avery immediately called the police.

The teenagers, who managed to elude the cops, were only

errand boys. They'd delivered three gift boxes to Avery's door, items he'd returned to Libby. But the Ralph Lauren sweater had ketchup splattered all over the front of it; a sportshirt had been slashed to pieces; and an expensive jogging suit had been partially torched—with ashes still in the box.

Beverly Hills' finest collected the evidence and called on Leslie Benita Stoddard. But Libby had left for Maui three days before. Avery pressured the police to contact authorities in Maui. When questioned, Libby claimed to have impulsively given the clothes—along with the autographed photo—to a couple of punk boys outside a thrift shop. They'd been asking people for spare change. She'd told them the clothes "weren't good enough" for Avery Cooper. That was her only contact with the teenagers. She said that except for leaving an angry message a week ago on Avery's answering machine (which— *golly, gee*—she now regretted), she hadn't tried to contact him.

Avery didn't believe a word. He'd hoped Libby's recent brush with the law in Maui had convinced her to back off. But now one of her creeps was on the phone harassing Joanne and him at seven-forty in the morning.

"Avery!" Joanne yelled from upstairs. "Oh, Jesus . . . Avery!"

He ran to the foot of the stairs. Joanne leaned over the upper railing. Her hair was a mess, and tears streamed down her face. Naked, she clutched the robe in front of her.

Avery raced up the steps to her. "What is it?" he asked, out of breath.

"In our bedroom—" She let out a gasp, then shook away a small black ant that had been crawling on her arm. Joanne shuddered and started swatting at her hair, trying to flick away bugs that may or may not have been nesting there. "Your sweater drawer," she cried, trembling. "Someone broke into the house. They've been in our bedroom. . . ."

Avery took hold of her arms. "What?"

Joanne cringed and backed away from him. "They left something in your sweater drawer." She took a deep breath, then pointed to the bedroom. "I think it's from your friend—what's her name, Libby. Take a look."

Stepping over the pillow on the floor, Avery glanced down at four or five ants scurrying along the wheat-colored carpet. They were moving toward his dresser, where their numbers grew. Just minutes ago, he hadn't noticed a single insect in the room. But now an army of ants crawled up the front of his cherry-stained dresser—all massing on the open bottom drawer.

Avery felt something tickle the top of his bare foot, and he swatted an ant away. Peering down into the drawer, he found what had attracted the swarm of black, crawling invaders. On top of his Irish knit sweater, someone had left a toy gun and a small baby doll—the kind usually dressed in a little bonnet and frock. But this doll had been stripped of its clothes, and swaddled in bloody, butcher-shop entrails. As the insects honed in on the rotting meat, they seemed to be devouring that cherub-faced toy baby.

With the police on their way, Avery and Joanne quickly got dressed. He'd managed to calm her down. He'd also taken care of the ant problem, using up a near-empty can of Raid. The smell of bug repellent drifted downstairs, where they now searched the house for anything that might have been stolen. None of Joanne's jewelry was missing, and all their silverware remained intact. Avery checked the shelves in the living room. Every item was still in place.

"I think you're right," he called to Joanne. "Libby must be behind this. Nothing's missing. She's rich. She doesn't want to steal anything, she just wants to harass us. She must have had one of her punks break in and plant that—that thing. She was always sending me sweaters. Not too subtle leaving it in my sweater drawer."

He couldn't stop wondering how the hell they'd made it past

the security system. "Joanne?" he called. "Did you go out yesterday?"

"We met with Dr. Nathan, remember?" she called back to him. Her voice was still a little shaky.

"Oh, yeah, sure," he muttered. They'd had an appointment with their fertility specialist. "Did you set the alarm before you left the house?"

"No, and I'm sorry, okay?" she called back, exasperated. "I'm never home long enough to memorize the stupid code."

The telephone rang.

"Ignore it," he yelled. "It's probably one of Libby's boys again." He could hear the answering machine in his study.

" . . . leave a message after the beep," the recording said. Then his own voice came on the phone: "Hey, honey . . . God, look at you. You're so sexy . . ."

He started toward the study. Joanne met him in the hallway. "Avery? What's going on?"

In the study his recorded voice kept talking over her: "I'm so hard. See what you're doing to me? Come here . . ."

Joanne clutched his arm. "What is that?" Tears came to her eyes as she listened to the sound of her own laughter.

"Oh, you wicked, wicked girl," he said on the recording.

"Jesus, they have our videotape," Avery murmured.

He hurried upstairs to the bedroom, still stinking of bug repellent. He headed toward the dresser, where Libby's errand boy had left that grisly calling card. A few surviving ants crawled amid the dead.

Avery could hear the police siren drawing near. He pulled open the drawer second to the top. He frantically dug through the underwear. T-shirts and shorts fell to the floor as he searched in vain for the videotape.

"Oh, God, no," he muttered.

The tape of Joanne and him making love was gone.

Five

"Thank you for your patience this morning," the flight attendant announced. "As soon as we've reached cruising altitude, we will begin our beverage service. . . ."

The plane had been delayed two hours. A limo had whisked Dayle to the airport at 6:30 A.M., only so she could wait and wait. She spent the time studying her script and reviewing today's scenes to the point of overkill. From the VIP Lounge, she was the last person to board the plane; and thanks to first class seating, she'd be the first to leave.

Her head tipped back and eyes closed, Dayle didn't dare look at the damn script again. Nor did she feel like chatting with the boring businessman in the aisle seat, who unfortunately recognized her. If she feigned sleep, the guy might leave her alone, and maybe she'd even drift off for a while.

But she kept replaying in her head that bizarre conversation with the room service waiter. She remembered what he'd said about Tony Katz receiving death threats: *He told me these*

*people were calling him at home, saying they were gonna kill
him and expose him as being gay. . . .*

Amid all the hate mail pouring in after Dayle had made
Survival Instincts, one note stood out. It wasn't among her fan
letters—or even in the mailbox at her apartment. She found
this one inside her car.

They'd been shooting at the studio into the early evening,
and it was dark when Dayle went to her green BMW, parked
in its spot outside the soundstage. She unlocked the door. The
interior light went on, and she saw the piece of paper taped to
the steering wheel. The note was printed up by a computer.
What it said made her heart stop: WHEN DAYLE SUTTON IS DEAD,
EVERYONE WILL KNOW THAT SHE WAS A LESBIAN DEGENERATE,
AND THUS YOU WILL DIE.

She didn't dare turn the key in the ignition. A police bomb
squad came to inspect the car, but found nothing. Dayle had a
couple of officers escort her home that night. It remained a
mystery how someone could have snuck past studio security
and broken into her locked car.

Dayle decided to start working her chauffeur full time, and
had him doubling as her bodyguard. After a couple of weeks,
the *Survival Instincts* backlash died down, and she forgot about
that note. She had enough on her mind with career worries.
Her box-office clout was slipping.

The good film roles were going to younger actresses. She
shouldn't have been surprised, but it still peeved her that—in
her late thirties—she was considered by the moneymen as too
old to play the romantic lead opposite Harrison Ford in one
project—and Robert Redford in another vehicle.

She couldn't lure the big-name leading men for films made
by her own production company. The guys wanted top billing
and too much money. So her recent on-screen lovers were
mostly second-echelon stars—all fine actors, but somehow
lacking the charisma for superstardom. If moviegoers didn't

see much chemistry between Dayle and her last few leading men, that was why.

Her leading men off screen weren't much better. In fact, for someone selected six times by *People* magazine as one of The 50 Most Beautiful People, her love life was pretty abysmal. It seemed predestined.

She'd gone to a numerologist once—on a dare, an old French-woman named Rene, who also did tarot readings. Rene must have dug up a few old magazine articles about her, because she accurately pegged Dayle as being an only child from a wealthy family. Perhaps she expected Dayle to be astonished when she pointed to the number nine on a chart, and declared in her thick accent: *Dis is how old you are when your father leaves you.*

Dayle nodded. Her parents' divorce was mentioned in that *Vanity Fair* cover story a while back. The article covered practically everything Rene was "unearthing": the years at a private boarding school, the need to escape through movies and books, the desire to pretend she was someone else that led to an interest in theater. *You do not trust many people,* Rene went on. *People like you, but you push dem away. You don't haff many close friends. I see walls dat you build. You are independent . . . cautious. You trust only yourself. You will not give up control. The relations in love*— Rene shook her head and sighed. *Dey are not so good. Maybe dis is because you need control? Or perhaps because of your caution?*

Dayle didn't remember Rene saying anything in particular that suddenly won her over. And maybe the old medium was merely conjecturing what might concern most single career women in their late thirties when she talked about Dayle's fear of growing old alone, her ticking biological clock, and the whole this-is-your-last-chance business. But by the time Rene started flipping over the various tarot cards, Dayle was busy taking notes.

Her love cards always looked so bleak: a man lying facedown

with dozens of spears in his back; a sword piercing a heart; a couple of paupers in the snow outside a locked castle. She and Rene finally began laughing over the utter hopelessness of it all.

Old Rene's cards didn't lie. Dayle felt cursed. The love of her life was Jeremy Caughlin, a brilliant young movie director, responsible for igniting her career. She was twenty-four and still a relative unknown when he picked her to star in *The Ivory Collar*, the film version of her off-Broadway hit. While shooting on location in Maine, Jeremy became Dayle's companion and confidant. He was a better friend than lover, but it didn't seem to matter.

They were a great-looking couple, favorites of the press, photographed wherever they went. Her future with Jeremy looked very promising indeed.

Jeremy told her that he was gay a few months before they got married. Dayle was smart enough to know that she couldn't change him, but Jeremy could change her—and make her into a major star. He was also a hell of a nice guy, her best friend, and he needed a wife for public appearances. He was very discreet with his boyfriends, while Dayle kept busy with her career. In seven years, she strayed only twice, the second time being the marriage breaker. Her affair with leading man Simon Peck made the tabloids. Jeremy was the one who filed for divorce.

Maybe she was looking for a way out with Simon Peck. He was sexy, yes, but she never really loved him. His real name was Simon Piccardo, and he admitted to stealing Gregory Peck's last name. That wasn't all he stole. Every time Dayle went to a party with Simon, he'd come back home with whatever item tickled his fancy at the host's house: a letter opener, paperweight, candy dish, or a CD. It was the same routine whenever they went shopping together. The studio had even established an understanding with various stores on Rodeo Drive that they would cover the cost of any items Simon stole. The store clerks merely had to keep tabs of the missing merchandise. Despite these precautions, Dayle still had to bail Simon out of jail twice. After the third arrest, she left him.

It was more or less the same scenario with her other show business boyfriends. She had a low tolerance level for their secret dysfunctions: the cokehead, the sex addict, the alcoholic, and the workaholic.

None of the men in Dayle's life really knew her very well—except maybe Jeremy. He'd remarried—another one of his leading ladies. As far as Dayle knew, he was still seeing his boyfriends on the side. His career had peaked during his time with Dayle. He lived on the East Coast now, and directed the occasional TV movie. They still kept in touch—holidays and birthdays mostly.

For lack of any competition, Dayle continued to think of Jeremy as one of her best buddies. Old Rene had called it pretty accurately: *You don't haff many close friends. I see walls dat you build. . . .*

The people who really knew her best were Bonny and Dennis. She was thinking about that last night, when Leigh Simone mentioned, "My best friend is my assistant, Estelle. And I pay her salary." Leigh said it was the same way with her band and backup singers—to a lesser degree. No matter how close she felt to them, they were still her employees. "Oh, the dilemma of being a diva!" she'd declared—before bursting into laughter.

Dayle kept her eyes closed as the plane encountered a little turbulence. Nothing severe. She smiled at the thought of Leigh Simone, and her offer of friendship. Here was someone very much like herself. How silly of her to worry about what people might think.

She opened her eyes. The boring businessman in the aisle seat didn't wait a beat before starting in: "The flight attendant came by for your drink order, but you were asleep. I ordered a Bloody Mary. What the heck, it's free. My wife's not going to believe I sat next to a movie star—"

"Excuse me, Ms. Sutton," the flight attendant interrupted, God bless him. "May I get you something to drink?"

Dayle smiled gratefully. "Yes, may I have a Diet Coke please?"

"I'd think a big superstar would order champagne and caviar," the man beside her remarked.

"I have a long day ahead," Dayle explained patiently. She glanced at her wristwatch, then reached for the air phone. "You've been very nice to let me sleep, thanks." She started dialing, then turned her shoulder to him.

"Oh, well, no problem," she heard him reply.

Dennis answered on the third ring. "Dennis Walsh speaking."

"Hi, it's me. I'm calling from the plane, which was delayed two hours. So—favor number one, let them know on the set that I'll be late. Favor two, call your buddy, Estelle, and see if you—"

"Estelle?"

"Leigh Simone's assistant, Estelle. Between you and her, maybe you can figure out some time when Leigh and I can get together this week. I figure—"

"Jesus, you don't know," he interrupted in a whisper.

"Know what?"

"I thought you sounded too damn cheerful."

"What are you talking about?"

"It's bad news, Dayle. Um . . . Leigh's dead."

Dayle told herself that she didn't hear him right.

But Dennis had confirmed it through a friend at Associated Press. Leigh had died from an apparent drug overdose in a rest room at the Imperial Hotel. "More bad news," Dennis went on. "Someone on the plane ID'd you and called somebody else. Long story short, you'll have a capacity crowd waiting for you at the gate—including our friends from the press."

"Oh, Jesus," Dayle muttered, rubbing her forehead.

"I'll get some extra security over to the airport for you."

"Thanks, Dennis," she said, her voice quivering. "Better have my lawyer there too. And for God's sake, see if you can get any more information about what happened to Leigh."

Camera flashes went off as Dayle emerged from the jet-way. Photographers elbowed and shoved each other for a good shot. Reporters screamed questions at her: What was her reaction when she heard about Leigh Simone's death? How well did she know Leigh? Did Leigh seem depressed last night? Did she know Leigh was taking drugs?

Dayle kept her gaze fixed directly ahead, neither smiling nor frowning. The extra security people controlled the crowd at the gate. Hank, her driver and part-time bodyguard, held the mob at bay with an intimidating look. A big guy with a blond crew cut, Hank was fifty-three. Without his glasses, he could have passed for an Aryan version of Oddjob, the deadly henchman in *Goldfinger*. In reality, Hank was a pussycat.

"Dayle, don't you have any comment about Leigh?"

On an impulse, she stepped up to the nearest microphone. "I don't believe for one minute that Leigh Simone took her own life," she announced. "Leigh didn't use drugs. When I saw her late last night, she was doing just great. I hope the police thoroughly investigate Leigh's death, because this overdose was not self-inflicted."

"Ms. Sutton, are you saying Leigh Simone was murdered?" one reporter asked. Then about a dozen others yelled out questions.

"I have no further comment," Dayle said.

"Thank God!" It was her lawyer, Ross Durlocker, who came to Dayle's side just as she turned away from the microphone. Balding and middle-aged, Ross compensated for his bland looks with frequent tanning sessions, eighty-dollar haircuts, and expensive designer suits. He hadn't come alone. Behind him were three men in not-so-expensive suits, who just had to be police. Neither Ross nor the plainclothesmen seemed too happy with her. "Dayle, sweetheart," Ross whispered. "The detectives here would like to talk to you before you say anything else to the media."

Dayle threw him a strained smile, then nodded. Hank went to claim her bags. The policemen led Dayle and her lawyer through the crowd, into an elevator that had a sign posted on the doors: AUTHORIZED PERSONNEL ONLY. They went up to the third floor, then followed the cops down the corridor to a narrow, windowless conference room with a long oak table and a dozen chairs. Blown-up aerial photos of the airport decorated the walls.

A thin, middle-aged Asian woman sat near the end of the table. She looked haggard. Her red jacket and skirt ensemble were slightly wrinkled. She gave Dayle and Ross a weary nod as she flipped open a steno pad.

"I could use some coffee," Ross whispered to Dayle. "You want coffee?"

"No, thanks." Dayle sat down at the table.

Ross settled next to her. He knocked on the table until the Asian woman looked up. "Honey, I'd like a cup of coffee, cream and sugar if you've got it."

The Asian woman nodded and smiled. But she didn't stand up.

"Don't call her honey," Dayle muttered. "You know that pisses me off."

"Me too," the Asian woman said. She shot a look at one of the cops. "Frank, get this asshole some coffee."

"Yes, Lieutenant Linn." He hurried out the door.

Dayle let out her first laugh since she'd stepped off the plane.

The woman turned to Dayle and her lawyer. "Well, you heard the man," she said. "I'm Lieutenant Susan Linn of the LAPD. I've been on the phone with the Portland Police Department since six forty-five this morning. I'm handling the investigation of Leigh Simone's death on this end."

Ross cleared his throat. "I'm here as counsel to—"

"I know why you're here, Mr. Durlocker," the lieutenant cut in. "You're Dayle Sutton's lawyer. I'll forget about your 'honey' crack if you forget what I called you. Now, let's cut to the chase. According to findings from the Portland police, Leigh's death was from an overdose of heroin—accidental or a suicide, they're still not sure."

Lieutenant Linn folded her hands and smiled at Dayle—the same smile she'd given Ross just seconds before calling him an asshole. "Now, Ms. Sutton. Since you were at the rally last night with Leigh, we wanted your cooperation in answering a few questions. It wouldn't have taken long. Of course, that was before you decided to share with the press your opinion about this case."

"I meant what I said," Dayle replied coolly.

"Your reputation for being forthright precedes you," the lieutenant said, glancing at her steno pad. "What makes you think, all evidence to the contrary, that Ms. Simone's overdose was—as you put it—'not self-inflicted?' "

Dayle leaned forward. "Leigh met me for a drink in my room late last night." Ross and the cops were staring at her, perhaps wondering about the lesbian angle; but Dayle didn't care. At least, she tried not to care.

"Go on," the lieutenant said. "I'm listening."

"We talked for thirty minutes or so," Dayle explained. "Leigh mentioned rumors about her sex life that simply weren't true. She said she didn't use drugs, and joked about being a 'disgrace to the rock star profession.' She wouldn't even take a drink when I offered. When she left my room at around eleven, she was in a good mood, not at all on the brink of suicide."

"So you two said good-bye at eleven o'clock," Lieutenant Linn remarked, glancing down at her notepad. "Did Ms. Simone say where she was going?"

"Back to her suite, her party."

"She never returned to her suite. It looks like you were the last person to see Leigh Simone alive."

"Except for the people who killed her," Dayle said,

"Ms. Sutton, Leigh's fingerprints were on the hypodermic. She'd trashed that ladies' room, and scribbled a note on the mirror in her own lipstick. Do you know what she wrote?"

Dayle shook her head.

"She wrote the word *Lies* twice. What do you think she meant?"

"Perhaps she didn't write it," Dayle said.

"Perhaps she did. Perhaps she'd been lying to you about not using drugs. How well did you really know Leigh Simone?"

"We met for the first time yesterday—after the concert. But I could tell she wasn't lying to me. Why should she?"

Ross's coffee finally arrived. The detective set it down in front of him. Ross pried off the lid and grumbled that he'd wanted cream and sugar.

"I'll take it if you don't want it," Dayle muttered, swiping the Styrofoam cup from him. She took a sip. The stuff fortified her a bit. She put the cup down. "Lieutenant, I might not have been in that rest room this morning. But I was with Leigh Simone last night. And the woman who left my suite was in a great mood, very much full of life. Your people in Portland ought to be looking into that hotel. Tony Katz was staying there the night he was murdered. And I happen to know that Tony was receiving death threats. Maybe his murder wasn't as random as it seemed. First Tony, then Leigh. Doesn't anyone in the Portland police or the LAPD see a connection here?"

"With the hotel? We see a coincidence. Where did you get this information about death threats toward Tony Katz?"

Dayle hesitated. "From someone who wishes to remain anonymous."

"That's not much help."

"But it should cast doubt on your theory that Leigh killed

herself. Somebody connected with the hotel could have been involved in both deaths.''

Lieutenant Linn shut her notebook and sighed. ''Ms. Sutton, I'm not investigating the death of Tony Katz. The Columbia County Police in St. Helens, Oregon, are handling that one. The bodies of Mr. Katz and his friend were discovered in a forest preserve seventy-five miles away from Portland and the Imperial Hotel. That was a double homicide. Leigh Simone took an overdose of heroin.'' The lieutenant gave her a perfunctory nod. ''I want to thank you for your time, Ms. Sutton.''

''Wait a minute,'' Dayle said. ''Is that all?''

Lieutenant Linn nodded. ''I'll send this information on to Portland.''

''And it won't change anyone's mind up there, will it?''

Linn got to her feet. ''I'll be honest, Ms. Sutton. What you've said hasn't changed *my* mind. I still think Leigh Simone took her own life. Despite what Ms. Simone might have told you, we know she was troubled about her sexuality and that she used drugs—including heroin.''

''That's a crock of shit,'' Dayle said, rising from her chair.

''No, that's gospel—according to someone who has known Ms. Simone for six years. We got it from her personal assistant, Estelle Collier.''

''I want a powwow with Estelle Collier ASAP,'' Dayle told Dennis over the phone in the back of her limousine. Hank was in the driver's seat, pulling out of the airport terminal.

''You want to meet with Estelle? Leigh Simone's assistant?''

''Yes. I'm sure everyone and their brother are trying to see her this morning, but do what you can. I need to talk to her.''

''Want me to get you an audience with the pope while I'm at it?''

''We're not talking. What's my schedule like today?''

''Mildly horrifying. You were due on the set an hour ago.

You have a lunch date with Maggie McGuire that I better cancel. Nearly every reporter in the free world wants to talk to you regarding Leigh Simone. And there's about a ton of other crap, but I took care of it.''

"Thanks, you're a prince," Dayle said. "One more favor. I want to talk with Tony Katz's widow, Linda Zane. She's someplace in Greece. See if you can dig up a phone number.''

"Will do. When can we expect you on the set?''

"We just left LAX. I'm on my way.''

"What were you saying back there?" Ross barked into his cellular. He sat behind the wheel of his Miata, a mile ahead of Hank and Dayle on Highway 405, near Culver City. "Do you really believe that Leigh Simone was murdered? That both Tony Katz and she were victims of some sort of conspiracy?''

"Maybe. For lack of a better word, call it a conspiracy.''

"Dayle, do you realize how nuts that sounds? One was gay-bashed. The other took an overdose. Except for the city and the hotel, there's no connection. Let's just drop this. The police are handling it. I don't want to sit through another session with Lieutenant Tokyo Rose, not on this. Besides, you hardly even knew Tony or Leigh. They both have a—a stigma attached to them. The wise thing to do right now is play down your brief association with Leigh—if you get my drift.''

"No, Ross. What is your drift?''

"As it is, people are going to talk about you and Leigh. Why give them more ammunition? I'm not your PR man, but even I can see that it won't do your image any good to keep harping on this whole Leigh Simone situation. It's bad press, box office hari-kari. Am I getting through to you?''

She had to salute Ross for his tact. He'd managed to put his point across without calling anyone a lesbian. "You sure sound like a PR man, Ross," she remarked.

"No, I'm your lawyer. I'm the one who'll have to sue some

tabloid to put an end to the talk. And you're not making it an easy case to win, Dayle.''

She told herself that gossip about her didn't matter, but it did. ''Listen, Ross,'' she said. ''Leigh didn't do drugs, and she wasn't gay. Her assistant is lying on both counts.''

''Well, why in the world would Estelle Collier lie?''

''I don't know,'' Dayle said. ''But I'm going to find out.''

Six

Libby Stoddard didn't look like an heiress. The plump twenty-seven-year-old had frizzy brown hair and a face that might have been pretty if she didn't appear perpetually bored. Her idea of dressing up for this meeting was a ratty black pullover and acid-washed jeans that hugged her wide hips.

The law office conference room had a panoramic view of Los Angeles. Seated at the long mahogany desk were Avery and his attorney, Libby, her lawyer, and an arbitrator.

Avery and Joanne had decided not to tell the police about the stolen videotape. They'd hoped to avoid any public embarrassment by meeting with Libby in private and persuading her to give it back. Avery's lawyer, Brent Cauffield, was very persuasive and charming. Always impeccably dressed, the tall, forty-year-old Brent had thinning brown hair and a confident smile. Avery wanted him to work his charisma on Libby: "We don't want to prosecute. If she returns the video, we won't press charges. I want to press her head in a vise, but we won't press charges."

Fueling Avery's anger were the calls to his house—more recorded snippets of conversation from their sex tape. He'd put a trace on the phone, and beefed up their security system. The Homeguard Company positioned four cameras around the house, one at the front gate, and another by the pool. All the cameras had twenty-four-hour videotapes that would be kept on file for a month before recycling. Joanne said it was like living in the Chase-Manhattan Bank.

The police never did figure out how the culprit had broken in. They said it must have been a pro. Avery surmised that Libby had upgraded from her punk errand boys.

As exasperating as Libby had been, Brent suggested that they bury the hatchet. It was why Avery had come along today—so Libby could finally meet him, and perhaps satiate her love-hate fixation for him.

Libby and her attorney had arrived fifteen minutes late. Her lawyer was a savvy black woman named Fiona Williamson, dressed in a yellow tailored suit. Libby seemed quite dumpy and under-dressed as she waddled through the door after Fiona.

Avery stood up and nodded politely.

Libby reeled back and vehemently shook her head.

"Ms. Stoddard and I would appreciate it if Mr. Cooper remained seated throughout the proceedings," her lawyer explained. "My client objects to his aggressive manner here—and his efforts to intimidate her."

"What?" Avery murmured, incredulous.

Rolling his eyes, Brent motioned for him to sit down. Avery took his seat. So much for burying the hatchet.

Fiona immediately started in about how her client felt persecuted and hounded by police during her Maui vacation. She stuck to Libby's original tale of unloading the returned gifts on some teenagers outside a thrift shop.

Brent asked why these destitute boys would ruin six hundred dollars' worth of merchandise and deliver it to Avery's door, rather than return the clothes and collect the refund money. Wouldn't that have made more sense?

"Probably," Libby replied, shrugging. That tired, bored expression didn't change. "I mean, whatever. . . ."

"Your client doesn't deny leaving an irate message on Mr. Cooper's home phone answering machine two weeks ago, does she?" Brent asked.

Libby snorted. Fiona shook her head. "Ms. Stoddard has already apologized for that unfortunate incident."

"We believe your client—still angry at Mr. Cooper—may have destroyed some gifts he'd returned to her. We also believe she paid those teenage boys to deliver the items to his door while she was in Maui."

"My client has already told you what she did with the merchandise in question," Fiona Williamson shot back.

"Does your client recall the name and location of the thrift shop?"

Frowning, Libby shook her head.

"It's important," Brent said. "Maybe we can track down these teenagers at the same place. We believe these boys may have broken into Mr. Cooper's home four days ago. They stole a very personal item."

Libby whispered something to her lawyer, then giggled.

Avery glared at her. She seemed to think this was all pretty amusing. He imagined her watching the video over and over. As much as she snickered at him and Joanne having sex, Libby probably relished the voyeuristic thrill. He could see her gleefully supervising the phone calls her errand boys made.

There had been several more in the last few days. They always hung up before a trace could be completed. At first, the same menacing voice crept over the line, spewing obscenities and quoting them in their intimate moments. A second person started phoning; he sounded older than the first. He said the videotape had been duplicated, and "My, won't the tabloids be interested."

Trying to maintain a brave front, Joanne said over and over that she refused to let the calls upset her. Nevertheless, Joanne's doctor had suggested that she go back on her antidepressants. But she ended up not taking them for fear it might hurt her chances of conceiving.

Seeing Libby so smug—almost enjoying this confrontation—Avery despised her. Beneath the mahogany table, he tapped his foot impatiently while his lawyer tried to tie her punk errand boys to last Thursday's break-in. Brent seemed headed in the wrong direction. Avery had already told him the cops thought a professional burglar had pulled the job. Why was Brent going on about these teenagers?

"Can you describe these boys outside the thrift store?" he asked.

"I don't remember." Libby shrugged and let out a little laugh.

"Ms. Stoddard, we're trying to track down the person or persons who stole an item from the Coopers' home last week."

"Listen . . . Libby," Avery broke in. "I'm not interested in pressing charges or anything like that. I just want this personal item back. I'm asking for your cooperation."

"Well, too bad you didn't want to talk to me last month," she sneered. "Too bad you sent back all the presents I bought you. I'll bet you're sorry now. Suddenly, you want to be my friend."

Fiona gently took hold of Libby's arm and whispered in her ear. Libby glanced down at the tabletop for a moment. "I don't know about any stolen stuff," she said coolly. "I can't help you."

Avery slapped the tabletop with his palm. "Goddamn it," he said.

"Mr. Cooper," the arbitrator said with a chastising look.

"Sorry," he muttered. Avery took a deep breath, then let it out slowly. He glanced across at Libby, who had a tiny smirk on her face. Avery leaned close to Brent. "God help me," he growled. "I'd like to strangle her. . . ."

"I beg your pardon, Mr. Cooper?" Libby's attorney asked hotly. She glowered at him. "Would you care to repeat it for the record?"

"No, that was between my attorney and myself," Avery said.

He didn't say another word for the rest of the hearing.

An hour after the meeting adjourned, Avery was back on the set for a love scene with Traci Haydn. It wasn't his day.

During a break in the shooting, he retreated to his trailer and caught Joanne on her cellular. She was in the car, returning from a lunch date. Avery gave her the bad news: "The arbitration was a disaster. And we aren't any closer to recovering that stupid video." He sighed, and sank down on his sofa. "The only thing to come out of this is—well, now I'm pretty certain Libby's not responsible for stealing the tape."

"What do you mean?" Joanne asked.

"When Brent asked her about those punks and their night delivery to the house, I could tell every answer Libby gave was a lie or an evasion. But when he focused on the break-in last Thursday and a 'stolen personal item,' I think Libby genuinely didn't know what he was talking about."

"Well, if it's not Libby, who's behind all this?" Joanne asked.

He'd been wondering the same thing. How could Libby know about their little home movie? Who else knew about the tape? Joanne admitted that she'd told a couple of girlfriends in New York, but no one else. Avery didn't trust most of Joanne's Broadway buddies. It was a gossipy, narcissistic crowd. Still, he doubted Libby or one of her people could have gotten to someone in New York. But seven weeks ago, the dead mice people had worked both coasts at the same time. They'd been in Joanne's dressing room, and they'd broken into his Vancouver hotel suite undetected. They could have first seen the videotape in his suitcase there. All those weeks went by, and nothing. How stupid of him to think that they had decided to pick on someone else.

"Are you still there?" Joanne asked.

"Yeah, sorry, I was just thinking."

"Listen, I talked to Saul again today," she said. "They still want me for that comedy. They've been holding off finding another actress, and the first read through is day after tomorrow in New York."

Avery sighed. "Well, I won't blame you if you need to go—"

"Honey, I told them no."

"Really?"

Joanne laughed. "You figured since things are getting rough, I'd start packing. Didn't you? Well, I'm sticking around, hon."

"Thanks," he said. "Listen, are you headed home?"

"Yes, home to all those cameras and security codes."

"I'll try to get out of here early. I love you."

As soon as Avery hang up, someone was knocking on his trailer door. "Avery? It's Bob!" the studio gofer said. "There's a call on your other line. It's Homeguard Security, something about the house. . . ."

"Um, thanks, Bob," Avery replied. He grabbed the receiver and pressed the blinking second-line button. "Yes, hello?"

"Hello, Avery Cooper? It's Homeguard calling. We don't mean to alarm you, sir. But we're a bit concerned by something we saw today and thought you might help clear it up for us."

"Yes?" Avery said.

"Well, we've been watching you on this video, licking your wife's snatch, and we're wondering how it tasted."

The line went dead.

* * *

With dinnertime just ahead, the Recipe Hotine was buzzing with helpful hints on Monday, October 27 at 4:43 P.M.:

ARLENE: My husband used to say that one of the worst things you can do to ground beef is make it into meat loaf, but then I got this recipe from my friend, Rachel. . . .

Mix 1 lb. lean ground beef with 1/2 cup of Pepperidge Farm Seasoned Stuffing (not cubed), 3 eggs, 1/4 cup of barbecue sauce, 1/2 pouch of Lipton's Onion Soup Mix (get plenty of the brown onion salt in there!), a dash of garlic salt, pepper, and just enough milk for consistency. Mold into Meat Loaf Casserole dish. If not on a diet, cover with a couple of slices of raw bacon. Slip into the oven at 350 degrees for one hour. It's delicious!

PAT: What do you usually serve with that? Baked Potato?

DOLORES: I have a garlic mashed potato that would complement it beautifully!

RICK: Request private chat with Pat, regarding pie recipe.

The following private mailbox interchange occurred at 4:46 P.M. on that same Monday afternoon:

AMERICKAN: Re: your inquiry, video has earned approx. $375,000 from various parties . . . SAAMO officers have broker handling it so we don't get R hands dirty . . . Understand stills will run in various adult mags, and B reproduced for Internet . . . 5000 copies of video being distributed . . . Copies can B easily duplicated to insure wider distribution . . . SAAMO high-ups congratulate U

for profitable & productive mission . . . that said, are U
aware of problems we've had with D.S.?

PATRIOT: She's mouthed off 2 press about R last job . . .
would like to muzzle her. We should have done job on
her 2 yrs. ago after lesbo vs. hunters movie.

AMERICKAN: Exactly . . . New orders to humiliate & ter-
minate D.S. as soon as possible . . . Details follow . . .
SAAMO Lieut., signing off.

Dayle had telephoned the Imperial Hotel several times, trying
to get a hold of Brian, the waiter. It was against hotel policy
to give out home phone numbers of their employees. Dayle
kept leaving her number, along with the message: "Call Ms.
Sutton as soon as possible." Brian never called.

Meanwhile, in the wake of Leigh's death, the tabloids
churned out their sordid headlines. Several publishers
announced forthcoming tell-all biographies, promising to
expose the secret life of Leigh Simone. Her CD sales boomed,
and Leigh Simone jokes made the rounds—with suicide or
lesbianism a part of the punch line. The new issue of *Time*
magazine presented Leigh on the cover, with the headline:
STARS AND DRUGS: THE SUICIDE OF LEIGH SIMONE.

Dayle wanted to prove *Time* magazine's suicide verdict
wrong. Ross warned her to stop "picking at the scab," and
Dennis said she was nuts. Still, he kept trying to reach Estelle
Collier for her, but to no avail.

Dennis did get a hold of Linda Zane, long distance at her
friend's villa in Greece. But Tony's widow couldn't tell Dayle
much. She'd spent little time with Tony in the final weeks of
his life, and knew nothing about any threats.

Frustrated, Dayle kept trying to reach the ever-elusive Brian.
He'd been dodging her for four days now.

She finally had the hotel operator put her through to the restaurant. Brian wasn't working, but one of his buddies was. He gave her Brian's phone number, and Dayle tried him at home. After two rings a young woman picked up. "Hi, this is Joy."

"Hello, is Brian there, please?"

She heard the girl call out: "Hey, Bry? Telephone!"

Dayle heard her mutter something, then Brian got on the line. "Hello?"

"Brian, this is Dayle Sutton."

Silence.

"Was that your girlfriend I was talking to just now?"

"No, that was my sister," he whispered. "This is my family's house. I wish you hadn't called me here."

"I'm sorry," Dayle said. "But you gave me no choice. I've left you several messages at the hotel. Is your sister still there with you?"

"She's in another part of the house now. But I can't talk long."

"Then I'll get right to the point. I think Tony Katz was killed by the people who had been threatening him. Your story makes it seem less and less like a random gay-bashing. The police don't know about the threats on Tony's life. I think the same people who killed Tony and his friend also murdered Leigh Simone."

"But she committed suicide."

"I have every reason to doubt that. So here's where you come in, Brian. You're the only one who knows about the threats on Tony's life. If you tell the police what you've told me, I'll do everything I can to keep your name out of the newspapers."

"But you can't guarantee anything like that, can you?"

"No, I can't," Dayle said. "I understand how you must feel, but if you keep quiet about the threats on Tony's life, the people who killed him could go on killing."

"No, I'm sorry, I can't help you," he said, his voice shaky. "The cops won't believe me unless I tell them about Tony and me. And I'm not doing that, no way."

Dayle said nothing. Brian was right. Admitting his sexual fling with Tony Katz was an unavoidable part of the package. And she couldn't guarantee anonymity for him. Dayle sighed. "Will you at least think about it, Brian?"

"I'm sorry, Miss Sutton," he whispered. Then he hung up.

"I'm Mrs. Richard Marshall, but you can call me Elsie."

"Hi, Elsie!" the studio audience replied in unison.

Elsie Marshall blew them a kiss. Today, she wore a purple suit, which showed off a lavender rinse in her hair. Elsie sat on the edge of the desk, the framed photo of Ricky beside her. "Well, isn't it a shame what Leigh Simone did to herself?" she asked her subjects in the studio seats. They all murmured in agreement.

"I'll admit, Leigh Simone was never one of Ricky's and my favorites. But that doesn't mean I'm not praying for her. It's sad, it really is, to see how certain people throw their lives away. Now, the way I understand it, Leigh Simone was at this wild party full of gays and lesbians like herself . . ."

Elsie hesitated, then frowned. *"Gay.* Remember when that used to be a perfectly good word? I certainly do."

She shrugged. "I'm just a housewife, and I don't know much about this crowd with their 'lifestyles' of indiscriminate sex and drugs. But I understand this party was connected to some benefit concert promoting special rights for homosexuals." Elsie frowned. "What do you think of these people who want special treatment, because they're homosexual? I'm sure my son, Drew, has a few things to say about that." She glanced stage right. "Drew?"

Drew Marshall strutted onto the set, wearing a clingy gray crew-neck jersey and pleated black trousers. This was one of the Best Dressed Man's casual days, and a chance to show off his well-toned body—usually hidden under designer suits. Drew had wavy, light brown hair, blue eyes, and cheekbones the camera loved. He seemed like the perfect, All-American hunk-hero. Never mind the rumors that a number of women had been paid off to keep quiet about their furtive one-night stands with the eligible bachelor. The stories—though unsubstantiated—went that Drew's cruelty in bed was matched only by his inadequacies. And the wholesome hunk, so often photographed shirtless while playing football or soccer, was said to be hot-tempered and arrogant on the field; "an incredible asshole," according to several former classmates at Harvard.

The reports never seemed to hurt Drew's popularity on the show. He always came across as a perfect gentleman. He stepped up to his mother's side and put an arm around her.

"Somebody forget to wear a tie today?" Elsie joked.

"Oh, c'mon, Mom," he said, blushing. "Give me a break."

The studio audience seemed to laugh on cue.

"Well, did you hear what I was saying?"

"I sure did." Drew nodded. "Y'know, Mom, I have to admit, I liked Leigh Simone's music. I have a couple of her albums."

Elsie rolled her eyes. The studio audience responded with a mild tittering. Elsie moved behind her desk, and Drew sat down in his chair.

"From what I read," Drew continued, "Leigh Simone was into drugs and had some deep problems having to do with her choice of lifestyle."

"Yes, indeed," Elsie said. "If you were listening to your mother instead of combing your hair backstage, you'd have heard what I said about that rally in Portland for homosexuals wanting special rights."

"I heard you, Mom," Drew said. He suddenly looked serious. "You know, unfortunate people like Leigh Simone—who promote the homosexual agenda and campaign to restrict our constitutional rights to bear arms—have no regard for American family values. We need to protect our homes, our families, and our impressionable youth. These homosexuals who want to take away our guns and prey on our children, they pose a direct threat to the American family. . . ."

Police had to control the mob of reporters and fans gathered outside the gated community of Malibu Estates. A parade of limos, Mercedeses, and BMWs slowly passed through the guarded entry. Each one carried a film or recording star. None of those famous people gave autographs or talked to reporters. They stayed in their cars—until the guard waved them through to the private cul-de-sac. Photographers still managed to take their pictures, while reporters wrote down what they were wearing and who they were with.

It may as well have been a star-studded film premiere—instead of the site for a memorial service.

Leigh's will requested a quick cremation and no funeral. Her producer, record mogul Morley Denton, invited a hundred of Leigh's friends to his beach-front mansion to "celebrate the life" of the late pop diva. Dayle was on the guest list. Morley had also invited some press agents and publicists. In addition to the crowd outside the gate, unwelcome tabloid helicopters hovered over Morley's house. Dayle's publicist had alerted the media that Dayle was attending the memorial with her current leading man, John McDunn.

One of the busiest actors in Hollywood, John had snatched up a Best Supporting Oscar three years before. Every one of his forty-six fast-living, hard-drinking years showed on his still-handsome face. Recently divorced, John costarred with Dayle in her new movie. Their steamy love scenes together had already generated some hot prerelease publicity for the film.

In fact, John had been Dayle's relationship number eight during the finalization of his divorce. She went into the affair knowing he had a roving eye. The romance was short-lived, but they remained friends.

John was the solution to Dayle's problems. He had no objections to a few publicity dates with her. They looked so right together, it silenced a lot of the whispered rumors about Dayle and Leigh.

Dayle clung onto John's arm as they stepped into the front hallway—an airy, marble atrium with a waterfall along one wall. She recognized a couple of press agents, staking out the arriving guests. They sized up John and her, then unabashedly scribbled in their notebooks.

"I really appreciate this, Johnny," she said under her breath. "I know there are a thousand other places you'd rather be right now."

John shrugged. "The Lakers game, in bed with you . . ."

Dayle nudged him. "Not anymore, honey. But thanks just the same."

The helicopters buzzing overhead had driven scores of guests from the terrace into the house. They gathered in Morley's huge living room, with its panoramic ocean view. Everyone still seemed in shock over Leigh's untimely death—and the news about her "drug problem." One of Leigh's noncelebrity friends confided in Dayle that she refused to believe any of the stories. "And by the way, Dayle," she said. "You should know, Leigh was so excited about meeting you. Before her Portland trip, that's all she talked about."

Dayle felt cheated of a friend.

She spotted Estelle Collier by the hors d'oeuvres table. In only six days, Estelle had gone from *celebrity-assistant* to *celebrity*. She knew Leigh better than anyone. Agents, publishers, and TV producers were tripping over each other for the rights to Estelle's story. She'd already appeared on several tabloid TV news shows, painting her dead employer as a pathetic, drug-dependent lesbian with a string of nameless, faceless lovers.

How Estelle could face Leigh's friends now was beyond comprehension. She looked like a white-trash lottery winner: too much makeup, too much jewelry, and a tacky purple dress that was too tight for her chubby figure. She loaded up her plate with food, and popped a cheese puff in her mouth.

Patting John's shoulder, Dayle excused herself and started across the room toward Estelle. Leigh's former assistant saw her coming. She put down her plate and started to turn away. "Estelle, we need to talk," Dayle said.

Estelle swiveled around with a professionally perky smile. "Why, hello, Dayle. I've been meaning to return your calls—"

"Tell me what's going on," Dayle said, her voice dropping to a whisper. "Why did you lie to the police about Leigh?"

Estelle nervously glanced around at the other guests. Frowning, she shook her head at Dayle. "I don't have to talk to you," she said.

"You didn't have to talk to the tabloids either, but that didn't stop you."

Estelle's eyes narrowed. "Be grateful I've left you out of it, Dayle. Take my advice and stay out of it."

"Leigh wasn't gay," Dayle whispered. "She didn't take drugs. And she didn't commit suicide. She trusted you. How can you betray her like this?"

"Let's drop it, okay?" Estelle whispered tensely. "You have no idea what you're getting into. Forget about it. Nothing can bring her back."

Dayle numbly gazed at her. "You know who killed her, don't you?"

"Please, leave me alone."

Dayle took hold of her arm. "Let's go someplace where we can talk. I want to help. If someone is threatening you—and making you tell these lies—"

"Please!" Estelle wrenched free from her grasp. She glanced around. They had an audience. Estelle cleared her throat. "I know how fond you were of Leigh," she said calmly. "We all were. There's nothing we could have done. She had so many problems. We mustn't blame ourselves." Estelle slowly shook her head. "Don't linger on it, Dayle. Let it go."

Seven

Twelve laps around her apartment building's rooftop track equaled a mile. Dayle was alone up there, twenty-one stories above the street. The heavy smog tonight made for a gorgeous sunset: billowing clouds of vibrant pink, orange, and crimson. But the smog also took its toll on Dayle's lung power. Eighteen laps, and already she was exhausted.

She took to the track whenever she was particularly frazzled, lonely, or blue; which meant she was in damn good physical shape lately. She'd hired a private detective agency, Brock Investigations, to check on Estelle Collier. Dayle figured Estelle was being blackmailed or threatened. There had to be some explanation for her lies. John McDunn had recommended the agency. He swore they were good, because his second wife used the sons of bitches to catch him cheating—and he'd been so careful. Dayle had spoken with Amos Brock three days ago. He'd assigned the case to his brother, Nick, who was supposed to have some results for her soon.

In the meantime, she felt uncertain and all alone with her

theories about the deaths of Leigh, Tony, and his friend. Hell, she felt all alone, period. Though they never had a chance to become friends, Dayle felt an inexplicable void in the wake of Leigh's "suicide."

Last night, she'd started to call Dennis at home—just to chat. But she hung up before she finished dialing. He wasn't on the clock. She had no right to bother him at home simply because she was lonely. Besides, Dennis had met someone, and supposedly he was in love. The way he kept talking about her—*Laura this, Laura that*—was rather nauseating. Dayle hated to admit it, but she was a little jealous. Dennis had found a life outside his job, he'd found someone more important to him than Dayle Sutton.

She wondered what people would say if she died the same way as Leigh had. Would her memory be marred by rumors and innuendo? Who knew her well enough to rush to her defense? She had no real intimate friends. All she had was her public image.

They'd probably rehash the lesbian rumors. Some enterprising tabloid reporter might even dig up evidence of the one time she'd "experimented" with another woman. It had happened almost fourteen years ago, the first of her two indiscretions while married to Jeremy. She was starring in a satire called *Positively Revolting,* about antiwar demonstrators in the sixties. The movie was shot in Mexico with a very hip, young cast and crew. Dayle often felt as if she was the only person on the production who wasn't high on something half the time. One night, during a weekend beach party, she indulged in too many margueritas. Everyone went skinny-dipping, and soon, twosomes and threesomes were ducking into the bushes or cars to have sex. Dayle wound up on a cheesy yacht that belonged to a friend of Cindy something. She didn't know what Cindy had to do with the movie, but she was pretty, with long, curly red hair, blue eyes, and freckles all over her slender body. Cindy also had a little cartoon of Winnie the Pooh tattooed on her ass—along with the words, BEAR BOTTOM.

The next morning, Dayle felt so sick and hungover as she crawled out of the bunk. She found her damp, sandy clothes amid beer cans and food wrappers on the cabin floor. Pulling on her panties, she squinted out the porthole and was relieved to see that they were docked at a pier with a couple of other boats, and not drifting somewhere in the middle of the Gulf of Mexico. But her hopes for a clean getaway were dashed when Cindy woke up and said something about going out for pancakes.

Dayle apologized and said she had to leave. Her memory of the night before was vague. She'd gone into the water with the others, but kept on her panties. Cindy had stripped all the way to nothing. Several of the guys were after her, but Cindy shot each one down, and eventually she swam to Dayle.

Having been married two years to a gay man, Dayle was curious about same-gender sex—and maybe just a tad interested in evening the score on her wandering spouse. She'd felt a rush of excitement sneaking away with Cindy. But by the time they began kissing and touching each other, it seemed silly. Dayle had to pretend she was someone else in order to overcome the awkwardness. The whole experience was like another acting assignment. She didn't enjoy it very much.

And she really didn't want to have pancakes with Cindy. Despite her urgency to get the hell out of there, Dayle tried to let Cindy down easy. She told her that the previous evening's activities had been a fluke, a drunken experiment. She couldn't get dressed fast enough. "Considering this kind of thing isn't my bag," she heard herself say. "I still had fun with you. . . ."

Cindy stared at her sleepily. Puffing away on a Newport, she lay naked in the bunk, an ashtray balanced on her stomach. "Bullshit," she said finally. "This *is* your bag. You're into girls. That's what I heard on the set. You dig girls, your old man is into guys, and the two of you got married to please the Hollywood establishment.''

Dayle didn't remember how long she stuck around trying to convince Cindy that she was wrong. But she vividly recalled the wavering boat, and feeling so sick. When she finally climbed up to the deck, she braced herself against a light post by the dock, and succumbed to the dry heaves.

The half-true rumors about her ''marriage of convenience'' periodically haunted Dayle and Jeremy during the eight years they were together. But the talk never grew above a whisper, and it stayed within the Hollywood community. Ironically, it took Dayle's affair with Simon Peck—along with the divorce, and Jeremy's subsequent remarriage—for the gossip to die down about both of them. Ending in all that mess, it didn't seem so much like a marriage of convenience anymore.

Of course, the tales about Dayle's lesbian leanings were resurrected after the release of *Survival Instincts*. And just as the gossip started subsiding, Leigh's ''suicide'' ignited all sorts of new speculation. What was Dayle's role during Leigh's last hours that night at the Portland hotel? Had a lover's quarrel provoked Leigh's overdose?

The publicity dates with John McDunn had helped take some of the heat off. The former lovers looked so right together, their claim that they were ''just good friends'' seemed like a smoke screen for some torrid affair. More damage control came from Dayle's publicist, who concocted a story about the meeting with Leigh on that fateful night. According to the press release, the two women had gotten together to discuss Leigh recording the theme song for Dayle's new movie. A lot of people bought the story. In fact, several recording artists expressed interest in taking over the vocal assignment.

Dayle had to look out for her reputation. Nevertheless, the more she thought about having to take these steps in the wake of Leigh's death, the less she liked herself.

She ran harder, pouring it on until she was sprinting around that rooftop track. Her lungs burned, and beads of sweat flew off her forehead.

When she'd started her laps a half hour ago, Dayle had been alone up there. The track encircled a glass-enclosed pool area—complete with lounge chairs, umbrella tables, blooming plants, and potted trees. There were also rest rooms and a mini-gym around the corner by the stairwell, on the other side of the elevator. The maintenance crew kept this semiprivate paradise spotlessly clean. Still, the place always smelled like chlorine and wet socks.

No one was using the pool right now. As dusk gave way to night, the inside lights—set on a timer—went on. Dayle tallied her twenty-eighth lap and began to slow down. Passing by the vestibule for the elevators, she caught a glimpse of someone on the other side of the glass door. He'd been standing there, watching her—a short, pale, mustached man in an aviator jacket. Despite the darkness, he wore sunglasses. Dayle didn't recognize him as one of her neighbors in the building.

Now that she'd spotted him, the stocky little man suddenly turned away and tried to look interested in the pool area. It wasn't a very convincing show. He opened the other door and stepped into the tropical atrium, but he kept sneaking these furtive glaces at her.

Dayle peered back over her shoulder at him. She veered along a bend in the track, and ran a half lap on the other side of the building. Taking another curve, she saw him again—still in the pool area. He hadn't strayed far from the vestibule door. He seemed to be staking out the elevators.

The distant blare of a car horn made her aware of the traffic several stories below—just on the other side of the chest-high railing. The wind kicked up a little, and Dayle suddenly felt cold. The sweat on her forehead turned clammy.

Warily, she watched him move back into the vestibule. She could tell that behind those sunglasses, the creepy man was staring at her. She must have been frowning at him, because he suddenly turned again, and reached for the elevator button. But he didn't actually press it, his thumb missed the button by an inch. The little arrow light didn't go on. Almost too casually, he glanced back at her again. He wasn't going anywhere. He was waiting for her.

Dayle couldn't quite catch her breath—even as she slowed down to a trot. Her skin felt prickly.

She kept her eyes trained on him—until she rounded another curve in the track. She jogged past the mini-gym, the rest rooms, and a stairwell on the other side of the glass. At the next bend, there was a door to the pool area. She hoped to duck inside and make it to the stairs before he saw her.

Approaching the pool entry, Dayle took a more deliberate stride. She didn't want to burst through the door and call attention to her flight. She couldn't let him know she was scared. Like a dog scenting her fear, he'd give chase if she ran. She pulled open the door and walked at a brisk clip toward the stairwell. The humid, chlorine-stagnant air hit her, but she didn't slow down. Navigating around the pool, she spied him— still by the elevators. He was talking on a cell phone. Dayle couldn't tell if he'd noticed her yet.

Then, as she neared the stairs, Dayle caught a glimpse of the door to the vestibule swinging open. She didn't look back. She heard his footsteps on the tiled floor—and him whispering some kind of urgent directions into his portable phone.

Dayle ducked into the stairwell and hurried down a few steps before she suddenly froze. She gaped over the banister. Two flights below, a figure pulled back from the stair railing and retreated into the shadows—along the cement wall.

Someone else was waiting for her.

For a second, Dayle was paralyzed. She turned and raced back up the stairs. She didn't see the stubby man with the sunglasses. She didn't even stop to look for him as she emerged from the stairwell. Everything was a blur. She found the ladies' room door, pushed her way inside, then locked it.

Catching her breath, Dayle leaned against the door. She couldn't stop trembling. She was covered with perspiration, and her jogging-wear clung to her body. She listened to the footsteps outside—then whispering. It sounded as though one of them said, "She's in there."

Dayle backed away from the door—toward the toilet stalls. One of the men outside began tugging and wrenching at the knob over and over—to no avail. Finally, a thin file slipped through the crack by the lock, and it started moving up and down.

Dayle frantically glanced around the lavatory, looking for anything she might use to defend herself. Out of the corner of her eye, she saw something move in the reflection of the mirror.

Gasping, she spun around. A shadow floated across the tiled floor—over by the corner stall. Was someone hiding in there? Did they have a third man working with them?

Dayle tried to scream, but no sound came out. Instead, the scream came from outside—from the pool area. It was the sound of a little girl. Dayle heard a woman and man talking, then water splashing.

Dazed, she stared at the door. The file wasn't there anymore. She didn't hear their whispered voices. They'd gone.

Dayle glanced back at that corner stall, then unlocked the rest room door and pushed it open. She peered out at the five people who had unwittingly saved her. Two children were splashing each other in the shallow end of the pool, while three adults—in their street clothes—settled down at an umbrella table. It looked like a young couple with a friend—one of Dayle's neighbors, probably an uncle to those kids.

She still didn't feel safe. Dayle stole one more glance at that stall in the corner. If someone was in there, he'd hidden himself well. And she wasn't going to start looking for him.

Dayle hurried out of the rest room.

* * *

"Then what happened?" Lieutenant Linn asked.

"I asked my neighbor over by the pool if he could escort me back to my apartment." Dayle spoke in a whisper. She glanced around the restaurant for a second, then sighed. "I told him that a reporter had somehow gotten into the building, and he was bothering me. Anyway, my neighbor rode down in the elevator with me, then walked me to my door."

Despite the noisy crowd at Denny's this Halloween morning, Dayle was certain someone would hear her. Already, a couple of loud, overly friendly women had come up to the table and asked for her autograph. They kept shrieking and laughing, like contestants on *The Price Is Right*. The women had left a few minutes ago, but people were still staring.

When Dayle had called her last night, Lieutenant Linn claimed that this particular Denny's was where she had all her breakfast meetings. A cardboard and tissue jack-o'-lantern centerpiece decorated their window table. The waitress, an older woman with glasses and a pink rinse in her hair, had seemed far too busy to notice that the order for dry toast and orange juice came from a bona fide movie star. Lieutenant Linn had ordered a Grand Slam.

"Don't you have someone handling security in your building?" she asked, while jotting in her notebook.

Dayle nodded. "We have a doorman and a guard. I called them immediately. But they never found the men. It's possible these guys slipped in past the front desk earlier. Someone on the eleventh floor was having a lot of work done on their place, and workmen were coming in and out all day."

Lieutenant Linn grabbed the brown plastic pitcher and refilled both of their coffee cups. "Why did you tell your neighbor that a reporter was pestering you? Why not just tell him the truth?"

"Because these men were after *me*," Dayle replied. "I saw no point in scaring my neighbor—or his friends."

"What makes you so sure they were after you—and only you?"

Dayle frowned. "I'm not paranoid—if that's what you're getting at."

"Well, isn't it possible that these men could have been reporters?" Lieutenant Linn said. "I mean, as you know, some of those guys are awfully aggressive."

Dayle sighed and glanced out the window for a moment. She'd hoped to avoid publicity by calling Lieutenant Linn last night—instead of reporting the incident to the police. She didn't want the press picking it up.

Their breakfast arrived. Dayle's toast was smothered with butter, but at this point, she didn't give a damn. "I know you think I'm overreacting," she said. "But something's happening here. Leigh's death wasn't a suicide, and what happened to Tony Katz was no random gay-bashing. He was getting death threats. I wish I could tell you where I heard this, but I can't. This person prefers to remain anonymous."

Susan Linn doused her pancakes with syrup. "So you think the men stalking you last night are the same ones who threatened Tony Katz—and killed Leigh Simone?" She gave Dayle a dubious glance. "Why should they want to kill you?"

Dayle shrugged. "I was at that benefit concert. I gave a tribute to Tony. Maybe I pissed somebody off. I had a ton of death threats a couple of years ago when I played a gay character in this movie."

Nodding, Lieutenant Linn jotted something in her steno pad. *"Survival Instincts.* I saw it. Listen, do you have a bodyguard?"

"My chauffeur doubles as my bodyguard."

"You should get somebody full time." She put down her pen. "When we last talked, you insisted we were wrong about Leigh's drug habits and sexual problems. Do you still feel that way?"

"Yes, I do," Dayle said.

"That would make her assistant, Estelle Collier, a liar, wouldn't it?"

"Has anyone ever bothered to confirm Estelle's claims about Leigh's 'secret life'?"

Susan Linn shrugged. "I suppose we're all rather quick to believe the worst about people, especially the rich and famous. Then again, why would Estelle Collier lie?"

"I might be able to answer that for you, Lieutenant. Very soon."

Amos Brock's brother, Nick, attracted a lot of attention as he swaggered to Dayle's trailer door. About thirty, and attractive in a cheap, hoody way, he was tan (probably all over), and wore a Hawaiian silk shirt, jeans, and cowboy boots. He had a sinewy body and his straight black hair was pulled back in a short ponytail. He looked like the male equivalent of a bimbo.

He'd shown up at the studio between scene setups. Dayle had managed to get in three hours of work since her breakfast with Lieutenant Linn this morning. She was in her trailer, chatting with Bonny, and primping for her next scene. She asked Bonny to leave them alone for a few minutes. Bonny gave her a lewd wink at the trailer door—as if Nick Brock were some hired stud service, not a private detective. Keeping a straight face, Dayle offered him a seat and a cup of coffee. He'd dowsed himself in Obsession, forcing Dayle to crank up the vent fan. She returned to her vanity, where she reapplied her lipstick. "Thanks for coming, Mr. Brock," she said to his reflection in the mirror. "I assume you found something."

"Correct-a-mundo, and you can call me Nick," he said, leering at her. "You know, you're one fine-looking lady, Ms. Sutton. And it doesn't take a lot of detective work to figure that out."

"Thanks," Dayle said. "But you can knock off the sweet talk, Nick. What did you find out about Estelle Collier?"

He opened a black leather-bound notebook. "Well, our gal, Estelle, has a lot of secrets. First off, she's got a kid, a love child, the result of her hippie period. His name is Peter, and he was born in San Francisco in 1970."

"Is this son still alive?" she asked.

Nick nodded. "Correct-a-mundo. And although she's been hanging out with liberal types like Leigh Simone, Estelle has kept junior a secret."

Dayle turned to stare at him. "What about the father?"

"It says 'unknown' on the birth certificate. But I know this much. The little bastard grew into a big bastard, despite mama busting her chops to make sure he got everything he wanted. Estelle has spent a small fortune bailing him out of jail again and again, and putting him into private rehab centers for substance abuse. Thanks to Peter, Mama Estelle was in debt up to her ass when Leigh Simone hired her. That was six years ago. At just about the time Estelle was climbing out of debt, Little Petee got bitten by the gambling bug. Three guesses how his luck was."

"Disastrous?"

He nodded. "Correct-a-mundo. A major loser."

"Could you do me a favor, Nick?" Dayle said. "Could you knock off the 'correct-a-mundo' bit? It's annoying."

Nick looked crestfallen. "Sorry," he grumbled. He glanced down at his notes. "Um, where was I?"

"The son had some gambling debts. I gather Estelle covered his losses."

Nick nodded. "Mama to the rescue. It was either that or sonny would get his legs sawed off at the kneecaps. To shell out the payments, Estelle borrowed from her boss—on the sly."

"She embezzled from Leigh?"

"Correct-a—" Nick caught himself. "Yes. Looks that way."

"How did you find out all this?"

Nick leaned back and sighed. "Detective work, Ms. Sutton. It's what I do. I talked to an ex-friend of Peter Collier's, and I found this in San Francisco." He handed her a copy of Peter Collier's birth certificate. "Plus I schmoozed with a clerk at the accounting firm for the late Leigh Simone."

"A clerk?"

Nick shrugged. "She's hot for me. I bat my baby blues, casually ask the questions, and she always spills more than she intends to. From what I could find out, when Leigh offed herself, right away, they noticed a lot of money had gone hasta-la-bye-bye from her accounts. So they pumped Estelle, and she cracked, fessed up to the whole thing."

"Why wasn't she arrested?"

"They were supposed to be keeping track of Leigh's doe-ray-me. If they blew the whistle on Estelle, they'd look like idiots. My guess is, they must have made a deal with Estelle to replace the money before anyone was the wiser. The day after Leigh was discovered in the ladies' lav, ever faithful Estelle played ball with the tabloids, slamming her dead boss. She raked in close to forty thousand that day, but you'd never know it, because it went right into Leigh's account to cover what she'd been skimming. Y'know, when it came to blowing the whistle on Madame Simone, Estelle promised the tabloids more than she delivered. She couldn't back up a thing she told them. No juicy photos or videos, no love letters in Leigh's handwriting, no proof. Bupkis. The tabloids weren't too happy with her."

"So Estelle couldn't prove she was telling the truth about Leigh?"

Nick nodded. "Correct-a . . . yes, correct, ma'am."

"Okay," Dayle said. "What I need is proof that she was

lying to the tabloids and the police. Were you able to dig any-thing up?''

Nick Brock shrugged. "Hey, sorry. I thought you were look-ing for something in her past, some good ammo for a black-mailer. Between the loser son she has stashed away and the embezzlement, I figured we had something.''

Dayle glanced at the copy of Peter Collier's birth certificate. She studied that line on the document: *Father: Unknown.*

"Mr. Brock, see what you can find out for me about this unknown father," she said. "And consider it a rush job.''

Eight

Traci Haydn refused to come out of her trailer, and all they could do was wait. Traci's assistant, a thin, pencil-faced brunette who had overdone the collagen injections, came out of the trailer at different intervals to explain that Traci had problems with her hair, problems with her makeup; she was on the phone with her astrologer, with her agent, with her husband; she had cramps, she had a headache. It was no secret on the set that Miss Big Lips was supplying Traci with cocaine.

Jotting notes on his script, Avery waited it out with the crew. A couple of technicians passed around the latest *US* magazine with Traci on the cover. "Says here," one read, " 'Traci makes friends wherever she goes. No prima donna, she's on a first-name basis with everybody on her movie set.' "

A soundman didn't look up from his newspaper. "That would be true, if we were all named 'Hey, Fuckhead.' " He glanced at Avery. "Want the paper?"

Avery shrugged. "Sure. Thanks, Fuckhead."

Chuckling, the soundman handed him the newspaper, which

was folded over to the Entertainment page. Avery checked out
CHASING AROUND TOWN by Yvonne Chase. The gossip column
featured tidbits on a dozen celebrities—their names in bold
print. The last blurb was an occasional gem Yvonne featured
to set Hollywood on a guessing game called I'M NOT SAYING
WHO, BUT . . .

Avery read the blurb:

*It's true what you've heard about a certain guy-next-
door TV-to-Film Star and his Broadway Babe wife. Proof
their Bi-Coastal marriage is A-OK is in the Porn! A
raunchy home video of these two in the sack is circulating
throughout the Hollywood Hills. One movie exec is said
to have paid ten thousand clams for a copy of the sexually
explicit tape. No comment from the frisky, unabashed
duo.*

Avery started to crumple up the newspaper, then became
aware of the soundman hovering over him. "Excuse me," he
managed to say. He headed toward his trailer.

It was happening. Copies of his and Joanne's sex tape were
out there now. People were starting to talk about it. Soon
bootlegged copies of the video would be available. And it
wouldn't be long before Internet users could download explicit
photos of Avery Cooper and Joanne Lane making love. The
last few days had been quiet, but he'd seen this coming.

He had already told his agent, Louise, about the new Avery
Cooper film for which she'd receive no commission. As Louise
said, "Well, you never know. Maybe some country will bomb
another country the day this video goes public, and no one will
give a damn about your little home movie."

Avery had also spoken to Brent Cauffield about legal avenues
they could take to stifle the video distribution and bootlegging.
His attorney wasn't very optimistic, but promised to do what
he could.

To handle "damage control," Louise had recommended a public relations wizard named Steve Bensinger. Avery had already talked with him on the phone. He seemed like a nice guy, very smart. They were scheduled to sit down and discuss strategies early tomorrow night.

Avery now needed to move up that appointment.

Once inside his trailer, he called Louise. They'd been playing phone tag all morning. She picked up this time: "Seers Representation."

"Hey, Louise. It's me. Did you see the blurb in Yvonne Chase's column?"

"Yes, I saw that tidbit," she said. "And I also heard from a friend of mine this morning. He says they showed your video last night during a party at Vaughn Samson's house. . . ."

"Oh, great." Avery muttered. "So we're party entertainment. . . ."

"If it's any consolation, you were quite a hit with Vaughn and the boys. He may just want to direct you in your next film."

"Swell," he grunted, pinching the bridge of his nose. He sat on his sofa. "Have any reporters called you about this yet?"

"Only about a dozen since breakfast," she answered dryly.

"I need to see Steve Bensinger as soon as possible," Avery said. "We shouldn't talk to the press until we've worked out an angle on this."

"I'll call Steve for you," Louise offered. "He owes me a favor. I'll make sure he sees you tonight."

"Good." Avery sighed. "I don't know how to thank you, Louise."

"Hmmm, maybe you could get me a copy of that video." She was the only one laughing. "Avery, it was a joke."

"Sorry. At the moment, I don't have a very good sense of humor."

"Honey, a sense of humor is what you need most right now."

He managed a chuckle. "Sound advice. Thank you, Louise."

Avery clicked off the line, but held on to the phone. He needed to call Joanne, and dreaded it. Despite the quiet calm before the storm of these last few days, she'd shown signs of increasing strain. Last night, she'd thrown a glass of red wine at the kitchen wall, because he'd made the fatal error of mentioning her mother again.

He'd brought up the topic a few days ago. Avery felt they had to warn their parents about the bad publicity ahead. He certainly didn't want Rich and Lo hearing about the video from someone else. They were still catching flack from church friends about his controversial TV movie. To brace them for this latest bombshell, he'd asked his brother to be at his parents' home when he called, then he got both his mom and dad on the line. At first, his mother didn't seem to comprehend what Avery was talking about: "What do you mean? What 'personal item' did these people steal?"

"They stole a video, Mom. It's—kind of a risqué home movie of Joanne and myself—in bed."

It was quiet on the other end of the line for a moment. Finally, his father cleared his throat. "Um, you made a video of the two of you—"

"Yeah, Pop. And they stole it." Avery's stomach was turning.

"Why?" his mom asked, incredulous. "Why did you do that? I can't believe Joanne would agree to such a thing. What were you thinking?"

"Honey," his father cut in. "Let's just listen to what he has to say."

"I'm really sorry, you guys," he muttered. "It gets worse. The people who took the tape, they say they're going to make copies . . ."

The more he tried to explain, the more upset his mother became. Finally, his father gently interrupted. "Avery? We'll have to call you back. Okay? Your mom's crying. We'll call you back, son.''

Avery heard a click on the other end of the line.

"I'm sorry," he said to no one.

They phoned back a half hour later. By then, his mother had calmed down, and his dad was even trying to joke about it. Avery apologized for the embarrassment they'd have to endure. But his dad reassured him, "Oh, so we'll get some flack. This too will pass. Comes with the territory when you have a movie star for a son. For the most part, it's a pretty sweet deal.''

As much as he'd hated making that call to his parents, Avery had known deep inside that they would be supportive—no matter what.

Joanne's relationship with her parents wasn't so ideal. She'd been estranged from her mother for several years—some bad blood over her mother's selling the house and all their furniture right after her father had died—without consulting Joanne. Though Avery had never met his mother-in-law, he encouraged Joanne to end their six-year standoff. Joanne told him to butt out. She claimed not to care one way or another what her mother thought once this sex video went public.

Avery had let the subject drop for a couple of days. Then he'd made the mistake of picking it up again last night. All he'd said was: "You sure you don't want to try getting in touch with your mom?"

Then the wineglass hit the kitchen wall. Joanne went on a tirade, calling her mother a bitch, and blaming Avery for bringing on this whole humiliating ordeal. "Why did you have to make that stupid TV movie anyway?" she screamed, banging her fist on the kitchen counter. "It's because of that movie they singled us out and stole the video. It's probably why I can't get pregnant. God's punishing us, because you played an abortion doctor—"

"Joanne, you can't mean that," he whispered, reaching out to her.

She reeled away. "Leave me alone!"

"All right, all right, just calm down," he said, pulling back. He glanced at the wine stain on the wall and the broken glass on the floor. "Listen to me for a second," he said. "I was wrong. Phoning your mother was a bad idea. Let's erase that. Okay? Everything's going to be all right."

She settled down a bit later, and took one of those pills that the doctor had prescribed. Avery cleaned up the broken glass, but the wine had made a noticeable mauve-colored stain on the white kitchen wall.

Joanne had gone to bed early. She'd still been asleep when Avery headed off for the studio this morning. He'd hated leaving her alone.

It was extra infuriating that he had to be here—while Traci hid in her trailer and held up production. An awful thought occurred to him: *You're dealing with two very temperamental actresses.* He refused to put his wife in the same league as Traci Haydn. Besides, Joanne was under a tremendous strain right now. This latest news about their video wouldn't help any.

Avery dialed home. The machine switched on. "Joanne? If you're there, pick up. . . ." He paused. "Okay, some things are starting to happen with the video. You can page me on the set—"

There was a click on the line. "Avery?"

"You're home. . . ."

"I'm screening calls," she said briskly. "The phone hasn't stopped ringing since eleven. And there are, one, two, three— I'm looking out the living room window—*six* TV news trucks parked outside the front gate."

"Then I guess you know already," he said. "How are you holding up?"

"I'm doing okay, believe it or not."

"You sure?" he asked.

She laughed. "Yes, I haven't smashed one single glass all morning."

"You had me worried last night," he admitted.

"Huh, I was pretty worried myself. But now that it's finally happening and the awful wait is over, I feel we can handle this. Really. Sorry if I gave you a scare. But c'mon, honey. You're married to an actress. The theater's in my blood. I can't have just a little hissy fit. Last night, Joanne Lane was playing to the balcony. But I promise, no more theatrics."

"Uh-huh," was all Avery said. The actress hadn't quite convinced him that she was all right. He was still worried about her. "Better not talk to any reporters until I get there," he said. "I'll be home soon."

The number of reporters and TV news vans outside their front gate had doubled in the last couple of hours. The police had arrived to redirect traffic on the block. Avery couldn't believe that a private home video of a married couple having sex was causing such a sensation.

"Is this a slow news day or what?" He nodded at the front windows. "It's like the Miracle of Fatima just happened out there."

Steve Bensinger chuckled. The public relations guru sat with them at their breakfast table. He had a tan complexion and a moussed mop of brown hair. "You're right, Avery," he said, sipping his coffee. "It's a slow news day. But your increasing star power is more of a factor. Plus you and Joanne are very high profile in print and on TV with those gun-control endorsements."

Joanne slouched back in her chair. "But how did it get so crazy so fast? This morning, it was only a blind item in Yvonne Chase's column."

"The thing just snowballed, Joanne." Steve checked some of his notes. "Several stills from the video began circulating on the Internet this morning. The owner of a video store in West Hollywood called into a radio station saying that within two hours he sold eighty-seven copies of the video at forty bucks a pop. News services picked it up within minutes.''

"So what can we do by way of damage control?" Avery asked.

"Well, I haven't seen the video yet, but I viewed some of the stills floating around the Internet."

Joanne squirmed at this news. Avery put his arm around her.

Steve glanced at his notes again. "The pictures are, of course, explicit, and undeniably you two. The good news is—well, you both looked great. We can make that work for us. You're a hot, sexy couple, who are married and very much in love. You made a video for your own fun, and it got stolen." He sipped his coffee. "I want you to keep that in mind during interviews. You did it for fun. . . . It was supposed to be private. . . ."

Avery stared at him. "You want us to talk to the press about this?"

"Practically every newspaper and magazine outside of the *Christian Science Monitor* wants to interview you two. Ditto the talk shows. We should be selective. I suggest you keep it down to very few—"

"How about keeping it down to *none?*"

"It's part of 'damage control,' Avery," Steve said. "Now, I suggest you appear on *Oprah, Jay,* and *Today*. And in print, give *People* magazine a few hours. They'll put you both on the cover, guaranteed."

Avery frowned at him. Though Steve was right, of course. They couldn't hang their heads in shame and go into hiding. They'd be playing right into the hands of whoever was behind this.

"Well, I'll consent to some interviews," Avery finally said. "But I don't see why Joanne has to subject herself to any of this—"

"Now, hold on," Joanne said. "I can talk for myself. And I want to do it. You shouldn't be on these interviews alone, Avery. Only the two of us together can make it work. Maybe we can turn this whole thing around."

He took hold of Joanne's hand. "You sure you're up to it?"

She laughed. "Darling, last year, I pulled off six performances—and a matinee—while fighting a fever of a hundred and two. I think I can handle a few interviews. This will be good. I'm all for it."

Avery nodded and tried to smile. He listened to her and Steve hatch a media strategy. But all the while, he kept looking across the kitchen—at a faint wine stain on the wall.

Avery and Joanne agreed to do the talk-show circuit. They wouldn't air any theories about who might have stolen the home video and why. Avery figured they should gloss over references to the break-in and the harassing phone calls. Those were police matters. Too much focus there, and they'd come across as victims. They had to keep the interviews light and entertaining.

Steve booked them on the talk shows he'd recommended. And *People* arranged to interview and photograph them at home. All these commitments would be fulfilled in the next seventy-four hours—including a trip to Chicago for *Oprah*.

Avery's agent reported that her phone was ringing off the hook with movie offers—hot, leading-man roles in big-budget productions. Joanne's agent in New York described a similar phenomenon at her office. Several publishers wanted them to write their autobiographies—as well as a how-to manual for married couples who wanted to keep the honeymoon alive. There was also an idea for a "tasteful, coffee table book" of them nude and making love, shot by a big-name photographer. They had countless proposals from clothing manufacturers, and cosmetic, cologne, and underwear companies to be spokesmodels. They politely declined all offers. No one could accuse them of cashing in on this scandal. Almost no one.

"I'm Mrs. Richard Marshall, but you can call me Elsie."

"Hi, Elsie!"

"God bless you," Elsie said, blowing a kiss to her studio audience. Today, she wore a royal blue First Lady suit and pearls. She picked up a newspaper on the desktop. "Well, I don't know about anyone else," she said, with a roll of her eyes. "But I'm pretty disgusted by all the attention these two—well, *pornographers*—have been receiving the last couple of days." She held up the front page of a tabloid with the headline: INDECENT EXPOSURE: AVERY COOPER AND WIFE BARE ALL IN EXPLICIT HOME VIDEO.

"Can you believe that some people actually consider these two 'role models for romance'?" Elsie asked. "I'm just a housewife, but it seems to me that decent people—people we're supposed to admire—don't make sexually explicit videotapes of themselves and *accidentally* let them get duplicated thousands of times for wide distribution. And they seem just as proud as punch about it! Did you see them laughing and making jokes on *The Today Show* this morning? I could barely eat my breakfast, watching those two snickering about this—pardon me—'sex tape.' " Elsie shook her head and sighed. "Now, from what I understand, Avery Cooper and Joanne Lane are supposed to have—what do they call it—a *bicoastal marriage?*" She glanced stage left, off camera. "Drew? Is that right? *Bicoastal?*"

Drew Marshall ambled onto the set to a swelling of applause. He wore a blue Armani suit today. "That's right, Mom, bicoastal," he said. He kissed her, then took the newspaper, glanced at it, and shook his head. "It means they're married, but live on opposite sides of the country. In most cases, it also means they can date other people. It's like how most of these so-called 'gay marriages' are. They say they're together, but they sleep with other people.''

''Well, that's not right,'' Elsie muttered.

''No, it isn't. You know, Avery Cooper and Joanne Lane are the ones who do those ads endorsing restrictions on our constitutional right to bear arms.''

''Oh, I've seen those commercials. They're awful!'' Elsie said.

Drew chuckled. ''Well, at least they have their clothes on in the commercials. We can be grateful for that.''

Elsie frowned. ''Wasn't Avery Cooper the one in that TV movie glorifying an abortion doctor?''

''That's right, Mom. And in his next movie, he plays a homosexual!''

''Well, all I can say is, 'It figures.' ''

''That goddamn homemade porn video has practically doubled their popularity! What the fuck is going on?''

His voice carried over the cries of seagulls and the sound of water lapping against the docks. A limousine and a rented Ford Taurus were parked side by side in the marina lot. The uniformed driver and another man leaned against the front hood of the Taurus. The second man was forty-five, with dark receding hair and a chalky complexion. He puffed on a cigarette, and glanced over his shoulder at the limo. The back window was cracked open, and he could hear his boss getting chewed out by one of the very-top dogs.

''The idea behind stealing and distributing the video was to ruin their reputations!'' the bigwig went on. ''But now they're America's goddamn fucking sweethearts. Their stupid gun-control commercials are pissing off my campaign contributors. I've made promises to them. And you can bet your ass, I'm going to deliver. Now, this porno-flick scheme was your fucking piece-of-shit brainchild. I want you to fix this. I want you to fix *them*. I want that faggot, Cooper, to suffer. I want his cunt of a wife to suffer. I want them disgraced. I want them both to wish they were fucking dead! Do you hear me?''

Propping his foot back against the rental car's front bumper, the man took another drag from his cigarette. ''Just listen to him in there,'' he said to the chauffeur, cracking a little smile. ''Hell, if old Elsie heard the way her son was talking, she'd wash his mouth out with Lifeboy.''

On Friday, November 7, at 5:52 P.M., a debate ensued over the Internet Movie-talk line about a film remake:

JOHN S.: Anne Heche played it too light. Janet Leigh was much better . . . with all that guilt and angst.

PAT: Plus Janet Leigh has a better set of knockers.

KARLA: Who is this pig? I liked Anne Heche's interpretation.

RICK: I don't go to movies that star lesbians. Request private chat with Pat, regarding another Hitchcock film.

The following private mailbox discussion took place a minute later:

PATRIOT: What's going on?

AMERICKAN: SAAMO high-ups not pleased over results of campaign to humiliate A.C. . . . Early reaction shows increase in his popularity due to video exposure . . . Very upsetting . . . Plans to enlist Leslie Bonita Stoddard to cooperate in another scenario are now a no-go . . . thorough background check on L. B. Stoddard shows she contributed $25,000 to handgun-ban campaign last yr. & also had abortion 3 yrs. ago.

PATRIOT: A bitch like that doesn't deserve 2 live.

AMERICKAN: Exactly . . . new plans re: A.C. under way . . . Details follow . . . SAAMO Lieut. signing off.

Nine

Rachel is at her desk, hunched over piles of legal briefs and a fast food dinner that she didn't finish. Enter Dianne. She comes behind Rachel and kisses the top of her head.

DIANNE
Come on, Rache. It's getting late. Let's go to bed.

RACHEL
In a minute.

DIANNE *(kissing the back of her neck)*
I know how important this case is. But so is our relationship. Now, take a break and come to bed.

Rachel surrenders, then turns and kisses her passionately. She unbuttons Dianne's blouse and kisses her breasts.

Quick Dissolve to:

SCENE 29: INTERIOR: RACHEL'S BEDROOM — NIGHT

Rachel and Dianne are in bed, making love. Various shots
show the two women in the throes of passion. . . .

"Oh, shit," Dayle grumbled, quickly closing the manuscript.
She was considering the role of Rachel, the fictitious name
they'd given to the real-life lesbian lawyer. This was Dayle's
first glance at the script, tentatively titled *In Self-Defense*.

For the past few days, she'd been trying to follow everyone's
advice, and stick to the business of making movies. She didn't
hire a bodyguard, but advised her chauffeur, Hank, that his
watchman skills were required. She let him carry a 9-mm Glock.
Hank assured her that he'd been practicing his marksmanship,
and was ready for any kind of "protective service emergency."
In other words, he was just itching for someone to take a potshot
at her so he could put his newly rehoned skills to use.

Nick Brock had called long distance from Estelle Collier's
old hometown, Monoma, Wisconsin. He'd left a brief message
on Dayle's machine: "Greetings from Dullsville, U.S.A. So
far, all I got is that Estelle had a fat, miserable childhood. I
hear later in high school, she was a pothead and bolted before
graduating. Nobody knows where. I'll try to dig up more. Ciao,
Ms. Sutton."

There hadn't been any more incidents like the one up on her
roof. But if things seemed calm for now, her playing a lesbian
in this next film would be inviting trouble back. The trades had
already reported her and Avery Cooper's interest in the project.

Dayle had the script in her lap, open to the sex scene. She
sat on the steps outside her trailer while the crew set up the
next shot. It was a scene with Maggie McGuire, an Oscar-
winning, forty-year film veteran, who played her mother. Mag-

gie wasn't averse to taking on small, juicy character roles like this one in *Waiting for the Fall*.

Her nose in a crossword puzzle, Maggie sat at Dayle's side, in a "star" chair with her name on it. For seventy-one years old, the silver-blond actress looked great thanks to a few nips and tucks. Maggie had recently gained media attention by marching with her HIV-positive son in the Gay Pride Parade in Los Angeles. The two of them had landed on the cover of *People*.

Dayle reread the lesbian love scene and sighed.

"The script can't be that bad," Maggie said.

"Actually, it's okay, but—well, here." Dayle handed her the manuscript, open to the sex scene. "They want me for the role of Rachel."

Maggie set aside her crossword puzzle and read for a moment. "Huh, I'd buy a ticket."

"Thanks for the vote of confidence." Dayle plucked the script out of her hands. "I mean, is this scene really necessary? Isn't it enough that my character's a lesbian? Do I have to prove it by making love to another woman on screen? Tom Hanks was gay in *Philadelphia*, but outside of a slow dance with Antonio Banderos, he hardly touched the guy. Meanwhile, I'm supposed to get naked and roll around with another woman to get the point across."

Maggie gave her a world-weary smile. "Haven't you figured out by now that heterosexual males call all the shots? Otherwise, there would be no wars, and we'd have a cure for breast cancer and AIDS."

"And I wouldn't have to kiss another woman's tits in this movie."

"Listen, you've got a gorgeous body. Why not show it off? As for the character, you're a method actress, you know what to do. Talk to some lesbian lawyers. I can have my son introduce you to some women—"

"That's all right, Maggie," Dayle cut in. "In fact, the film's based on a true story. This afternoon, I'm meeting the lawyer I play.''

''The breast-kissing Rachel?''

Sighing, Dayle nodded. ''Her real name's Sean Olson.''

''Something else about this movie bothers you,'' Maggie said, studying her. She set aside her crossword puzzle book. ''It's not just this sex scene. What is it? Tell your mama.''

Dayle managed a chuckle, then shrugged. ''Oh, maybe it's the subject matter. It really seems to unnerve people. Stick your neck out, and someone always tries to chop it off.''

''No kidding,'' Maggie said. ''Certain folks have been grinding an ax for me since I appeared on the cover of *People* with my son. I've had a ton of hate mail. But that's when I get on my high horse. No one's going to tell me to shut up—especially when I'm defending the civil rights of my son. I'm a fighter, Dayle. I think you are too.''

Frowning, Dayle glanced down at the script in her lap.

Maggie started to reach for her crossword puzzle book. ''I've made you uncomfortable, I can tell.''

''No, it's okay. Really. You're helping me figure this out, you are.''

Maggie sat back. ''Well, then here's my two cents. You're a big star, Dayle. You could help launch this film. I know what the script's about. It's a movie that might make a difference for people like my son. If I'm picking away at you, that's why. I have a personal investment in the subject matter. People will talk, and it's a risk. I know you have an image to maintain, Dayle. But you shouldn't rationalize your way out of doing this film.''

Dayle felt herself blushing. Maggie McGuire could see right through her. She shrugged. ''Well, maybe I'll feel more of a personal investment myself once I meet Sean Olson this afternoon.''

''I hope so,'' Maggie said with a knowing smile.

* * *

"They're still back there," Dayle said to Hank, glancing out the rear window. "What's it been—twenty-five minutes?"

"More like fifteen, Ms. Sutton," he replied, his eyes on the road ahead. The glass divider between them was down.

He was driving her across town to Sean Olson's office. A white Corsica had persistently remained two cars behind the limo ever since Hank pulled out of the studio gate. Dayle couldn't quite see their faces, but two men sat in the front. "Do me a favor and keep a lookout, okay, Hank? I'm getting a crick in my neck." Dayle turned forward.

She didn't know this Sean Olson. Dayle almost hoped to be unimpressed by her; then she could turn down the film role. Why risk her career, her reputation, and even her life to play this stranger? She had no personal investment in Sean Olson at this point, and she wanted it to stay that way.

Sean Olson's law office was above a HairCrafters salon on Hollywood and Vine. Hank announced that they'd eluded the white Corsica at about the time he started searching for a parking place. Usually, he'd just double-park, and escort Dayle to the door. But he didn't leave her side nowadays, so they had to park the limousine in a lot down the block.

Two flights above HairCrafters, they could still smell the perfumed hair products and chemicals. The doors along the hallway were old fashioned, with windows of bubbled glass. On the door numbered 307 someone had taped a sign, written in green marker: SEAN OLSON, ATTORNEY — COME ON IN!

She and Hank went on in. They heard a woman singing "Moon River," along with the radio. The small waiting room was a shambles. Paint-splattered plastic tarp covered every piece of furniture, and there was more of the same beyond the open door to the office. Dayle cleared her throat loudly.

"Who's out there?" someone called.

"Us," Dayle said, stopping in the office doorway.

The woman stood barefoot on a stepladder with a paint scraper in her hand. She wore jeans and a frayed T-shirt that had WORLD'S GREATEST MOM written across it—along with a photo of herself. She was a very attractive woman, slender and tall with high cheekbones and dark brown eyes. A red bandanna covered her hair, but from the tacky photo on her T-shirt, it appeared wavy, chestnut-brown, and shoulder length. Dayle guessed she was in her early thirties. Poised on the ladder, she put a hand on her hip. "And who is 'us'?" she asked, staring at them.

"I'm Dayle Sutton," Dayle said. "I have an appointment with Ms. Olson."

Stepping down the ladder, the woman scrutinized Dayle, then let out an embarrassed laugh. "Ha! Well, hi. I'm Sean Olson." She tore off a work glove and shook Dayle's hand. "I didn't expect you until tomorrow."

"Our appointment was for today, Monday," Dayle pointed out.

Sean Olson shrugged. "Well, move aside some tarp and pull up a chair."

"Um, nice meeting you," Hank said quietly. Then he touched Dayle's arm. "I'll be out by the stairs, reading the latest, Ms. Sutton."

"Thanks, Hank. Let me know how it is." Dayle waited until Hank left, then gave Sean Olson a cool smile. "He's a big fan of true crime and detective novels. Looks like I caught you at a bad time."

"Oh, don't sweat it." Sean pulled back a piece of paint tarp to reveal a minirefrigerator. "What can I get you? I have Evian, Evian, Diet Coke, Evian, Lemonade, Evian, and Evian."

"Evian, please."

"Sorry about the looks of the place. I just moved in. Kind of a dump, but at least I won't have to go far to get my hair done." She handed a bottle of Evian to Dayle. "Everything has gone to hell because of this move. Some of my law books are still in Eugene. But I've passed the California state bar, thank God.''

Dayle raised her Evian bottle to toast her. Pushing aside the tarp, she found the corner of a gray leather sofa and sat down. "I like your T-shirt," she lied. She wondered to whom Sean Olson was The World's Greatest Mom.

Sean glanced down at the photo of herself. "Isn't it awful? I'm going straight to hell for wearing it while painting. My kids gave this to me, and for the last few months I've been forced to wear it on practically every family outing. I figure after this week, I can say it has too much paint on it. They'll probably run out and buy me another just like it—except in pink.''

"How many kids do you have?" Dayle asked.

"Two." She reached under the tarp covering her desk, then pulled out a framed photograph and handed it to her. "Danny, eleven, and Phoebe's seven.''

The sweet, gawky, dark-haired boy and the little redheaded girl were quite cute, and Dayle said so. The screenplay hadn't mentioned any children or an ex-husband. Maybe the kids were adopted, or conceived by artificial insemination. Sean offered no explanation.

She took the framed photo back, then sat on the edge of her desk. "So are you here to check me out?" she asked.

"Well, yes. Also I might ask the director to take you on as a technical advisor—that is, if you're interested.''

Sean frowned. "Depends. Would I advise you movie folks about how true-to-life everything is?''

"Probably," Dayle answered, puzzled by a sudden edge in Sean's voice.

"Well, I'd probably last two hours on that set before you guys kicked me out on my butt." She took a swig of Evian, then shook her head in resignation. "You know, for years I've watched this story get twisted inside out, soft-pedaled, commercialized, and bastardized by Hollywood and I'm fed up. How can you even stand this business? You want the truth, Ms. Sutton?''

Dayle laughed. "Do I have a choice?''

"I think you're all wrong to play me. You're a glamorous superstar. This part requires a serious actress, maybe someone from the theater. I'm not trying to insult you—''

"It's comforting to know that," Dayle said, sitting straighter. "For the record, Ms. Olson, I'm a serious, working actress with theater origins—''

"Are you going to play me as a lesbian?" Sean interrupted.

"Yes, I was planning on it."

Sean put down the Evian bottle and folded her arms. "I'm so sick and tired of this Hollywood hypocrisy. Talk about a bunch of phonies. Are there actually lesbian sex scenes in this latest script?''

"As a matter of fact, yes," Dayle heard herself say, suddenly defending them. "The scenes are thought-provoking, and necessary to the story line."

Sean rolled her eyes. "I was afraid you'd say that."

Dayle stood up. "Your slams against Hollywood don't impress me. They've paid you a lot of money. I think you're the hypocrite, Ms. Olson. You're also rude." Dayle headed for the door.

"Listen, I should explain . . . ," Sean started to say.

But Dayle kept walking and pretended not to hear.

She hated asking Hank to escort her up to the apartment. Lately, she even had him come inside until she'd turned on the lights. Of course, Hank loved playing her protector. But Dayle found it humiliating.

They stepped into the lobby together, and the doorman greeted them. The spacious atrium was decorated with a modern cubic fountain sculpture, several tall potted Fichus trees, and three long, leather-covered sofas.

Sean Olson sat on one of the couches, reading a book. Dayle's first instinct was to breeze toward the elevator and simply ignore her—as she had her two phone messages since their awful meeting yesterday. But Sean sprang up from the sofa. "Dayle? Do you have a minute?"

She stopped and gave her a frosty stare usually reserved for obnoxious reporters. "Yes?"

"I'm sorry if I offended you yesterday, Dayle." Groveling wasn't her forte. The apology had a brisk and businesslike tone.

Still, Dayle's stony expression softened a bit. Sean Olson cleaned up nicely. She wore a pale green suit, and in her beige heels, she stood close to six feet tall. Her shiny, chestnut brown hair was casually swept back.

Dayle patted Hank's shoulder. "I'm okay, Hank. Go home, get some rest."

He nodded. "G'night, Ms. Sutton."

Sean watched him lumber toward the door, then she turned to Dayle. "About yesterday," she said. "You're right. I was rude to you. I apologize."

Dayle managed a smile. "Okay. Apology accepted."

"Contrary to how I came across, I really do want to see this story realized into a film. But it should be an honest film."

"And I'm too much of a Hollywood hypocrite for you, is that it?"

"That's not it at all." Sean sighed and shook her head. "The only problem I have with you, Dayle, is that you're a beautiful movie star, and I'm no glamour queen. I can just see you trying to *deglamorize* yourself for this film. I'd be really insulted." She rolled her eyes.

Dayle laughed. "Are you kidding? If anything, I'll have to look younger for the role."

"Well, thanks, but I wasn't fishing for a compliment."

"What are you fishing for, Ms. Olson?"

"Please, call me Sean," she said. "You have the clout to demand script changes, don't you?"

"I suppose so," Dayle said. "Within reason."

"Well, I managed to snare a copy of the new screenplay. There have been several versions over the years. Each time, they shrink further away from the truth. This new script really takes the cake. If you knew the extent of creative license here, you'd die laughing. For example . . ." Sean trailed off and gave Dayle a wary look. "Is this okay? Am I offending you?"

"No, it's all right, I'm interested," Dayle said. "In fact, would you like to come up, maybe have a glass of wine?"

Sean's face lit up. "Oh, thanks, that would be great."

They lapsed into small talk on the elevator. Dayle gave her a brief tour of the apartment, and Sean praised her decorating choices—especially the Oscar pedestal created from dilapidated footwear. Dayle poured them each a glass of wine, and started toward the living room.

"Could we sit in here?" Sean asked, pointing to the area off the kitchen. "Seems more like home to me. Do you mind?"

"I don't mind at all," Dayle said. She turned on the gas fireplace, and they settled on the sofa. Fred took an immediate liking to Sean, and curled up in her lap. Dayle kicked off her high heels, and watched Sean follow suit. "You were about to tell me how the latest screenplay isn't very accurate."

Stroking Fred's back, Sean sipped her wine and nodded. "Well, for starters, the lesbian sex scenes and the glamorization of my character. During the trial, they have me—this super-beautiful, super-lesbian—taking an occasional break from the law books to have super sex with my gorgeous girlfriend in this huge tastefully decorated loft. In reality, Dayle, I was averaging three hours of sleep a night and living in a dump of a house with very little furniture or knickknacks, because my darling toddler boy was destroying everything he could get his sweet, sticky hands on. And I hardly spent any time with him, which had me in tears constantly. Plus I was in a very chubby, nauseous stage of pregnancy with Phoebe and starting to stretch out my good court clothes. In short, Dayle, I was a mess."

Dayle let out a stunned laugh. "Well, um, I see. Well, yes, that's a big difference. So—both your children are your own. They weren't adopted?"

"No, I gave birth to them," Sean replied. "What did you think?"

Dayle shrugged. "Well, I figured . . . I mean, who's their father?"

"Why, my husband, of course." Sean Olson's mouth dropped open. She tossed back her head and laughed. Fred was startled for a moment, until she hugged him. "Oh, my God, I thought you knew!" she cried. "It's one reason this screenplay is such a crock. Dayle, I'm married. I'm not a lesbian. That was the notion of screenwriter number two or three. He figured only a lesbian would so valiantly defend a gay man, and suddenly—poof!—my character's this gorgeous lesbian. They figured a pregnant, married lady was too boring."

Dayle shook her head. "Oh, no."

Sean nodded. "Oh, yes. That's why I asked you yesterday if you intended to play me as a lesbian—with all those soft-focus, curtains-blowing-in-the-breeze sex scenes." She settled Fred back into her lap, then sipped her wine. "That's all from the imagination of some horny screenwriter. The death threats I received during the trial, the letters and phone calls, it's true, they called me 'lesbo,' 'dyke,' and 'fag-loving bitch,' but they also promised to kill me—and my family. That wasn't in the script. They said they'd burn down the house with my children in it, these 'good Christians' with their 'family values' told me that. But it's not in the script. . . ."

Dayle sat in a dazed silence as Sean explained the truth behind the cheaply glamorized screenplay. Gary Worsht, the gay doctor Avery Cooper would portray, was actually a waiter. He had picked up a fraternity pledge in a gay bar. They started necking in an alley by the tavern, when the kid went berserk and attacked him. Then the boy's frat brothers came out of hiding to help "beat up the fag." In self-defense, Gary killed the reluctant pledge with a broken beer bottle. The dead boy's youthful handsomeness played against the defendant's promiscuity, blurring the lines of guilt and innocence. It was a tough case to win, because the frat boys—all A-students from good homes—were the real culprits. They were fine, upstanding boys who happened to like getting drunk and beating up queers for fun. Ironically, the same group of lads also enjoyed forcing their pledges to march down to weekend breakfasts naked—in a line with each boy holding the penis of the pledge behind him.

"There isn't a scene like *that* in the script," Dayle remarked over her glass of wine. And yet, she was supposed to kiss this totally fictitious other woman's breasts. She thought about what Maggie McGuire had said: *Haven't you figured out by now that heterosexual males call all the shots?*

"The screenplay has no guts," Sean said. "They made it so black and white—with Gary Worsht coming across as a saint, and the frat boys as these lowlife thugs—including the poor victim, who was just a scared, sweet-faced pledge forced into playing gay bait. This was a complex case, Dayle, and they whitewashed it. Can you see why I'm such a pain in the ass on the subject?"

Dayle nodded thoughtfully. "There'll be some changes made; otherwise I won't do this movie."

"You mean that?"

"Yes," she said. "I'll be glad to have a husband in this movie instead of a lesbian supermodel or whatever she was."

Sean laughed. "Well, my husband will sure be delighted. He's a real movie nut. In fact, could I get an autograph for him before I leave tonight?"

"I have some glossies in my desk. No problem. What does he do?"

"Dan? Oh, he . . ." She hesitated. "At the time of the trial he was a chef."

Dayle gave her a slightly puzzled look. "What does he do now?"

"He—um, well, he stays at home and looks after the kids." Sean shifted a little on the sofa, and she let out a slightly uneasy laugh. "So—enough about me. Let's talk about you *playing* me." She sipped her wine, then smiled. "Seriously, why did you want to take on this part—this fake-lesbian lawyer?"

Shrugging, Dayle stared at the fireplace. "I must admit, I had a tough time warming up to the role. But now, I can certainly relate to what you said about death threats, and the lesbian accusations. It's happened to me recently. Everyone thinks I'm paranoid, but I'm sure somebody—some group— has been following me." Dayle sighed and shook her head. "I wasn't willing to put my career on the line for this role as written. But if I could play you, Sean, in a truthful account of what really happened, it would be worth the risk."

They talked for over an hour. Dayle kept remembering the intimate chat with Leigh Simone that night at the Imperial Hotel, how they'd instantly bonded. It was like that tonight— with Sean Olson. The similarities were almost unsettling. Dayle told her so. She also told her about how Leigh Simone might have been murdered by the same people who had killed Tony Katz. "Do you think I'm nuts?" Dayle asked.

"Not at all," Sean replied. "You said earlier you thought some people were following you."

"Yes?"

Sean got to her feet and wandered over to the window. "While I was waiting for you in the lobby, I noticed this man sitting alone in a Chevy, parked across the street. He sat there for a half hour. Then a silver car came up behind him. The guy in the first car nodded, pulled out, and the second guy took his spot. It was like a changing of the guard. Fifteen minutes later, your limousine turned into the drive. The man in the silver car took out a cellular phone and called someone."

Dayle stood up and moved to the window. Cradling the cat

in her arms, she stared down at the front driveway to her building. A silver car was parked across the street.

"He's still there," Sean said. "You're not nuts, Dayle. Someone's watching you."

"Hi, it's me again, and I'm fine," Sean reported to Dayle on her cellular. "Traffic's running smoothly here along the coastal highway. No accidents, no tailgaters, no claw hooks dangling from my car door handle. I'll have another traffic update for you in fifteen minutes."

"Thanks, I'm making a mental note to play you as a grade-A smart-ass," Dayle replied. "How are you, really?"

"I'm making great time," Sean said.

Dayle Sutton hadn't liked the idea of her driving alone at night this long distance. She'd made Sean promise to call on her cellular every fifteen minutes until she reached her in-laws' house.

"At this clip," Sean said. "I'll be home in ten minutes."

"Well, call me for touchdown so I'll know you're okay," Dayle said.

"Will do, Dayle. Thanks again." Sean clicked off the line. She glanced out her window at the dark, choppy waters of the Pacific. This time of night, all she could see were the curled whitecaps. Behind her, a series of distant headlights pierced the darkness. Something about the long, lonely drive in the dark—and that cool, ocean breeze whipping through the car window—made her feel so lost and melancholy. She'd even allowed herself a good cry a few miles back. In this vulnerable state, she realized that Dayle Sutton was the first friend she'd made on her own in California. But Dayle was also a movie star, and in Hollywood, friendships were transitory. Maybe that was why she didn't tell Dayle about Dan.

Sean glanced in the rearview mirror—at the Jeep that had been following her since she'd merged onto the coastal highway thirty-five minutes ago. She hadn't noticed it when she'd left Dayle Sutton's apartment building. Instead, she'd focused on the lone dark figure in the silver car. He'd called someone from his cellular as soon as she'd emerged from the building. Had he phoned the person in this Jeep?

Sean told herself to stay calm. The highway wasn't exactly deserted; plus the Jeep kept a safe distance behind her. Testing things, Sean eased up on the accelerator. The speedometer dropped to sixty-five . . . sixty . . . fifty-five. Other cars began to gain on her, the Jeep among them. One by one, they pulled into the fast lane and passed her, but the Jeep stayed behind.

Dayle answered the phone. "Hello?"

"Dayle? It's me, Sean. We have touchdown. I'm walking up the driveway as I speak."

"And you don't think anybody was following you?" Dayle asked.

"Well, for a few minutes after the last call, this Jeep behind me gave me a case of heebie-jeebies. I couldn't shake him. But he pulled off an exit before me, so I guess it was nothing." She paused. "Oh, Phoebe's waving at me from the front window. Anyway, I'm fine, Dayle. Thanks for worrying about me."

"We'll talk tomorrow," Dayle said. "I'll call you."

"Sounds good. G'night, and thanks again." Sean clicked off, and waved back to her daughter. The petite, redhaired seven-year-old wore her pink ballerina outfit from Halloween. She jumped up and down excitedly, then made fish faces against the window for her mother. Sean laughed and blew her a kiss. She started up the walk to the front door.

Dan's brother Doug and his wife, Anne, owned a large, cedar shaker on beachfront property—with a wraparound terrace and beautiful gardens. At one time, Sean had dreamt of having a home like this one. But now all bets were off.

Approaching Anne and Doug Olson's front door, she thanked God for having such great in-laws. Dan and Doug were close, but even the most devoted of siblings might have cracked under the pressure of putting up a brother, nephew, and niece, a rotating series of baby-sitter nurses, and a sister-in-law, who checked in on her family from time to time between business in the city. Yet Doug and Anne never complained.

Phoebe opened the door as Sean reached the front stoop. "Well, my goodness!" Sean declared. "Look at my pretty ballerina!" She gave Phoebe a kiss. "Did you wait up for me?"

Phoebe nodded, and began telling her about what had happened in school today. She chattered nonstop as they stepped inside. The TV was blaring in the family room toward the back of the house. It was a beautiful, spacious room with a stone fireplace and an ocean view. Since coming to stay at Doug and Anne's, she'd tried to keep her kids from trashing the place—and for the most part, she'd succeeded. Sean noticed a few things scattered about: papers and school books, a pair of gym shoes, and one of Phoebe's sweaters. She also found her eleven-year-old, Danny, lying on his stomach directly in front of the television. Despite a trace of adolescent acne and an unruly mop of brown hair, he was a cute boy, with long-lashed blue eyes and an endearing smile. Barely looking up from the TV, he muttered, "Hi, Mom."

"You'll go blind," Sean announced. "No, don't get up. You haven't seen your mother since yesterday morning, but God knows, that shouldn't tear you away from the boob tube and *Babe-Watch.*"

On TV, a bikini-clad, blond silicone case ran through a dark corridor from a man with a butcher knife. "This happens to be PBS," Danny said. "And I'm watching it for homework."

Sean laughed. "You're a twisted young man. God knows why I love you. Please tune it down a bit—for Uncle Doug and Aunt Anne's sake."

Danny sighed and lowered the volume with the remote.

Without the TV noise, Sean heard a mechanical *whosh-whosh* from another part of the house—as constant as those waves crashing against the rocky shore outside. It was a sound she'd grown to love and hate; a reassurance of life continuing, and a reminder that living was hard as hell.

Sean stooped down and kissed Danny. "I've missed you. Is Dad asleep?"

"Nope. He's right here!" Doug Olson announced over the steady *whosh-whosh* of Dan's respirator. Coming from the guest room down the hall, he pushed Dan in his wheelchair.

Their favorite nurse, Julie, trailed behind him. Julie Adams-Smart had saved Dan's life twice already—when his respirator had malfunctioned. The petite, pretty, strawberry blonde had a lot of guts. Dan loved her, the kids loved her, Doug and Anne loved her.

Sean's feelings for this young woman were more compli-cated. She was grateful, resentful, beholden, and in awe of Julie. Dan now depended more on Julie than he did on her. Only last week, she couldn't understand something Dan was trying to say, but Julie had picked it up. She'd become better than Sean at reading his lips and anticipating his needs. Julie was smiling at her now. "Dan insisted on getting dressed for you," she said.

Dan grinned. He wore his gray sweats, which had been cut to accommodate the feed tube in his back. Another tube—for his respirator—was connected at the base of his throat and hooked up to a portable machine. Julie had obviously shaved him today, and overcombed his hair until it was flat. Sean preferred Dan a bit more scruffy, because he used to look sexy with a five o'clock shadow and his thick light-brown hair mussed. Too much grooming now made him appear waxy and lifeless—ready for the coffin.

The disease had rendered him totally immobile. His head was propped back against a small pillow. His hands—now puffy and mannequinlike—had been placed palms-down on his thighs. He appeared older than forty. Sometimes, Sean looked at that helpless, old man in the wheelchair, and she didn't recognize her husband. But then Dan would smile, or show a gleam in his eye, and she'd see the man with whom she had fallen in love. He was still there.

He gave her one of those looks now, and she read his lips. "Hi, honey," he said. "How did round two go with Dayle Sutton?"

Sean kissed him. "I'll tell you after the kids are in bed," she whispered. She kissed him again and held her face against his. "Thank you for waiting up and getting dressed, sweetie. You're a sight for these sore brown eyes."

The constant *whosh-whosh* of Dan's respirator was like a clock ticking. Depending on the night, it could keep Sean awake or lull her to sleep. Tonight, she was awake. She'd been up forty-five minutes before, working the suction tube to clear Dan's mouth of excess saliva and phlegm that might obstruct his breathing. When she was done, she read his lips: "Go to back to sleep, honey. I'm fine. Good night."

Sean kissed his forehead, then crawled back under the sheets. The respirator machine separated his hospital-type bed from her single. Sean was so anxious and desperate for sleep, she couldn't nod off. Finally, she threw back the covers and climbed out of bed. At least Dan was asleep, thank God.

Tiptoeing into the family room, Sean opened the cabinet where they kept the videos. She found the one she wanted, and popped it into the VCR. Switching on the TV, she turned down the volume so not to wake anyone. Sean sat back on the couch, and watched her handsome, young husband playing on the beach with their two kids. Phoebe was four at the time, and Danny, nine. They were on vacation here in Malibu. Sean watched Dan swimming with Danny, and building sand castles with Phoebe. He had such a beautiful, tan body, strong arms and a hairy chest. Dan's brother must have taken the next shot, because Dan was picking her up and carrying her into the water. They were cracking up. With the volume down, she could only imagine his laughter—a sound she hadn't heard in over a year.

At the moment, accompanying their old home video was the constant *whosh-whosh* of Dan's respirator machine down the hall.

At first, they'd thought Dan had arthritis or carpal tunnel syndrome, because his hands kept cramping up. Why else would a healthy, athletic thirty-seven-year-old man find it hard to hold on to things? As a chef, it became utter misery. He'd drop utensils and pans. So many of his culinary creations ended up on the floor, and he'd have to start over again—at the price of an expensive cut of meat, fowl, or fish. Customers often complained about having to wait forever for their dinner.

The evening before his doctor's appointment, he and Sean were talking in bed. "I know what's wrong with me, honey," he whispered. "The muscles are going. It's like Gary Cooper in *Pride of the Yankees.*"

"Lou Gehrig's disease," Sean said quietly, stroking his arm. "ALS, I looked it up last week."

"I did my reading in the library a month ago," Dan said.

Sean held him tighter. "We don't really know yet. Both of us are being melodramatic. Let's not drape the black crepe yet, honey."

"Yeah, let's hope we're wrong," he said. "We'll laugh about this later."

After a barrage of tests, when the doctor diagnosed his ailment as ALS, amyotrophic lateral sclerosis, they nodded and said the initials in unison with him. Dan's body had already started wasting away, and would continue to deteriorate in the coming months. The ironic cruelty to this disease was that his mind would remain clear.

Sean and Dan had prepared themselves for the worst, and

they got it. He wouldn't be around to watch Danny and Phoebe grow up. At the most, he had two more Christmases with them.

Sean silently watched her handsome, athletic husband slip away. He needed to feel independent as long as he could. So while she longed to tie his shoelaces for him, she'd pretend not to notice his frustration as the simple task took him nearly ten minutes some mornings. Later, she let Dan decide for himself when he was ready for a wheelchair. And Sean sat beside him as he told Danny and Phoebe that he wouldn't be getting any better.

Dan could no longer work at the restaurant. They went in debt experimenting with expensive drugs and holistic remedies. Dan began having difficulty speaking and breathing. Sean spent many nights waking up to the sound of him choking on his own phlegm. She'd drag her husband out of bed, plop him into his wheelchair, then push him into the bathroom and turn on the hot water full blast. The steam helped clear Dan's lungs, so he'd eventually cough up whatever was choking him. With all the nightly interruptions, Sean had to function regularly at the office on an average of three hours of sleep. The ordeal harkened her back to those days and nights with the kids when they were babies. It had been easier then, because there would be an end to the nocturnal feedings, and Dan was helping her.

Now, the only end in sight was Dan dying.

They put him on a respirator and a feeder. Machines did his eating and breathing for him. Yet all the while, those eyes of his were so alert. He could communicate with her and the kids—not as an invalid, but as a husband and father. The kids still turned to him for advice or praise. Danny and Phoebe were able to read his lips almost as well as their mother could.

Sean missed his voice, and his touch.

In the silent video, she and Dan emerged from the surf together and kissed for the camera. Phoebe ran to him, and Dan hoisted her in the air. Danny jumped up and down in front of them, making a goofy face.

For a moment, she thought Phoebe's faint cries were coming from the nearly muted television. Then she realized the screams emitted from her daughter's room downstairs. Sean switched off the video, then raced down the steps. She found Phoebe sitting up in bed. Except for her Little Mermaid night-light, the room was dark.

"Honey, it's okay, I'm here." She sat down on the edge of her bed.

Phoebe immediately hugged her. She was trembling. "There's a man looking in my window!"

Sean glanced over at the window across the room. This part of the house stood at ground level, with the ocean view blocked by shrubs. The leafy branches shook in the wind, occasionally scraping at the windowpane.

"It's just the bushes outside, that's all," Sean assured her—and herself.

"No, I saw a man," she whined. "I did."

Sean kissed the top of her head. "Well, I'll just sit here with you for a while and chase him away if he comes back. In the meantime, don't you worry about it, honey. I'm here."

Sean gently stroked Phoebe's head and listened to her breathing grow more steady. All the while, she stared out the window—just in case Phoebe wasn't dreaming.

Ten

Dayle had a great respect for the stars of yesteryear—even the ones long ago forgotten by the public. She'd revived the careers of several veteran performers by campaigning for them to play pivotal roles in her movies. Months before Maggie McGuire had found herself back in the limelight and on the cover of *People* with her gay son, Dayle had approached her to play the mother in *Waiting for the Fall*.

The crusty old actor set to play Dayle's long-lost father had recently suffered a minor stroke, and they needed to find a replacement. Dayle had promised the director she would review applicants, "the Geritol guys," Dennis called them. She sat with Dennis at a conference table—along with the casting director and his assistant.

"Our next old-timer did this commercial earlier in the year," the casting director said. A handsome man with silver-black hair, he wore a blazer over his gray silk shirt. Leaning back in his chair, he popped a Tic-Tac in his mouth. "Check him out. His name's Tom Lance."

The casting director's assistant, a pale, thirtyish blonde with a bad perm and too much rouge, slipped a tape into the VCR. A McDonald's ad came on. A kindly looking, bespectacled old man shared some french fries with his grandson. A real heart-warmer. It was a shame that Dayle, with her reverence for forgotten stars, didn't recognize the actor in that McDonald's commercial.

"So—what do you think?" the casting director asked. "Name's Tom Lance. Want to meet him? He's right outside."

Dayle nodded. "Fine. Show him in."

The assistant opened the door, then called for Tom Lance. He looked younger than the grandfather in the ad, but not as gentle and sweet. The old man had an embittered, edgy quality to him. He hobbled through the doorway, trying to stand tall. He wore a tie with a powder-blue blazer and madras slacks—pro-shop clothes, the colors a bit too bright, the material too stiff.

Dayle smiled at him, then spoke loudly. "Hi, Mr. Lance. Thanks for coming today."

He grinned. "You don't have to shout. I may be old, but I'm not deaf." He pronounced it so it rhymed with leaf.

Dayle nodded cordially. "Do you mind telling me how old you are?"

"I don't mind telling you that I'm seventy," he said, slurring his words. "Those McDonald's people wanted somebody older, so I came up with the glasses and whitened my hair. I—I can play older or younger, you name it."

Dayle kept a pleasant smile fixed on her face. Tom Lance clearly had indulged in a few shots of courage before this interview. He weaved a little as he stood in front of them. She felt sorry for him.

Dennis leaned over and whispered in her ear. "I think this guy's had a belt or two or five. The hook or what?"

Sighing, Dayle sat back and caught the casting director's eye. He nodded. "Thank you, Mr. Lance. We'll—"

"That's all? That's it?" he asked.

"We'll be in touch."

"Bullshit!"

"Now, wait a minute—"

"No, you wait a minute," the old man shot back. "I made fifty pictures before any of you were born! I deserve some respect. Instead, I'm forced to sit out in that hallway for an hour. Then I'm called in here like a pet dog by blondie there. Nobody bothers to get off their rear ends to greet me. I—" He shook his head and swatted at the air. "Oh, forget it!" He swiveled around, almost lost his balance, then lumbered out the door.

"Sorry about that," the casting director said.

"It's all right." Dayle sighed. "The seventh actor is good enough for me if Noah likes him."

The casting director and his assistant started to collect all the résumés and videotapes.

"You seem in the dumps," Dennis whispered to her. "Is it Grandpa? I'll go beat the shit out of him if you want."

Dayle worked up a chuckle. "My knight in shining armor." She waved to the casting director and his assistant as they left the room. Then the smile fell from her face and she turned to Dennis again. "I—I've had these people following me around for a couple of days now. This morning, a tan Chevy tailed Hank and me from my place all the way to the studio."

"Maybe it's the tabloids. They've done this to you before, Dayle."

She shook her head. "No, I'm sure it's something far more serious. These people have me under a kind of surveillance."

"Why don't you call the police about it?"

"They'll just say I'm paranoid."

Dennis cleared his throat. "Well, you've been under a lot of stress, Dayle. I mean, ever since Leigh Simone committed suicide—"

"Suicide?" Dayle asked sharply. "Haven't you been listening to me at all these last few weeks? Leigh was murdered! Suicide? Did you say that just to get a rise out of me?''

"I'm sorry." Dennis shrugged. "It's just—well, you seem to be the only person in the free world who doesn't believe Leigh killed herself. Laura, she's a nurse, and she has some background in psychology . . .''

Dayle just glared at him. The last thing she wanted right now was to hear his girlfriend's theories.

"She said what you're feeling is normal. You were the last person to see Leigh Simone alive. Naturally, you feel responsible. You can't help asking yourself if you could have done something to prevent it—"

"No, Dennis. What I'm asking myself is—Where the hell do you get off talking to Laura about me? You've only known her two weeks."

Dennis didn't respond. He stared down at the desktop.

Dayle rubbed her forehead. "Just get out of here and leave me alone."

Without a word, Dennis slunk out of his chair and headed toward the door. He glanced back at her for a moment.

"I'm not crazy, goddamn it," Dayle whispered.

Dennis nodded, then left.

The old man's Plymouth Volare was parked on a high, winding dirt road just below the HOLLYWOOD sign. Sitting at the wheel, he glanced around, then decided the coast was clear. He reached into the glove compartment and pulled out a .380 semiautomatic.

Nobody at the audition had recognized him. If they'd bothered to look at his résumé, they'd have seen who he was. Instead, he was just some old actor from a McDonald's ad.

Why, only two nights ago, one of his movies had been on television. None of his films had made it to video yet, so he was always on the lookout for when they were broadcasted on

TV. Tom Lance saw this one listed in the *TV Guide,* which he bought every Tuesday:

> '26-MOVIE-Western; 1hr, 35min (BW) **
> "Fall From the Saddle" (1952). Rancher turns outlaw
> when wife is killed by a crooked sheriff. Predictable. Tom
> Lance, Louise Reimen, John Clemens.

The movie aired at 2:30 A.M., and was chopped to pieces with commercial interruptions for diet centers and 900-number sex lines. Yet Tom looked forward to each break, because the announcer would say: "We'll return with more shoot'm-up action in *Fall from the Saddle* with Tom Lance."

Yesterday, Tom had stayed inside his tiny apartment, not wanting to miss any calls from friends—or possibly a producer—who had seen the movie. But the phone never rang. So Tom called a few actor acquaintances. One of them mentioned that Harry somebody had just suffered a stroke. He'd been set for a featured role in the new Dayle Sutton movie, and now they were recasting the part. For a while, Tom had such high hopes.

How stupid he'd been, thinking he had a chance.

He looked down at the gun in his hand. It was right that he should blow his brains out here by the HOLLYWOOD sign. Not very original, but appropriate. Plus they'd find him here within a few hours. Hell, if he killed himself at home, it might be days before they discovered his decaying body.

He thought about writing a farewell note to Maggie, but didn't want to cause her any bad publicity. Maybe Tom Lance and his films were forgotten, but folks still knew who Maggie McGuire was. She had a plum part in the new Dayle Sutton film, the one for which he'd just auditioned—and lost.

How ironic, since he'd helped start Maggie's career—way back in 1950. He'd starred in *Hour of Deceit,* and had been engaged to Maggie at the time. He'd practically browbeaten the director into giving her the small but showy role as the mistress of an underworld boss. She'd gone on to bigger and better films, and won an Oscar. Meanwhile, he'd floundered in B-movies and low-budget westerns. Then she'd dumped him.

Not long ago, he'd brought Maggie a book, *The Illustrated Movie Star Dictionary*. It was still inside a gift bag on the backseat of his car. Tom dug it out. *Over a Thousand Stars Listed,* the book's jacket bragged, between a photos of Sylvester Stallone and Greta Garbo. *Lavishly Illustrated, Concise Accounts of the Stars' Careers and Their Films. From Bogart to Brad Pitt! From* It Girl *Clara Bow to* Material Girl *Madonna!*

He wasn't listed, not even mentioned. But they gave Maggie a nice write-up, and featured a beautiful glamour shot of her. Seemed like such a waste that Maggie would never get her gift. Then again, he could deliver it to her, and say good-bye. He imagined Maggie wanting to pay him back—not just for this token gift, but for her whole career. She owed him. She might even have some influence in getting Dayle Sutton to change her mind.

The sound of gravel crunching under tires made him glance up. A police car cruised from around the bend a few hundred feet in front of him. Tom quickly stashed the gun inside the book bag. Then he straightened up and gripped the steering wheel with both hands. As the squad car crept by, the cop spoke into a mike, and his voice boomed over a speaker: "No parking on this road. Please move your vehicle."

Tom waved and nodded. He started his engine and followed the cop car—keeping his distance. Sweat slithered down his temples, and his shirt stuck to his back. Once they were off the dirt road and the police car went in another direction, Tom loosened his tie.

Driving to Maggie's house in Beverly Hills, Tom imagined a revised edition to that movie book. This one would include him.

LANCE, Tom, it would say, under his favorite early portrait

of himself, smoking a cigarette, his black hair tousled and wavy.
*(1925– , b. Thomas Lancheski, Chicago, Illinois). Handsome,
dark-haired leading man in a number of RKO westerns and
crime dramas in the early fifties. But within a decade, he was
relegated to guest-star appearances on* Perry Mason, Ben
Casey, *and* Bonanza; *then Lance seemed to fade into obscurity.
Hollywood misused Tom Lance, and it is a great travesty that
his talent went unappreciated until, at age 76, he took a supporting role in the Dayle Sutton starrer,* Waiting for the Fall. *Lance
made every minute of his screen time count. Critics raved, and
he nabbed a Supporting Actor Oscar nomination . . .*

Tom's daydream took him all the way to Beverly Hills.
He turned onto the winding, palm-tree shaded road that was
Maggie's cul-de-sac. He drove past the beautiful houses and
carefully manicured lawns. By comparison, Maggie's ranch
house looked rather modest—albeit respectable.

He pulled into the driveway and parked behind a white
Mercedes. Glancing in the rearview mirror, he suddenly regretted this impulsive visit. He looked grimy and tired. He was
about to restart the car and leave, but he heard a dog bark. All
at once, the Doberman leaped up toward the car door, its paws
on the window. Tom reeled back, clutching his heart. The huge
dog growled and snapped at him on the other side of the glass.

"Tosha, get down from there!" Tom heard Maggie call. He
glanced out his rear window. She came around from the side
of the house. She wore jeans, a white sweater, and gardening
gloves. "Tosha? Tosh, get down! Who's there?"

The dog finally shut up. Tom opened the car door and stepped
outside. He patted Tosha's head and smiled at Maggie, who
came up to his Volare.

She frowned for a moment. "Oh, Tom . . ." She pulled off
the gloves. "To what do I owe this surprise visit?"

He wasn't too good on his feet today—with his gout flaring
up. He tried not to limp as he made his way around the Volare.
"Hi, Maggie—"

"Say, listen," she interrupted. "Did you call me last week?"

"Someone called pretending to be me?"

"Someone called *threatening to kill me,*" Maggie said. "He sounded like you. I wasn't sure. Phoned twice. He said, 'You promote perversion, and thus you will die.' Then he quoted the Bible to me—I forget what exactly."

Tom shook his head. "Why would I say something like that?"

She shrugged. "Forget it. Some crank. I've gotten a lot of crank letters since those cover stories in *People* and that gay magazine. But crank calls to my home phone are another story. I just thought—well, forget I asked."

"I brought you a present." Tom reached inside the car for the gift bag. It felt a bit heavy, and he remembered that the gun was in there. Turning his back to her, he transferred the gun to his pocket inside his jacket. Her dog sniffed at his crotch. Tom handed Maggie the gift bag.

"Sweet of you. Tosha, stop that," she said in one breath, with an apathetic glance inside the bag. "I suppose I should ask you in. Would you like some ice tea?"

"Oh, I don't want to be a bother."

She laughed. "Yeah? Since when?" She sauntered toward the side of the house and gave him a beckoning wave. "C'mon, it's no bother. I was about to pour myself a glass." She snapped her fingers at the dog. "C'mon, Tosh."

Tom and the dog followed her to the fenced-in back section of the house. There was a large kidney-shaped pool, and a rock garden. "It's the leash for you, Tosh," she said, grabbing the Doberman by his collar. She led him to a chain attached to a palm tree at the garden's edge. "Tosha, keep still." She dropped the gift bag to fix the dog to his leash.

"I hear you're in the new Dayle Sutton film," Tom said.

"Yeah, sort of an extended cameo."

"That's quite a coincidence, because I've been considering

a part in the same movie. Maybe you could put in a good word
for—''

''Okay, Tosha, there you go,'' she said to the dog. ''Stay
put now.''

Tom bit down on his lip.

Maggie retrieved the bag, straightened up, then opened the
sliding glass door to the house. ''Okay, here we go. After you,
Tom.''

He tried not to hobble, but he caught her staring. ''What's
wrong with your foot?'' she asked.

''Oh, I twisted my ankle jogging this morning,'' he lied.

''Jogging? You?'' Maggie laughed. ''I'd buy tickets to see
that.''

Tom was careful of the step up to the recreation room. He
loved this room, because it definitely belonged in a movie star's
home. The floor was Mexican tile, with a lambskin rug in front
of the large stone fireplace. The sofa, love seat and chairs were
covered with soft, cream-colored leather. Above the sofa hung
an arrangement of framed photographs, Maggie's magazine
covers from a *Life* portrait in 1953 to a shot of her and her gay
son on the front of *People*. There was Frank Sinatra planting
a kiss on her cheek as she clutched her Academy Award;
Maggie shaking Princess Grace's hand at some formal reception; Maggie and her ex, Pierre Blanchard, attending a film
premiere with Elizabeth Taylor and Mike Todd; Maggie and
President Kennedy laughing over what seemed to be a private
joke at some Hollywood political function. Her Academy
Award took center spot amid the pictures, the only three-
dimensional object on that wall. A sconce held it up.

''I saw you on that Burger King commercial,'' Maggie said.
She was in the kitchen, pouring their ice teas. Her kitchen was
incorporated in the large, all-purpose room, separated by a
counter bar.

Tom climbed onto one of the tall, cushioned stool-chairs at
the counter. ''It was a McDonald's ad,'' he said.

"Whatever," she shrugged, handing him a glass of ice tea. "I thought it was cute." She lit a cigarette. "Those ads can be pretty lucrative."

"I've had film offers," Tom lied. "They're interested in me for Tom Hanks's father in his next movie."

"Tom Hanks," she said, deadpan.

She knows I'm lying, Tom thought. "It's nothing definite yet," he said. Playing father to Kevin Costner or Tom Hanks was one of his fantasies lately.

"Tom Hanks," Maggie repeated, then she shook her head. "Well, that's just terrific. I'm thrilled for you." She took a drag from her cigarette, then reached for the gift bag. "I may as well open this—before you head out."

"I hope you don't already have it," he said, grinning.

She pulled out the book. "Oh, look, one of these things," she said, glancing at the cover. "They reduce your whole career to a couple of brief paragraphs. Hope you got it on sale."

"You don't like it," he murmured.

"Actually, I'm a sucker for these books," Maggie said. She flipped through its pages, and Tom noticed her stopping in the M's.

" '. . . But her career never fulfilled its early promise,' " Maggie read aloud, sneering. "Well, isn't that sweet? Thank you for buying this for me, Tom."

"That's just their way of saying Hollywood didn't do right by you. I think it's a nice review. The only thing they failed to mention was the guy who helped get you started. I should have gotten some credit. I mean, if it weren't for me, you'd still be—"

"I'd still be a cocktail waitress," she finished for him. Maggie rolled her eyes. "I don't have to see it in print. I hear it enough from you—practically every time you come over here on one of your surprise visits: 'You'd still be a cocktail waitress!' " She laughed. "Don't you think that by now, Tom, I'd have been promoted to hostess?"

"I don't bring it up that often," Tom argued. "And I don't drop by that often either. Lord, you make me sound like a pest."

"Huh, no comment," she mumbled over her ice tea glass.

Wounded, Tom gazed at her. "Is that what you think I am? A pest?"

"Every time you come over here, you make me feel like I owe you something. And I'm sick of it, Tom."

"I don't mean to make you feel that way, Maggie." Yet he liked the idea that she still felt beholden to him after all these years. He reached a hand over the counter toward her. "I'm proud to be the one who helped you—"

"May I remind you for the umpteenth time that I wasn't exactly on poverty row when you 'discovered' me? I'd done some modeling and commercial spots. I would have made it into the movies with or without you—eventually."

Tom stared at his empty hand, palm up. She didn't seem to notice that he'd been reaching out to her. He climbed off the stool, and pain shot through his foot as soon as he put some weight on it. He grabbed the counter to keep his balance.

"Are you okay?" she asked, eyes narrowed. "Should I call you a taxi?"

She thought that he was drunk. Tom shook his head. "Thanks, but I'm all right. Sorry I bothered you."

"Oh, Jesus, the martyr role now." Maggie reached for her Merit 100's.

"Do you feel even an ounce of gratitude toward me?" he asked.

"Now that's a laugh." She lit her cigarette. "I only lived with you and put up with your crap for practically three years. If that ain't gratitude, I don't know what."

"I thought it was love," Tom murmured.

Maggie shook her head and sighed. "Good exit line, Tom. Now, just let that hang in the air as you make your way to the door. And you can take this book with you." She pushed it too far across the counter—over the edge. The book toppled to the floor, just missing Tom's sore foot.

Clutching the stool, he bent down to retrieve the unwanted gift. The .380 fell out of his pocket. Tom wondered if she saw it. Quickly, he stashed the gun back inside his jacket. Then he retrieved the book and pulled himself up. "Do you know why I came here, Maggie?" he asked.

"Obviously, to bring some sunshine and happiness into my day."

"No. It's because I thought you were the only one who would miss me. I wanted to say good-bye to you before I killed myself."

She started sorting through some mail left on the countertop. "Oh, Tom. Give me a break, will you?"

"I'm serious, for God's sake!" He pulled out the .380.

But she wasn't looking at him. "Yeah, you're serious all right," she said, studying her phone bill. "Like that business about playing Tom Hanks's father. *Sure.* See you in the movies, Tom. You're pathetic, you really are."

"And you're an uncaring bitch," he whispered.

Maggie looked up from the phone bill. Her eyes widened at the gun in his hand. "My God, you stupid—"

The moment the gun went off, Tom felt a sensation he hadn't experienced in years. He felt powerful. The shot still echoed in his ears, and an electriclike jolt rattled his hand. He blinked and looked down at her.

Maggie's thin body twitched and convulsed on the kitchen floor. Blood covered her face, yet her eyes remained open. She still wore that baffled, openmouthed expression from when he'd turned the gun on her. The spasms in her arms and legs halted. But blood continued to leak from her forehead. Wedged between her fingers, the cigarette she'd been smoking still smoldered.

"Maggie?" he whispered.

He heard the dog barking outside.

Beneath her head, a pool of dark blood bloomed on the tiled floor. The cigarette was burning down to her fingers, but she didn't move. He'd done this to her. His heart beating wildly, he gazed at the gun in his hand. He'd meant to take his own life today. This wasn't supposed to happen.

Tom glanced toward the sliding glass door. Had anyone heard the shot? Were her neighbors calling the police right now? The dog continued to bark furiously. It was as if the dumb animal knew what had happened to its master.

Tom began to tremble. *Fingerprints.* He shoved the gun back inside the bag, then pulled out a handkerchief. He wiped the edge of the counter, the bar stool, every place he'd set his hands. He rinsed out his ice tea glass, then put it away. He found the gift bag and stuffed the book inside it.

With the handkerchief wrapped around his hand, Tom slid open the glass door. He clutched the bag to his chest. As soon as he stepped outside, the Doberman lunged at him. Then, with a yelp, the animal abruptly stopped a few feet shy of him, restrained and choked in midjump by the chain attached to his collar.

Tom hobbled around the side of the house. The dog's barking started up again—like some beastly alarm that alerted the entire neighborhood. Tom expected to see a police car blocking his Volare in the driveway. But there was no one. He climbed inside his car, fumbled with the keys, then started up the engine. He crept out of the driveway. Reaching the palm-tree-lined street, he didn't see anyone. He didn't hear a police siren either. But the dog's barking still echoed inside his head.

They had a huge whirling fan trained on her. Dayle's hair fluttered in the breeze. Shadows of trees, phone poles, and headlights raced across her face and reflected on the windshield of her mock convertible sports car. That was the front screen projector working. The rear screen had the seaside road on which Dayle's character drove while intoxicated. Clutching the steering wheel, Dayle rolled her eyes ever so slightly. She'd been "drunk driving" on and off for about two hours now.

During one of the off moments, she'd retreated to her trailer and telephoned Nick Brock. He was still digging around Estelle Collier's hometown. Dayle caught him in his room at the Holiday Inn in Madison, Wisconsin.

"Nothing new on the father of Estelle's kid," he told her. "I'll have to pick up the pieces in San Francisco. But this you'll be interested in. I've talked to about twenty people, just casually fishing about our Miss Collier, and it turns out I'm not the first person to come here with a lot of questions about Estelle. This one yokel told me that a guy calling himself a reporter was digging around here four months ago with the same kind of questions."

"You mean, before Leigh's death?"

"At least three months before," Nick said. "I think you're right about a blackmailer. Somebody was looking for a skeleton in Estelle's closet."

"They must have found something," Dayle said. "Listen, Nick. I need to know more about that 'unknown' father. It's what they must have used to get her to lie. Maybe we can use the same thing to squeeze the truth out of her."

Once Dayle had clicked off, she phoned Sean Olson's office and left a message on her machine—relaying what Nick had just told her. In only two days, Sean had become her confidant. Concerning this conspiracy, no one else took her seriously except Sean.

"Cut!" the director yelled. "Beautiful, Dayle. Let's break for lunch."

Dayle sighed and let her hands drop from the steering wheel. Dennis helped her out of the mock sports car. A tall, stunning redhead stood behind him. She wore a lavender suit that showed off her jazzercised-thin figure and long, shapely legs. "Dayle," Dennis said. "I want you to meet Laura."

"So you are *the* Laura," Dayle said, shaking her hand. She wondered what this woman saw in good old pudgy Dennis. Snuggling alongside him, Laura stood an inch taller than Dennis. She had a sweet, nervous smile, and seemed starstruck in Dayle's presence. "Dennis has told me all sorts of nice things about you," Dayle said. "How does it feel to be on a movie set?"

"Oh, I love it!" Laura exclaimed. "It's so exciting!"

Dayle gave her shoulder a pat. "Someone once said that your first day on a movie set is an incredible thrill. And your second day is so dull it couldn't cut butter. Glad you're enjoying yourself, Laura. My big question for you is—how do you put up with this character?" She nudged Dennis.

Laura just giggled nervously.

Bonny handed Dayle her Evian water. Dayle winked, then turned and toasted Laura with the bottle. "Nice meeting you," she said, heading to her trailer. "Keep this guy out of trouble."

Laura giggled again. "Sometimes I call him Dennis the Menace!" she called. "You know, Dennis the Menace?"

Dayle looked back and nodded. "Yes, that—that's very cute. Well, see you around, Laura." She continued toward her trailer.

Dennis caught up with her at the door, leaving Laura behind to chat with the assistant director. "So what do you think of her?" he whispered.

"Oh, she's nice—and very pretty." Dayle stepped into the trailer.

Dennis followed her in, then shut the door. "So—am I still in the *casa de fido?*" he asked warily.

"Why should you be in the doghouse?" Dayle sat down at her vanity table. "You mean for suggesting I was paranoid yesterday?"

He nodded. "I was out of line, Dayle. I'm sorry."

She smiled at him in the mirror. "Okay, no sweat. You're forgiven."

He just stood by the door, looking at his feet. "Um, listen.

I heard some bad news from the studio publicity folks a few minutes ago.'' He took a deep breath. ''Maggie McGuire's dead. Somebody shot her.''

Dayle turned to stare at him. ''What?'' she whispered.

''It was on the AP wire. Happened in her house. Her dog was barking all night long, and one of her neighbors called the cops. They found Maggie on her kitchen floor early this morning, before dawn.''

Dayle kept shaking her head. Tears stung her eyes.

''The cops are pretty certain an obsessed fan did it,'' Dennis sighed. ''But considering everything that's happened lately, I don't know. Anyway, I'm sorry, Dayle. I know you liked her.''

She nodded. ''I want to send flowers to Maggie's children.''

''Consider it done,'' he replied.

She turned toward her vanity once more. ''Dennis, I think I need to be alone for a while,'' she said, her voice quivering.

''I'll make sure no one disturbs you.'' He paused in the doorway, and caught her reflection in the vanity mirror. ''For the record, Dayle,'' he said quietly. ''If I ever thought you were paranoid—I don't any more.''

The *Noon News Report* on TV led with their coverage of Maggie's death. Tom Lance watched a jerky clip of the sheet-covered corpse on a gurney as it was loaded into an ambulance. A police barricade held people back; it could have been a star-studded film premiere, judging from the curious crowd. A pretty, black woman reporter in a red suit stood in Maggie's driveway—just about where Tom had parked his car yesterday. She announced that the police didn't have any clues. ''One theory here is that Ms. McGuire's killer is an obsessed fan. But police are still gathering evidence.''

Tom found himself smiling. The cops didn't know.

He'd wiped away his fingerprints. No one except the dog had seen him arriving and leaving. On the way home, he'd stopped by Santa Monica Beach, and from the pier, he'd tossed his gun in the ocean.

All morning, he'd sat in front of his TV, waiting for the story to break. There hadn't been anything in the morning paper. For a change, one of the other tenants hadn't stolen it today. Most of his fellow occupants in the ugly, three-story gray stucco apartment building were lowlifers. But Tom's place was nicely furnished—if not a bit cluttered with mementos. Framed lobby cards from his films hung on the living room walls, and his career scrapbook sat on the coffee table. His old landlady used to browse through it with him occasionally, but her kids stuck her in a nursing home a few years back.

The telephone rang, startling him.

This was the third time today. Tom didn't answer it. He hardly ever got any calls—except for the occasional wrong number or salesperson. This had to be the police. Last night, he'd been convinced that at any minute they'd break down his door and arrest him. Several shots of Jack Daniels had helped calm him down. He'd fallen asleep on the sofa, drunk and weepy.

Even with the pretty reporter on TV assuring him that the police had no clues, the ringing phone made Tom feel hunted. He got to his feet. The painful gout had subsided a bit. He hobbled over to the window, moved the old lace curtain and glanced at the street below. He half expected to see a line of police cars in front of the building. But there was nothing. His Volare was still parked down there. He wondered if the police already had a description of it from one of Maggie's neighbors.

At last the telephone stopped ringing, and the moment it did, Tom realized something: cops didn't phone murder suspects, they came to their homes. No one had knocked on his door yet, and they probably wouldn't either, because *they knew nothing.* Maybe those calls were from reporters wanting to interview him. After all, he'd discovered Maggie and made her famous. "Damn!" Tom muttered, falling back on the couch.

The first time in years—decades—that the media would want to interview Tom Lance, and he'd been too scared to answer the phone.

Maggie's death captured the lead spot on the noon news. He could look forward to a big, fat obituary in the evening papers, and certainly a tribute on *Entertainment Tonight*. Murdered movie stars were the stuff that made tabloid covers, best-sellers, and TV movies. Every time a film star died, their costars were interviewed on TV and quoted in newspapers and magazines. He'd made Maggie famous again. And he would become famous again too.

"You want the official findings, Sean? Leigh Simone OD'd in the ladies' room at the Imperial. Her fingerprints were on the hypodermic. She had almost two grand worth of heroin in her purse, and she wrote something on the bathroom mirror about her life being a lie, I forget the exact wording."

"So the case is closed?" Sean asked, the phone to her ear. Sitting at the desk in her half-painted office, she had her pen poised on a legal pad. After Dayle's last phone call, Sean wanted to find out just how much the Portland police knew about the deaths of Leigh Simone, and Tony Katz and his friend. Were they even close to suspecting a conspiracy? From her years as an attorney in Eugene, Sean had established ties with many law enforcement officials in Portland—from policemen to prosecuting attorneys.

On the other end of the line right now was Vincent Delk, a well-respected cop who became a desk jockey after getting shot in the knee during a drug bust. Vinnie had his hand on the pulse of the whole force. He was an excellent source. And it helped that he had a crush on her.

"You're hesitating, Vinnie, my love," she said, tapping her pen on the legal pad. "Is the Leigh Simone case closed or not?"

"Well, darlin', it hasn't officially reopened, but quite frankly, I want to dig a little deeper into this sucker. Now, don't quote me . . ."

"I told you," she said. She stopped taking notes for a moment, "This isn't for anyone but me. I just want your personal take, Vinnie."

"Well, from day one, this case smelled fishy to me. That message Leigh Simone wrote on the mirror, it always struck me as bogus. I mean, how often do we find a suicide note with someone who has OD'd on heroin?"

"Huh, not very?" Sean murmured.

"Nope. That dog don't hunt. Another thing sticking in my craw is the timing. It happened less than two weeks after Tony Katz and his buddy bought it in those woods outside St. Helens."

"You see a connection?"

"At first I thought it was the hotel. They were both staying at the Imperial at the time of their deaths." Vincent Delk let out a long sigh. "So we checked the registration and found a handful of guests who were there during both Tony Katz's and Leigh Simone's stay. But all of the people cleared. Ditto the hotel staff. I still see a connection. But I'm a minority opinion."

Sean stopped writing for a moment. "So what's the connection?"

"One word: *planning.*"

"I'm listening," Sean said.

"The scene in the ladies' room looked like a suicide or an accidental overdose, right? But in case of any doubts, we get this weird message on the mirror, spelling it out for us. To me, that's the result of deliberate planning."

"Go on."

"I'm not sure you want me to," Vincent said. "It's got to do with what happened to Tony and his friend. It's not pretty, Shawny."

"I'm a big girl," Sean said. "I can take it."

"Well, you probably heard that the two guys had been stripped naked, tied up, and killed. Looked like a gay-bashing."

"Yes, that's what I heard."

"Well, Tony and his friend were abducted and taken to that forest. We know this, because both men had come to the gay bar by taxi. They didn't have a car to drive fifty miles to that forest preserve. Some of the more gruesome details were kept out of the papers. This part's on the hush-hush. Tony Katz was found with a whittled-down tree branch shoved up his butt. And he'd been sexually mutilated. The other guy died execution style, shot in the head. But he also sustained sixty-one stab wounds and a slit throat."

"My God," Sean muttered.

"Now get this. The coroner is pretty sure he was already dead when they went to work on him with their knives. Which brings me back to what I was talking about earlier: *planning*."

"What do you mean?"

"The excessive stabbing occurred *after* they killed the boyfriend. Shows they didn't so much want to prolong his agony as they wanted to make a sensational impression. Like I say, *planning*. Next. From checking out the tire tracks and footprints, the FBI estimated anywhere from six to ten people were there in the woods—in two or three cars. Yet not a beer can or cigarette butt in sight. This wasn't the work of some drunk teens who let a gay-bashing get out of hand. No, this is a tight-knit group. Possibly eight people participating in one of the most grisly, sensational murders here in recent years. Headlines every day for well over a week—"

"Until Leigh Simone's suicide," Sean interjected.

"And despite all that sensationalism, none of those six, eight, or ten participants talked. No one bragged to anybody about it. That's unheard of. No leaks. Tight as a drum. As freakish and insane as this double murder appeared, in actuality, it was carefully orchestrated and performed without a flaw. A bunch of people got together and planned it, Shawny. You can bank on that. And they're still together, you can bank on that too.''

"So you think these same people killed Leigh Simone, and made it look like a suicide?"

"As I said, seems like deliberate planning there too. But I'm flying solo on this. I'm the only one around here who thinks Leigh's assistant is a liar."

"Listen. What if Estelle Collier stepped forward and said she'd been forced to lie about Leigh's—drug and sexual problems?"

"Are you trying to strike a deal for her?"

"I'm hoping she'll change her story. Knowing she can do so without incriminating herself might make it easier for her to tell the truth. Might make it easier for everyone."

"Well, Shawny, if anyone can swing a deal for this gal, it's you."

"Thanks. Listen, Vinnie. What if I told you that I believe this same group is now after Dayle Sutton?"

"Then I'd say Dayle Sutton is a dead woman."

Eleven

"So—do you recognize us with our clothes on?" Joanne asked the audience at the beginning of *The Tonight Show*. She and Avery came across as good sports, and the host clearly enjoyed exchanging zingers with them:

INTERVIEWER: What's the deal with this home movie? So you just decided one night to set up a video camera, and get the whole thing on tape, huh?

AVERY: Well, it's not like we were the first couple to come up with the idea. I just figured it might add a little spice to things.

JOANNE: I like being married to a guy who, after four years, is still interested in spicing it up. The fact that he's still interested is wonderful. Though I must admit, had I known the damn thing would end up being seen by hundreds of thousands of people, I'd have insisted on better lighting, a good makeup person, and a stunt double.

When the interviewer asked who might have stolen the video, Avery became serious, yet not too solemn. He said it was a police matter, but he suspected the responsible party didn't agree with Joanne's and his politics.

"I think someone was trying to humiliate us," Joanne added. "And it's embarrassing this video—we made for ourselves— has been seen by so many people. But you know, I'm not sorry we made it. What's the big deal? Why the scandal? We're an old married couple, for God's sake."

They applauded her. Avery had forgotten about Joanne's ability to connect with a live audience. She instinctively knew what to say, when to be serious or irreverent, when to shut up, and when to shut him up.

Braving a barrage of intimate questions, she'd held up through an insane schedule the last three of days. And the phone calls wouldn't stop: film offers, and a long list of magazines wanting to shoot cover stories, including *Vanity Fair*, who asked for them both in a sexy Herb Ritts portrait.

The producers of *Expiration Date* couldn't have been more pleased that Traci Haydn's costar had grabbed the media spotlight. They talked about moving up the film's release date, and giving Avery top billing over Traci. Suddenly he had clout. Dayle Sutton e-mailed Avery to use his influence with their director to hire another writer to rework the gay-bashing script and make it more honest. On her recommendation, he also phoned Gary Worsht, the gay man he'd be playing—a nice guy, but definitely not the milksop saint from the script.

Gary had high praise for Sean Olson: "That lady really went to bat for me." The least Avery could do was go to bat for her and Dayle Sutton. To his utter amazement, the director listened to him, and a new screenwriter was hired. Almost overnight, he'd acquired that kind of pull.

If someone had been out to sabotage Avery's career by releasing that video to the public, their plan had backfired. Proof of their failure might have been gauged by the loud applause for Avery and Joanne as they strolled off *The Tonight Show* set. Holding hands, they waved to the audience.

Joanne ducked behind the curtain, and her grip on Avery's hand became tighter. A few members of *The Tonight Show* staff, two NBC pages, and the reporter and photographer from *People* waited for them backstage. Blinded by camera flashes, they made their way toward their dressing room. Joanne's hand remained like a vise around his.

Avery opened the door for her. "What's going on?" he whispered.

Joanne shut the door behind them, then suddenly bent over. "Oh, God, Avery," she gasped. "Something's wrong."

He sat her down in a chair. All the while, Joanne trembled and clutched her abdomen. Avery grabbed the phone and got through to the studio operator. "This is Avery Cooper calling from my dressing room in—in Studio B. We have a medical emergency. We need an ambulance or a doctor here at once. Can you help us?"

"Yessir, I can."

He noticed blood seeping down Joanne's legs. "Tell them to hurry."

Tom was fed up. He'd left three messages on his agent's machine, and the son of a bitch still hadn't called back. In fact, the phone hadn't rung all day, not one lousy call since the one he should have answered around noon. Now he was about to videotape *Entertainment Tonight,* assuming they'd have a tribute to Maggie McGuire. But like an idiot, he'd forgotten to buy blank videos. He had to tape over one of his old movies from *The Late, Late Show.* He was frantically trying to find some leftover time on the tape of his 1950 western, *Trigger Happy,* when *Entertainment Tonight* started.

"The entertainment world is shocked and saddened today by the passing of one of its most durable talents. Academy-Award-winning actress Maggie McGuire was shot to death in her Beverly Hills home last night. . . ."

Tom kept having to go back and forth from the broadcast to the videotape until he finally found the end of his western. Then he switched back to the broadcast and started recording. They were showing Maggie's ranch house, police cars jammed in the driveway. " . . . as investigations continue," the anchorwoman said. "Maggie McGuire's career spanned four decades. She played a Mafia mistress in her first movie, *Hour of Deceit. . . .*"

"My God, there I am!" Tom gasped. He stared at a scene from the movie. He'd cornered Maggie in a bar. His back was to the camera, but his face was visible in partial profile. "I'm not gonna sing to any cop," Maggie said, puffing a cigarette. She wore a sexy, off-the-shoulder cocktail dress. It was before Hollywood had groomed her for stardom, and she looked so fresh, raw, and beautiful. Her wavy black hair fell down to her bare shoulders. Tom now remembered why he'd fallen in love with that gorgeous young girl. "I've had a bellyful of you cops," she continued. "Besides, Frankie treats me nice. . . ."

Tom still remembered his line that followed: "I think you're scared of him, Miss Gerrard." But they cut to another film clip. "More bad-girl roles followed for McGuire," the anchorwoman announced. "She received a Best Supporting Actress Oscar for *Strange Corridor,* in which she played—"

The telephone rang. For a moment, Tom was torn. Was it a friend who had just seen him on TV? His agent? A reporter? A movie offer?

He pressed the mute button on his remote and reached for the phone. "Hello?" he said, tentative. He watched a clip of Maggie with Robert Mitchum.

There was a mechanical click on the other end of the line. A strange humming sound followed, and over this, a muffled barking—as if a dog was outside the caller's house.

"Hello?" Tom said again. "Who's there?"

The dog continued to bark, only louder. Tom realized it was a recording. Someone turned up the volume. Why would anybody want to tape a dog howling and yelping repeatedly?

He was ready to hang up. The barking was like some sort of alarm that wouldn't shut off. Then he realized that he was listening to Maggie's dog, Tosha. The recording must have been made yesterday, at just around the time when he was killing her.

"Hello?" Tom whispered. He could hardly breathe.

The volume went down on the tape, and the dog's barking faded away. Tom listened to the quiet for a moment. Then he heard another click, followed by Maggie's recorded voice: "Tom. You're pathetic, you really are."

Entertainment Tonight had another headline story—besides Maggie McGuire's death. Behind the anchorwoman's right shoulder appeared a blowup photo of Avery Cooper and Joanne Lane. "Doctors released Joanne Lane from Cedars-Sanai Medical Center today after emergency treatment for an undisclosed ailment," she announced. "The Broadway actress and her husband, Avery Cooper, have been embroiled in a media furor over the public release of their very private home-video sex tape. *E.T.* correspondent, Charles Platt, has the story from outside the Coopers' home in Beverly Hills."

A swarthy, square-jawed young man stood by Avery and Joanne's front gate. "Sally-Anne, I'm here outside the home of Avery Cooper and Joanne Lane," he said into his microphone. "The couple had just filmed a segment for *The Tonight Show,* and while backstage at NBC studios in Burbank, Avery Cooper telephoned for an ambulance for his wife. Joanne Lane was rushed to Cedars-Sinai Medical Center. There have been conflicting reports as to the nature of this medical emergency. However, sources at the Cedars-Sinai have unofficially told *E.T.* that Joanne Lane suffered a miscarriage. . . ."

The picture switched to a clip of Avery helping a shaky, frail Joanne into a black BMW at the hospital's side entrance. Camera flashes illuminated them like a flickering strobe. "The Coopers left the hospital together at two-thirty this afternoon," the reporter continued. The camera pulled back to show him standing in front of Avery's driveway—along with about a hundred people. Bouquets of flowers and cards had been left by the front gate. "The Coopers' house here in Beverly Hills is far from quiet tonight—"

"Which explains why the Coopers are here," Sheila Weber said, switching off the TV set on their kitchen counter. Demurely pretty, Sheila had a creamy complexion and curly blond hair. She was five months pregnant with her first child. "How are you holding up?" she asked, refilling Avery's wine-glass.

Avery nodded. "I'll be okay." He sat at the Webers' break-fast table. George Weber stood behind him, rubbing his shoulders. With dark eyes and prematurely gray hair, he was a handsome guy. A psychologist, he must have had patients constantly falling in love with him. "Relax, eat something, buddy," he said. "You look like shit."

Avery managed to chuckle. He patted his friend's hand, but didn't touch the sandwich in front of him. Joanne was asleep in the Webers' guest room.

George and Sheila Weber were his closest friends—and in a way, his second family. Avery had known George since high school. When he'd moved to Los Angeles, Avery stayed in George's one-bedroom garage apartment. He'd had a roll-out futon in the living room, and paid half of the rent. For three years, the struggling actor and the medical student had lived together.

Avery had been best man at George's wedding. The Webers had already asked him to be godfather to the baby. Sheila's sister would be godmother. Avery hated seeing Joanne left out of the loop. Yet he had a hunch Joanne merely went through the social motions with the Webers, the same way he couldn't quite bond with her Broadway cohorts. Maybe bringing her here wasn't such a smart idea, what with Sheila so healthy, happy, and pregnant.

In the hospital emergency room, Joanne had told him that she'd taken a home pregnancy test last week. The results had been positive. She'd planned on seeing their doctor once this media blitz campaign was over. *The Tonight Show* was their last obligation. "I wanted to tell you tonight, honey," she whispered, tears streaming down her face. "I wanted to surprise you."

As he and Joanne had left the hospital, photographers had fought each other for a good shot. One of the most painful times of their lives needed to be recorded for the public by these vultures. Pulling away in the black BMW, they'd had at least a dozen cars on their tail. Steve Bensinger had quickly assigned several other black BMWs to converge with Avery's car on their escape route from Cedars-Sinai. The strategy worked. By the time Avery and Joanne reached the Webers' block in Brentwood, they'd lost the bloodhounds.

"Why don't you lie down for a bit?" George suggested, sitting down at the table with Avery. "You can crash in our bedroom. You won't wake Joanne."

"No," he said. "I need to pick up some things from home if we're spending the night."

George offered to come along, but Avery said he wanted to be alone for a while. Before leaving, he checked in on Joanne once more. She was still napping. Neither of them had caught much sleep during the last three days. In fact, the strenuous schedule had probably contributed to her miscarriage.

Curled up beneath the blanket, she lifted her head and squinted at him.

"I'm going home for some stuff," he said. "You need anything, honey?"

Joanne shook her head.

He leaned over and kissed her. Joanne's cheek was wet with tears. Avery took hold of her hand and squeezed it. "You— you just rest, okay? I'll be back in about an hour."

He didn't drive directly home. He swung by a small, secluded ocean-view park, halfway between home and the Webers'. There wasn't much to the place: a couple of wooden benches, and a low rock wall at the bluff's edge. Avery sometimes came here when he felt blue. He sat down on one of the benches. The smog made for an achingly beautiful sunset: layers of bright pink and topaz streaked the darkening sky, and reflected in the choppy waters of the Pacific. A cool ocean breeze stung the tears in his eyes. He could cry here. He didn't think anyone was around to see him.

But a rented white Taurus idled at the side of the road less than half a block from the little park. Avery and Joanne had lost the pursuing reporters after leaving the hospital, yet this car had managed to remain inconspicuously on their tail. One of the two men in the Taurus was now talking on a cellular phone. He had urgent instructions regarding Avery Cooper's exact location.

Avery had no idea how much time had passed while he sat on that park bench, but a drab darkness had consumed the beautiful sunset. He'd been so worried about Joanne grieving around the very pregnant Sheila. But he was the one who ached at the sight of his friend's pregnant wife tonight. He saw the promise of a family there. For a short while, Joanne had been carrying his child, and he hadn't even known.

Avery wiped his nose. He noticed a woman coming up the winding dirt path by the rock wall. She stared at him from behind a pair of black cat-eye glasses that seemed as sixties retro as her auburn page-boy wig. She kept her hands in the pockets of her shiny black raincoat.

Avery heard a car pull up. He stood and glanced back for a moment.

"Excuse me?" the woman said. "Aren't you Avery Cooper?"

He turned to her. "Yes, but I—"

Her hand came up so quick, he didn't even realize what she was doing until her fingernails tore at his cheek. He reeled back. The woman ran away, then ducked inside the white car that had just pulled up. Dazed, Avery watched the car peel away and speed down the street. There was no time to get a license plate number, no time to even process what had just happened.

Dazed, he wandered back to his car, climbed inside, and checked the rearview mirror. Whoever the woman was, she'd done a number on his face: four claw marks weeping blood on his cheek. He thought about calling the police to report the incident. But what could they do about it?

He drove home. The crowd outside his front gate had dwindled down to about twenty people, most of them reporters. Avery opened the gate with a remote device. The mob fought for a look at him, shouting questions, mostly about Joanne—where she was, how she was holding up. All the inquiries seemed to blend together—except for one reporter, whose voice dominated the others as he asked, "How did you get that scratch on your face, Avery?"

Avery stared straight ahead, pressing the remote device to shut the gate behind him.

Once inside the house, he tended to the scratches on his face. He'd forgotten he was still wearing makeup from his *Tonight Show* appearance. He washed his face, then put peroxide on the scratch marks. After collecting some things for Joanne, he phoned George to let him know he'd be back soon. "How's Joanne doing?" he asked.

"Still napping," George said. "Where are you? Did you *just* get home?"

"Yeah, I made a stop along the way," Avery replied.

He'd spent almost ninety minutes in that park. It was a lapse of time the police would later question. They would also ask about the scratch marks on his face.

Twelve

As was now the custom, Hank entered the apartment first, and turned on the lights for her. Then Dayle stepped inside. She didn't pay much attention to the ringing telephone. Hank forged ahead into the kitchen, letting Fred out. The cat scurried toward her. Dayle scooped him up and hugged him.

The answering machine in her study was picking up the call: *Beep*. "Hello, Ms. Sutton? Nick Brock calling from nowheresville, Wisconsin. Hold on to your socks. I got the goods on who Peter Collier's daddy is, and it's one for Ripley's, a badseed story. Small wonder Estelle has kept junior a secret. I think you're right about her being blackmailed—"

Dayle grabbed the telephone. "Hello? Nick?"

"Ms. Sutton?" Nick was saying. "Hey, cool. Glad I caught you . . ."

"I'm sorry, Danny, I don't want you spending the night at this Greg's house." The cordless phone to her ear, Sean stood on a ladder, painting her office walls. "I don't know Greg or his parents—"

"Well, geeze, Mom, maybe if you were home more, you'd know him. He's practically my best friend."

Working the roller over the wall, she sighed. "I thought Jason was your best friend."

"He is, but Greg's new. Ah, c'mon, Aunt Anne said it's okay with her."

"Well, it's not okay with me—not yet. Tell you what, have Greg's mom call me here at the office, and I'll get back to you and let you know." Sean paused for a moment by the roller-tray full of sea-foam-green paint. She wore a baseball cap, a paint-splattered T-shirt, and old jeans. "Are you still there, Danny?" she asked. "I just want to talk to Greg's mother—"

"Forget it," her son grunted. "I never get to go anywhere, and you're never home. Fine. This sucks."

"Hey, this isn't very fun for me either," she said.

After Danny hung up, Sean went back to painting her office. Her son had a point. She was hardly ever home, and missed so much of her children's lives. But she had to set up her business. Dan wouldn't be around too long, and she couldn't expect to keep living off the generosity of her in-laws.

The phone rang again, and she snatched it up. "Yes?"

"Sean? It's Dayle. How are you?"

"Oh, my son hates me, but otherwise I'm all right." She put down the paint roller. "Did you get my message?"

"Yes," Dayle said. "In fact, the timing is impeccable. I think you're right. Estelle Collier will be more cooperative if she has a lawyer to work out a deal for her. Could you meet me at Estelle's place tonight around eight?"

Sean hesitated. She'd wanted to be home by eight.

"By the way," Dayle added. "I don't expect you to do this for free. I'm paying for your services here, Sean, whatever you charge."

"Well, I'm not going to pretend that I can't use the money." She reached for a pen on her desk. "What's Estelle's address?"

As Hank pulled out of the driveway, Dayle watched the Corsica start after them. It stayed on their tail for a half hour. Twice, Dayle made Hank stop for amber lights, because she didn't want to lose the Corsica just yet.

They turned into the Valley Ridge Condominiums complex. The three tall buildings, constructed in the early Reagan years, compensated for their lack of charm with a clean, spartan style. Hank pulled up to the entrance of the middle tower. Stepping out of the limo, Dayle spied the Corsica at the edge of the parking lot—one building over. Its headlights went out.

Hank escorted her to the lobby door. Dayle toted a Nordstrom bag. She buzzed number 501: *F. & B. LASKEY.* Laskey was Bonny McKenna's married name. It would take some time and research for anyone to connect Dayle's stand-in with this address. "Hello?" the voice over the intercom asked.

"Hi, it's me."

"Oh, howdy. I'm buzzin' ya up."

Dayle took the elevator to the fifth floor. Bonny was waiting in the hallway. "So what does our hair look like today?" she asked.

Within minutes, Bonny emerged from the building and strolled toward Hank and the limo. She looked exactly like her employer, right down to Dayle's confident strut. Bonny climbed into the backseat of the limo. Once Hank pulled out of the lot, the Corsica started following them.

Dayle watched from the fifth-floor window. For the next two hours, Bonny would go shopping on Rodeo Drive—with Hank at her side. She knew enough about surveillance to keep her shadows at a distance—and eventually lose them without raising any suspicions.

Dayle changed into the outfit she'd brought along in her bag:

jeans and a purple jersey. From the phone in Bonny's kitchen, she called a cab.

The taxi dropped Dayle in front of a U-shaped two-story apartment building. The place looked as if it had once been a hotel in the early sixties. At the front gate, two tiki torches with Polynesian masks on the poles stood like relics of the bygone era. Each unit had its own entry off a balcony walkway overlooking the pool and patio.

Dayle found Estelle's apartment on the second level. She rang the bell. It seemed a gauche place to live for someone who had worked alongside such a high-profile star. Then again, Estelle's bad-seed son had depleted most of his mother's income. Maybe this dump was all she could afford now.

Dayle rang the bell once more. Estelle opened the door. She'd obviously just gotten out of the tub. Her broad face was framed by dark, damp ringlets. She wore a pink robe, and her feet were bare. She frowned at Dayle.

"Can I come in and talk with you, please?" Dayle asked.

"God, what now?" With a roll of her eyes, Estelle opened the door wider, then plodded to the kitchenette. She poured herself a glass of wine, ignoring Dayle, across the counter from her. "We've already been through this at Leigh's memorial service, Dayle. I have nothing more to say."

Dayle sat down at the kitchen counter. It was a continental kitchen, the kind incorporated with the living room. Estelle's apartment looked like a modest suite in some southwestern resort—all brown, beige, and rust colors, with Aztec art on the walls. The only personal touch to her living room was a framed photo of a younger Estelle holding a toddler, probably the son. He didn't look much like his famous dad. Lucky kid.

"Does Peter know who his father is?" Dayle asked quietly.

Estelle's eyes widened for a moment. She put down her wineglass. "You can't prove a thing about Peter's father. You're just guessing."

Dayle sighed. "I know where you spent the spring of sixty-nine, Estelle. Wasn't Peter conceived during your time at the ranch?''

"I wasn't at there when those murders happened—"

"I know," Dayle said grimly. "The Tate-LaBianca murders were in August. You left Spawn Ranch in March. But you lived there nine weeks."

"Guilt by association, right?" Estelle said. "You're just like those monsters who were harassing me. They thought Charles Manson was Peter's father too. It's so damn ridiculous! I wasn't one of his women!"

"But, Estelle, amid all that drug use and group sex, can you remember for sure?" Dayle studied her face and sighed. "The truth is, you can't prove Charlie *isn't* the father. That's how these people got to you, isn't it? Charlie had targeted dozens of celebrities. Who in the entertainment industry would have hired one of his disciples? Who could trust you?"

"I want you to leave," Estelle said.

"And in the end, you couldn't be trusted. Look what you did to Leigh."

"That's so unfair! Do you think they gave me a choice?"

"Are we finally talking about the same 'they'?" Dayle asked. "How did they approach you? Did you meet any of them?"

Estelle took another gulp of wine, then shrugged. "I never met a single one. They started calling me about four months ago. I was in trouble. I'd taken some money out of Leigh's account to pay my son's debts. Somehow, these people found out about it, and they called me—"

"You said 'they.' " Dayle remarked.

"Yes. About five different people phoned me over the next few months. They kept asking how I planned to replace the money from Leigh's account before someone noticed. They knew I'd spent time at Spawn Ranch too." She shook her head. "Who would have understood? I was a fat, unwanted teenager. That spring at the ranch was the first time I ever felt like I *belonged*. You and Leigh, women like you, pretty all your lives.

You wouldn't know what it's like to be repulsive to people, to be that hungry for love. At the ranch, they took me in. And yes, my son was conceived there.'' She sighed. ''Only I saw how some of the other girls got passed around. So I left. After I had Peter, I worked hard to make a good home for him. The truth is, I don't know who his father was. And that's what I told the police and FBI when they rounded everyone up after the Tate murders.''

''These people calling you, how did they get their information?''

Estelle took her wineglass around the counter and sat on the stool beside Dayle. ''I heard someone was in my hometown asking questions about me a few months back. A couple of high school friends knew about my time at Spawn Ranch. Maybe somebody got to them. Is that how your man found out?''

Dayle nodded. ''I just want your cooperation, Estelle.''

She let out a cynical laugh. ''Ha, those monsters only wanted my cooperation too. Oh, they were very clever. They merely *suggested* I could replace the money I borrowed by selling the tabloids a story about Leigh Simone's involvement with drugs, and her secret lesbian lifestyle.''

''This was *before* her death?'' Dayle asked.

''Yes, months ago.''

''Did you try to talk to Leigh about this?''

Estelle's mouth twisted into a frown. ''I didn't want her to know I'd stolen from her. She trusted me! I just kept hoping these people would go away. But it only got worse. They started following Leigh around like stalkers. And they were so blatant about it, as if they were untouchable. They'd park outside her house for hours at a time—''

''But Leigh had bodyguards.''

Estelle shook her head. ''Only when she was on tour. Otherwise, she had a retired cop who handled security for the house, and a chauffeur who carried a gun. By the time one of them came out of the gate, the car would always take off. But another car just like it would be back an hour later.''

''Another car just like it? What do you mean?''

''They were rentals, you know, midsize cars, Corsicas, Cavaliers—''

''And Tauruses,'' Dayle murmured. ''Last couple of days, they've been following me around too. What did Leigh do about it?''

Estelle stared at her for a moment, then sighed. ''Leigh thought they were from the tabloids. She called them the 'rental mentals.' Sometimes she'd flip them the bird as she came out of her driveway in the limo. She wasn't afraid of them. But I was.''

''You had to know they were going to kill her. . . .''

''I thought they were out to destroy Leigh's career. The night before we left for Portland, I got another call. They knew about the trip. This man told me, 'If anything should happen to Leigh, her accountants will discover the money is missing. You'll have to square things with them.' He said that the tabloids would pay for the *inside story* on Leigh. I could replace the money very quickly if I gave them what they wanted. He told me, 'Remember, she was a lesbian, and she used heroin. She was very unhappy.' I thought at the time, 'Why is he saying, *she was, she was*?' ''

Dayle frowned. ''In the back of your mind, you had to know.''

''I didn't want to believe it.'' She shook her head. ''I didn't even believe it when the police told me she was dead. The cop, right away, he said to me, 'Did Leigh Simone use heroin?' And I knew that I had to answer yes.''

Staring at her, Dayle almost felt her pain. ''Did they contact you again?''

Estelle nodded. ''Two days later, this woman called. She just said, 'Good job, Miss Piggy.' They used to call me 'Miss Piggy.' She said, 'Good job, Miss Piggy. Now keep your fat mouth shut.' '' Estelle refilled her wineglass. "I did what I was told. And I managed to replace the money in Leigh's account.''

Dayle rested a hand on her shoulder. "Listen. If you're worried about changing your story for the police, I have a lawyer friend. I think she can swing you a deal. I'll pay her fee. I asked her to come here tonight.''

"Generous of you," Estelle murmured, in a stupor.

"Also if you're worried about a job, you can work for me.''

Estelle let out an abrupt laugh. "But you're going to die too," she said, staring at her as if she was stupid for missing something so obvious. "You just said, they have you under surveillance. It's already started.''

Dayle automatically shook her head.

"They've probably already gotten to somebody close to you, Dayle, the same way they got to me. It's most likely someone you trust, a loyal, old friend, or a new acquaintance. Whoever it is, have some compassion for them.''

"I have compassion for you, Estelle. I want to help. I know a police lieutenant who's handling Leigh's case here. She's a good woman. I'd like you to talk to her. Tell her what you told me.''

"Sure, why not?" Estelle ran a hand through her damp hair, then stood up. "There's nothing more they can do to me. Go on, call the police. I'll give them a statement. Let your lawyer friend in. I need to get dressed.''

Dayle watched her plod into the bathroom and shut the door. She heard the hair dryer start. Sifting through her purse, Dayle found Lt. Susan Linn's business card. Then she reached for the phone.

He'd already packed his scrapbook in the suitcase, and now Tom was pulling clothes out of his closet. Another call had come in an hour ago; but he'd let it ring. Right now, he just wanted to get out of there before they called again. These people knew he'd killed Maggie, and they were torturing him. Why? He had a feeling they were watching him this very minute.

The telephone rang again. Tom stepped into the living room and gazed at the phone for a moment. Finally, he picked it up, but didn't quite bring the receiver up to his face. The voice seemed tiny and distant: "Hello? Mr. Lance? Mr. Tom Lance? Is anyone there?"

Tom brought the receiver closer to his ear. "Yes? This is him."

"Hi. My name's Hal Buckman. I'm a reporter for *Entertainment Tonight.* I'm calling because we've discovered that Maggie McGuire made her movie debut with you. I was wondering if you'd be willing to give us an interview." He paused. "Would that be all right? Mr. Lance? Are you still there?"

"Yes, I—I'm still here," he said numbly. "You want me to be on TV?"

"That's right. We'd tape the interview tomorrow morning for tomorrow night's show. Could you fit us into your schedule?"

Tom closed his eyes and smiled gratefully. "Yes," he said, past the sudden tightness in his throat. "Yes, I—I think I can fit you in. . . ."

Someone knocked. Dayle peeked out the window, then opened Estelle's front door. Sean wore a navy blue silk blouse and a black skirt. Her hair had been pulled back in a ponytail. "So where's my new client?" she asked.

"In the bathroom, getting dressed. I've already put a call in to a police lieutenant I know. I think she'll work with us on this."

Sean glanced at the closed bathroom door. Estelle still had the hair dryer on. "Is she ready to talk?"

Dayle nodded. "She's told me an earful. These people forced her to lie about Leigh's problems with sex and drugs. They were calling her up long before Leigh died—practically admitting they were going to kill her.''

"Does she have proof that these people actually murdered Leigh?''

Dayle shrugged. "I can't say. You'll have to ask her yourself.''

Sean nodded and sighed. "I'll need to ask her a *lot* of questions before we talk to the police. Might be a long night ahead.''

"You can sleep over at my place if you want.''

"Thanks,'' Sean said, putting down her briefcase. "But I want to fix breakfast for my kids tomorrow. Plus my husband has had a few bad nights lately, and I need to be with him.''

Dayle squinted at her. "You mentioned he was sick. Is it serious?''

"Dan was diagnosed three years ago with ALS, Lou Gehrig's Disease.'' Sean spoke in a matter-of-fact way. She even managed a smile. "The doctor originally gave us only eighteen months, so we're doing better than expected.''

"Oh, Sean, I'm so sorry,'' Dayle murmured. "Are you getting any help?''

She nodded. "My in-laws came to our rescue. It's one reason we moved here from Eugene. We had to sell our house. Don't get me started talking about the debt. Anyway, the UCLA Medical Center is doing great things in the treatment of people with ALS. So this is the place for us to be right now.''

"Sean, I wish you would have told me. I wouldn't be bothering you with all this—''

"No, you're helping me out. We could use the money—''

The phone rang.

"That's probably Lieutenant Linn.'' Dayle grabbed the receiver. "Hello?''

"Dayle? Susan Linn, here. I got your page. I'm on my way. I'll be there in fifteen minutes if traffic allows. Is Estelle there with you now?''

"Yes. She's in the john,'' Dayle said, watching Sean wander

toward the closed bathroom door. "And I have a lawyer here to represent her."

"Fine. I'll see you soon." Susan Linn hung up.

Sean turned to Dayle. "That dryer's been on for at least ten minutes. . . ."

Dayle put down the phone. She rapped on the bathroom door. "Estelle?"

No answer. Dayle pounded on the door again. "Estelle? Can you hear me? Estelle!" She jiggled the doorknob. Locked. At the crack under the bathroom door, blood seeped past the threshold onto the beige shag carpet. "Oh, my God," she whispered. "Sean, call an ambulance. . . ."

Dayle threw her weight against the door. "Estelle! Oh, Jesus, no. . . ."

Sean hurried to the phone. Dayle kicked at the spot just below the doorknob until it finally gave. But the door didn't move more than a couple of inches. Something was blocking it—something heavy and lifeless.

Dayle peeked into the bathroom and gasped. She saw the blood on the white tiled floor, and Estelle's nude body, curled up in a fetal position. She hadn't cut her wrists. All the blood leaked from a slice across her throat. And in her hand, she still clutched a razor blade.

Thirteen

"Are you okay, Dayle?" Sean asked. Sitting at the steering wheel, she took her eyes off the road for a moment to glance at her.

Dayle was slumped in the passenger seat. She gave Sean a limp smile. "I'll be fine," she said, her voice scratchy from talking to Lieutenant Linn for the last ninety minutes. She'd been crying a little too. A pair of approaching headlights illuminated her pale, tearstained face; and for a moment, Dayle Sutton didn't look anything like a glamorous movie star. "You're keeping it together really well," she said.

Sean studied the traffic on the highway. "Well, I didn't know Estelle," she reasoned. "And I'm not the one who was talking to her just ten minutes before we found her in there—like that. I'd say you absorbed most of the shock for us, Dayle."

Sean patted her shoulder. Dayle probably thought she was a real cold customer for not breaking down at all. But that scene in Estelle's place was all too familiar. Because of Dan's seizures, Sean had almost become accustomed to dealing with death and near-death, 9-1-1, paramedics, and answering a ton of stupid questions while under stress.

She and Dayle had sat in Estelle's beige living room an hour ago, watching them carry the draped corpse out on a stretcher. She'd told Susan Linn everything she could—which wasn't much. She shared some of Vince Delk's theories with her, but didn't mention that she had a source within the Portland police. The burden was really on Dayle, who told the lieutenant everything Estelle Collier had so desperately concealed for such a long time.

"This is all hearsay, you know," Lieutenant Linn had warned them. Her dark, almond eyes appeared tired. She wore jeans and a sweatshirt, and her black hair was tied back in a loose bun. She sat on the sofa with them, a tape recorder in her lap. She shut the machine off. "I'll send this tape to the Portland police, suggesting they reopen the Leigh Simone investigation. But I can't guarantee anything. Meanwhile, we'll give this place a thorough going-over. Maybe Estelle kept a journal, something to back up what you've told me. Dayle, I'll call you if we find anything." She loaded the recorder into her purse. "Have you thought about hiring yourself a full-time bodyguard?"

Rubbing her eyes, Dayle nodded. "I probably will, yes."

"I could try to fudge the police report on this," Lieutenant Linn said, shaking her head. "But the press will still get wind of the fact that you discovered the body, Dayle. They'll want you to make a statement." She glanced at Sean for a moment. "I think your lawyer friend here would agree with me, it's not a good idea to comment on this. It might screw up the investigation. And if what you say is true, you could be putting yourself in danger."

Sean offered to drive Dayle back to her apartment building. For the last half hour in the car, Sean couldn't stop thinking about the press coverage—and what it meant. She'd be included in the story on page one tomorrow: DAYLE SUTTON DISCOVERS

SUICIDE OF LEIGH SIMONE'S AIDE. These people who had targeted Dayle would now go after her—and possibly her family.

Tightening her grip on the steering wheel, she glanced over at Dayle, who had dozed off. Up ahead, a white Cavalier was parked across the street from the apartment building. Sean could just barely make out someone in the front seat. "Dayle?"

She sat up, suddenly alert. "What?"

"Is there a another entrance to your building?"

For a moment, Dayle didn't seem to understand. Then Sean nodded at the Cavalier—and the lone figure inside it.

"There's a side entrance," Dayle said. "But I have to call the night watchman to let me in."

"Cellular's in my purse," Sean replied. She turned down the cross street in front of Dayle's building. The Cavalier was too far away for her to tell if its occupant had noticed them. While Dayle fished out the cellular and called the night man, Sean studied the other cars parked along the street. All of them looked empty. She found the building's side door, and pulled up to the loading zone beside it.

"We're waiting here now," Dayle was saying into the phone. "Thanks." She clicked off and handed the cellular to Sean. "He'll just be a minute."

"Let's stay in here until he shows," Sean said, putting her phone away. She nervously glanced around—particularly at shadowy bushes alongside the building. Then she checked to make sure the car door was locked. "Why didn't you tell Lieutenant Linn about these guys who have you under surveillance?"

"I really wasn't thinking about them." Dayle shrugged. "Besides, she'd only think I was paranoid. She'd say these guys are with the tabloids. I've been through this before with her. Ditto my assistant, Dennis. You're the only one who really seems to believe me, Sean." She sighed. "Listen, I can't thank you enough. If you weren't with me tonight—"

The sudden noise gave Sean a start, and she swiveled toward

her window. It was only the night man, pushing open the side door for Dayle. He smiled and waved at them.

Dayle finished thanking her, and said good-bye. Sean watched her trot around the front of the car to the door. Once Dayle was inside, Sean pulled forward and turned at the next intersection. Near the end of the block on the cross-street, she saw someone leaning against a parked Taurus, talking to the driver inside. He looked about forty-five, with sneakers, white pants, and an ugly, shortsleeve turquoise blue shirt. He puffed on a cigarette. Only a couple of cars behind was the Cavalier with the front door cracked open and the interior light on.

Sean remained idling around the corner from them. She must have caught them during the changing of the guard. They didn't seem to notice her. The man in the ugly shirt was still talking to his friend. He was laughing about something. He tossed away his cigarette, slapped the hood of the Taurus a couple of times, then started toward his own car. Then the Cavalier's headlights went on, and it started to pull away from the curb.

Sean turned the corner and began to follow him. She passed the parked Taurus, then glanced in her rearview mirror. The man inside didn't seem to notice her. He had his window rolled down, and he was looking up at Dayle's building.

Forty-five minutes later, the Cavalier turned into the parking lot of a seedy-looking hotel called the My-T-Comfort Inn. It couldn't have been all that *comfortin'*, located right off a busy highway, with cars and trucks whooshing by. Someone had rap music cranked up to full volume; it was either from the Dairy Barn Kwick Stop next door or a resident of the trailer park across the street. The hotel was a shoddy, late-sixties cabin-row-style setup with about forty rooms. Below the blinking VACANCY sign, a yellow-lit billboard heralded in black letters: FREE HBO — HAPPY BI THDAY ANITA!

Sean pulled over to the curb, near the motel sign. She watched the Cavalier wind around to the back of the hotel. Grabbing her purse, she climbed out of the car. The November night air had turned chilly, and Sean shivered as she crept along the wild shrubbery that bordered the parking lot by the hotel. She ducked behind a Dumpster, then watched the man with the ugly shirt step out of his car. He'd parked beside two Corsicas. He ambled to room 18, and let himself in. Sean pulled a piece of paper and a pen from her purse. She started scribbling down license plate numbers from the rental cars.

After a couple of minutes, Ugly Shirt Man emerged from his room again, an ice bucket in his hand. He knocked on the next door down, number 17. The door opened, and a stubby man with a mustache and greasy brown hair stepped outside. He wore army fatigues and a gray T-shirt, which revealed a tiny beer gut. Sean watched him punch his buddy in the arm, very macho friendly. The traffic noise from the street was too loud for her to hear what they were saying. Inside the room, she could see his TV was on. A laptop computer sat on the desk. The two men laughed about something, then both stepped inside the room and shut the door.

Sean finished jotting down the plate numbers and car descriptions. Another midsize, rental-type car pulled into the lot, the beams from its headlights sweeping across the bushes for a moment. Sean stepped back. The car, another white Taurus, parked in a space in front of her. She had a good view of the driver as he opened the car door. He didn't look like the others. He was about forty, with strawberry-blond hair; the boy next door, grown-up handsome. He wore a navy crew neck and khakis. At first, Sean thought he wasn't with them. But then he reached below the driver's seat and took out a handgun. He glanced around for a second, then checked the gun for something. After a minute, he slipped it back under the seat, climbed out of the car, and locked the door.

Crouched in the bushes, Sean kept perfectly still and watched him. Suddenly, the cell phone in her purse rang. She almost jumped out of her skin. She ducked further back, and grabbed the phone out of her purse. It rang again—louder this time, without the purse to muffle the sound. Mr. Boy Next Door stopped and glanced in her direction. A truck roared by on the street, drowning out the third ring. Sean switched off the phone, then held her breath and waited to see what the man would do.

He gave a little shrug, then walked across the parking lot, where he knocked on the door to room 17. Mr. Stubby Macho answered it. They shook hands. Sean noticed that the nice-looking one wore a pager. Then she realized they both sported pagers. These guys were soldiers, on call. They had a ringleader somewhere, pulling the strings. The two men stepped into cabin 17, and shut the door.

After jotting down Boy Next Door's license plate number, Sean scurried around to the front of the hotel. She peeked past the finger-smudged glass doors toward the front desk. She needed to know how many of them there were; she wanted names, where they lived—information the desk clerk might provide. At the moment, her potential source was leaning against the front counter, lazily paging through what looked like a skin magazine. He might have been handsome with some grooming, but he was too gaunt, and his long brown hair looked unwashed. Dayle guessed he was about thirty. His T-shirt hung on him as if draped over a skeleton.

Sean turned away from the door. Opening her purse, she checked her wallet: eleven dollars and some change—hardly enough for bribe money. She sighed, then caught her reflection in the window of a nearby parked car. Frowning at herself, Sean put down the purse, then unbuttoned her navy blue blouse. Despite the cold, she tied the shirt up in a Calypso fashion so her bare midriff showed. She didn't look much like a hooker, but this was the best she could do. Rolling her eyes, she retrieved her purse, then started into the lobby.

She was hit with a waft of warm, moist air that smelled of moldy carpet and stale coffee. The lobby had two orange plastic, bucket-style chairs and a Formica coffee table with a dusty, fake fern that had seen better days.

The desk clerk quickly stashed his skin magazine under the counter. "Want a room?" he asked.

Approaching the desk, Sean saw a ratty, tired-looking German Shepherd curled up at the clerk's feet. The dog gazed up at her with disinterest. "Atta girl, Anita," the clerk mumbled. *Anita, the birthday girl,* Sean thought. The clerk caught her eye again. "What can we do for you? You want a room?"

"Actually, I'm supposed to meet someone," Sean whispered, with her best coy smile. "There's these guys in a block of rooms—like sixteen, seventeen, and eighteen? I can't remember this particular guy's name or which room actually. Could you tell me the names of the guys in those rooms? I think they all checked in together a couple of days ago."

The desk clerk gave her a wary look. "Well, I dunno . . ."

"Oh, c'mon, be a sport," she said. "I don't want to knock on the wrong door tonight. C'mon, whaddaya say?"

He frowned. "It's against the law to give out peoples' names. I've got to be careful about stuff like that with these cops around."

"Cops?"

"Yeah, they checked in tonight. The squad car is on the other side from where your buddies are."

"What are they here for?" Sean asked. "Are they with the others?"

Shrugging, the skinny clerk glanced over her shoulder. "Huh, maybe you can ask these guys. They're with that group. . . ."

Sean swiveled around. From outside, Mr. Stubby Macho and Boy Next Door came toward the lobby. Stubby Macho pushed at the glass door.

Sean turned to the clerk. "Don't give me away," she whispered. "This is supposed to be a surprise! Don't say anything. Please!" Her head down, she quickly started for the door, hurrying past the two men.

Stubby Macho stopped and leered at her. Meanwhile, his pal continued toward the desk. "If I knew you were stocking this place with whores, I never would have booked us here," he said loudly—obviously for her benefit.

Sean glanced back for a second. He slapped some money on the counter. "Listen, I'm expecting a limousine early tomorrow morning. . . ."

Stubby Macho turned and started coming toward her. He was smirking. "Hey, girlie," he whispered. "You want to party?"

Sean quickly shook her head, then ducked outside. The cold night air nipped at her. Shivering, she ran across the lot to her car, parked at the curb. She jumped inside and ground the key in the ignition. Her heart was racing as she pulled into traffic. Sean glanced in her rearview mirror. No one seemed to be following her.

"Oh, Sean, thank God," Dayle said into the phone. "I've been trying to get a hold of you. . . ."

Dayle sat in the study, her second shot of brandy in a glass beside her on the desk. She'd poured the first one just minutes after the night watchman had escorted her up to her apartment. Then she'd checked her phone messages—eleven in all, but only two were important. One of those was from Bonny McKenna: "Hi, Dayle, this is your evil twin, Bonny. Hank and I lost those guys around nine thirty on La Brea Ave.; then I met up with my hubby, and he drove me home. No problems See you at work on Monday. Bye."

The other message was from Dennis: "Hey, Boss Lady, it's me. First off, Laura really enjoyed meeting you. Second, flowers and a card in your name went to Maggie's kids this afternoon. Now, if I may eat some crow-burger, I think it wouldn't hurt if you got yourself a full-time bodyguard. Hank's the salt of the earth, but The Terminator he ain't. Laura and I met a guy at a party last week, a pro, with references. He's thinking of retiring, but I could persuade him to work for us. His name is Ted Kovak. His phone number is 555-3641, or I can contact him for you. Mull it over. We'll talk later. Bye.''

Dayle jotted down the messages. She thought a shower might relax her. But as she stood under the warm spray from the duel shower heads, she couldn't help remembering Estelle's body. Even with her eyes closed, she could still see Estelle—pale, bloated, and naked—curled up on that tiled floor in a pool of blood.

Dayle didn't linger in the shower. She'd dried off, slipped into her terrycloth robe, and poured that second brandy. She'd called Sean's cellular number. It had rung three times before the line went dead. Dayle tried again every ten minutes after that.

She'd been ready to call Sean's in-laws' house—or the police—when her phone rang.

"I got your call, and I shut off my cellular," Sean explained. "I'm sorry. I was in no position to talk to anyone at the time. I'll explain later—"

"Well, are you okay?" Dayle asked. "Where are you?"

"In the car," Sean replied. "I should be home in about an hour. I'm okay. Nobody's following me. Anyway, sorry I cut you off. I saw it was you who phoned. I was going to call you anyway. Listen, Dayle, I pulled a switcheroo and followed one of these guys who's had you under surveillance. They're all holed up in this hotel called the My-T-Comfort Inn. There are at least four of them—if you include the guy parked outside your building tonight. I checked out this hotel, and some cops are staying there too. At least, there's a police car in the lot. I don't know what that's about. But I wrote down the plate numbers on the rental cars. Do you still have that private detective working for you?"

"Yes," Dayle said numbly.

"I'll fax or e-mail these numbers to you when I get home

tonight," Sean said—over some static on the line. "Maybe your guy knows a good computer hack who can come up with the credit cards used at the car rental agency. We might be able to find out who these guys are—and where they're from."

"The reception's getting choppy," Dayle said. "Listen, why not just call the police now? They can go to that hotel and—"

"Dayle, the police are already at the hotel," she replied. "For all we know, they could be involved. Let's first just find out who these guys are. Dayle? Can you hear me?"

"Yeah, but you're breaking up."

"I know. My phone's running out of juice. I better hang up. I'll send you that list tonight. Okay? Bye, Dayle."

"Okay, be careful." With uncertainty, Dayle hung up.

She took another sip of brandy, then moved to the window. Hiding behind the curtain, she glanced down at the white Taurus parked across the street. She remembered something Estelle had said earlier tonight: *But you're going to die too. . . . They have you under surveillance. . . . It's already started.*

Fourteen

Tom had bought five different Saturday morning newspapers from the kiosk down his street. They were scattered across his living room floor like a paper drop cloth, each one open to the story about Maggie's death. Only the *Los Angeles Times* mentioned his name: *McGuire had her screen debut in the film noir sleeper, 'Hour of Deceit,' co-starring William Wagner and Tom Lance, her fiance for a brief time.*

Tom's heart ached. All those tributes to Maggie, and he'd been reduced to playing a bit part. Still, he took solace in the *Entertainment Tonight* interview. The *E.T.* people were due to pick him up at 7:15. Tom checked his wristwatch. *Any minute now.*

He was dressed in his new blue suit (only three years old), a crisp white shirt, and his favorite tie. Tom combed his hair again, then pulled out a scissors and trimmed his wild eyebrows and ear hair. He took another look at his wristwatch: 7:45. Where were they?

What if this Hal Buckman was some sadistic crackpot, the

same one making those calls earlier? They'd never called back; no more recordings of Maggie or that barking dog. Maybe this whole thing was an elaborate trap.

"It's real," Tom whispered resolutely. "It's *Entertainment Tonight.* That guy was telling the truth. And he'll be here any minute."

Tom's heart leaped when he saw a limousine finally pull up in front of his building. He watched the driver get out, and a moment later, the downstairs buzzer sounded. He pressed the intercom. "Yes?"

"Mr. Lance? This is Arnie, your driver. Sorry for the delay, sir."

Grinning, Tom pressed the intercom again. "I'll be right down. Thanks."

He grabbed his scrapbook, then paused in the doorway for a moment, long enough to whisper, "God, please, don't let me screw this up."

Hal Buckman waited for him in the limo's backseat. He looked about fifty years old, with receding black hair, an affable smile, and thick jowls. He wore gray slacks, a black turtleneck, a blue blazer, and sunglasses. "We appreciate you taking time out of your busy schedule for this interview, Mr. Lance," he said, shaking Tom's hand. The limo started to move. "I realize this isn't easy for you. This whole thing must have been an awful shock."

Tom sighed. "I still can't believe it. What's this world coming to?"

"You and Maggie McGuire remained close, didn't you?"

"Yes. We kept in touch." He tapped the cover of his scrapbook. "I brought pictures—some really good ones of Maggie and me together. Maybe you can show them during part of my segment."

"Super," Hal Buckman said. "I understand that you helped Maggie get started in movies. You landed her the part in *Hour of Deceit,* didn't you?"

Tom felt himself blushing. "I talked to the director," he said. "But Maggie's beauty and talent won her the role."

"So—in a way, she owed you her career."

"Well, I wouldn't go so far as to say that," Tom replied. At least he wouldn't say it on national TV.

"So tell me, Tom," Buckman said, moving even closer to him until their shoulders touched. "Can I call you Tom?"

He nodded. "Certainly, please do."

"So tell me, Tom," he whispered. "How did you feel when you shot that ungrateful bitch in the head?"

"Thanks for coming on such short notice," Dayle said, heading into the kitchen with Dennis.

She wore jeans, a black pullover, and no makeup. She didn't plan on going outside the apartment today. She was the reluctant star of The Story on Page One. This morning, her "rental mental" surveillance man had a lot of company—at least a dozen reporters gathered in front of her building. But Dayle wasn't talking with anyone—not even her own public relations people. She decided to let Dennis handle them. That was why she'd asked him to come over this morning. "I hope I didn't screw up your Saturday with Laura," she said, sitting down at the kitchen table.

"She wanted to go to the mall," Dennis said. He took a mug from the cupboard, then helped himself from the Mr. Coffee pot. "So I owe you big time for getting me out of it. Where's Hank?"

"He's at his place. I'm staying home today. I don't need him." She moved aside the newspaper she'd been reading. "In fact, Hank's one reason I wanted to talk with you today. That bodyguard you mention, your friend, Kojak—"

"Kovak," Dennis said, sipping his coffee. "Ted Kovak. He's a real pro. Nice guy too. Want me to set up an interview?"

Dayle nodded. "You read my mind."

Dennis glanced down at a story in the newspaper she'd been reading: AIDE TO LEIGH SIMONE COMMITS SUICIDE.

"Must have been rough," he said.

"Huh, you don't know the half of it."

"Did Estelle talk?"

"What?"

"Did she tell you anything?"

Dayle stared at him, eyes narrowed. "What do you mean?"

"Before she killed herself, did Estelle tell you anything?"

Dayle hesitated. It was an innocent question, but he seemed to be asking it for someone else. Dayle shook her head. "Um, no, it's just like the newspaper said, Sean Olson and I came in and found her in the bathroom."

Frowning, Dennis shook his head. "Too bad."

Dayle was thinking about what Estelle had said: *They've probably already gotten to somebody close to you.* . . . Dennis had been working alongside her for over three years now; she trusted him. Then again, Estelle had been with Leigh Simone twice that long.

"Dennis, do you like working for me?" she asked.

"You're the bane of my existence," he said over his coffee cup.

"I'm serious," Dayle said. "I want to know if you're happy with me. I know I piss you off sometimes. Do you ever want to get even?"

He laughed. "Get even? What? Dayle, I happen to love working for you." Dennis cocked his head to one side. "What's going on?"

"Nothing," Dayle muttered. "Nothing at all. Forget it, honey."

The limousine glided down a street where palm trees adorned meridians, and gates didn't quite obscure views of immaculate lawns and seven-figure houses. Inside the limo, Tom listened

to a tape from that afternoon at Maggie's. The man calling
himself Hal Buckman smirked during Maggie's harangue:
" . . . See you in the movies, Tom. . . . You're pathetic, you
really are."

"Oh, here it comes," he whispered.

"And you're an uncaring bitch," Tom heard himself growl.
"My God, you stupid—"

The loud gunshot cut her off. Tom winced at the sound of
her body hitting the kitchen floor. He hadn't heard that when
it was really happening.

Hal Buckman pressed a button on the armrest, and the tape
stopped. He took off his sunglasses, then cleaned them with a
handkerchief. "We had her under surveillance for three weeks,"
he explained. "We planted eight thousand bucks' worth of bugging devices in her place. Lucky for you, we had enough time
to get back in and collect it all before the police came to check
out your handiwork. Otherwise, we'd be pretty upset with you,
Tom."

" 'We?' " Tom asked timidly.

Buckman smiled, and puffed his chest out a bit. "Have you
ever heard of SAAMO, Tom?"

He shook his head.

"Good," Hal said. "You're not supposed to hear of it.
SAAMO stands for Soldiers for An American Moral Order,
and we have chapters all over the United States. We're the
good guys, Tom. We're going to clean up this country, make
it a decent place for our children." Buckman glanced out the
car window. "Maggie McGuire's son is a sexual deviant. He
has AIDS, thanks to his homosexual lifestyle. Some folks think
that's mighty sad, but certain individuals get what they
deserve."

"What does all this have to do with me?" Tom asked quietly.

"You gave Maggie McGuire what she deserved, Tom. Here's
a lady—and I use that term lightly—who appeared on the cover
of *People* magazine, saying how proud she was of her queer

son. She was endorsing deviant behavior. This is a war we're fighting, Tom. Maggie McGuire was the enemy, preaching her propaganda. We wanted to stop her somehow, but you took care of that for us." He slapped Tom on the shoulder. "You fixed her—for good."

"I didn't mean to kill her," Tom argued. "I—I still don't understand any of this. What do you want with me?"

"You're a good shot, Tom. You obviously know how to handle a gun from all those great westerns you made. You sure hit the bull's-eye with Maggie McGuire. We might need you to silence another morally corrupt actress."

"Who?" he murmured.

"She's a big name, Tom. That's all you need to know right now. We'll give you the details at the appropriate time. We have a very exciting plan. We'll need you to do some acting too. I think you'll enjoy it. Of course, you're in no position to refuse. But we'd like to have your enthusiasm nevertheless."

"But I'm not a killer," Tom whispered, shaking his head. "What happened with Maggie was an accident."

"What happened with Maggie was *practice*," Buckman said.

"Well, how do you expect me to pull it off?" Tom asked. "I'm not a *hit man*, for God's sake. I'm seventy years old!"

"You're seventy-six, Tom. And we'll tell you in due time how you'll pull it off. You'll like this plan, I guarantee it."

The old scrapbook had been poised on his lap for nearly an hour. It felt heavy—and useless. Tom glanced out the limousine window as they drove past his neighborhood Thrifty Mart. They were taking him home.

"I know you're confused," Hal said, with a gentle smile. "We'll tell you more within the next couple of days. In the meantime, don't do anything foolish, or worry about the police. They still don't know who killed Maggie McGuire. Our men who retrieved the equipment from her house did a very thorough job of wiping away evidence. You were sloppy, Tom. Your fingerprints were on her counter. But they're gone now. You should thank us, Tom, you really should.''

"Thank you," Tom muttered obediently.

The limo slowed down as it approached his apartment building. Tom sighed. "You went to a lot of trouble to—to *procure* me for this job. What happens if I refuse? What if I surrender to the police, and tell them all about you and this SAAMO outfit?''

Hal Buckman appeared very concerned for a moment, almost tortured. "Oh, Tom," he whispered, shaking his head. "You'll disappear before you even utter a second word to the police."

Nick Brock stood in Dayle's doorway. Her cordless phone to her ear, Dayle waved him inside, then shut the door. He followed her to her study, all the while checking out her "plush pad" of an apartment. Dressed in a tight black T-shirt and gray pleated pants, he carried a slim leather briefcase. Dayle sat back behind her desk and finished up on the phone with Bonny, thanking her again for acting as decoy last night. Then she clicked off and smiled at Nick. "Sorry to keep you waiting," she said.

He pulled a magazine out of his briefcase and dropped it on her desk. "You might be interested in page thirty-four."

It was a *Playgirl.* Dayle didn't understand, but she picked up the magazine and turned to page thirty-four. She stared at a full-page photo of Nick naked, except for a shoulder holster and gun. His back was to the camera, but he grinned over his shoulder. Shaking her head, Dayle turned back a page, and read the pictorial's title, PRIVATE DICKS.

Dayle was momentarily stunned, but only momentarily. "Well, good for you, Nick. Nice butt." She shoved the magazine across her desk. "Now, let's get down to business. I have more work for you." She handed him the license plate listing that Sean had faxed her. "Those are license numbers to five rental cars. These guys have been following me around for the last few days. I'm wondering if you can come up with the credit card numbers that paid for these rentals. I also want names and addresses off those cards. And I need to know if there were any hotel or car rental charges on these cards in Portland when Leigh Simone and Tony Katz were killed.''

Nick frowned. ''Ms. Sutton, unauthorized access to credit card files is against the law.'' He waited a beat, then broke into a cocky grin. ''It'll be a cinch for our resident computer nerd. The guy can tap into just about any system—from Aunt Ida's home computer to Command Center in the Pentagon. He hasn't gotten laid in like eight years, but the guy's a whiz on that PC.''

''I'm both happy and sad for him,'' Dayle said with a patient smile. Then she sighed, and the smile fell away. ''You heard about Estelle Collier.''

Nodding, Nick frowned. ''Yeah. It's a pisser.''

''Don't you feel accountable?'' Dayle whispered. ''I know I do.''

''Huh?''

She shook her head and sighed. ''Nothing. Only—I can't help thinking, 'What goes around, comes around.' Maybe they're digging up something about me right now—something from my private past. Estelle said they operate that way. For all I know, they're rattling some skeletons in my closet right now.''

Nick grinned at her. ''What do you have to hide?''

''Nothing much.'' Dayle answered. She glanced down at the desktop and gave a little shrug. ''But enough, I guess—so that it worries me.''

Tom poured himself another Jack Daniels. He kept hearing that tape over again in his head: Maggie insulting him, the gunshot, and her body hitting the floor.

Now they wanted him to do it again, all planned out this time.

He had the TV going, but there was nothing about Maggie on the six o'clock news. Glancing out the window, he wondered if Hal's men were watching him now.

"Stay tuned for *First Edition,*" the TV announcer said, as the titles for the evening news scrolled up on the screen. "*F.E.* has an exclusive look at the film Maggie McGuire kept secret for forty years! Viewer discretion advised."

Tom fumbled for the remote control and turned up the volume. What were they talking about? He'd seen every movie Maggie had made. What did they mean by viewer discretion advised?

He turned up the volume on the TV. "Tonight on *First Edition!*" the announcer proclaimed. "A shocking exclusive! The Maggie McGuire film that she didn't want anyone to see!" A grainy, black-and-white image came on the screen. It was Maggie, fondling a beer bottle and licking the stem in a provocative fashion. She was topless; but a computerized checkerboard grid obscured the bottom half of the TV picture to hide her breasts.

Tom watched in stunned silence. Indeed it was a young Maggie in the rickety old stag movie; probably a desperate measure from her struggling modeling days, before she'd met him. The sight of her youthful beauty left him feeling weak; he still wanted to protect her. The love of his life, and here she was, naked and debasing herself, for all to see.

They broke away from the stag movie, so the *First Edition* anchor, a perky blonde in a pink blazer, could introduce the show. Then they started the film again—with portions of the screen still blurred by the computerized grid. But Tom could tell what was going on. After pouring beer over her breasts, Maggie appeared to be doing something down there with the empty bottle. The movie had no sound. The anchor handled the voice-over, explaining that *First Edition* had uncovered the

one-reel film today, less than forty-eight hours after the shocking murder of its star, Maggie McGuire. The film had been
made in 1947. Miss McGuire's costar hadn't yet been identified.

Not that anyone had much chance to see his face. The
scrawny, balding man's back was to the camera as he strolled
onto the set. The grid obscured his buttocks. Maggie, sitting
at the edge of a bed, set aside the beer bottle and reached out
to him.

They switched back to the announcer, who explained that
they couldn't show any more footage from the movie, titled
Thirsty Lady. Adam Blanchard, the late star's forty-year-old,
HIV-positive son, had no comment regarding the newly discovered film.

Tom began to cry. His greatest contribution to the movies
was Maggie McGuire. Yet after this, who would remember
her years of hard work? Who would remember the Academy-
Award-winning performance? Her impressive career was now
eclipsed by scandal, and most people would only remember
Maggie McGuire's dirty movie.

"This is the worst she's ever been, George," Avery said to
his friend on the phone. He sat at his desk in the study. "You
saw how she was today. They put her back on the antidepressants at the hospital. But I don't think it's doing any good."

"Be patient, give Joanne a little time," George said. "Where
is she?"

"Right now, she's napping upstairs."

Joanne had slept the entire time at George and Sheila's—
except for a couple of trips to the bathroom, and an episode at
around three in the morning.

Avery had woken to the sound of her crying, distant whimpering that escalated to screams. Avery switched on the light and
saw her across the room. Joanne stood by the guest room
window, shrieking, with tears rolling down her cheeks. He

managed to quiet her down and guide her back into bed. "I'm so tired," was all she could say.

In the morning, he told his friends that Joanne had had a nightmare. It was almost the truth. She didn't come down to breakfast. She didn't utter a word all morning—not even when George and Sheila hugged her good-bye at the door. Avery led her to the car. He hated to think that perhaps Joanne was pulling some theatrics here. His actress wife wasn't beyond "playing to the balcony" at times—as she herself had admitted. How much was a real breakdown—and how much was drama—he couldn't tell.

About a dozen reporters hovered around the front gate. They peered into the car, and shouted questions. A couple of them asked about the claw marks on Avery's cheek. All last night and this morning, Joanne hadn't even noticed. As they pulled into the driveway, she turned away from the cameras and covered her face. Once inside the house, she plodded up the stairs to their bedroom, pried off her shoes, and slipped into bed.

That had been over four hours ago. He'd checked on her several times. To be safe, Avery had gone into their bathroom and removed all the razor blades and an old bottle of sleeping pills.

"Keep a close eye on her," George recommended over the phone.

"I'm way ahead of you," Avery said soberly.

"Good. Well, call if you need anything. I love you, buddy."

"Thanks, George. Love you too. Bye." Avery hung up the phone, and wearily reclimbed those stairs. He crept into the bedroom. Joanne was still dressed, still in bed—but awake.

Avery sat down at her side. "Hey, sweetheart," he said. "Why don't you go freshen up? I'll throw something together for dinner. Okay?"

"Dinner?" she said vaguely. She didn't even look at him.

"Yeah," Avery caressed her arm. "C'mon, Joanne, I'm tired

of talking to myself here. Please?'' He started to laugh and cry at the same time. ''You're scaring me. . . .''

The telephone rang. Joanne didn't even seem to hear it.

Avery sighed and grabbed the phone off the nightstand. ''Hello?''

''Avery? Hi. It's Steve Bensinger.''

''Oh, Steve. You know, now is not a good time to talk.''

''Well, then you're going to hate me, because I'm on my cellular, in front of your house. I'm sorry, Avery, but it's urgent I see you.''

He rubbed his forehead. ''Okay, give me a minute. I'll open the gate for you.'' Avery hung up the phone. He kissed Joanne's cheek, then hurried down the stairs and flicked the wall switch for the gate. He met Steve at the door.

''Holy shit, what happened to you?'' Steve asked, gaping at the scratch marks on Avery's cheek.

''Tell you later.'' Avery closed the door. ''What's the emergency?''

Steve stepped into the foyer. He wore a V-neck sweater and jeans. ''Okay, no song and dance,'' he said grimly. ''I have a contact in the Beverly Hills police force, and he knows I work for you. He called me an hour ago and asked if I had any clue as to my client's whereabouts last night. . . .''

Avery shook his head. ''I don't understand.''

''A certain Libby Stoddard was stalking and harassing you last month. I talked to your lawyer about it on the way here—''

''Yeah, okay, so?'' Avery said impatiently.

''She's dead, Avery.''

''What?''

''Libby Stoddard's gardener has a key. He discovered the body this afternoon. She'd been stabbed several times. There's also evidence of rape.''

''God, no,'' Avery whispered.

''They think she let the guy in,'' Steve explained. ''It happened last night. Coroner's still working on an approximate time. . . ." He glanced up toward the top of the stairs.

Numb, Avery followed his gaze and saw Joanne at the second-floor landing. Her hair was a mess, and her clothes were wrinkled. She clutched the banister as if it were the only thing supporting her. She had heard everything. Avery stared at her. "Joanne, you shouldn't—"

She began to laugh.

Avery hurried up the steps to her. As he led her toward their bedroom, Joanne's laughter became louder and louder. She sounded like a crazy woman.

He'd just fallen asleep when the telephone rang. Blindly, Avery reached toward the nightstand. "I have it, hon," he mumbled, trying to focus on the digital alarm clock: 5:13. He cleared his throat. "Yes? Hello?"

"Mr. Cooper? This is Aaron Harvey from Homeguard Securities. Our cameras have picked up some activity in your backyard pool area—"

"What?" Avery rubbed his eyes. It took him a moment to put everything together. The guy was talking about the cameras they'd installed outside their house after the break-in last month. "What kind of activity?" he asked.

"I've taken the liberty of sending over an ambulance—"

"An *ambulance?* What?" He sat up, then swiveled around. Joanne's side of the bed was empty.

"I think your wife's had an accident," the man said. "She seems to have fallen in the pool."

"Wait, wait a second." Avery jumped out of bed and ran to the double doors to the balcony. He pushed them open and stared down at the pool.

Joanne's robe billowed out as she floated facedown on the water's surface. She barely moved—expect for the water lapping around her. She drifted in the shallow end like a fallen leaf.

In the distance, he could hear the wailing siren. Avery snatched up the phone again. "Tell them we're around back."

He hung up and bolted down the stairs. In the hallway, he flicked the switch that held open the front gate. Then he ran through the kitchen and out to the pool. Jumping into the frigid water, Avery grabbed Joanne. He hoisted her out of the pool, and set her down on her stomach. She wasn't breathing. He frantically pushed and pushed on her back.

He could hear the ambulance down the street, then voices and footsteps. People were coming up the driveway.

He continued his efforts to resuscitate her, but Joanne didn't stir. Headlights swept across the backyard bushes as the ambulance came down the driveway. Avery heard more voices: "Something's happened!" one reporter shouted to another. "I need this on video!"

Avery wouldn't give up. He kept trying to force the water from her lungs. The paramedics rushed through the back gate, followed by several reporters and photographers. Camera flashes popped in the murky dawn light.

Joanne coughed, regurgitating a stomachful of water onto the pool deck. Hovering over her, Avery let out a grateful cry. She was still coughing when the paramedics relieved him.

Drenched, and clad only in his undershorts, Avery rolled over and caught his breath. He could see Joanne moving. Camera flashes illuminated everything. He managed to stand up, then glared at the handful of paparazzi at his back gate. "You guys are trespassing," he said evenly—between gasps for air. "You're blocking the ambulance. Get the hell out of here. Now."

Incredibly, they obeyed him.

One of the paramedics asked him how it had happened. Avery just shook his head.

"Your wife seems to have swallowed a mixture of barbiturates and alcohol. We need to move her to the hospital right away.''

''Yes, of course,'' Avery whispered. He gazed down at the other medic inserting a fat plastic tube in Joanne's mouth. Her eyes were half open.

Avery began to shiver from the cold.

He stepped into the dimly lit hospital room. Joanne was asleep. As Avery moved closer to the bed, he saw the restraining straps around her wrists—attached to the bed's side railings. She looked so frail and sickly. Her damp hair had dried into flat, greasy tangles.

He still smelled of chlorine from his plunge into the pool five hours before. He'd found the empty bottle of sleeping pills in the kitchen garbage. Joanne had had the prescription filled in New York. She'd washed down the pills with several shots of vodka—before jumping into the pool.

The doctor had allowed him only a brief visit, so Avery stayed just a few minutes. He gently kissed her forehead. ''G'night, honey,'' he whispered, though he knew she couldn't hear him.

Outside Joanne's private room, a slim Asian woman, about fifty, waited by the security guard's desk in the hallway. She had a pen and pad, and wore a red cardigan with black pants. Avery was a bit disappointed the guard hadn't chased away this reporter. He frowned at both of them.

''Mr. Cooper?'' She dug into her purse. ''I know my timing is awful. But I need to ask you some questions.'' She pulled out her badge. ''I'm Lieutenant Susan Linn, Beverly Hills police. Could I buy you a coffee in the cafeteria? I promise this won't take long.''

Avery sighed. ''I've talked to you people all day. How many times do I have to go over this? My wife wasn't herself. She's been through a lot—''

"This isn't about your wife, Mr. Cooper. I need to ask you some questions about Libby Stoddard. I believe you knew her."

They'd caught the hospital cafeteria during a lull between the breakfast and lunch crowds. Only a handful of other customers were scattered about. A janitor was mopping up; he'd placed chairs upside down on several tables.

Avery sipped his Coke. "So what did you want to ask me?"

Susan Linn frowned. "Well, first you should know that— um, you're not required to answer any of my questions. You're entitled to counsel, and anything you say might be used against you."

Avery gave her a wary look. "Am I a suspect?"

Lieutenant Linn shrugged. "It's standard jargon. You've seen the cop shows. Hell, you've *acted* in the cop shows."

Avery nodded. "I'll let you know if I feel the need for a lawyer. For now, go ahead, ask away."

"The scratch," she said, unwrapping her prepackaged Rice Krispies Treat. "How did that happen?"

Avery touched his cheek, then shrugged. "I was at this little ocean-view park last night, just to—well, collect my thoughts. Suddenly, this nut—this woman—came out of nowhere, and she scratched my face. Then she ducked into a car and drove off."

"When did this happen?" Linn asked.

"Around five-thirty. Joanne and I were staying with friends. I was on my way home to pick up some things, and I swung by this park."

Lieutenant Linn nodded pensively. "Your friend, George Weber, concurs—you left his house at five-fifteen. One of the reporters outside your front gate saw you come home at seven-twenty. You spent a lot of time at this scenic spot, collecting your thoughts. Did you go somewhere else?"

Avery shook his head. "Only the park. I had a lot on my mind. My wife had just had a miscarriage—"

"I know all about that," Lieutenant Linn said, over her coffee cup. "You were filming a talk show when your wife had to be rushed to the hospital. Were you wearing any stage makeup for this television appearance?"

Sipping his Coke, Avery nodded. "A little."

"Did you have a chance to wash it off before this trip to the park?"

"No, I didn't." He drummed his fingers on the tabletop.

She put down her Rice Krispies Treat. "Can you believe these things are low-fat? They're so sweet. Only a few more questions." She scribbled on her notepad. "Um, what's your blood type, Mr. Cooper?" she asked, not looking up.

"Type O."

"Hmmm." She kept scribbling. "Between the time you left the Webers' and arrived at your home, did you meet up with anyone besides this scratch-happy woman in the park?"

"I'm afraid not." Avery straightened in his chair. "Am I a suspect in Libby's murder?"

Lieutenant Linn sighed. "Well, I've done my homework. I know Libby was your 'number-one fan' as well as a thorn in your side. According to her attorney, you threatened Libby at an arbitration hearing last month."

"I didn't kill her," Avery said quietly.

Lieutenant Linn flipped through her notebook and scanned a particular page. "Um, on top of being your number-one fan, Ms. Stoddard was also a very rich young woman. With no evidence of a break-in, and not a single item missing from her home—we can eliminate robbery as a motive. So it looks like a crime of passion or revenge. Libby was stabbed eleven times. The coroner estimates the time of death was between five and eight o'clock." Lieutenant Linn glanced at him for a moment. "Apparently, Libby put up a fight. There's evidence of a struggle. We know she scratched her assailant, because skin fragments were found under her fingernails. We also found traces of stage makeup mingled in with the loose skin tissue. Ms. Stoddard was also raped. We were able to draw a semen sample, and determine the blood type.''

"Type O?'' Avery whispered.

She nodded.

Avery swallowed hard. "Why is this happening?'' he murmured.

"Would you agree to giving us a semen sample?'' she gently asked. "It might eliminate you as a suspect.''

"I can't say right now,'' Avery muttered, shaking his head. "I think I need a lawyer. I better not say anything else.''

Fifteen

Dayle turned off the duel shower heads, grabbed a towel, and stepped out of the stall. Patting herself dry, she moved through a cloud of steam and wiped the condensation from the mirror. She frowned at her reflection. Her eyes were puffy from lack of sleep last night. Thank God for Oil of Olay—or the stuff she called Oil of Olay. It was from some clinic in France, and worked just like Oil of Olay on wrinkles—only it cost seventy bucks an ounce.

She had an interview with *Premiere* magazine in ninety minutes. It was just a one-page fluff piece—with an accompanying full-page photo that had been shot in a studio over a month ago. But she still had to look good for the interview—to be held over an intimate lunch at the Beverly Hills Hotel. They always reported how she looked, what she was wearing, and what she was eating during these things. Dayle planned to pin her hair up, pick at her Cobb salad, and on her bed, she'd already laid out the black Givenchy short-sleeve dress that always made her look thin.

Dennis had already let them know that she wouldn't be answering any questions about Leigh Simone or Estelle Collier. She'd hibernated inside her apartment all day yesterday, screening her calls.

Dayle dried her hair and fixed her face. With the towel wrapped around her, she stepped out to the bedroom, and glanced over at her dress on the bed. She suddenly froze. A chill raced through her. Pinned to the dress was a page torn from a magazine. Someone had just been in her bedroom. For all she knew, they could still be in the apartment.

For a moment, Dayle stood paralyzed. Then she took a step toward the bed and gazed down at the calling card they'd left. The magazine clipping was of a woman on a sailboat. It looked like part of an ad for a vacation getaway. In black marker, they'd scribbled across the top of the page: WE FOUND CINDY ZELLERBACK.

Dayle didn't know what it meant. She backed toward her nightstand, reached for the phone, and called down to the front desk.

"This is the lobby, Ms. Sutton."

"Hello, Todd?" she whispered urgently. "I've had a break-in. . . ."

"Hey, Mom, your cell phone's ringing!" Danny called from the front door.

"Well, find out who it is, sweetie!" Sean was loading her collection of law books into the car. She planned to haul them over to the office this afternoon. Shoving another box in the back, she straightened up and wiped the sweat off her forehead. She glanced over at her son.

Danny stood in the doorway, the cellular phone to his ear. The color seemed to drain from her son's face, and his mouth dropped open.

"Who is it?" she asked, hurrying up the front walkway.

Danny covered the mouthpiece. "It's *Dayle Sutton!*" he exclaimed.

Sean laughed. "It's okay, honey. Thanks." She took the phone, and gave him a thumb signal to go play. "Hello, Dayle? How are you doing?"

"I've had better days," Dayle said. "Could I possibly come see you?"

Sean hesitated. Watching Danny run out to the front yard, she thought about the people who were following Dayle around. Except for three reporters who had called her office, there had been no backlash from having her name mentioned in that news story yesterday; no calls at home, and no strange cars parked on her block. She wanted to keep it that way. "Um, rather than you come out here, I'd just as soon meet you in the city."

"Will I be dragging you away from your family?"

"No. Actually, I'm dropping off some things at my office at four-thirty. I'll be a couple of hours. Could you meet me there?"

"Yes, your office would be great. Thanks."

"Are you okay? You sound tense."

"I just need a friend right now."

"If it's any help, Nick, this woman spent some time in Mexico years ago. My guess is that she's back in California now." Dayle fought the inclination to whisper into the limousine phone. She stared at the back of Hank's head. The glass partition was up, but she wondered if he could still hear her.

They weren't far from Sean's office. Dayle had been with Hank for the last four hours. He'd arrived while the police were still searching her apartment. They didn't find anything, and nothing was missing. In fact, there was no evidence of a break-in. Todd, at the front desk, said he couldn't understand how somebody might have slipped past him. The cops probably had her pegged as a total paranoid.

Dayle didn't show them the note. Once she'd remembered Cindy and their one-night stand on the boat, she didn't want to explain the message to anyone. She lied to the police and said she'd discovered the front door open after emerging from her shower. Actually, she hadn't dead-bolted the door—in case Hank came early to pick her up for the interview. He had his own key to the apartment. He was the only one with a key—besides her.

She'd been a half hour late for her interview—and terribly distracted through the whole ordeal. She kept thinking about the "positively revolting" shoot down in Mexico so many years ago, Cindy something with the Winnie the Pooh tattoo, and that sailboat. Dayle barely touched her Cobb salad, and twice she had to ask the interviewer to repeat a question. Nevertheless, by the time it was all over, she'd still managed to charm the guy.

Hank had waited out by the limo during her lunch. Dayle couldn't help wondering about old reliable Hank. Had he been forced into letting someone duplicate his key to her apartment? Or had he left that note himself? He'd been with her for seven years, but how well did she really know him? He was just this simple, sweet—almost neuter—lump of a guy who liked mystery novels and The Beatles trivia. In all the miles they'd driven together, she'd barely scratched the surface with Hank. Yet her trust in him was unwavering—until now.

She'd raised the limo's glass partition for her call to Nick. She needed him to track down the whereabouts of Cindy Zellerback: Caucasian, red hair or possibly blond, late thirties. It was a rush job.

Dayle wasn't sure how much damage this Cindy affair could cause. After all, it was an isolated incident from fifteen years ago. Was this the only ammunition these people had to use on her? If so, maybe it wasn't such a big deal. At least, that was what she kept telling herself.

She wanted Sean to tell her the same thing. Cradling the

limo's phone against her ear, Dayle dug into her purse. "Listen, Nick, if you find something in the next hour or so, here's where I'll be ..." She read Sean's office phone and fax numbers from her business card.

"I'm on top of it," Nick replied. "And I should have that license plate and credit card trace for you by tomorrow."

"Good boy," Dayle said.

"Ciao, Ms. Sutton." Nick hung up.

Dayle listened to the dead air. She was still looking at Hank in the front seat. "Hank, can you hear me?" she said, into the phone.

He didn't flinch at all. Dayle hung up the telephone. She continued to stare at him on the other side of the glass divider. "Hank?" she said. "Hank, you can hear me, can't you?"

He didn't flinch. He seemed totally focused on the road ahead.

Dayle pressed the button on the armrest, and the divider window descended with a low mechanical hum. "Hank?" she said.

His eyes met hers in the rearview mirror. "Yes, ma'am?"

Those eyes were so guileless. He patiently waited for her to say something. Good old Hank. What was she thinking?

With a tired smile, Dayle sat back again. "Never mind. For a moment there, I thought you'd made a wrong turn, but I was mistaken."

"It happened so long ago," Dayle said, handing Sean a book from the packing box. "I vaguely recall someone taking my picture with Cindy while we were on the beach. God help me, I think we were topless at the time."

Sean stood on a ladder, filing law volumes on the top shelf of her bookcase. Her office was taking shape: sea-foam green walls with white trim. No more drop cloths.

"Well, Dayle," she said. "I don't think your career will

suffer. Like you say, it happened too long ago—and with some nobody. It's old news.'' She held her hand out. ''Volume seventeen, please.''

Frowning, Dayle gave the law book to her. ''You're probably right. But I want to be prepared when this thing goes public. I mean, maybe it's *out there* already. Right now, this Cindy could be talking to Jane Pauley.''

Climbing down from the ladder, Sean chuckled. ''If it'll make you feel better, have a look.'' She found the remote, and switched on her TV. ''But I think all the show business news is about your future costar, Avery Cooper.''

The TV came on: ''I'm Mrs. Russell Marshall. But you can call me Elsie.''

''Hi, Elsie!''

''Oh, shit,'' Dayle muttered, plopping down on the sofa.

''Maybe I'm just a housewife,'' Elsie said. ''But as a mother and a good Christian, I think my opinion counts for something. . . .''

''She kind of makes you wish they'd start feeding 'good Christians' to the lions again,'' Sean remarked, ready to switch channels.

''Wait a minute,'' Dayle said. She heard Elsie mention Maggie McGuire.

'' . . . and I'm sorry she's dead. But if you'll excuse me, I wouldn't exactly say she was a shining example of motherhood—as some people maintain. She claimed to be proud of her homosexual son who now has AIDS. Well, I'm sorry, but 'proud'? Come on! How exactly did he get AIDS? Was she proud of that?''

''My God,'' Sean said. ''How does she get away with it?''

On TV, Elsie was now meandering toward her desk. ''Quite frankly, I hope people have sense enough to see the truth behind the tragedy here. We've all seen her hard-core porn movie. I have a difficult time respecting a woman who would make a movie like that. . . .''

''What's she talking about?'' Dayle asked. ''What porn movie?''

Sean stared at her. ''You don't know?'' She turned down the volume. ''Maggie McGuire did a stag film back in the late forties. Now it's suddenly resurfaced. Her body's barely cold, and last night they were showing Maggie's old skin flick on *First Edition.*''

Dayle glanced back at the TV. Elsie was still talking, but with the volume so low, Dayle could only make out her saccharine tone, and the audience laughing. She'd missed the joke. That was what Maggie McGuire had now become: a joke. The accomplishments of her forty-year career suddenly took second place to this scandal. ''My God,'' Dayle murmured, gazing at Elsie on the screen. She looked so superior and smug. This humiliation of the late Maggie McGuire was a victory for Elsie Marshall and the radical right.

Maggie's personal crusades and causes suddenly seemed wrong, and Elsie's logic rang true. Maggie McGuire had stood by her gay son, *but this was a woman who had appeared in pornographic movies. Her opinions couldn't count for much. She was a bad example of motherhood.*

The same thing had happened to Tony Katz and Leigh Simone after their untimely deaths. ''They all died in shame,'' Dayle murmured, staring at the TV.

Sean squinted at her. ''What?''

Dayle got to her feet. ''There was a scandal when each one was killed—Tony, Leigh, now Maggie. Their reputations were ruined. Tony—caught with his pants down, and Leigh—a drug addict. Now, Maggie, a porn star.''

Sean was shaking her head. ''I don't understand. Slow down—''

''It wasn't enough that they killed them. They had to ruin their reputations too, disgrace them, take away their credibility. Tony, Leigh, and Maggie, they were outspoken liberals, and they all got killed—''

The telephone rang.

"Go on, I'm listening," Sean said. "It's just my fax machine."

"Their names were dragged through the mud," Dayle continued. "They died in shame. Their careers and their causes became like a joke."

"What do you mean by 'causes'?"

"They advocated gun control—or gay rights. They were pro-choice, or they fought against censorship and capitol punishment, you name it. These are the kind of hot issues that make certain people crazy—crazy enough to quote the Old Testament—or march and protest, or even kill."

"So where do you come in?" Sean asked.

"Maybe I pissed them off when I spoke out about Leigh's death. They might know about the movie we're going to make. I keep thinking about this Cindy business. Maybe that's how they're going to drag me though the mud—once they've killed me."

Sean frowned. "No. It's just not sensational enough. So you got drunk one night fifteen years ago and experimented with another woman. This is the new millennium. Who cares?"

The telephone rang again. "The machine will pick up," Sean said.

"But whoever is behind this isn't living in the new millennium," Dayle said, over the phone recording. "They don't want any liberal martyrs and cult heroes. So they're making their celebrity victims look sleazy—"

"Yo, this is Nick Brock, and I'm calling for Dayle Sutton—"

"Oh, grab it, grab it!" Dayle steered Sean toward the phone on the desk. Sean picked up the receiver.

"Hello, Sean Olson speaking." She listened for a moment, then rolled her eyes. "Well, I'm not your 'honey doll,' but yes, she's right here." Sean put a hand over the mouthpiece. "It's your detective friend. He sent the fax."

"Don't hang up on him," Dayle said. She checked the fax machine.

"I'm not supposed to hang up on you," Sean said into the phone. "Though I'm sorely tempted."

Dayle glanced at the first fax page. Nick had scribbled a note on the cover sheet: *Cynthia Zellerback's current address and phone number are on page 4. Chow! Nick.*

"Tell him I'll call him in a couple of minutes," Dayle said. She watched the fourth page inch out of the machine.

"She'll call you right back, Romeo," Sean said, then hung up.

Two pages of the fax were from a four-month-old article in the *Los Angeles Times*. Dayle hardly recognized the dowdy, middle-aged woman in the news photo as that girl from the boat. The once lustrous, long red hair now appeared short and brittle. Cindy's features had turned hard. The picture had been taken outside, with some steps in the background, perhaps a church or courthouse. Cindy looked so hardened and bitter, squinting in the sunlight.

Dayle read the headline: KILLER OF HUSBAND AND CHILD PAROLED, WOMAN SERVED 12 YEARS FOR MURDERING HER FAMILY.

Dayle read on, cringing at the details surrounding the stabbing deaths of two-year-old Sunshine Zellerback and her father, Andrew, a 29-year-old motorcycle repairman. Cindy had been convicted of the murders in 1988. Claiming she'd been reborn to Christ while in prison, the "reformed" Cynthia Zellerback blamed her earlier actions on drug use and a promiscuous lifestyle, which had included lesbian sex.

It was the type of stuff tabloids devoured and spit out at the public with relish. Dayle imagined the headlines: DAYLE SUTTON IN LESBIAN LOVE-NEST WITH CONVICTED CHILD-KILLER! The murders had occurred only a few years after that episode on the boat down in Mexico. Dayle showed the fax to Sean. "This is the girl I was with," she said.

Sean took a couple of minutes to read the news article, then shrugged. "Well, it's not like *you* murdered anybody."

Frowning, Dayle shook her head and sighed. "I had sex with a child killer. It's guilt by association. The tabloids will eat it up."

"What are you going to do?"

"I don't know," Dayle muttered. "I'll probably spend tonight drinking too much and sleeping too little while I fret about it. And after that break-in today, I don't feel very safe there. Maybe I should check into a hotel—"

"Don't be silly," Sean said. "Come spend the night with us in Malibu. My husband, the movie fanatic, will be so excited to meet you, he'll probably climb out of his wheelchair and do the hokeypokey."

"Oh, I wouldn't want to impose," Dayle said.

"Nonsense," Sean said, dismissing her with a wave of her hand. "My in-laws would love to have you. Phoebe can bunk in with Danny, and you can have her room. You and I can burn the midnight oil and hatch a strategy to deal with this Cindy business. You shouldn't be alone tonight, Dayle."

She gave her a fleeting smile. "Thanks, Sean. But . . ." She turned toward the window. Three stories below, a white Taurus was parked half a block away on the other side of the street from Hank and her limousine. She could barely see the man sitting behind the wheel. "If I came over tonight, I'd be bringing some excess baggage—and possibly endangering your family."

Sean stepped up to the window. She stared at the rental car. "You could leave now—and lose him somehow. Then come back here, and we'll drive to Malibu together."

"I'll phone my friend, Bonny," Dayle said. "Maybe she's available to play decoy again. After we make the switch, I'll circle back here by cab."

Sean nodded. "Use the delivery entrance. I'll give you my cell phone. Call me, and I'll let you in." She dug the tiny phone from her purse, then handed it to Dayle. "It's good that you're getting a professional bodyguard. Your driver, Hank, seems very nice, but well . . ."

"I know," Dayle replied.

Sean took her hand and squeezed it. "Be careful, okay? I have a weird feeling about tonight. It's one reason I think you shouldn't be alone."

"It's really not fair to you, Hank," Dayle said from the backseat of the limo. The divider window was down. "You didn't hire on as a bodyguard, and that's what I need right now. Dennis says this guy is a pro, with years of experience. The people who are out to get me, they mean business. They may have hired professional killers. So I need a professional bodyguard, some guy who's a real pain in the ass. And I'm not going to like him, because he'll make me take all sorts of silly precautions. But most of all, I'm not going to like him, because he won't be you."

Hank's eyes met hers in the rearview mirror. "I understand," he said, nodding. "Is it okay if I don't like him either?"

Dayle patted his shoulder. "I wouldn't have it any other way, Hank."

They pulled into Bonny's apartment complex. The Taurus had kept a steady pace behind them. Dayle made out only one person in the car. The driver turned off his headlights as he followed them into the parking lot. He took a spot near one of the other buildings.

Dayle quickly donned her trench coat and sunglasses. Hank walked her to the front door, and she rang the buzzer.

"Sunglasses at night? I'll be as blind as a bat." Bonny stood in front of the mirror in the hallway, arranging her hair to look like Dayle's.

"Sorry," Dayle said. "They're parked pretty close. I didn't want to take any chances they'd see a switch."

Bonny laughed. "Make them wear these shades. They won't see squat."

"Be extra careful out there tonight," Dayle said. "I think they might try something pretty soon."

"Well, in that case I'll bring a friend along." Bonny pulled a gun and holster from her closet shelf. She strapped on the holster as if it were part of a backpack. Dayle watched her, amazed by the former policewoman's cool composure. Bonny climbed into Dayle's trench coat.

Dayle gave her a quick hug at the door. Then she phoned for a taxi. The dispatcher said a cab would be there in ten minutes. From Bonny's living room window, she watched Hank, leaning against the limo. The white Taurus was still near the lot entrance. Dayle hadn't noticed before, but a police car was parked only a few spaces down. It must have just pulled in. Someone stood outside the patrol car, talking to the cop inside.

Directly below, Bonny approached the limo. With the sunglasses and trench coat, she was Dayle's duplicate. Hank opened the limo door for her.

Across the way, the person talking to the officer a moment ago was now gone. Dayle glimpsed a figure darting around some shrubbery by another building in the complex. Then he disappeared in the shadows.

Something's wrong, Dayle thought, pressing her hand to the window. Below, Hank was steering the limo toward the exit. At the same time, the police car started to move, but its headlights remained dark.

Dayle remembered Sean mentioning a cop car had been parked in the lot at that cheesy hotel where they were all staying.

"Oh, Jesus, no," she gasped. She grabbed Sean's phone out of her purse.

Five stories down, Hank pulled onto the road. The patrol car crept to the lot exit; then the headlights went on—as did the red strobe on its hood.

Dayle dialed the number of her limo. Helplessly, she watched the police vehicle speed up behind Hank, less than half a block from the lot exit. On the third ring, a recorded message told Dayle that the number she'd dialed was no longer in service.

"Goddamn it!" she hissed. She dialed again. Then she looked at the limo, now stopped by the side of the road, the cop car in back of it. *One ring.* The officer got out of the patrol car. He was reaching for his gun.

Two rings.

"Pick up, Hank!" Dayle hissed. "Goddamn it, please pick up!"

The policeman had his gun out. He approached Hank's side of the limo.

"Hello?" Hank said, on the other end of the line.

"Hank, it's a trap!"

The cop was at his window now.

"What?" Hank asked. "Just a minute—"

"No, no, it's a trap. Please, Hank! Don't you see?"

She could hear him: "What's the matter, officer?"

"Hank, get out of there!" Dayle screamed.

"Hey, wait a minute, *wait a minute, WAIT A MINUTE!*"

The noise on the phone was like someone hitting a knife against hollow pipe. A metallic echo. Three times. The cop, or whoever he was, had a silencer on his gun. She heard Hank dropping the telephone.

Dayle could see the cop firing into the open window of the limousine's front seat. He must have shot poor Hank in the face.

A loud shot rang out. It had to be Bonny firing in self-defense. The cop reeled back, then managed to aim his gun again—this time, at the figure in the backseat.

Over the phone, Dayle heard two more of those metallic

echoes. Then a loud pop from Bonny's gun. The cop retaliated with another two shots.

Still, Bonny must have hit him, because he was clutching his side as he staggered back to his patrol car. He peeled away from the curb, passing her limousine and speeding up the street.

Meanwhile, the limo didn't move. Dayle could hear moaning on the telephone line. She wasn't sure if it was Hank or Bonny. But someone was dying.

Sixteen

The 9-1-1 operator told Dayle to stay by the phone.

"I'm on a cellular," Dayle said. She rattled off the number as she grabbed a couple of towels from Bonny's bathroom. "I'm headed out to the limo right now. Please, tell them to hurry."

Dayle threw the phone in her purse and raced down to the lobby. Five floors. She couldn't wait for the elevator. She ran out to the street. The limo was up ahead, under a street lamp. She could see the beaded windshield-like raindrops, only they were on the inside of the car, and the droplets were blood.

She saw Hank, and let out a strangled cry. He was slumped forward over the steering wheel. A steady stream of blood dripped off the tip of his nose and chin. The limo phone had fallen on the floor—beside Hank's latest true-crime book.

"You called somebody, I hope," she heard Bonny whisper.

Dayle opened the back door. "The ambulance is coming," she said. She swallowed hard at the sight of her friend. The sunglasses had fallen on the car floor. Sprawled across the car seat, Bonny had a laceration above her eyebrow, along her right temple, where a bullet must have grazed her. Under the open trench coat, her pale green sweater was soaked with blood.

Dayle quickly reached into the limo bar and found some bottled water. She drenched a hand towel and pressed it to the side of Bonny's face. Bonny shivered a bit. "I—I nailed the SOB, Dayle. Got him in the gut. He'll bleed to death if he doesn't get help soon." She winced. "Damn, this hurts."

"Oh my God, Bonny, I'm so sorry." Dayle held her hand. "Hang on. The ambulance will be here soon."

Bonny's husband, Frank, had on his policemen's blues. He'd been on patrol when Dayle called 9-1-1. Tall and lanky, Frank Laskey had receding, wiry black hair. At the moment, his blue eyes were bloodshot from crying. His wife was in surgery. He sat beside Dayle in the trauma unit waiting area, a drab room with orange Naugahyde couches, fake plants, and faded Norman Rockwell prints on the walls.

Dayle's clothes were still stained with blood. She kept her arm around Frank. "She'll pull through," Dayle assured him. "Our Bonny's a fighter. She'll be okay. Can I get you anything? You want some coffee?"

He nodded. "Thanks."

She wandered out to the corridor in search of a vending machine. The place might have been mobbed with reporters if Frank's buddies on the force weren't guarding the hospital entrances and taking down names. The rumor among the press was that Dayle Sutton and a police officer had been shot.

Dayle had already talked to their chief of surgery on the phone. He'd promised to call in their best doctor for Bonny. Dayle had also arranged for a private room and notified hospital administration to bill her.

It was too late to do anything for Hank. His only family was a married brother in Milwaukee; no close friends except for a book group that met every other Sunday to discuss mystery novels.

Dayle couldn't afford to break down yet. She hunted through her purse and found Susan Linn's business card. With a shaky hand, she dialed the number, then got a recorded greeting: "... if you'd like to speak with another officer, press zero, otherwise—"

There was a break in the message. "Lieutenant Linn speaking."

"Susan?" Dayle said. "Thank God. Listen, this is Dayle. Someone shot my friends. My chauffeur, Hank, he's dead. And my other friend, Bonny, they shot her too—"

"Hold on," Susan said. "Calm down, Dayle. Where are you?"

"I'm at the hospital," she said. Dayle did her best to retell the shooting and keep her composure. "Listen, there's a place I'd like you to send somebody, okay? Maybe send a whole squad if you can."

"Where?"

"These people who have me under surveillance, I found out where they're staying. A friend of mine followed one of them. They're all holed up in this hotel in the Valley, a dive called the My-T-Comfort Inn. They're in a bunch of rooms around the back—numbers fifteen through twenty, I think. I didn't want to tell you about it until I had more information on these guys. I have a private detective working on it. But we shouldn't wait anymore."

"I'll go check out this place right now. From what you tell me, I better give myself some backup."

"Good," Dayle replied. "Get those bastards, Lieutenant. Get them before they hurt someone else."

"I've been hit," Lyle Bender gasped into the pay phone.

"Where?"

"Twice in my gut. I'm bleeding like a stuck pig. Can you get someone?"

There was a pause on the other end. "We'll find a doctor for you, Lyle. Can you still drive, or should we send someone to pick you up?"

"I'll stay with my vehicle," Lyle said resolutely.

"Good boy. Think you can make it to the designated spot?"

"Affirmative," Lyle said. "Get me somebody good. No quack. I promised my son I'd take him hunting next week, and I don't intend to let him down."

"See you in twenty minutes?"

"Affirmative. Over and out." Lyle hung up the telephone, smearing his blood on the handle.

Thirty-eight years old, Lyle Bender had a stubby build, straight brown hair, and a pale complexion. An hour ago, he'd thought he looked good in his police uniform. He'd always wanted to be a cop. Now the blue uniform was blood-soaked from the chest down to his knees. His belly was on fire. Lyle could hardly get a breath without it hurting. He staggered back to the police car and got behind the wheel, only to sink into a puddle of his own blood. Starting up the engine, he headed south toward Long Beach.

This was a test of his strength. He'd deliver his vehicle to the designated spot. Hal and the doctor would marvel at his dedication and stamina. Hal might even admit how wrong he was about a lot of things and apologize. Lyle resolved to forgive him. It was the Christian thing to do.

Hal had accused him of getting "carried away" with his job. Maybe he was overzealous at times, but he believed in what they were doing. He believed Tony Katz had to be taken down a few notches after they drove him and his fellow deviate to the forest. So he whittled a tree branch and shoved it up the pervert's ass. But Hal didn't understand; he was too concerned about following the SAAMO big shots' instructions to the letter.

Hal just didn't get it. In that hotel room with Leigh Simone, after they'd dragged her in from the corridor, Lyle had threatened to rape her. He had no intention of actually going through with it. He was simply having a little fun, as guys do. And the threat worked. When he began to feel her up, that smug black bitch suddenly seemed terrified. She looked as if she might whimper an apology for promoting her twisted lifestyle to the youth of America. But Hal pulled him off her, whispering that there couldn't be any evidence of an attack. Her death had to look like a suicide.

He could tell Hal looked down on him. It was the way some of those SAAMO higher-ups treated the guys in the trenches. They were too full of themselves and their college educations to get their hands dirty. Hal was a SAAMO lieutenant. All he ever did was give orders and handle communications on the Internet, calling himself *Rick*—or sometimes *Americkan.* Lyle knew the real backbone of the organization was made up of people like himself, the soldiers. And after all, they called themselves Soldiers for An American Moral Order. There were fourteen SAAMO chapters in various cities and small towns throughout the United States, with a total of fifty-three members. But those thirty-nine men in the field, all soldiers like him, they were the unsung heroes.

Hal hadn't wanted him to pull the job tonight. SAAMO had enlisted an amateur from the outside to do it next week. Hal kept saying that Dayle Sutton was too much in the spotlight right now. It was too risky for one of them to handle the job.

Lyle had set off tonight to prove Hal and the SAAMO big shots wrong. He'd expected some interference from the bodyguard; but he hadn't counted on Miss Lesbo Pro-Abortion Gun Control to be carrying a piece. He'd put down the bodyguard, close and fast, almost a mercy killing. The guy didn't even know what hit him. Then suddenly from the backseat, Dayle Sutton was firing at him. In those silly movie star sunglasses, she still got a couple of lucky hits. But he managed to get her back, and *he* was still alive.

"Stay with me, Jesus," Lyle whispered. His knuckles turned white as he tightened his grip on the steering wheel. It was as if something were eating away at his gut, sharp teeth gnawing at him. He was losing a lot of blood. He felt it slithering down the back of his legs, wetting his socks.

Lyle pressed hard on the accelerator. Switching on the siren and red strobe, he headed for the highway exit. He ran a light at the end of the off-ramp, then made a sharp turn, almost tipping over the car. A stop sign didn't slow him down. He sped through it, heading into an industrial area. Only a few more minutes, and he'd be at the prescribed meeting place.

"You better be there with a doctor, Hal," Lyle whispered, gritting his teeth at the agonizing pain. He'd bleed to death if he didn't get help soon. Up ahead, he saw Newell Avenue, and he turned into the cul-de-sac. NO OUTLET, the sign said. He drove over a set of railroad tracks. The full moon illuminated a silo and a couple of smokestacks in an abandoned chemical plant. Lyle saw the entrance gate, closed and padlocked; and he saw the Corsica, parked across the street, waiting for him.

"Thank you, Jesus," he murmured, tears in his eyes. Lyle killed the police lights on his roof, then straightened up the best he could. He imagined the bullets lodging deeper inside him with every movement. Despite his agony, he had to smile when the Corsica's headlights flashed on and off.

Lyle shifted to park and shut off the engine. He started counting the seconds as he waited for his friends to climb out of the car. He counted up to seventy. The puddle of blood in which he sat had turned cold. He was losing feeling in his legs. "C'mon, guys," he grumbled. "I'm dying here."

Hal and the doctor finally emerged from their vehicle. They were sure taking their sweet time about it.

"Fuck," Lyle growled, and he punched the horn.

Startled, the doctor jumped a little. Lyle could see him now as he walked into the headlights: an old man in a loose trench coat. He seemed timid and scared. Hal must have bullied him into coming. He had a grip on the old guy's arm as they approached the car.

Lyle fumbled for the handle, then pushed the door open. The interior light went on. Hal walked up to the car, practically dragging the old guy. "Lyle, my God, look at you." His eyes widened at all the blood. "Well, listen, it's okay. I brought someone who's going to take care of everything."

Slumped over the steering wheel, Lyle managed to grin at his friend. "Praise the Lord," he said in a raspy voice.

"I also have some bad news," Hal said, frowning. He let go of the old man's arm. "Our source close to Dayle Sutton phoned a few minutes ago. She's very much alive. That was her stunt double you shot. She's the wife of a cop. It's a real mess you've created, Lyle. Once again."

"Oh, fuck," Lyle said, clutching his stomach. "You can't be serious—"

"It's okay. We've already started the cleanup." Hal grimaced and shook his head. "Damn, Lyle, you're hurt bad. Pray for forgiveness of your sins, all right? You hear me, Lyle?"

"What do you mean?" Lyle started to reach out toward them. Then he saw the old man pull a gun out of his coat pocket. All at once, Lyle realized he was going to die. "No, NO, NO!" he screamed.

The old man shot him in the shoulder. Then he fired again, putting one more bullet into Lyle's gut. Stunned and mute, Lyle gazed at Hal as if to ask why they were doing this to him.

"It's part of the cleanup, Lyle," Hal said soberly.

Lyle Bender barely felt an impact from the next bullet, which blew off the side of his head. He recoiled, and then his lifeless body flopped across the seat, blood splashed up from the wet cushion.

The old man dropped the gun. He staggered back to the chemical plant's chain-link fence, bent forward, and vomited.

"Well, that's that," Hal said. He picked up the gun. "You'll need some work on your aim, Tom. Otherwise, you did a fine job.''

Tom Lance wiped the dark spittle from his mouth with a shaky hand. "Is it Dayle Sutton?" he asked. "Is it Dayle Sutton you want me to kill?" He nodded at the corpse in the front seat of the patrol car. "I can't do that again! I can't! Please, don't ask me ..."

"We aren't *asking* you, Tom," Hal said. "When the time comes, you'll do what you're told. You understand that, don't you?" Hal frowned. For a moment, his face was illuminated by headlights. A minivan cruised down the cul-de-sac toward them.

The cleanup guys. Hal had explained to Tom on the way to Newell Avenue that a couple of their men were handling disposal of the body, repainting the car, cleaning it up. They would do whatever was necessary.

"Just in time," Hal said, with a glance at the approaching minivan. "C'mon, Tom. I'll take you home. You did well tonight."

The cellular phone inside her purse rang.

Dayle lay faceup on a padded examining table while they pumped blood from her arm. A stout, middle-aged black nurse tended to the needle and tubes. She wore a lavender sweater over her white uniform, and had a kind but homely face. Dayle had volunteered to donate blood for the hospital reserve, which Bonny was tapping. She was still in surgery. Meanwhile, they'd given their celebrity donor a private room.

"Could you hand me my purse, please?" Dayle asked the nurse. One-handed, Dayle managed to retrieve the phone and click on by the fourth ring. "Hello?" she said, tipping her head back to the cushion. The sudden movement had made her a bit dizzy.

"Dayle, this is Susan Linn. I'm here at the My-T-Comfort

Inn. The characters you told me about, if they were here, they've checked out—"

"What do you mean, 'if they were here'?" Dayle asked. She remembered to keep clenching and unclenching her fist for the nurse. "Did you check those room numbers I gave you?"

"I came up with a couple of families in those rooms. None of them looked like killers to me. Obviously, these guys cleared out."

"Have you examined the registration records?" Dayle asked. "Did you talk to the desk clerk?"

Susan Linn let out a long sigh. "Yes, Dayle. He said those families registered here two days ago, and before that, the rooms were vacant. They haven't had any police staying there either."

"But that's not true—"

"Ms. Sutton?" the nurse whispered. "Please, keep pumping your hand."

Dayle nodded distractedly. "Listen, Susan," she said into the phone. "That desk clerk must be lying. Maybe they paid him off. Can't you check his bank accounts or something?"

"I'm sorry, Dayle. It's a dead end here."

"But I can prove . . ." Dayle hesitated. She had that list of license plate numbers. By tomorrow, Nick might have the credit card numbers, names, and addresses of those men. "Listen, Susan," she said. "I didn't send you on a wild-goose chase tonight. Give me a day or two at the most, and I'll prove that this group was there. . . ."

"Well, you call me when you come up with that proof, Dayle."

She chose to ignore the slightly patronizing tone. "I will, Lieutenant." Working one-handed, Dayle clicked off.

The nurse removed the needle, then pressed a cotton swab to Dayle's arm. "Keep applying pressure there for a minute or two, Ms. Sutton,'' she said. ''Just lie still, and I'll be back with some cookies and juice.''

Following her instructions, Dayle managed to smile. ''Thank you.''

''Oh, thank you for donating, It's a very nice thing you're doing for your friend.''

''She was doing a nice thing for me,'' Dayle whispered.

In her bloodstained clothes, Dayle sat alone in the hospital corridor, sipping her orange juice and eating a Chips Ahoy cookie. She looked like a little girl outside the school nurse's office after falling down on the playground. She tried not to cry. She'd checked with Frank a while ago; Bonny's sister had arrived, and was with him. Bonny was still in surgery.

Gazing down the hospital corridor, Dayle recognized Dennis in one of his Argyle sweaters. He carried a shopping bag, and walked alongside a tall, lean man with receding blond hair and a healthy tan. The man wore a sweatshirt, plaid shorts, and sandals, very casual. He looked about thirty-five years old.

Dennis winced at the dried blood on Dayle's skirt and blouse. In the shopping bag, he had a change of clothes from her studio wardrobe. ''Oh, boss, I was so sorry to hear about Hank,'' he said.

Dayle nodded. ''Thanks for coming,'' she said.

''I brought you some new threads. I also brought you Ted Kovak. This is the man I was telling you about. . . .''

She reached up and shook his hand. ''Pleased to meet you.''

''Hi, I'm Ted.'' He smiled. ''Sorry about my appearance. Dennis called and said you needed me immediately.'' He casually lifted his sweatshirt to reveal a taut, hairy stomach and a gun in a shoulder holster. ''So I just strapped this on and flew. Dennis has my list of references. If you don't go with me, that's fine. But while you decide, I'll be happy to act as a temp.''

Dayle nodded cordially. Was that flash of stomach supposed to impress her? There was something about him she didn't like. She couldn't quite put her finger on it. Then again, maybe she just missed Hank, and wanted to make good her promise to dislike his replacement.

"Well, down to business," Ted Kovak said. "Our boys in blue have this hospital sealed pretty tight. How soon do you want to go home?"

"Actually, once I get an update about my friend in surgery, I was going to call a cab."

"Let me handle it," Ted said calmly.

Dayle nodded. "Thanks." She took the shopping bag full of clothes from Dennis, then retreated to the ladies' room, and ducked into the last stall. Quickly, she peeled off her soiled clothes. The blood had already dried to a dark rust color. Down to her bra and panties, she stopped for a moment, lowered the toilet seat lid, sat down, and allowed herself to cry.

"Are you okay?" Dayle asked, sounding anxious on the other end of the line.

"I'm all right," Sean said. "Don't worry. I'm just getting ready to go home."

She was alone in her office. The place was deathly quiet.

Two hours ago, when Dayle had called from the hospital with news of the shooting, Sean's building had been buzzing with activity: music from the salon downstairs, phones ringing, people in the hallway, someone's Xerox machine working overtime next door. Sean had had no reason to feel vulnerable. She'd only felt bad for Dayle and her friends.

While setting up her office computer, she'd periodically glanced out the window for what Dayle called the "rental mentals," but saw nothing suspicious.

She hadn't noticed how quiet the building had become until this second call from Dayle. Better news this time: her friend

Bonny had made it through surgery all right; and Dayle wouldn't have to be alone this evening. Her assistant had come to the hospital with a new bodyguard for her, and both of them were staying over at her place tonight.

"But I don't like the idea of you all alone in that office," she said. "And it's getting late."

"I know. I'm about to head out of here right now. Don't worry, Dayle."

"Well, thanks for being such a good friend. You were there for me this afternoon, and I really appreciate it. Be careful on that drive back to Malibu. Call me if you—oh, I still have your cellular . . ."

"I'll survive without it for one night. You get some rest and I'll talk to you tomorrow, okay?"

After Sean hung up, she glanced out her office window at the street below. She didn't see anyone sitting in a parked rental car. But that didn't necessarily mean they weren't out there.

In the window's reflection, she thought she saw a shadow pass behind her. Sean gasped. She grabbed a letter opener from her desk and crept out to the corridor. Her footsteps echoed on the tiled floor. No one. None of the other office lights were on.

"You're creeping yourself out," she muttered. "Quit it."

Ducking back in the office, she quickly collected her coat and purse. The telephone rang. The sudden noise hit her like a jolt. She snatched up the receiver. "Yes, hello?"

Silence.

She didn't need this right now. "Hello?" she said louder.

"Sean Olson?" The voice was raspy and guttural.

"Who's calling?"

He cleared his throat. "This is Avery Cooper. I—I'd like to make an appointment to see you tomorrow. I need a good lawyer."

Seventeen

"It's kind of ironic. I might be defending him for murder, and in the movies, he'll be playing a man I defended for murder." Sean sighed. "I tell you, only in Hollywood."

She hovered over her husband, shaving him and talking over the buzz of his cordless razor. Dan sat propped up in bed, a towel tucked under his chin. Sean was still in her bathrobe. "He said on the phone last night that Gary Worsht sang my praises. Plus he's been reading up on the case—all my old clippings. His regular attorney is one of those smooth-talking entertainment lawyers, not at all qualified to handle a murder trial. Unfortunately, Mr. Cooper very quickly agreed when I suggested that perhaps, in a rape-murder case like this one, he was indeed better off represented by a woman rather than by a crew of high-priced, slick male lawyers. It bothered me, he saw an angle in that."

Dan smiled, and mouthed the words: "You're the one who suggested it."

"Yeah, I know." She chuckled. "But he didn't have to be

so quick to agree. Anyway, I have to admit, he came across as a real sweet guy on the phone, but his alibi is one for the birds. Really shaky. I just don't know. . . .''

She switched off the razor, then reached for the Old Spice aftershave—a present from Danny last Christmas. Sean shook some into her hand, then smoothed it over Dan's face and neck. "Hold on, sweetie," she said, pulling out a Kleenex. "You have a little glop in your eye here." She dabbed it away. Dan joked to her and the kids about his "sleepy peas," but he'd been a handsome and somewhat vain man before all this had started. She knew it killed him to have mucus around those once-beautiful eyes. The blinking reflex was just another part of his body shutting down.

"There now." Sean tossed the crumpled Kleenex on the nightstand, then leaned back to look at him. "All finished."

Sean read his lips: "This sounds like a high-profile case. Could make a lot of money, help you build up a reputation, a client base . . .''

"I know." She sighed. "But it'll keep me busy day and night. I'm away from you and the kids too much right now as it is."

Dan's eyes wrestled with hers. "This is about your future, honey," he said, visibly straining to form the words. "It's about your career. We owe money. I want you to be okay when I'm gone."

Sean touched his cheek. "You know I hate that kind of talk."

Those clear blue eyes were beautiful for a moment as he focused on her. His lips moved again. "So you can't play nursemaid. If I leave this world knowing you're building a future for you and the kids, that's something I want, that's something good."

Sean felt herself tearing up, and she quickly hugged her husband. He smelled of the Old Spice aftershave, and she inhaled it, cherishing every breath.

RECOOPERATING: Actress, Joanne Lane, 32, (wife of TV and Film Star, Avery Cooper, 34) is recovering after a fall into the pool of her Beverly Hills home early yesterday morning. The Tony-nominated actress had recently suffered a miscarriage. She was heavily sedated at the time of the accident. Upon discovering his wife unconscious in the pool, Cooper called paramedics. Lane was rushed to Cedars-Sinai Medical Center, and held overnight for observation. She is expected to be released later today.

So said the blurb in the entertainment section of *U.S.A. Today*. Avery tossed the dog-eared newspaper back on the security guard's desk. "Thanks," he muttered to the lanky, uniformed black man. Avery was sitting beside him in a folding chair outside Joanne's hospital room. Her door was closed.

Most papers ran similar versions of yesterday's incident. None of them mentioned the murder of Libby Stoddard. Avery figured the police would officially question him within the next day or two. He had an appointment with Sean Olson later this morning, but he couldn't give the case much thought beyond that. He had enough on his mind with Joanne.

The hospital's head psychiatrist, Dr. Wetherall, had mentioned possibly transferring Joanne to a sanitarium if her condition didn't improve. He'd been in the room with her for the last half hour. The door finally opened, and Dr. Wetherall emerged. He was a wiry, handsome, balding man in his late forties. "She'll see you, Avery," he whispered. "Only a couple of minutes. Okay?"

Avery stepped into the room. Joanne lay very still, staring at him as he approached the bed. She was pale, and her unwashed hair had been brushed back. She must have bitten down on her lower lip too hard, because it was bleeding a little. "Hi, sweetheart," Avery said.

She wiggled her hands to show the straps around her wrists. "Was this your idea?" she asked, her voice raspy.

"Of course not," he replied. "They're just worried you'll hurt yourself."

She sneered at him. "Yes, I'm a dangerous character."

"Are you getting any rest at all?"

She said nothing. She gazed up at the ceiling.

"Joanne?"

"You know who I feel like right now?" she said at last. She sounded as if she were in a trance. "I feel like Natalie Wood in *Splendor in the Grass*. She just got crazier and crazier, and couldn't help it. Remember how they finally had to send her away to that sanitarium? Actually, it looked nice, the art therapy classes, the sprawling lawns, people in rocking chairs . . ."

She turned and gave him an icy stare. "Why don't you send me away to a place like that?"

Avery shook his head. "You don't mean that."

"I'm tired," she said, closing her eyes. "You can go now."

"Joanne—"

"GET THE FUCK OUT!" she screamed. "LEAVE ME ALONE!"

Dr. Wetherall hurried in, then he steered Avery toward the door. A nurse rushed in after them. Down the hall, Avery could still hear Joanne screaming.

Later, he sat in a stupor as Dr. Wetherall gave him a folder for Glenhaven Spa in Palm Springs. The doctor knew the facility, very private with a tranquil environment and a top-notch staff. He talked up the place as if it were a Shangri-la for nutcases. Dr. Wetherall said that it was *almost inhumane* to keep Joanne here, drugged and strapped to a hospital bed, when they could do so much for her at Glenhaven.

Avery wandered out of the doctor's office, the folder under his arm. He hadn't signed anything yet. He passed by the hospital's newsstand gift shop, where the clerk was placing the new issue of *People* on the magazine rack. On the cover was a flattering photo of Joanne and him, wrapped in each other's arms. They looked so healthy, decked out in jeans and crisp white T-shirts, standing in front of their pool. He was kissing Joanne on the cheek. AVERY COOPER & JOANNE LANE, said the caption. HOLLYWOOD'S HAPPIEST & SEXIEST COUPLE.

Sean heard a knock on the anteroom door. She put down the new issue of *People,* stashed it in her desk drawer, then sprang to her feet. "Come in!" she called. Her chestnut hair pinned back, she wore a burgundy suit with an ivory blouse—a chic, professional look. Guilty or innocent, Avery Cooper was her first potential client here, and she needed to make a good impression.

They met in the doorway. "Hi, I'm Avery," he said, very somber as he shook her hand. "Thanks for agreeing to see me." He wore a denim shirt and khakis. His black hair was a bit mussed. She noticed the scratch marks on his left cheek.

Sean only knew Avery Cooper's public persona: the cute, happy-go-lucky guy next door. Considering the purpose of this visit, she'd figured "happy-go-lucky" wasn't on today's menu. But she hadn't expected him to be so damned attractive. Or perhaps she was simply drawn to his sadness. Sean had to remind herself that he was the suspect in a murder-rape case.

She briskly pumped his hand. "Come in, sit down. Did you have a tough time finding the place?"

"No," he said, settled on her sofa. "Though I thought you were kidding on the phone when you said your office was above a hair salon."

She paused by her mini-fridge. "Are you sorry now that you didn't go for a crew of high-priced, slick male lawyers?"

He smiled and shook his head.

"Something to drink?" She opened the refrigerator door. "I

have Evian, Evian, Diet Coke, Evian, Evian, just plain Coke, and Evian.''

"Evian, please.''

Sean poured Evian into two glasses, and handed him one. She sat down across from him in the easy chair. "So tell me your story, Mr. Cooper.''

"Call me Avery.'' He tried to smile, but his eyes watered up, and his voice cracked. "I've never been in this type of trouble before. And my wife, she's . . .'' He trailed off, then wiped his eyes and took a sip of water. "Damn,'' he muttered, looking down at the carpet. "I'm sorry. It might work better if you just started asking me questions.''

Sean's heart broke for him. "Would you rather do this some other time?''

He waved the question away. "No, this is good. Really, I'm all right. Ask me whatever you want to know.''

Sean studied him, at the way he held back. "You—'' She was about to say, *You remind me of my husband.* But she cleared her throat, and asked, "You sure you're okay?''

"Yeah, fine,'' he said, straightening up.

She reached for a recorder on the coffee table. "Mind if I tape this?''

Avery shook his head. "No problem.''

Sean switched on the machine, then sat back. "I've thought about what you told me over the phone yesterday, Avery, and maybe you can explain a few things to me. First, can you think of anyone who might have seen you at that park—I mean, besides the woman who scratched you?''

"No. And I probably wouldn't recognize her again. She wore these weird glasses. I'm afraid I didn't catch a good look at her—um, *getaway* car either.''

"Did *she* drive off?''

"No, someone picked her up. I saw her duck into the passenger side.''

"On your way to this park, did you sense someone was following you?"

Avery sighed. "Not at the time. Everything was so muddled. That was the day Joanne had a miscarriage—"

"Yes, I know, I'm sorry," Sean interrupted gently. "Avery, one of the most damning pieces of evidence against you is that you received that scratch at just about the time Libby Stoddard was fighting and clawing her killer. Under her fingernails, they found skin tissue matching your blood type, and traces of a certain makeup they use backstage in NBC Burbank Studio B, where you'd filmed *The Tonight Show* earlier that day. Do you have any explanation for that?"

Frowning, he shrugged. "Only a vague, half-baked theory. To be honest, I've been so worried about my wife these last couple of days, I haven't given much thought to anything else."

She smiled sympathetically. "I understand. But I'm going to steer you back to my question earlier. Even if it's 'half-baked,' I want to hear your theory about those scratch marks and the skin tissue under Libby's nails."

Avery leaned forward. "You'll think I'm nuts, but I figure someone was following me, waiting to catch me alone. And—this is the crazy part—they must have been watching Libby too. They saw a chance to frame me for Libby's murder. I think the woman in the park was sent there to scratch my face. I don't know forensics, but is it possible they could have transferred my skin tissue from that woman's fingernails to Libby's?"

"I suppose." Sean studied him with uncertainty. "But that would mean Libby was raped and murdered for the specific purpose of framing you."

"Well, isn't it obvious?" Avery said. "For a while now, someone's been trying very hard to make me look bad. They stole that home video, then distributed copies of the damn thing. At first, I blamed Libby. In fact, I told several people that I'd like to see her dead. If you were going to kill someone and frame me for it, Libby Stoddard was the perfect victim.''

"Let's put the theories on hold for a minute," Sean said. "Last night, on the phone with me, you said that you were hesitant about furnishing the police with a sperm sample. Why? If you're really innocent of this rape-murder, a sperm sample would eliminate you as a suspect."

"I know that," Avery replied. "But I'm afraid my sample will somehow match with they've found."

Sean slowly shook her head. "I can buy the skin tissue transferred from under one set of fingernails to another. But manufacturing this other piece of evidence requires some cooperation from you, Avery."

"I know it sounds hokey and paranoid—"

"I'm sorry," Sean interrupted. "But if these people want to destroy you, they're sure going at it in a very roundabout way. They killed an innocent woman for the sole purpose of framing you for murder? Wouldn't it be a lot easier just to kill you?"

"But it's not about killing me. Hell, they've broken into my hotel room and my home. They could have gotten at me any time. No, these people want to bring me down, ruin my reputation, make me look horrible."

"Why do you think they're doing this?"

He shook his head and shrugged. "I don't know for sure. I was in a TV movie a couple of months ago that ticked off a lot of people. Joanne and my commercials for gun control have made us a lot of enemies too."

"So—you think the same group that's after Dayle has targeted you?"

Avery squinted at her. "What are you talking about?

"You mean, you haven't talked to Dayle Sutton?" Sean asked.

He shrugged. "We've exchanged e-mail about the movie—"

"Dayle hasn't told you about these people who want to kill

her? She hasn't mentioned a possible conspiracy linking the deaths of Tony Katz, Leigh Simone, and Maggie McGuire?''

Avery slowly shook his head.

For a moment Sean studied that guileless expression on his handsome face. Somehow she knew he was a good, honest man. She'd felt the same way when she'd first set eyes on Dan. "You're telling me the truth,'' she said.

"Well, yes, of course,'' he replied.

"You said a minute ago that the police would probably find a match if they tested your sperm alongside what they discovered in Libby. How do you think these—conspirators were able to pull that off?''

He shook his head. "I don't know.''

"Well, since I'm going to be your attorney, Avery, we'll have to figure out an answer to that question.''

Tom waited for Hal in front of his apartment building. They had a noon appointment. He had a rolled-up *Los Angeles Times* in his hand. The headlines told of an ambush on Dayle Sutton's limo. There was nothing about a shooting death outside a deserted chemical plant in south Los Angeles. But on page two, they carried a blurred photo of Maggie—from that stag movie. The caption read: MAGGIE MCGUIRE, EARLY SEX FILM BLOT ON A DISTINGUISHED CAREER.

Leaning against the entryway, Tom felt so tired. Last night, Hal had given him something to make him sleep. It was probably still in his system. Killing that man had been like watching himself in a movie. Reality hit him a moment after pulling the trigger. Then he threw up. Drops of vomit—and the man's blood—had gotten on his clothes, so Hal made him strip. Tom was shivering, nearly naked, standing in a darkened, deserted cul-de-sac. He tried not to cry. They gave him a pair of coveralls, and the "cleanup'' crew took his clothes away. Thank God

Hal's sleeping pills had worked. For a few hours, he'd forgotten everything and slept.

Hal had said he needed to work on his aim; and so they were heading out to the desert for target practice this afternoon.

A white Corsica pulled up to the curb. Hal was behind the wheel. Tom reluctantly climbed in beside him. He saw coffee from 7-Eleven in the cup holder. Hal held up a bag. "Cream and sugar. Plus a couple of donuts. If you took those pills, you probably slept through breakfast."

Pulling into traffic, Hal announced that there was a cooler of beer in the trunk for later. He cranked up the air conditioner, and popped in a Glen Miller tape. "I also have Perry Como here, and Sinatra. I wasn't sure about your taste in music."

Tom said nothing. He wondered why this sudden VIP treatment.

Hal kept his eyes on the road. "You did well last night," he said. "I know it was rough, but you really proved yourself. Our SAAMO officers were impressed. Are you comfortable? Is the air-conditioning too cold?"

"It's fine. Thanks." He pried the lid off his coffee.

"So—what do you think of your old girlfriend's porn movie?" Hal asked, glancing at the newspaper on Tom's lap. "Have you seen her little epic?"

Tom cleared his throat. "No, I haven't," he replied. "She—she must have needed the money very badly. You weren't behind this, were you?"

"Behind what?"

"Releasing that old stag movie, making her into a joke. Is your SAAMO group responsible for that?"

"Why, no. Like I told you, Tom, we were investigating Maggie. But we didn't release the porn tape. Someone else must have."

Tom wasn't entirely convinced.

Hal briefly smiled at him, then studied the city traffic. "I'm glad you asked me. Until now, we've had to keep you in the dark about certain things, and I'm sorry. We don't want you left out of the loop anymore. If there's something on your mind, just ask.''

Eyes narrowed, Tom stared at him. "Okay, I have a question,'' he said. "How do you expect me to kill Dayle Sutton? I'm no marksman. You saw how close I was to that man last night, and it still took me three shots.''

"We'll get you close enough to her, Tom.''

"That's another problem. If I'm too close, she might recognize me.''

"What are you talking about?'' Hal asked.

"Dayle, her assistant, her casting director and his secretary— they all met me the afternoon Maggie died. I auditioned for them. It didn't go well. I got a little miffed. I'm afraid there were some—heated words.''

Hal gave him a perturbed glance. "Better watch that temper of yours, Tom. It keeps getting you into trouble. Give me a blow-by-blow.''

When Tom finished explaining about the disastrous audition, Hal pulled a cellular phone out of the pocket of his windbreaker. "Sounds as if you wouldn't mind killing Dayle Sutton—with or without our help.'' He unfolded the little gizmo, then pressed the numbers on the dial pad. "Hi. I'm with Tom, and we're on our way to target practice,'' Hal said into the cellular. He was merging onto the freeway.

Tom sipped his coffee and pretended he wasn't interested in Hal's phone conversation. "Yeah, well, he'll just have to agree to it,'' he said at one point.

Tom glanced down at his half-consumed jelly donut and the cup of coffee in his hands. For a while there, Hal had almost made him feel important. He wondered what he'd "just have to agree to.''

After another minute, Hal clicked off and slipped the tiny phone back in his pocket. "You won't mind wearing a disguise, will you, Tom? Maybe glasses or a fake mustache? Worst we might do is shave back your hairline a bit.''

"I'll just have to agree to it," Tom said, frowning. He let out a long sigh. "Listen, why me? I mean, why not hire a professional hit man?"

"You're a good actor, Tom." Hal said, his eyes still on the road. "It's a shame Hollywood didn't use your talent better. See, when you take care of Dayle Sutton for us, there will be a lot people around. One of our men will be a security guard at the scene, and he'll shoot you with blanks. Our own special ambulance will whisk you away. Now, a hit man might be a good shot, but he won't play dead very well, not like you. I saw your death scene in *Fall from the Saddle*. You made it look real, Tom. I even cried. I saw that picture a couple of times. Is it your favorite?"

"Well, it's one of the better westerns I made. . . ."

For the rest of the ride, he and Hal talked about his movies. They listened to Glen Miller, then Perry Como. He found himself liking Hal. Tom actually forgot for a few minutes that he had to put a bullet in Dayle Sutton's head for these people. And when he did remember, it didn't seem like such a terrible thing.

"What time is it?" Dayle muttered, rubbing her eyes. She wore her ivory silk robe. Her head felt like a wad of chewing gum, and her mouth was so dry she could barely swallow. She tried to focus on Dennis, seated at the kitchen table. He looked as preppie as ever in jeans and a pink oxford shirt.

"It's a quarter to one, and you can blame me for your hangover," he said. "I got you drunk last night. Why don't you go back to bed? You aren't going anywhere today. Might as well take it easy. You want an aspirin?"

"I just took three," Dayle said, sitting at the table with him. "Did you talk to the studio?"

"Oh, I've spoken with a ton of people today." He got up and poured her a cup of coffee. "First off, don't worry about the movie. They'll shoot around you. They don't expect you on the set any time before lunch tomorrow."

Dayle swept back her tangled hair, then sipped some coffee. "What was I drinking last night? I can't remember. . . ."

"You had a couple of glasses of wine. But you gave blood yesterday, so it went right to your head."

Dayle nodded with recollection. The new bodyguard, Ted, had arranged for transportation from the hospital to home. Her initial assessment of Ted now seemed unfair. Procuring the limo, he'd thoroughly inspected it for tampering or sabotage, and he interviewed the driver. While still at the hospital, he'd had his girlfriend fax them a copy of his résumé. Ted had protected some high-profile people: politicians, multimillionaires, and several entertainers—including Vegas singer-actor Gil Palarmo, who had died from AIDS last year. Despite his ladies'-man image, everyone in the industry knew Gil was gay and something of a lecher. The fact that this handsome, straight guy remained at Gil's side for eleven months was a testament to Ted Kovak's tolerance.

He was kind of a hard-ass, and maybe she needed that. She'd told him about yesterday's break-in, but didn't mention the note pinned to her dress. Before she could set foot inside her apartment, Ted spent twenty minutes combing the place over for booby traps, bugging devices, and bombs. Then Dennis arrived with carryout for everyone. And the wine started flowing.

Dayle took another sip of coffee. "I can't believe I'm this hungover after only two glasses of wine," she muttered.

"Oh, you were still pretty wired, so I put you to bed with a couple of brandies and unplugged the phone in the bedroom. I crashed in the guest room, and Ted pulled an all-nighter. He went home a few hours ago. He hired two more security guards, one for the hallway outside and another for the downstairs lobby. This place is like Fort Knox. Ted's due back around six o'clock. Meanwhile, we're under strict orders to stay put.''

"How's Bonny?'' Dayle asked quietly.

Dennis patted her hand. "She'll be okay. They're moving her out of intensive care this afternoon.''

Dayle nodded, then took a deep breath. "Um, Hank has a brother in Milwaukee. We need to get a hold of him—''

"It's taken care of, Dayle,'' Dennis cut in. "I talked with the brother this morning. He's having Hank's body flown home. They're not planning a funeral or wake. The burial's in Milwaukee on Thursday. It's family only.''

Tears brimmed her eyes, and she shrugged. "I thought we were Hank's family.'' Dayle recalled with aching regret those few minutes yesterday when she'd suspected Hank of betraying her, and she began to cry.

"It's all right, Dayle,'' she heard Dennis say. He squeezed her hand. "Just rest up for now. I'm here. I'll handle everything. . . .''

The Budweiser can flew off the railing, hit the wall, then ricocheted to the floor and rolled around for a moment. It was the only thing moving on the front porch of the deserted, dilapidated old ranch house.

"Damn, you're good!'' Hal said, slapping Tom on the back.

Tom smiled. He focused on the next target along the railing, a Coke bottle. He aimed the .380 semiautomatic and carefully squeezed the trigger. The bottle toppled forward. The bullet had hit the railing, but not the target.

"Close enough,'' Hal said. "Just think, if you were aiming for Dayle Sutton's head, you'd have shot her in the throat. And that ain't bad at all.''

Tom caught himself grinning. His aim had been a bit rusty at first, but he relaxed and eased into it.

"We'll get you a better gun, Tom. We just needed to make

sure you know how to handle fire arms. I must say, I'm impressed. How about a cold one?'' Hal said, once Tom had shot all the targets off the railing.

They leaned against the car, and sipped icy Michelobs. Tom twirled the gun on his finger. He was exhausted and sweaty, yet he felt like a young man today.

For every diploma on the walls of his office, Dr. Nathan had two framed Monet prints. It certainly created a serene environment for frustrated couples consulting Dr. Nathan about their unsuccessful attempts to conceive.

The Coopers' fertility specialist had his practice on the top floor of a new, six-story medical center. He'd carved out some time for his famous client. Dr. Nathan was a thin man with a mop of curly gray hair, glasses, and a droll manner. Sean guessed he was about fifty. She immediately liked him. He seemed very sincere in his condolences to Avery about the miscarriage, and he was optimistic about Joanne's chances of becoming pregnant again. Avery didn't mention his wife was on the verge of being institutionalized.

Sean didn't say anything either. They were waiting for a call back from the lab where Avery's sperm samples were stored. If any of those samples had disappeared, Sean would have her explanation for Avery's semen having been found inside the murder-rape victim.

When Dr. Nathan's phone finally rang, Sean and Avery anxiously leaned forward in their chairs. He grabbed the receiver: ''Yes? Yes . . . uh-huh . . . we have nine samples on record here. . . .''

''What's the count over there?'' Sean interrupted.

Dr. Nathan covered the mouthpiece. ''Nine, none are missing,'' he said, then spoke into the phone again. ''That's all I needed, thanks for—''

''Don't hang up yet,'' Sean cut in again.

"Just a second," he said into the phone. He gazed at her over the rims of his glasses, eyebrows raised.

"Sorry to keep interrupting," she said. "Did they verify that all nine samples are from Avery?"

The doctor spoke into the receiver again. "Thanks for waiting. I need you to run a test on the nine samples, see if they all match. How long will that take?" He listened for a moment, then covered the mouthpiece. "Is tomorrow afternoon okay?"

"That would be great," Sean said. She waited until Dr. Nathan hung up the phone. "Would it be possible to furnish us with a list of employees both here and at the lab who might have had access to those sperm samples?"

Dr. Nathan nodded. "I'll talk to someone in administration about it."

"Could we pick up that list tomorrow?"

"I'll see what I can do," he said.

"Thanks," Sean said. "And security here is pretty tight?"

"We don't leave specimens sitting around, if that's what you mean." He shrugged. "And besides, who would want to steal or switch a sperm sample?"

"That's exactly what we're trying to find out," Sean replied.

Avery studied Sean at the steering wheel, a steely, determined look on that beautiful face. Her soft brown hair fluttered in the breeze from the open window as she watched the road ahead. She had an aristocratic face, yet there was something very down-to-earth about her.

He'd asked this woman to be his lawyer based on gut instinct and a brief conversation with a gay man she'd once defended. So far, she hadn't disappointed him. He imagined a team of slick, expensive lawyers padding their billing hours and weaving strategies, never for one minute believing his innocence. But Sean Olson had integrity and guts.

She glanced at him. "Is your place much further?"

"Only a few more minutes. I'll tell you when it's coming up."

"FYI," Sean said, her eyes on the road again, "our boys in blue are probably obtaining a search warrant for your house this very minute. I wouldn't put it past this group to plant incriminating evidence in your home."

"I doubt anyone could have gotten past the cameras and the alarms. We upgraded security after the break-in."

"Tell me about these cameras," Sean said.

"We have six video cameras recording twenty-four hours a day at different points outside the house."

"What happens to the tapes?"

"If I remember right, the security guy said they hold on to them for a month before they recycle them."

"I want to review those tapes as soon as possible."

"Okay, I can arrange that," Avery said. "I'll reserve us an editing room at the studio for tomorrow."

"Good. Maybe we can catch something on videotape that might have slipped past your security people." She stole another look at him. "Maybe you should find yourself a body-guard, Avery. These people have killed before. If they did away with you now, you'd die a murder suspect, which would suit them fine."

"That's a cheery thought," he replied, glancing out his car window. "Anyway, I'll be okay. My biggest concern right now is my wife. Until she's up and feeling better, nothing else really matters."

"Huh. You remind me of my husband," she said.

Avery turned to look at her. "Really? What does he do?"

"Dan used to be a chef. But he's been sick. He has ALS. You know, Lou Gehrig's Disease? We have him on a respirator and a feeding machine."

"God, I'm sorry," was all Avery could say.

"Yeah, it's a lousy deal." She sighed. "Take my advice, people recover from nervous breakdowns. Your wife's chances of getting better are very good. Don't you worry. She has doctors and nurses looking after her.''

A sad smile flickered across her face as she stole one more glance at him. ''You need to look after yourself, Avery. Promise me you will.''

She thought she saw something on the monitor, a figure skulking outside the house by the pool. Then again, after viewing the security videos at fast speed for three hours, Sean's eyes were probably playing tricks on her. She and Avery sipped coffee to sustain themselves while watching the flickering black-and-white images on four small monitors. They sat at the control desk in a tiny room stocked with film and video equipment.

''Take a look at this,'' Sean said, setting the tape in reverse, then slowing it down.

Their chairs had wheels on the feet, and Avery scooted over to her side. He'd dressed casually for their video marathon today: a white shirt and jeans. Sean looked very much the legal eagle in a gray linen suit.

''Someone's sneaking around your pool area at four fifty-two in the morning,'' Sean read the time and date along the top of the screen. A woman in a robe emerged from the shadows on the Coopers' patio.

''That's Joanne,'' Avery murmured.

Sean watched Joanne Lane stagger toward the edge of the pool. Obviously drunk, she lost her balance and fell down. She had a hard time standing up again.

''I haven't seen this before,'' Avery said, his voice strained. ''I think it's when she tried to kill herself.''

''Oh, God, I'm sorry.'' Sean found the switch and shut it off. ''Stupid of me—''

''It's okay. You didn't know.'' He rubbed his eyes. ''Listen,

I could use an intermission. Do you want to go for a walk or something?"

"No, thanks. You go. I need to make some calls." Sean waited for Avery to leave, then she rolled her head from side to side. Staring at the blank screen, she finally pressed the play button. The tape came on: Avery's wife lowering herself into the pool, dog-paddling toward the deep end. Her robe billowed out around her as she tried to make herself sink to the bottom. It was almost a struggle for her to kill herself. As much as Sean pitied this woman, she couldn't help feeling a bit annoyed by her too—this showy attempt at suicide. There was something very theatrical about it. After a while, Joanne seemed to relax and sank beneath the pool's surface. For nearly two minutes, she drifted facedown in the water, her hair and robe spread out and swaying around her still body.

At last, Avery ran out of the house in his undershorts. Plunging into the pool, he swam to his wife and dragged her limp body onto the deck. According to the numbers across the top of the screen, it took him fifty-six seconds to revive her. But the time seemed to drag on and on as he struggled over that lifeless form. It was gut-wrenching to watch. This was punishment for her morbid curiosity—and for starting to think about him the way she did. She watched Avery hover over his wife until the paramedics finally arrived and loaded her on a stretcher.

Sean sighed, then switched off the tape.

Avery bought a pack of red licorice vines and a roll of butter rum Lifesavers from the vending machine on the first floor. Starting back up the steps toward the editing rooms, he popped a Lifesaver in his mouth—part of his balanced breakfast. He'd only eaten a few spoonfuls of Special K this morning when the police had buzzed him from the front gate intercom. They had a search warrant. At least he was shaved and dressed for their surprise visit. Avery remained calm. It was almost surreal now, the way his whole world had turned upside down. He put a pot of coffee on, and the four officers combing his house for evidence appreciated the Starbuck's Kona Blend served to them by a genuine movie star murder suspect.

As far as he could tell, the police hadn't found anything. They'd filed out the front door after an hour—with only some carpet fiber samples.

Avery washed out the policemen's coffee cups, then called the hospital. The news from Dr. Wetherall wasn't good. He advised Avery not to visit Joanne today. She'd tried to attack a nurse yesterday, and was still under sedation. Had he given any more thought to Glenhaven Spa?

Avery said that he'd have a decision for him by tomorrow. In other words, he was hoping for a miracle within the next twenty-four hours.

Munching his Lifesaver, Avery wandered up the corridor, past offices and editing rooms. He found Sean, seated at the video controls and talking on her cell phone.

"I have nothing to tell you," she was saying. "No, you're way out of line . . . and please, don't call me again." She clicked off, then tucked the phone in her purse.

Avery tossed the red licorice vines on the desk. "Thought you could use a sugar fix," he said. "Who was that?"

"Some asshole reporter—if you'll pardon me. I don't know how he got my cell phone number." She picked up the red vines. "Thanks."

"What did he want?"

Sean tore at the cellophane wrapper. "I'm not even sure he was a real reporter. Hell, he could have been part of this hate group. He wanted to know if you'd been formally charged with Libby Stoddard's murder yet—the *yet* part really burned me. He also wanted to know how we intended to plea."

She got to her feet. "Listen, you were right earlier. I could really use a break. Let's go for a walk."

* * *

They strolled through a studio back lot, which depicted a small town circa 1958. Long, fin-tailed cars lined the curb, and the Movie Palace played *Vertigo*. Down the block were Smitty's Malt Shop, Deedee's Millinery, and Christoff's Five-and-Dime.

Sean pulled a very anachronistic cellular phone out of her purse, then checked the last call. The reporter from before had a blocked number. Frowning, she slipped the phone back in her purse. "That stupid call still bothers me. Do you think it was really a reporter?"

"Maybe even a reporter working for them," Avery said. They strolled past Tony's Barber Shop. "If this group wants to ruin certain celebrities' reputations, they'd need media people on their payroll. Yeah, that was probably a legitimate reporter just now. And I can tell you how they describe a conversation like the one you just had: 'When asked about Avery Cooper's homicidal tendencies, his attorney, Sean Olson, offered no comment.' " He shrugged and grinned. "That's typical in this business."

Sean found herself half smiling back at him. Avery didn't seem to have let *the business* corrupt him. He was more worried about his wife than his career. In a town dominated by phonies often trying to pass themselves off as "just plain family folk," this guy was the real thing. His sweetness and his wholesome good looks were perfectly suited for this small town setting from the fifties. He even looked a bit like Ricky Nelson. Sean almost wanted to hold on to his arm as they continued walking down this magical street together.

Her cellular rang, jarring her from the momentary daydream. She pulled the phone out of her purse again and clicked it on. "Sean Olson speaking."

"Ms. Olson, it's Doug Nathan at the clinic. I have the results from the lab tests on those nine sperm samples from Avery Cooper."

"Yes, Dr. Nathan," she said, her eyes meeting with Avery's.

"All nine samples match," he reported.

Sean turned away from Avery. "Are you sure?" she said into the phone.

"Yes. All nine samples are from the same subject-donor: Avery Cooper. Also, I'm trying to untangle some red tape from administration for those employee records you requested. Could I call you tomorrow on it?"

"Yes, of course," Sean murmured. "Thanks, Dr. Nathan."

"Talk to you tomorrow. Bye." Then he hung up.

Sean clicked off the phone, then slipped it back into her purse. She couldn't look at Avery. "All the sperm samples match," she said.

"You're kidding," he muttered. "Are they sure?"

"They're sure."

Avery said nothing. Shaking his head, he backed away until he bumped against a Studebaker Coupe parked along the curb.

Sean rubbed her forehead. "Avery, is there something you haven't told me? Did you have sex with Libby? Maybe consensual sex?"

Leaning against the car, he rolled his eyes. "God, no. The only time I even met Libby Stoddard was with our lawyers at that hearing. I didn't even shake her hand."

"Okay," Sean said, nodding patiently. "And you're pretty sure the police will find a match with the victim if you furnish them with a sperm sample?"

"Yes. I don't think these people would go to all the trouble of murdering Libby and setting me up for it without somehow matching up that important piece of evidence. They must have paid off someone in the lab." He shook his head. "I'm stalling for time here, Sean. Don't you see? If I give the cops a sperm sample, and it's a match, I'll be thrown in jail immediately, right? I won't be able to see my wife or do anything to help with this investigation."

"I understand," Sean said, patting his arm. "Well, I can

question people at the lab. Maybe somebody's lying. You're not a sperm donor, are you?''

He kicked at the pavement. ''No.''

''Can I get personal?'' Sean asked.

''Hell, we're talking about my sperm. We've already *gotten* to 'personal.' ''

''You and Joanne spend a good deal of time apart. Is it possible you were with someone who might have kept some of your semen from a diaphragm or a condom?''

Avery shook his head.

''The truth, Avery,'' Sean said. ''You haven't strayed once?''

''I'm sorry. I haven't been with anyone else since I met Joanne.''

''Well, don't be sorry,'' Sean managed to say. ''It's actually very sweet.''

He looked at her again with the same guileless expression that had first won her over. ''Sean, you don't really think I killed Libby Stoddard, do you?''

''No, I believe you're telling the truth, Avery.'' It was beyond all logic, but Sean meant what she said.

Eighteen

Tom Lance emerged from Lowell's Guns & Ammo Stop, carrying a .38 caliber and a box of bullets in a brown paper bag. This was the gun he would use to kill Dayle Sutton. Authorities would trace its purchase here by a Tom Lance whose appearance was slightly altered.

He wore his disguise for next week's mission: nonprescription glasses with black frames, and a gray mustache. Hal, standing under the awning of a nearby pawnshop, joked that he almost didn't recognize him. He suggested that they grab a late breakfast at the McDonald's across the street.

"I see you've made a purchase," Hal said, nudging Tom as they headed toward the restaurant. "Have any trouble? Any sticky legal red tape?"

"No, not at all."

"Well, good. You know, Tom, if people like Dayle Sutton get their way, we won't be able to buy a gun anywhere—except from criminals."

They ordered Egg McMuffins. For a moment, Tom harkened

back to his glory days months earlier, when—because of his TV commercial—the folks at his local McDonald's gave him a free apple pie with lunch. He almost told the haggard-looking black girl behind the counter about the ad, but she wouldn't have given a damn.

The bag with the .38 caliber sat on the table between them. Hal had insisted Tom take it inside the McDonald's. "You have to feel comfortable carrying it around."

Hal now folded his hands in prayer over his Egg McMuffin. Some teenagers at the next table seemed to think this was pretty damn funny. Snickering, they imitated Hal, who became red in the face as he crossed himself. He glared at the kids, then picked up his sandwich.

He started to review their itinerary for the next few days. But after a while, he practically had to shout to compete with the loud teenagers across from them. "I can't talk over these foul-mouthed niggers," he grumbled.

Tom pushed away his Styrofoam plate and he too glared at the kids.

"What the fuck you looking at, asshole?" one of the boys sneered.

Tom turned away, but his face flushed with bottled-up rage.

"Little do they know," Hal whispered. "You could just reach into this bag here, couldn't you? *Erase* them. What good are they? Look at those ones." Hal nodded at three punk teenagers at another table. Their clothes were filthy and they had pierced eyebrows and noses. One of them, an Asian girl, had blue hair. "Who would miss them?" Hal asked. "Killing them is just a reach away."

Tom stared at the bag.

"And check out the two queers over there," Hal whispered, his eyes darting toward a couple of young men with dyed-platinum hair, pierced ears, and white T-shirts that were a little too clean and a little too tight.

"In a way," Hal went on, "when you eliminate Dayle Sutton,

you'll help rid our country of this scum we're now forced to share breakfast with. We're waging a war against these degenerates, Tom. The queer sodomites, these slant-eyed aliens, welfare blacks, you name it. Would you take your child or grandchild to eat here among these creeps?" Hal nodded at the bag between them. "I mean, without that for protection?"

Tom glanced over at the teenager again, the one who called him an asshole. The kid was arguing with his girlfriend. "They have no idea how close to death they are right now," Hal was saying. "Doesn't that make you feel powerful, Tom? Knowing what you could do?"

Tom smiled and nodded.

Carrying a flower arrangement and a small boom box, Avery stepped inside the hospital room. The blinds were open, baking the place in sunlight. A pine-scented air freshener failed to completely camouflage the sharp smell of urine. Someone had cranked up the bed, so Avery's night-owl wife had no choice but to sit there, squinting in the harsh morning glare. They'd combed her unwashed hair back behind her ears. Her wrists were still bound, but now a padded material cushioned the encircling straps to prevent bruises. As Avery walked into the room, Joanne didn't seem to notice. She continued to stare out the window, her pale face pinched up.

Setting the flowers and the boom box on her nightstand, Avery tried to smile. "I figured you might want to listen to some of those homemade tapes. You know, the ones you take on the road? Jesus, it's hot in here. What are they trying to do to you?" He moved to a window, opened it a crack, then lowered the blinds. "Is that better, Joanne?"

She said nothing. She didn't seem to know he was there. At least she'd stopped squinting. Avery returned to her bedside and kissed her cheek. "Do you feel like talking today?" he asked gently.

No response. She stared at the window.

"How about some music? This is your seventies tape." He pressed the button on the boom box. Joni Mitchell came on, singing "Morning Morgantown."

Grimacing, Joanne began to squirm. She sucked air between her clinched teeth. It was as if the music were fingernails on a blackboard.

"Oops, sorry." Avery switched off the recording. "Joni isn't cutting it, huh?" He felt so lame. He couldn't reach her.

Joanne sighed, then went back to gazing at the window.

He caressed her arm, and at least she didn't pull away. That faint, underlying smell of urine became more pungent. Avery realized that she'd wet herself. He kept stroking her arm. Joanne was gone. He could no longer hope that she was simply "playing to the balcony." This was real.

After a while, he rang for the nurse. A tall, big-boned, twenty-something blonde came to the door. "Yes, Mr. Cooper?" she said.

"Um, my wife wet the bed," Avery explained in a raspy voice.

"Oh, well, that's all right," the nurse said gently. "We have her in diapers. I'll change her as soon as you leave."

Avery hesitated. "Well, I—I'll take off now so you can do that. Thanks."

He leaned over Joanne and gently kissed her forehead. "See ya, honey."

She still didn't seem to know he was there.

Avery thanked the nurse again. He stepped out to the corridor, then started toward Dr. Wetherall's office, where he would sign the necessary papers to have his wife transferred to a mental institution.

He aimed and squeezed the trigger. Something was off today. He missed the Dr Pepper bottle on the ranch's front porch railing. "Damn," Tom muttered. He was hot and sweaty. The Egg McMuffin from breakfast wasn't sitting too well in his stomach.

"It's okay, Tom," Hal said patiently. He stood behind him, nursing a Sprite from the cooler. He wore sunglasses and a baseball hat. "It's a new gun. You need to become accustomed to the feel of it. That's why we're here."

Tom fired and missed again. "When am I supposed to do this for real?"

"Next Tuesday morning," Hal said.

Lowering the gun, Tom turned to gape at him. "My God, so soon?"

"It's six days away," Hal said, with an amused grin. "You'll be fine. It's all planned out. No room for error. We have a friend in Dayle *Slutton*'s camp, which gives us access to her schedule—among many other things. On Tuesday morning, she'll be shooting scene eighty-seven, in which her character addresses an AA meeting with about twenty-five extras. All those people will provide just the right amount of commotion once you start shooting. She'll be at a podium, an easy target. We'll give you instructions where to stand." He gulped down some more Sprite, and stifled a burp. "Get in at least two shots. Go for the head. Before you even fire a third shot, our security guard will turn on you with the blanks, and you'll go down quick. That's the tricky part. You don't want any Johnny-come-lately guards wanting to get their two cents in."

"This sounds pretty complicated," Tom said warily.

"We'll practice. It's all choreographed and staged, Tom. You won't have to play dead for more than a minute before the second ambulance arrives. That'll be us. Remember, everyone will be paying more attention to Miss *Slutton*, and she'll get the first ambulance—though it might as well be a Hearse picking her up. Right?"

Tom shrugged. "Well, I can't guarantee—"

"I have confidence in you, Tom." He finished off his Sprite, and tossed his empty can on the dusty ground. "An hour after pulling that trigger, you'll be cleaned up and on a plane with enough money to retire in Mexico or Rio de Janeiro or some-place. Not bad, huh? Can't you see yourself living out your golden years at a tropical villa—sipping cocktails, a ceiling fan swirling overhead, exotic birds chirping? Take a day to think about where you'd like to go. By the way, we're paying you a quarter of a million for your efforts."

Tom stared at him in disbelief. Was this guy on the level? He wiped the sweat off his brow. "I had no idea," he managed to reply.

"Sure," Hal nodded. "Least we could do, Tom. Any more questions?"

"Only a ton," Tom said, with a dazed chuckle. It was all coming a little too fast at him. "I mean, how are you getting me on the set when they're shooting this scene eighty whatever it is?"

"Scene eighty-seven." Hal smiled reassuringly. "Like I said, we have someone working close to Dayle Sutton. You'll have clearance. It's being taken care of right now, as we speak. You'll use the name Gordon Swann."

"His name is Gordon Swann," Dennis told the head of studio security over the phone. "Be sure they allow him on the set Tuesday morning."

"I'll make a note of it, Dennis."

"I've also cleared him with the assistant director, because I won't be around. I have Tuesday off. I'm helping my girlfriend move. Page me if there's a problem. Okay?"

"You got it."

"Oh, and one more thing," Dennis said into the phone. "Do me a huge favor, tell the guard not to stick him in another time zone. It's important that he gets a good look at Dayle during the shoot. So give him a spot close to the action. Will you make sure about that?''

''For you, Dennis, I'll make dead certain.''

The man on the other end of the line couldn't see Dennis Walsh smile.

Dennis handed her a bottle of Evian water. ''Here. Don't say I never gave you anything.'' He sat on the steps to her trailer door.

''Thanks.'' Dayle said, twisting open the bottle. She rested in her ''star'' chair outside the open door of her trailer. For another flashback sequence, she sported a sixties look: a Petula Clark–influenced auburn wig, coral frost lipstick, and Twiggy-style, inch-long false eyelashes. She wore fat plastic earrings, a miniskirt, and a ribbed turtleneck. According to Dennis, she looked like *The Girl from U.N.C.L.E.*

Providing her with a fresh Evian bottle every couple of hours had been Bonny's self-appointed undertaking. Dayle had briefly talked to her on the phone this morning. Bonny sounded tired and doped up, but still managed to get in a dig about ''human target'' not being part of her job description. She was supposed to be out of the hospital by next week, in plenty of time for Thanksgiving at home. Meanwhile, Dayle had a temporary stand-in.

The telephone rang in her trailer. ''I'll pick it up,'' Dennis volunteered. He ducked into the trailer. A few moments later, he emerged with her cordless phone. ''It's Slick Nick the Private Dick. Want to 'rap' with him?''

''Nick?'' Dayle sat up. ''Yes, I'll take it. Thanks.''

Dennis gave her the phone, then settled back on the trailer steps.

''Hello, Nick?''

''Yo, you got me. Y'know, that assistant of yours is a real wiseass.''

"No kidding," Dayle said. "Do you have any news for me?"

"Sure do," he said. "One of the five license plate numbers you gave me doesn't go with the others. It's some schmuck from Burbank, probably boinking his secretary. But the other four rental plates matched with credit cards that seem to belong to a group. I don't know if the names on these cards are real, but feature this: three of these same dudes were renting cars and staying at the Sandpiper Motel in Portland, Oregon, when Tony Katz and his boyfriend bought the farm. And two of them had a return engagement a couple of weeks later when Leigh Simone cashed in her chips. All those credit cards have the same mailing address, a post office box in Opal."

"Opal?"

"It's a little town in Idaho. So here's the skinny. I'm catching a plane to Boise or Spokane tomorrow morning. But it might be a few days before I can track down who in Opal is paying these hotel and car rental bills."

"A few days?" Dayle said.

"Yeah, we'd need a court order to find out who has that PO box. Even El Nerdo, our computer expert, can't help us with this one. I'll have to go to Opal and stake out the post office. Eventually, somebody's got to pick up their mail. And Nick Brock will be on them like ugly on an ape."

"That's good, I guess," Dayle said. "Listen, we better give this information to the police. Maybe you can fax it—"

"Woah, wait a minute, Ms. Sutton. The last thing you want right now is for the cops to catch on. Once the feds descend on Opal, this group will scatter in a dozen different directions, and we're back to square one. They have to think it's business as usual. That's how I'm gonna catch them with their pants down. I'll fax you the info at home, in case something should happen to yours truly—God forbid. But don't hand it over to the cops just yet, okay? Give old Nick forty-eight hours at least."

"Well, all right," she said with a sigh. "I'll give you 'til Sunday."

"Fantastic. I'll call you from Opal tomorrow."

"Well, good luck, Nick," she replied. "And, hey, for the record, you're pretty damn good at what you do."

"Hey, think I'm good on the job? Check me out during playtime."

Dayle shook her head. "Nick, you're a pig, you really are. God knows why I like you. B'bye." She clicked off and handed the phone to Dennis.

"So who's Opal?" he asked with a curious smile.

"It's a little town in Idaho," Dayle said. "Nick's on his way there tomorrow."

"Well, this place is pretty nice, Mom," Avery said into the cordless phone. Exhausted, he sat slouched in a deck chair by the pool. For the last hour, he'd been putting off this call to his parents.

Joanne had been transferred by ambulance to Glenhaven today. Avery had gone there to say good-bye and drop off some of her clothes. They discouraged visitors for the first week. He saw her only briefly, and she didn't seem to recognize him. Coming home, he felt the house to be so empty. He was used to being alone here, but this was a totally different kind of solitude. Joanne wasn't in New York, passionately working on a play. She was in a sanitarium. And if she came back, would she ever be the same? It was as if something about the house had died. Avery aimlessly wandered from room to room, and finally settled by the pool—with a beer and the cordless phone. Maybe Joanne truly didn't want to be rescued out here the other morning.

By the time he called his parents, he was pretty much cried out. He even managed to sound upbeat for them. "The people at Glenhaven gave me a tour yesterday," he said. "They have these beautiful gardens and walking paths, a pool, private jacuzzis, saunas, messages, lots of personal attention.''

"Did they say if she'll be out in time for Thanksgiving?" his father asked on the other extension. "Or do they think it might be longer?"

"They're really not sure, Pop. But I know she's better off there than she was in the hospital."

Someone buzzed from the front gate. Avery hopped off the pool chair and hurried into the house. "Somebody's at the door. Can you hold on for a sec?" He stole a glance out the front window. A police car waited at the end of his driveway. Avery went to the intercom and pressed the button. "Yes?"

"Mr. Cooper, this is Sergeant Rick Swanson of the Beverly Hills Police. We'd like to accompany you to the station for some questioning. It shouldn't take too long. Could you let us in?"

Avery covered the mouthpiece of the phone so his parents wouldn't hear. "Am I under arrest?" he asked.

"Oh, no, Mr. Cooper. They simply want to ask you some questions down at headquarters, that's all. We've been instructed to escort you."

"Um, I'm not dressed," Avery said. "Let me put some clothes on, then I'll buzz you in." He brought the phone back up to his ear. "Mom? Pop? Can I call you back? It might not be until tomorrow. I have something going on here that's kind of important—"

"What happened?" his father asked. "I can tell from your voice that something's wrong. . . ."

"I'm fine, Pop, really. Let me call you later. Okay?"

As soon as he disconnected with his folks, Avery phoned Sean's cellular number. He caught her at the lab where they'd analyzed his sperm samples. He explained about the police waiting outside his house.

"Don't let them in," Sean said. "Dayle's chauffeur and stand-in were gunned down by a man dressed like a cop, driving a patrol car. No. Don't do a thing until I check on this. What's this police sergeant's name again?''

"Swanson," Avery said.

"Okay. Sit tight until you hear back from me."

She hung up. Avery glanced out the window again—at the police car parked by his front gate. The cop stood near the intercom on the post.

With the cordless in his hand, Avery went back and closed the sliding glass door to the pool area. A feeling of dread gnawed at his insides. He checked out front again. The cop was now staring up at the house, arms crossed.

The telephone rang, and Avery quickly answered it. "Yes, hello?"

"Hi. It's me," Sean said. "I checked. These guys are on the level. They're taking you in for some questioning. I'll meet you at the station. Don't tell them anything until I get there. Okay?"

"Right. Thank you, Sean."

Avery hung up, took a deep breath, and walked into the front hall. He pressed the switch for the front gate. Then at the window, he watched the police car slowly pull into his driveway.

Sean clicked off her cellular and apologized to the lab supervisor for the interruption. Avery's sperm samples had been stored and analyzed here at Kurtis Labs. The receptionist up front had given Sean a lab coat to wear, then sent her to this supervisor, a fidgety man in his mid-fifties named Alan Keefer. He had dark hair, a rubbery smile, and beneath his white lab coat, he wore a yellow polyester shirt and a tie that just had to be clip-on.

They sat in his office, which looked into one of the main labs. Through the window, Sean had a view of everyone at work, hunched over microscopes, transferring test tubes back and forth from refrigerators to centrifuges, punching data into computers.

Keefer explained that they'd run tests on all nine sperm samples and come up with the same donor, Avery Cooper. He also insisted that his lab team was beyond reproach. But Sean had cross-examined enough people in her day to trust her instincts that Alan Keefer was hiding something. And while he talked, he seemed to be leering at her.

Someone else wouldn't stop staring at her. An obese bearded man in a lab coat kept shooting her looks through the office window. Sean had been about to ask if she could talk with some of the other technicians when Avery had called on her cellular.

She slipped the phone back in her purse, pulled out a business card, and scribbled on the back of it. "I'm sorry, I have to run," she said, placing the card on Keefer's desk. "I wonder if I could come back at a later date, maybe interview some of your staff."

"Well, speaking of dates, maybe I could interview you over dinner some time?" Keefer asked with his rubbery smile. He walked her to his office door.

"Oh, that sounds nice," Sean said. "But I'm awfully busy with this case, and any free time I have, I spend with my husband and children."

"Well, I'm busy too," he replied coolly, the smile gone. "If you'd like to see me again, you'll have to make an appointment in advance. And I'm sorry, but I can't have you taking my people away from their jobs for these interviews. You'll have to make some sort of other arrangements."

Sean nodded. "I see. Well, thank you for your time, Mr. Keefer. I left my card on your desk. Avery Cooper's phone number is on the back. If you have any new information about those samples, I trust you'll call one of us."

"Yes, of course," he grunted.

Turning to leave, Sean caught the overweight lab technician

staring at her again. Something told her that this visit to Kurtis Labs wasn't quite the dead end it seemed. But she didn't have any time to ponder that now. The police were about to interrogate Avery, and she needed to be there with him.

Rain pelted the hood of Sean's car, and the windows were fogging up. Neon lights from the drive-in burger joint illuminated droplets on the windshield. Sean sat at the wheel, nibbling her french fries while Avery devoured his cheeseburger like a starving man. The session with the police had left him tired and ravenous.

Riding in the back of that patrol car on his way to the station, Avery had been so sure he wouldn't return home for at least a couple of days—or however long it took to post bail. The policemen had led him into a small conference room. He'd seen enough movies to know that the large mirror on the wall was a two-way job—with someone else on the other side. They started asking about his activities on Friday night, November fourteenth. Avery politely refused to answer any questions until his lawyer was present.

Sean arrived within five minutes, and sat down beside him at the table. She was professional and courteous. Avery could tell the detectives liked her despite themselves. She whispered to him at the start, "Don't mention any conspiracy right now. It's too soon and we don't have any evidence to back that up yet. Okay?"

She didn't interrupt him much, and instinctively knew when to rescue him. "I'm sorry, guys," she'd say with a smile. "My client can't answer that at this time. Do you have another question?"

Eventually, they asked if Avery would furnish them with a sperm sample. Sean Olson jumped in before he could answer. "For the time being, I've advised my client not to submit to that," she said.

The interrogation lasted three hours. Although he hadn't been formally charged, Avery remained a suspect in Libby Stoddard's murder.

"End of round one," Sean told him, picking at her order of fries. She glanced out the rain-beaded window. "I think our boys in blue are jerking you around a bit. My guess is that they already have a DNA match on the sperm sample from Libby and your skin tissue under her fingernails. If you had a hairbrush lying around when they were in your house the other day, they probably collected and tested a sample of your hair too. They don't really need your sperm, Avery. But it looks good for their case if they asked for a sample and you refused."

"Looks even better for them if I furnish a sample and it matches."

"Exactly," Sean said, sipping her Coke. "Either way, you're screwed. We're on borrowed time here."

Avery crumbled up his food bag. "Huh, could you tell me some good news?"

"Well, you have a lawyer who believes you're innocent," Sean offered. "I'd like to talk to your friends, the Webers, at their place tomorrow evening. Then we'll go through and retrace everything you did that Friday night. Think you're up for that?"

Avery nodded. "I'll call George. I can also review those security videos with you again during the day—if you'd like. I'm not working this week. I don't have any plans."

"You aren't seeing your wife?" Sean asked.

Frowning, he shook his head. "This new place doesn't allow visitors the first couple of weeks."

For a moment, there was just the patter of rain on the roof, and paper bags rustling as they put their uneaten food away. Avery turned and caught her gazing at him. Sean quickly turned away.

"It's horrible to see someone you love slip away in front of you," he said. "I feel so powerless, so sad and angry at the same time. I can't quite describe it. . . ."

"You don't have to describe it for me, Avery," she murmured.

It took a moment for him to realize what she was talking about. He felt so stupid. "Of course," he said. "I'm sorry, Sean."

"Don't sweat it," she replied, setting the food bag aside. Sean started up the car, then switched on the lights and the windshield wipers. "I should take you home." She backed out of the space, then turned out of the lot.

Avery stared at the wipers fanning back and forth. "I'm used to Joanne being away. But this is different. I've never felt this kind of loneliness. I don't know how you handle it, Sean."

"You keep going, Avery," she replied, studying the road ahead. "You just keep going."

Nineteen

POLICE QUESTION AVERY COOPER IN BRUTAL RAPE-MURDER. So said the headline running across the bottom half of the morning's *Los Angeles Times*'s front page—along with a somber photo of him.

A mob was waiting at the end of the driveway as Avery left his house. Behind the wheel of his BMW, he slowly cruised toward the wrought-iron doors. About thirty reporters and fifty spectators had amassed outside the gate. Several of them carried signs: KILLER COOPER, BEVERLY HILLS BUTCHER, and AVERY COOPER: PRO-ABORTION, PRO-GUN CONTROL, PRO-RAPE, PRO-MURDER! This last wordy placard was held by a middle-aged woman in a pink sweatshirt that identified her as a FOXY GRANDMA. Avery caught a closer look at Foxy's handiwork when she slammed the sign against his windshield.

Riding the brake, he tried to ignore the angry shouts, the people spitting on his car and pounding on the hood. Avery crawled through the crowd, then picked up speed. He watched them growing more distant in his rearview mirror. But a white

Taurus emerged from the throng, one of the "rental mentals," Sean had told him about. Avery had to cut someone off, then speed through a yellow light to elude the car. By the time he reached Sean's office building, he figured he'd lost him. He parked in back of the hair salon.

Sean appeared tired when she met him in her office doorway. She wore houndstooth check, pleated pants and a clinging black, crew-neck sweater that showed off her figure. On their way to Avery's car, she admitted she wasn't in a good mood. She'd slept on her office sofa last night, and had to find out this morning that her husband's respirator had gone on the blink at three A.M. He'd been turning blue from lack of oxygen. It had taken the nurse on duty fifteen minutes to find the blockage in his tubes and fix it.

"At least we avoided another trip to the hospital," Sean said. "But I should have been there for him. I would have known what to do, because it's happened before." She put on her sunglasses and rolled down her window. "So how about you?" she asked. "Did you phone this Glenhaven place yet?"

"I'm waiting until this afternoon," Avery said, eyes on the road. "I called my friends, George and Sheila, and they're expecting us around six."

"I hope my mood improves by then," Sean said. "I feel eight different types of lousy this morning."

"Well, maybe the tide will change," Avery offered, with a shrug.

"Yeah, the tide can change," she said, nodding tiredly. "What the heck? Maybe today's the day we'll find something in those security videos to prove you were set up. You never know."

Avery glanced in his rearview mirror. He didn't see anyone on his tail. But it suddenly hit him. "The 'rental mentals,' " he said. "I never noticed those guys until you told me about them. But on the videos, I've seen cars parked down the street across from the front gate. Haven't you?"

"I assumed they were your neighbors."

"Maybe," he said. "Maybe not. I never thought to check the car types or if anyone was sitting inside. Maybe we could prove—as part of a set up—someone was watching me and the house before Libby was murdered. . . ."

"My God, you're right," Sean muttered. "I made a list of license plate numbers from the rental cars that have been following Dayle. If we match one of those plate numbers with a car in front of your house, we can introduce the conspiracy angle, establish reasonable doubt." Sean patted his shoulder. "We might need certain images from the security video blown up. Do you know someone at the studio who could do that for us?"

Avery nodded. "Yes, it should be easy."

"Except I don't have my copy of the list." Sean frowned. "I took it home for safekeeping—in case those people broke into my office. Only my little girl decided to clean off my desk for me, and threw it away, God love her." Sean bit her lip. "Hmmm, I faxed the list to Dayle. If I remember right, she gave it to this private detective she hired. We might have to track him down. . . ."

Wasn't there a single *Playgirl* at Spokane's airport? Nick Brock had time to kill before picking up his bags. But the search for his magazine proved in vain. None of the newsstands carried it. Disappointed, he plodded down to baggage claim, then rented a car. The three-hour drive to Opal, Idaho, had scenery right out of a beer commercial, real "Land of Sky Blue Waters" stuff.

Opal lay smack-dab in the middle of all this mountain splendor. The quaint city center, located three blocks off Opal Lake, seemed like the type of place that shut down by six P.M. Very clean and friendly. Dull as hell.

But on the edge of town, Nick noticed a couple of taverns,

a McDonald's (open until the unholy hour of ten P.M.), and several hotels to accommodate the tourists taking advantage of Opal's natural wonders—hunting, fishing, hiking, and in the summertime, camping, boating, and swimming.

Nick had made reservations at Debbie's Paradise View Motor Inn. Tackle equipment and mounted fish decorated the lobby walls, and the furniture was made of unfinished logs with Indian-weave cushions thrown on top—stylized rustic crap. A cute, young blonde worked the front desk. Her hair had been teased and curled, and there was a touch of teenage acne on that pretty face. Nick couldn't resist flirting with her. Her name was Amber. "Debbie" was her grandmother, and the old witch had skipped to Reno for the week.

Amber happily gave him directions to the post office. It wasn't yet noon, and the leaser of PO Box 73 probably hadn't picked up the mail today. Nick winked and thanked Amber. Blushing, she smiled and stepped back. He noticed her spandex miniskirt showed off a great set of legs and a sweet butt. He also glimpsed a small magazine rack behind the desk, and there it was: his *Playgirl*.

"Hey, you got it!" Nick said, pointing to the rack. "Check it out, the *Playgirl*. Page thirty-four. You might be interested, honey." He grabbed his suitcase and headed for the door. Nick glanced over his shoulder at Amber. She was thumbing through the magazine; then she stopped suddenly—on *his* page, he was sure. "Omigod!" Amber squealed, obviously impressed.

Smiling, Nick moved on. Made his day.

"I think we found something to prove there's a conspiracy," Sean said on the other end of the line.

The phone to her ear, Dayle sat at the vanity table in her trailer. She'd been touching up her "old" face for a scene in which her character has aged into her mid-sixties. Her hair had been spray-dyed a mousey gray, and they'd added some crow's-feet, laugh lines, and liver spots. She wore a tweed suit and pearls. "What did you find?" she asked, turning away from the mirror.

"Avery and I are here in this editing room at his studio, looking at security videos taken outside his home. We noticed some rental cars parked across from his house."

"They're following him too?"

"Looks that way," Sean said. "We're having a few of the video images blown up and enhanced so we can see the license plates. Here's where you come in, Dayle. Do you still have that list of plate numbers I faxed you? Or did you give it to that Nick character, the centerfold?"

"I still have a copy at my place," Dayle said. "I can fax it to your office when I get home tonight. Would seven-thirty be too late?"

"No. That would be fantastic, Dayle. Thanks a lot."

"We'll talk tonight, okay? Take care."

As Dayle hung up the phone, she heard someone on the steps to her trailer. She went to the door and opened it. Dennis stood there.

He looked startled. "I was just about to knock," he said. "I need to talk to you. It's important."

"All right," she said, mystified. "C'mon in."

Dennis stepped inside, and closed the door. "You better sit down for this. It's not good news."

"Okay." She sat across from him at her vanity. "What happened?"

"Does the name Cindy Zellerback ring a bell? A distant bell?"

Dayle kept very still. "What about her?"

"She—um, recently completed a prison sentence for killing her husband and baby. She claims that she had sex with you a long time ago. Apparently, she's now born again or something. The point is, at this very minute, Elsie Marshall is interviewing her in front of a studio audience. They're taping this afternoon's show.''

Dayle felt a little sick. She just stared at him.

''I only now found out,'' Dennis continued. ''The reporters are banging down the studio door for a statement. Publicity wants to talk to you as well.''

Dayle reached for an Evian bottle on her vanity. It was empty. Sighing, she pitched it in the wastebasket. ''Wouldn't you know, they'd leak the story to Elsie? She'll get lots of mileage out of it.''

''Then the story is true,'' he said quietly.

''Yes, Dennis. It's true.'' She took a deep breath. ''Listen, I need some time alone right now.''

''You got it.'' Dennis started for the door, but he hesitated and turned to her. ''You can trust me, Dayle. You know that, don't you?''

She nodded. ''I'm counting on it.''

''Hi, Elsie!'' the studio audience cheered in unison.

''Hi, and welcome back to *Common Sense!*'' Elsie Marshall said. ''I know I'm breaking a lot of hearts out there when I tell you my Drew won't be here today. He's in Washington, D.C.''

There was a wave of feminine sighs and murmurs of disappointment from the studio audience. Elsie held up her hands. ''But we have an unusual guest this afternoon, and you won't want to miss what she has to tell us!''

The camera pulled back to show Elsie sitting at her desk. She wore a white dress with red piping and a sailor collar. She hadn't yet introduced her guest: a dowdy dishwater-blonde with bad posture. She sat across from Elsie, studying the studio audience with some readable contempt and trepidation. She had on a pale, flowery dress that had gone out of style ten years ago.

Dayle barely recognized Cindy. She watched Elsie's show on a big-screen TV in the studio's VIP visitors' lounge. She was still in her matronly makeup and wardrobe. She'd agreed to work late if they filmed around her for the next couple of hours.

"Today we're talking some *common sense* with a real survivor," Elsie announced. Then she turned to Cindy with a sudden, phony concern. "I understand you had an *intimate, lesbian* relationship with an established film star when you were only nineteen years old."

"Oh, Jesus," Dayle groaned. She reached for a memo pad and a pen.

"Yeah, I was nineteen," Cindy said. She leaned toward Elsie. "But I want to make it clear that I've rejected the sinful lifestyle I once had."

With a little pout, Elsie gazed into the camera. "My guest today is Cynthia Zellerback, who was drawn into drugs and the gay scene eighteen years ago. Cindy's here to tell us her story—which included a sexual relationship with film personality Dayle Sutton. . . ."

Elsie paused to give the studio audience a chance to gasp—and gasp they did—while she nodded emphatically. "Yes, it's true!"

People were still murmuring when Elsie turned to Cindy. "Eventually, you tried to reject this lesbian lifestyle and lead a normal, Christian life. But even with a husband and baby, you wouldn't 'go straight,' would you?"

Frowning, Cindy shook her head. "No. And if it weren't for my drug and sexual dependencies, I don't think—*it* wouldn't have happened."

"For the studio audience and our friends at home, Cindy," Elsie said in a whisper. "What exactly happened?"

"I killed my husband and baby daughter," she answered with hardly a tremor in her voice. "I was convicted, and I spent twelve years in prison. . . ."

More gasps and murmurs from the studio audience. Dayle took notes, scribbling furiously while Cindy described the murders as if someone else had committed them. Cindy said how much she missed her husband and her two-year-old, Sunshine. She even cried a little. If only she hadn't been doing drugs and having gay sex. She discovered the "power of God's forgiveness" in the federal pen.

Elsie patted her shoulder, and chimed in to announce a commercial break. "When we return, we'll talk some more *common sense* with Cindy about her lesbian affair with none other than Dayle Sutton. Don't go away!"

Dayle didn't go away. On her cellular, she phoned Dennis to let him know that she would read a brief statement for the press after Elsie's show.

"Hi, Elsie!"

"God bless you," Elsie chirped, coming back on and blowing a kiss to her audience. Now that everyone had Cindy Zellerback identified as a reformed drug-addicted, child-killing lesbian, Elsie didn't waste any time linking this *survivor* with a certain *liberal actress*. After less than a minute of chitchat with the audience, she turned once again to her guest.

"Cindy, you were only nineteen when you met Dayle Sutton. That's a young and impressionable age, isn't it?"

Cindy shrugged. "Sure."

"What was it like, meeting a movie star?"

"It was pretty cool," Cindy answered. "I was in Mexico with some friends, and heard they were shooting a movie nearby. So I started hanging around the set. I even got to be in a couple of crowd scenes."

"You also met Dayle Sutton," Elsie said. "Tell us, Cindy, were you doing drugs at the time?"

She sighed. "Yes, I was."

"Were a lot of people on this movie set doing drugs?"

"Oh, yeah."

"Including Dayle Sutton?"

Cindy nodded. "Sure, I guess."

"And Dayle Sutton was married at this time, wasn't she?"

"I think so," Cindy replied.

"Who initiated this—gay sexual encounter?" Elsie asked, with a sour look, as if it pained her to discuss this sordid business.

"It was mostly her," Cindy said. "I could tell before this, y'know, particular night that she was interested in me. And it was kind of exciting, because she was a movie star and all that. Plus, I heard people talk on the set about her being a lesbian. . . ."

Dayle studied Elsie's face, and as much as the old bitch tried, she couldn't contain a smile.

Dayle faced the press, flanked by Dennis and Ted. About forty reporters and several cameramen gathered outside the soundstage where she was filming *Waiting for the Fall* for this impromptu press conference. In her "old lady" garb, she looked very sweet and matronly. Yet Dayle had modified the makeup a little so that the pretty movie star shined through. Security was tight, with guards stationed every eight feet at a roped-off section around the podium where Dayle addressed the crowd.

"I'm in the middle of making a movie right now," Dayle announced. "Which explains why I'm dressed and made up this way. I'm sorry I won't have time to answer questions. But I'd like to make a statement for anyone who cares to listen." Dayle smiled at them. She needed these journalists on her side. "Actually, I'm not wearing any makeup. I've simply aged twenty-five years in the past hour while watching a certain 'talk show.' "

There were some laughs and titters among the reporters, and she heard Dennis behind her chuckling—almost too enthusiastically.

Elsie's show had ended only forty-five minutes ago. Dayle

had scribbled out a brief speech. She felt a strange calm. The "scandal" was out there now, thanks to Elsie Marshall. That left Dayle with damage control, an assignment the studio brass tried to entrust to their public relations department. "It's my ass on the line," Dayle had told a studio bigwig over the phone. "I'll handle this."

They wanted to check her speech, but the only person she let read it was Dennis, whose thumbs-up gave Dayle the confidence she now needed.

"I take enormous pride in the fact that I'm on Elsie Marshall's hate list," Dayle announced. "Elsie had a guest on her program today, a woman named Cindy Zellerback, who murdered her husband and child thirteen years ago. Now, the widow Marshall—to my knowledge—has never had a murderer on her show—morons, yes, but not murderers."

A few reporters laughed, but Dayle kept a straight face. "The reason Elsie put Cindy Zellerback on her show was that this particular convicted murderer claimed to have had sexual relations with me a few years before she killed her family. Ms. Zellerback's story first came to my attention earlier this week, by way of an anonymous note from someone who seemed to have extortion in mind. I chose to ignore it. Obviously, this mudslinger turned to the widow Marshall with this story. So in her attempt to publicly humiliate me, Elsie Marshall has consorted with an extortionist and a murderer."

Dayle shook her head and sighed. "Well, I'm a little embarrassed, but not humiliated. The story this woman told is indeed true. One night, sixteen years ago, while shooting a movie in Mexico, I went to a beach party and had too much to drink. While under the influence, I experimented with a nineteen-year-old named Cindy. The widow Marshall would like you to believe I corrupted this young woman, but I'd like to point out that I was the ripe old age of twenty-three at the time, and not much of a party girl. I have very little memory of my evening with Cindy Zellerback. I do, however, recall that the 'experiment' wasn't my idea of a good time. I never saw—or heard about—Cindy Zellerback again, not until the anonymous note last week.''

A wave of murmurs rippled through the crowd. Dayle shrugged. ''That's the extent of my association with this''— she shook her head—''this pathetic woman who killed her family. I can't understand how someone who preaches the power of God's forgiveness can also preach hate toward gays and lesbians. She blamed the murders of her husband and toddler daughter on drugs and her lesbian lifestyle—as if she herself weren't responsible at all. That's just not right. I'd feel sorry for Cindy Zellerback if she still weren't doing harm— this time with her demented moralizing. I'm glad my association with this pitiful woman was so brief, and forgettable—when my mind was clouded with drink. The widow Marshall, however, chose to associate with her in front of a television audience, and seems to consider her a colleague. What's clouding Elsie's mind? A powerful dose of hate, I'd say. Listen, Elsie, when you resort to the testimony of convicted murderers to trumpet your homophobic rhetoric, it's time to reevaluate your beliefs.''

A few reporters started to applaud, and others joined in. By the time Dayle stepped down from the podium, they were cheering her.

But in a deluxe penthouse suite at the Hyatt Regency in Washington, D.C., the reporters on hand scoffed at Dayle Sutton. Her speech was broadcasted live on the Entertainment News Network. Over thirty supporters of Drew and Elsie Marshall—many of them from the press—crowded the huge suite. Plied with drinks and hors d'oeuvres, they watched the telecast on a big-screen TV. They hadn't expected Dayle Sutton to respond so soon. The group had originally assembled with their host, Drew Marshall, to watch his mother interview the convicted murderer who had once been Dayle's lesbian lover.

Elsie's interview had been a great victory for Drew. The excitement and enthusiasm buzzing through the room had everyone nearly giddy. Dressed in a white linen shirt and jeans, he held court in a stuffed easy chair. He led the group in applause every time his mother got in a zinger against Dayle *Slutton*.

Then a call had come in saying that ENN would provide a live telecast of Dayle Sutton's response to today's *Common Sense* segment. Everyone stayed to witness Dayle Sutton's humiliation. They couldn't wait to see her squirm.

In reverence to Drew—and out of respect for his mother— several of the guests hissed at Dayle during her speech. But some people seemed uncomfortable, their mood plummeting from the zealous fever of an hour before. A few of them even left the room—very quietly. But the loyal ones stayed on to criticize and ridicule Dayle Sutton. Drew insisted that today was a moral victory for everyone who believed in family values.

With his beer in hand and a confident smile on his face, Drew turned to one of his associates. "Listen carefully to me," he said, under his breath. "When they shoot that whore next week, I want a piece of her goddamn brain for a souvenir. I don't care if they have to scrape it off the fucking floor, make sure someone brings it to me."

Drew caught a reporter's eye from across the room. He hoisted his beer stein as if to toast him and broke into his charming, boyish smile. "Hey, you're running on empty, Duane," he called. "Have another round!"

A pair of fuzzy dice dangled from the rearview mirror of the blue '89 Chrysler LeBaron. It pulled into the Reservations Only space in front of Debbie's Paradise View Motor Inn. Things were slow at the front desk. Amber had her nose in a

Cosmopolitan quiz, "Are You Getting the Most out of Mastur-bation?"

She glanced up from her magazine as the driver of the Le-Baron stepped into the lobby. With his mustache, receding gray-brown hair, and windburned face, he looked like a cowboy. He wore a denim jacket and tan sans-a-belt pants that rode low under his belly. He leaned against the counter. "I need Nick Brock's room number, honey."

Setting down her magazine, Amber consulted the guest file. "Brock?" she asked, snapping her gum. "There's nobody here by that name."

"You sure? Maybe he checked in under an alias."

Amber simply shrugged.

"Good-looking guy, about thirty, my height. Black hair—"

"Omigod, yeah, sure," Amber said with a smile. "Nick Brock. I remember thinking he didn't use the same name when he checked in." She grabbed a *Playgirl* from the magazine rack, then flipped through the pages until she found Nick Brock's butt shot. She set the open magazine on the counter, under the man's nose. "Is this the guy you mean?" Amber asked.

Sean felt as if she'd made a couple of friends this evening. Sheila Weber was a salt-of-the-earth type. Sean recalled going through that same stage of pregnancy, and Sheila lapped up the advice. George was cute, congenial, and obviously a wonderful friend to Avery. The Webers insisted that they stay for dinner. Sheila made a terrific chicken pasta.

Sean had to remind herself that the Webers were tight with Avery and his wife. There was no room for a fifth wheel.

Still, tonight had been special, and for a few minutes she'd stopped worrying about respirators and catheters. She hadn't thought about conspiracies and grand juries. She'd actually fooled herself for a while, and felt like part of a normal couple again.

They were now on their way to the park, where Avery's mystery woman had scratched his face. Sean had a tiny buzz from the Chianti the Webers had served with dinner. She glanced over at Avery in the driver's seat, watching the road ahead. She studied his profile, the strong jawline, and those long eyelashes. He was playing a tape of seventies music. He'd brought it to his wife in the hospital, but she hadn't wanted it.

Out of respect for James Taylor, and "Fire and Rain," neither of them talked. Sean sat quietly, enjoying the pretty drive along the coast. The cool air smelled sweet through the car window.

Avery pulled off the highway to a little alcove with six parking spaces. "This is it," he announced. He hopped out of the car, and hurried around to open the door for her. The wind had kicked up. Sean rubbed her arms from the chill. Avery dug a flannel-lined jacket out of the backseat, then placed it on her shoulders. They strolled down to the park benches and a little stone wall. The Pacific stretched out before them, rippling and moonlit.

"I watched the sunset that night," Avery said. "So it was earlier."

"When we go back to the car, remind me to call the weather bureau and find out what time the sun set on the fourteenth."

Avery nodded. "I stayed until dark, I remember." He pointed to a path by the rock wall. "That's where the woman came from. The trail dips down, then comes up to the other side of the parking alcove."

"Did you hear a car?"

"Yes. She asked if I was Avery Cooper. I heard the car. Then when I turned for a moment, she scratched my face."

"Was this car parked where yours is now?"

"Yes. But I don't recall the car type. It could have been a rental type. I'm not sure. I remember it was white. I was kind of dazed, and I didn't think to look for the license plate."

Sean glanced over at the small parking lot. "You couldn't have seen it very well from here anyway."

"You look cold," he said. "Why don't you put your arms in the sleeves?" Stepping in back of her, Avery helped her on with his jacket again. It carried a subtle musky fragrance she'd come to identify with him. "The zipper's a little tricky," he said, turning her around. "Let me help you."

Sean let him zip up the front of his jacket. He pinched and tugged at it for a moment. The jacket was roomy, its cuffs covering her knuckles. Without thinking, Sean reached up and touched his cheek. "You can barely see the scratch anymore," she said.

His eyes met hers. Avery hesitated, then smiled. Her fingertips lingered on his handsome face. She was filled with such longing and tenderness. She ached inside.

Sean made herself turn away. She swept back her windblown hair, and gazed out at the water. "It's beautiful here," she said. "But there's something—I don't know—very lonely about this spot. Didn't you say you often stop by here?"

Avery nodded.

"It's funny. Your public persona is one of this carefree, light-hearted guy. But there's a sadness in you—and I think it's been with you a long time. These last few days have been like a crash course in getting to know you, Avery. I learned a lot tonight. I really like your friends." She realized she was babbling, but couldn't help herself. "They—they'll make excellent character witnesses."

For a moment, they simply looked at each other. Finally, Avery turned away and glanced at the ocean. He shoved his hands in his pockets. "Is there anything else you need to ask me about that night?" he said.

"No," she replied. "Not right now. We can go if you'd like."

They went back to the car, and he opened the door for her. Sean touched his arm. "Thanks, Avery," she whispered. Then she climbed inside.

As he started up the car, the James Taylor song came on

again. Avery backed out of the parking spot. Neither of them said a word. The seventies tape serenaded them, and Sean kept her head turned toward the window, so he couldn't see the tears in her eyes.

They didn't notice any rental cars following them on their way back to her office. Avery had broken the awkward silence by talking about the case. He kept it all business. They parked behind the hair salon, and used the service entrance into the building. Avery carried Sean's briefcase for her.

In the dimly lit upstairs corridor, Sean fished the keys from her purse, opened the office door, and switched on the light. She headed for the fax machine. "The photos your friend made for us are in my briefcase—in the blue folder on top."

On the security video, they'd spotted three different cars parked at various times in front of Avery's house; rental-company favorites: a Taurus and two Corsicas. They'd enlisted the help of a starstruck, young videophile from production named Jamie. He'd blown up and enhanced three video images, each showing the cars' plate numbers.

Avery found Jamie's photos in the blue folder, while Sean examined the latest incoming fax. Dayle had scribbled on the cover sheet:

Dear Sean,
  Hope this is what you need. Attached is the list you originally gave me on a fax from my private detective friend. He's in Idaho, following this up. I'm home if you want to call. Don't show this list to the police until you've talked to me. Okay?
  Take Care, Dayle

Sean glanced at Nick Brock's note to Dayle, scribbled below the list of license plate numbers. He'd traced credit card payments for the rental cars to a PO Box 73 in Opal, Idaho. He was on his way there to stake out the post office. If Dayle needed him, he was registered as Tony Manero at Debbie's Paradise View Motor Inn in Opal.

"Does the name *Tony Manero* sound familiar?" Sean asked.

Avery shut her briefcase, and bought the photos over to her. "Wasn't that John Travolta's character in *Saturday Night Fever?*"

She nodded. "Huh, figures." Sean laid the photos down on her desk beside the listing. Two plate numbers matched: a Corsica, AOB-829, and a Taurus, EMK-903. Sean and Avery were both quiet for a moment, hunched over the desk together, shoulders touching. Finally, she patted his back. "At the very least, we've established some reasonable doubt, Avery."

"Thank God," he sighed, laughing. He slid his arm around Sean, and pulled her closer. "You're beautiful. You really are. . . ."

For a moment, Sean's whole body stiffened, and she could tell he sensed it. Except for the occasional consolation hug from her brother-in-law, she hadn't felt a man's arms around her for more than a year. And now this sweet, attractive man was holding her. "Um, Avery, I—"

"Oh, sorry," he said, stepping back. "I didn't mean to get so—enthusiastic."

"It's okay," she said awkwardly. "But I think we ought to call it a night. Maybe I can make it home in time to tuck my kids into bed."

"Oh, yeah, good idea," he said.

Sean took a deep breath, then started to put the papers in her briefcase. "Maybe you should spend the night at your friends' house. You shouldn't be alone. These same people tried to kill Dayle two nights ago. We have to be careful, Avery."

"Yeah, I know. George and Sheila are expecting me back." He moved toward the door. "I'll walk you down to your car."

Sean felt herself blushing. She wished she hadn't pulled away earlier. She wanted so much for him to hold her again— just for a moment. But she could never tell him that.

She closed her briefcase. "Yes," she said resolutely. "We both have to be very careful, Avery."

Twenty

George and Sheila's guest room was like his home away from home, and sleep should have come easily. But Avery had been tossing and turning for hours. He glanced at the nightstand clock for umpteenth time: 3:27 A.M. The house was quiet. He'd heard Sheila a while ago, padding to and from the bathroom. As she recently pointed out, she was peeing for two now.

It seemed so long ago that Joanne was healthy and they were trying to get pregnant. He remembered how she'd appeared to him on the balcony that morning he'd been swimming, how she'd dropped her robe and stood before him naked. It was hard to connect that sexy, fun woman with the catatonic he'd had committed to an institution three days ago.

His dad had asked if Joanne would be out by Thanksgiving— only a week away. Not very likely. He wasn't even sure if she'd be home in time for Christmas. He couldn't imagine the holidays without her. Even when they'd had conflicting schedules, Joanne and he had always managed to spend Christmas Eve together. It was quite possible that he'd be spending the Yuletide in a federal prison—and Joanne would still be in that place. *Think you're lonely, scared, and hopeless right now? Just wait a few weeks. . . .*

Avery sat up, switched on the light, and reached for the phone. Maybe all he needed was to hear another person's voice, any familiar voice. He dialed home and listened to the messages he'd forgotten to retrieve last night. His agent and Steve Bensinger had left messages, and so had his parents.

He didn't know what to make of the last call—at 9:52 P.M.: "Hello, Avery Cooper? This is Gene Clavey. I'm a technical analyst here at Kurtis Labs. I recently examined your sperm samples for Dr. Nathan. Your attorney was asking some questions around here yesterday. I'm curious about a few things. We might help each other out. Why don't you give me a call?"

He tried Gene Clavey's office number at 8:45. Hunched over the Webers' breakfast table with his second cup of coffee, Avery anxiously counted four ring tones until a man answered: "Kurtis Labs, this is Gene."

"Hello, Gene Clavey? This is Avery Cooper returning your call."

"Oh, hello," the man replied tentatively. There was an awkward pause.

"Can you talk right now?" Avery asked.

"No, not really."

"Why? Is someone there?"

"Oh, yeah, you bet," he replied cheerfully.

"You have information about the sperm samples?"

"That's right."

"Tell me this much. Did all those sperm samples match?"

"Not right now. But lunch would be great—if you're buying. How about meeting me at Pink's Famous Chili Dogs on Melrose? Say eleven-thirty to beat the crowd?"

"Can I bring my lawyer?" Avery asked.

"Yeah, why not?"

"Do you know what I look like?"

"Of course. See ya at Pink's. Take it easy."

There was a click on the other end of the line.

"Was anyone following you?" Sean asked. She locked her office door, and they started down the corridor toward the back stairs.

"Yeah, but I think I lost him." Avery reached for Sean's briefcase.

"I got it, thanks," she said, briskly. Sean had a strange, all-business energy about her this morning. And she'd barely even made eye contact with him so far. "I've been a busy girl," she announced, starting up the car and backing out of the space. "I called your Dr. Nathan. He faxed me a list of employees at the clinic and the lab—everyone who had access to your sperm samples. Gene Clavey is on the list, so he's no phony. I think he's this overweight man I saw there the other day." From the alley, she merged into traffic. "Six employees have either been let go or quit since you and Joanne started going to the clinic. If those samples were tampered with, my guess is that one of these six 'former employees' is the responsible party."

She glanced in her rearview mirror. "By the way, keep your eyes peeled for any 'rental mentals.' "

"Will do." Avery checked the side mirror, and didn't see anything.

"I called that hotel in Idaho where Dayle's detective pal is staying," Sean went on. "But he wasn't in. How much further to this Chili Dog place?"

"A few more blocks," Avery said. He stole a glance at her. "Are you okay, Sean? You seem a bit distant this morning."

"I'm fine," she answered, staring straight ahead. "I actually cooked pancakes for my kids before they went to school. And my husband slept through the night. So I have no complaints. How's your wife doing?''

"Better. She let one of the nurses feed her some dinner last night. I'll know more this afternoon when I call for an update.'' He caught her eye and smiled sadly. "It's ironic we got thrown together—with our similar situations.''

"I don't know what you mean,'' she said coolly.

"Well, sure you do. In fact, I think that's why we're drawn to each other. I understand what you're going through, because our situations—''

"I don't agree at all,'' Sean said, eyes on the road.

"I beg your pardon?''

"Your wife has been sick, what, a week? And she has a very good chance of getting well. My husband won't be getting well. For the past year, he hasn't been able to walk, eat, breathe, shit, or pee without some kind of assistance. In all that time, I haven't heard him laugh or say my name. He can't even squeeze my hand. Our situations are different, Avery.''

He stared at her. "I didn't mean to offend you. I just—''

"I'm your attorney, Avery,'' she continued. "I don't need you understanding me—or trying to understand me. My job here—my main concern—is proving your innocence in this murder case. Can we please keep this on a professional level?''

Frowning, Avery sat back. "I didn't know it was against the rules for us to be friends.'' He nodded at the upscale greasy spoon on the corner of Melrose, half a block away. "That's Pink's Chili Dogs on your right.''

Sean steered into the parking lot. She didn't say anything, and neither did he. They climbed out of the car, and walked around the squat chrome, glass, and neon diner to the front entrance.

"Mr. Cooper?''

Both Avery and Sean turned. A rotund man waved at them from one of the outside picnic tables. The sun reflected off his glasses, and illuminated the sweat on his forehead. He had a beard, and wild, curly strawberry-blond hair that needed trimming. He took up nearly half a picnic bench, which seemed ready to splinter from the strain.

"Are you Gene Clavey?" Avery asked.

"Yes, sir." He made a token attempt to stand up by leaning forward as he pumped Avery's hand. "Sorry I acted so weird over the phone. My boss was in the room, and I didn't want him knowing about this." He glanced at Sean. "You're the lawyer. I saw you in Keefer's office the other day."

She nodded. "Sean Olson. Yes, I remember. Pleased to meet you."

Again, he inched up for a second, then shook her hand. "They'll be coming out with my food soon. You can order here. Sit. Take a load off."

They sat down across from him.

Gene grinned at Avery. "You know, I've lived in L.A. for over two years, and you're the first movie star I've ever met. It's kind of a kick."

"Well, the thrill's all mine—depending on what you have to tell me. You examined those specimens for Dr. Nathan's clinic?"

Gene nodded. "I saw the newspaper yesterday, and realized why you were asking about those samples a couple of days back." He smiled at Sean. "After you showed up at the lab, I snuck a peek at your business card on Keefer's desk. You folks think somebody stole one of those sperm samples and planted it in the dead woman. The old turkey baster transfer. Am I right?"

"Something like that, yes," Sean said. "The report we received from Dr. Nathan was that all nine of Avery's sperm samples matched."

"It figures." Gene scratched the side of his beard with his big, chubby hand. "Keefer must have covered it up and lied to Dr. Nathan. He's probably afraid you'd sue—and you should."

"Then the samples didn't match?" Avery asked.

Gene chuckled cynically. "Hell, those nine samples were like a Kellogg's Variety Pack. Only two were from the same donor—you. Someone must have switched the labels on the other seven."

Sean grabbed Avery's arm and squeezed it. He patted her hand, and she didn't pull away. "Do you have proof?" he asked.

Gene took a folder out from under his thigh. "Presto chango. The lab report." He handed it to Sean.

A waitress arrived with a tray of three chili dogs, large fries, and a supersize soft drink. Avery ordered a chili dog and a Coke; Sean asked for a hot dog and a Sprite. Once the waitress left, Sean opened the lab folder. "That's an original," Gene said, nibbling a fry. "The copy I made is in the files at Kurtis Labs. I hear photocopied documents don't stand up in court."

"You're a very smart man, Gene," Sean said, studying the report.

He bit into his chili dog, then wiped some food off his beard. "You might not understand the lingo," he said. "Basically, I reported that only two of the nine samples are from the same donor—Avery Cooper. I think it's on page four that I describe the other specimens. But this wasn't just a plain old switcheroo, folks. It's far more—um, *dastardly* than that. . . ."

They waited while Gene took another bite of his chili dog. "Hell's bells," he said finally. "When you stop to think that some of these samples might have been used to inseminate *Mrs.* Cooper, it's damn scary."

"What do you mean?" Avery murmured.

"I ran some tests. One of the more healthy bogus specimens was from a black man with hepatitis. So if your wife became pregnant from that specimen, odds are your baby would have been black—a sick little black baby at that."

"And wouldn't the tabloids have had a field day?" Sean remarked.

Gene nodded over his hot dog. "Four specimens were

infected with HIV,'' he said, his mouth half-full. ''The other two samples contained a German measles bacteria, which would have insured your baby was born retarded or deformed. Somebody was really out to destroy you and your wife, Avery.''

A napkin clenched in his fist, Avery slowly shook his head.

''Do you have any idea when a switch might have taken place?'' Sean asked. ''An educated guess?''

Gene sipped his Coke. ''The two most current specimens—both around mid-September—are yours.'' He nodded at Avery. ''The tampering must have taken place before then.''

Sean riffled through her briefcase, then pulled out a folder and handed it to Gene. ''This is a list of employees from both the clinic and Kurtis Labs. The ones with stars by their names have either quit or been fired since Avery and his wife started going to the clinic.''

Wiping his fingers on his napkin, Gene took the list and studied it.

''If you think anyone there might have been responsible for making the switch, it would really help us a lot. We think it's someone ultra-ultra right wing. Do you know what I mean?''

Reaching for a pen in his pocket holder, he nodded. ''Yeah, off the scale. Just on the sunny side of white supremacy. Can I mark on this?''

''Go ahead,'' Sean replied.

While he scrutinized the list, the waitress returned with their meals. Avery paid the check, then pushed his plate away. He'd lost his appetite. ''What about your boss as a possibility, Gene?'' he asked. ''I mean, he lied to Dr. Nathan about the lab results.''

Gene shook his head. ''He's too stupid. I read Keefer pretty well. He went into a total tailspin when I told him the results of my tests on those samples. He was genuinely surprised. No, he lied to avoid a lawsuit.''

''I'll need you to testify about this lab report,'' Sean said. ''Will that get you in trouble with Keefer?''

Gene grinned at her. "Hell, ma'am, that's why I'm here. I want to show him for the worthless, lying scumbag he is. Maybe I'll even get him fired. The S.O.B. doesn't do a damn thing around there except give me crap about my weight. He calls me 'UFO,' says it stands for *Ugly Fat Oaf*. Well, okay, now I've caught him in a lie, and this Ugly Fat Oaf is going fry his ass."

Between sips from his soft drink and picking at his fries, Gene Clavey studied the list and mumbled to himself. "Hmmm, no way is it Maggie Freeman, and not Mitch, he's too P-C. . . ." He glanced up from the paperwork. "You know who you guys should be looking for? The part-timer who was holding down another similar job. Probably a nurse working at another clinic, where he or she had access to these unhealthy specimens." He shrugged. "Just a theory."

"It's a good one," Sean said, nodding. "A part-timer who quit around mid-September. That's very good. Thanks, Mr. Clavey."

He reached for his second chili dog. "You're welcome."

The head of administration at Dr. Nathan's clinic had a thing for frogs. A stout woman in her mid-fifties with short blond hair, she wore black-rimmed glasses and a frog pin on her blouse. The bookcase behind her desk was adorned with ceramic frogs, a philodendron in a frog-shaped planter, seashells glued together to look like frogs, and a frog made out of pipe cleaner and bottle caps. She also had a wall poster of a toad on a lily pad, with a slogan beneath it in script: LEAP AHEAD TO SUCCESS!

The frog lady's name was Brenda Dreyfus. She wanted Avery's autograph for herself and three friends. While he scribbled his personalized Best Wishes on Brenda's frog stationery, Sean persuaded her to dig out records on two part-time employees who had quit the clinic in September: Bob Donnellon and Lauren Schneider, both nurses.

"Bob Donnellon worked here as a nurse for three years," Brenda said, consulting his file. "Though some of the guys prefer 'medical assistant.' He worked part time for both Dr. Nathan and Dr. Konradt. He gave us a month's notice, and his last day here was September third. He now works full time for the Visiting Nurses Association."

She took out another tablet of frog stationery and started writing. "I'll jot down the number at the VNA for you."

"And his current address and phone," Sean said. "If you have it."

"I sure do," Brenda said, scrawling on the pad. "Oh, by the way, Avery, could I have one more autograph? This one for Marlys. M-A-R-L-Y-S. Thanks." She reached for another folder. "Okay, onto the next. Lauren Schneider. She worked part time for Dr. Jans and Dr. Nathan. She was here from May twenty-seventh until September fourteenth."

Avery looked up from his writing. "May twenty-seventh?" He turned to Sean. "That's only three weeks after my TV movie aired, the one that ticked off so many people. Joanne and I had been seeing Dr. Nathan for about two months. Hell, we could have bumped into her."

"Do you have a photo of this Lauren Schneider?" Sean asked Brenda.

The frog lady shook her head. "No, I'm sorry—"

"How about her age? Is her date of birth listed?"

Brenda glanced at the folder. "Um, yes, she's thirty."

Sean turned to Avery. "Any help?"

He shrugged and shook his head. "Joanne might remember. I—" He caught himself, and tried to smile. "I'm sorry. . . ."

Sean patted his arm.

"She worked part time," Brenda said. "And she gave us a week's notice. I don't show another employer listed."

"What about her address and phone number?" Sean asked.

Studying the records, Brenda Dreyfus frowned. "I have a Linden Avenue address in Beverly Hills, but it's no longer current according to this note my assistant jotted down here. Her last paycheck was sent to a post office box in Opal, Idaho."

While none of the network newscasts yesterday had focused on such a gossipy item as the Dayle/Elsie war, the local affiliates went crazy. Most stations seemed to take Dayle's side. Channel 8 even had an editorial, blasting Elsie and suggesting that she make a public apology.

As Dayle turned off the shower in her trailer bathroom, she could hear Dennis in the next room. He was singing "Do You Know the Way to San Jose?" in a falsetto.

"Hey, Dionne," she called, slipping into her bathrobe. "Where's Ted?"

"Outside, on the phone, making security arrangements for that citadel that used to be your home."

"Have there been any public rejoinders from Just-Call-Me-Elsie?"

"No, not a peep from The Scary Widow," Dennis answered from the other side of the door. "I hear from a couple of sources that she's mega-pissed. Seems no matter how it's served, fried or fricasseed, Elsie won't eat crow. You came out ahead yesterday." She heard him laugh. " 'The widow Marshall,' I loved the way you kept saying that to the press. They ate it up too."

"Yeah, it was pretty good, wasn't it?" Dayle said, emerging from the bathroom. She sat at her vanity and vigorously worked a towel over her wet hair. "Did Nick Brock call today?"

Dennis was ensconced on the sofa with the ever-present clipboard in his lap. He munched on a Kit-Kat bar. "Nope, no messages from Opal, Idaho, and Mr. Golden Buns."

She turned to him. "Did I tell you Nick was in Opal?"

"Sure did." He glanced at his clipboard. "Listen, The Hollywood Walk of Fame Award dinner next week, it'll be packed with press folk. Might be a good idea to attend. John McDunn indicated he's available, if you'd like.''

She stopped drying her hair for a moment. ''I'll think about it. Thanks.''

''There are several events coming up, and it wouldn't hurt to be seen with John at your side. It's good for appearances—for the movie, I mean.''

She caught his eye in the mirror. ''I know what you meant, Dennis.''

''Just trying to help.'' He consulted his clipboard. ''Um, a reminder. I'll be here Monday, but I'm not working Tuesday. I have to help Laura move. She's getting an apartment closer to mine.''

''That's nice,'' Dayle replied. ''Listen, you can go over all this with me on Monday. It's late. You don't have to stick around.''

Dennis stood up. ''Oh, before I forget, a friend of my parents is coming from out of town. He's like an uncle. I've cleared it with security and Ted. He's visiting the set Tuesday.''

''Remind me on Monday. Let me know what time so I can look for him.''

''Midmorning. But that's okay, Dayle. Don't make a fuss. I only wanted to let you know that he'll be on the set. No biggie.''

She shrugged. ''Okeydoke. No biggie.'' She started to brush her hair and smiled at him in the mirror. ''Now, go on. Get out of here before I give you something to do. Have a great weekend.''

At a stoplight on the way back to her office, Sean glanced over at Avery and caught him gazing at her. He smiled tentatively, then turned toward the window. The light changed, and she moved on. They were tired, and hadn't said much for the last few miles. As the streetlights flickered on against the darkening sky, Sean didn't want this car ride to end.

Avery had talked to his wife's doctor this afternoon. Apparently, Joanne was better, eating more and responding to the nurses. In a strange way, this news made Sean feel sad, and more alone. Avery was due back on the set Monday. He'd asked if she needed his help over the weekend. Sean had said that she didn't know yet. She found herself trying to think of an excuse to be with him tomorrow or the next day.

But there wasn't much to do. They'd uncovered enough circumstantial evidence to establish reasonable doubt. Actual proof of a conspiracy now depended on what Nick Brock could find in Opal, Idaho. Unless Sean decided to join him in Opal, all she and Avery could do now was wait.

She should have been happy tonight. They were on the verge of exposing these criminals and proving Avery's innocence. But she was on the verge of losing him too.

Sean switched on her indicator and began to slow down as they approached the parking garage where Avery had left his car this morning.

"Don't stop, keep going," he said urgently.

He didn't have to explain. Sean glanced at him, and out the passenger window, she saw a white Corsica parked across the street. Two men sat in the front seat. Sean stepped on the gas.

"We'll go back to my office," she said. "We'll call a taxi to meet you around back." She checked her rearview mirror. The Corsica hadn't moved yet. "This weekend, I want you start shopping for a bodyguard, okay? What time are George and Sheila expecting you tonight?"

"They have theater tickets. I'm going home."

"Alone?"

He chuckled. "Don't worry. I have a dozen reporters and a lynch mob camped out by my front gate. I won't be lonely."

Sean turned into the alley by her building, then parked around back. As they climbed out of the car, she let him carry her briefcase. They started up the back stairwell. "Listen, Avery," she said. "I want to apologize for snapping at you this morning—you know, in the car?"

He paused on the landing and smiled at her. "It's okay."

"I didn't mean to imply that I have it a lot worse off than you. What you said was right. Our situations *are* similar—in many ways. I don't know why I was so disagreeable."

"Maybe you were just setting some boundaries," Avery said. They started down the hallway to her office. "I probably had it coming. I was a bit too familiar last night."

Sean gave him a questioning look. "When?"

"Here. After we read the fax, I hugged you. It was inappropriate."

She opened her office door. "It felt nice, Avery," she admitted. "I think I just got a little scared."

For a moment, he gazed at her in the darkness of her office. He set down her briefcase, then touched her arm. "All this time, you've never been unfaithful to him, have you?"

Sean shook her head. Her first instinct was to step back, but she didn't.

"And he hasn't been able to hold you or kiss you?"

"Not for the last fifteen months."

He sighed. "Jesus, what a waste."

She let out a sad little laugh. "That's what Dan says."

"Sean, do you think it would be okay if I—put my arms around you? Just for a little while?"

"I think so," she whispered.

Avery gently pulled her toward him, and she gratefully sank into his embrace. He stroked her hair. She couldn't keep from crying. He kissed the tears on her cheeks, then his moist, soft lips slid down to her mouth.

Sean trembled at the feelings awakening inside her. She kept

thinking that this wasn't supposed to happen, it was wrong.
Yet she surrendered to every sensation.

He whispered her name and kissed her neck hungrily. His
beard stubble was scratchy, but felt wonderful. It seemed like
forever since she'd heard her name spoken in the height of
passion. His warm breath was swirling in her ear. Sean ran her
fingers through his wavy black hair. Avery's mouth met hers
again, and she parted her lips against his. She clung to his
shoulders. It was as if a giant, warm wave had washed away
that huge wall of protection she'd built around herself and her
feelings.

Sean's head was spinning. They sank back on the sofa
together. He kissed the hollow at the base of her throat, and
she sighed with pleasure.

Avery pulled back for a moment to unbutton his shirt. She
ran her fingers through his chest hair. She could feel his heart
racing. Avery had a movie star physique, but what captivated
her most were his beautiful hands—manicured, masculine, and
so skillful in the way they caressed and aroused her. Sean
brought those exquisite hands to her mouth, kissing his fingertips, sucking on them. It had been so long since she'd experienced a man's touch. She couldn't help thinking about how
Dan's hands had become bloated, pale, and hairless—deadened
by disease. Suddenly, a panic swept through her.

Avery kissed her again. Sean fiercely clung to him. "I'm
sorry," she whispered, crying. "Please. I'm sorry, Avery. We
have to stop. I'm so sorry."

He just held her, his face pressed against her breast. He
rocked her in his arms. "I know," Avery replied, his voice
raspy. "It's okay."

Sean realized he was crying too.

* * *

From a window in the back stairwell, she watched Avery climb into the taxi. Looking up, he gave her a melancholy smile, then shut the cab door.

They'd spent the last hour and a half on her office sofa, just holding each other. Occasionally, he'd kiss her forehead, or bring her hand up to his lips. Neither of them said anything. They huddled together in the darkness, listening to the traffic outside. There were moments when she remembered how it been with Dan, and she could feel Dan's arms around her again. But she never forgot that it was Avery rescuing her from the emptiness of the past fifteen months. With his tender kisses and caresses, he'd resurrected those feelings in her.

She'd missed dinner with her family. But she wouldn't have given up one minute of intimacy with Avery—not even for Dan and her children. It had scared her to realize that.

Sean had been the one to say it was getting late. She'd phoned for his taxi, and given him a fleeting good-bye kiss in the stairwell.

She watched the cab pull away; then she wandered back toward her office. She didn't want to go home right now. Maybe she should have made love with him tonight. She couldn't imagine feeling any more guilty and torn than she was now.

If only she could go away for a couple of days, and not have to face Avery or her family. Right now, she felt such an urgent need to put some distance between the people she loved and herself.

Her eyes had become accustomed to the darkness in her office. Without turning on the lights, she found Dayle's fax from Nick Brock on her desk. Sean sat on the edge of her desk for a few minutes.

Finally, she picked up the phone, dialed Debbie's Paradise View Motor Inn, and asked for Tony Manero's room. He answered after two rings. "Yeah?"

"Is this Nick Brock?" she asked.

"Who's calling?"

"I'm Sean Olson, Dayle's attorney friend. We talked the other day."

"Oh, yeah. You're the one who said you wouldn't hang up on me, though you were tempted. What can I do you for, doll?"

"I just thought you should know," she said. "I'm flying out there tomorrow to work with you."

Twenty-one

After a three-and-a-half-hour drive over snowy mountain roads, Sean arrived in Opal to find the post office closed. She'd been trying to reach Nick Brock since this morning. She'd phoned from LAX, Portland, and Spokane. No Nick. No one even picked up at Debbie's Paradise View Motor Inn.

Last night, he'd been surprisingly agreeable to having her work with him in Opal: *Might be a couple of days before I nab these creeps. In the meantime, this burg is dullsville, I could use some company, doll.*

Sean didn't need the company. She made reservations at another hotel, a mile away from Debbie's. But she wanted to touch base with Nick Brock today. She knew his motel was on the same street as the post office, but almost drove past the place. The sun had set an hour ago, but no one had switched on the illuminated sign yet. Sean turned into the parking lot. The two-story modern stucco stretched a quarter of a block. It didn't appear deserted. Lights were on in the lobby, and plenty of cars were parked in front. But yellow police tape sectioned off the back part of the lot. Sean drove up to the tape line, and stepped out of her rented Chevy. She didn't see anything unusual. Still, she felt uneasy.

She spotted a 7-Eleven across the street. Ducking back into the warm car, Sean steered out of the lot and pulled up to the convenience store. From a pay phone outside, by the store entrance, she dialed Debbie's Paradise View. After six rings, a woman picked up. She sounded young, and frazzled. "Uh, yeah, Debbie's Motor Inn."

"Yes, hello," Sean said. "Nick—I mean, Tony Manero's room, please."

"Oh, um . . . ," the girl replied. Sean heard her talking to someone else, the words muffled.

"Hello?" Sean said. "Are you still there?"

"Can I help you?" a man piped up on the other end of the line.

"Yes, could you connect me with Tony Manero's room, please?"

"May I ask who's calling?"

"Um, this is his employer," Sean said. "Is he there or not?"

"I'm afraid there's been an accident."

"What kind of accident?" she asked. Across the street, through the naked trees, she could see the motel lot and the yellow police tape fluttering in the breeze.

"From what we can figure," the man said. "Mr. Manero must have been smoking in bed. I don't know why the smoke detector didn't work. The only damage was to his room and a vacant room next door."

"How badly is he hurt?"

"He was burned up pretty bad. He—he was dead before the firemen even got to him. Happened around seven this morning. Tony Manero doesn't seem to be his real name. The police are trying to track down a next of kin. Perhaps you could help, ma'am—"

Sean hung up before he finished. She gazed at the motor inn

across the street. The cold November wind kicked up, and she started to shiver.

The people in the room next door could probably hear her crying. So Sean switched on the TV and cranked up the volume to a *Dukes of Hazard* rerun. Then she went on sobbing.

The Opal Lakeside Lodge wasn't so horrible—just cheesy enough to keep her wallowing in remorse, loneliness, and fear. Screwed to the paper-thin wall were two framed faded prints of rabbits in a grove. The carpeting was an ugly brown shag—with beige stains by the bathroom door. On the desk with all her paperwork was a plastic turquoise ashtray with burn marks.

She hated being alone in this place. Part of her wanted to jump in her rental, drive to Spokane, and fly home. But she'd be going back to Avery and Dayle with nothing.

Dayle had no idea she was even out here—and for that, Sean felt guilty. They were supposed to be friends, yet Sean still couldn't confide in her about Avery. She couldn't explain her urgent need to get away. Even now, with Nick dead, she didn't want Dayle knowing she'd come here. Dayle would only send in the police—or insist that she fly back home immediately. And Sean felt duty-bound to stick it out here—at least through Monday, so she could see who was picking up mail for this group. Also she needed to track down that nurse, Lauren Schneider.

She missed Avery. She would have given anything to have him with her right now. Last night, she'd been in such a hurry to get away. She'd wanted time alone. Now Sean kept thinking about that tired, old saying, *"Careful what you wish for. . . ."*

Even though they hadn't carried it any further than some kissing and hugging, she and Avery were still guilty of betrayal. He'd just placed his wife in an institution days ago, and she was the voice, hands, and legs for her disease-paralyzed husband. Last night, the idea of working here in Opal with Dayle's detective seemed like the perfect escape from guilt and temptation.

She couldn't afford to let Dan know this junket was anything more than a boring weekend away—chasing down a lead. Last night, she'd made it back to Malibu just after dinnertime. She'd sat out on the deck with Dan, watching the kids play along the beach with her sister-in-law, Anne.

"What's going on?" he'd asked silently, the constant *whosh-whosh* from his portable respirator competing with the sound of the ocean waves. "You're acting funny. Did something happen while you were in the city?"

Her eyes watering up, Sean had shrugged and managed a smile. "Oh, you know me. I always get blue before a plane trip. That's all, honey."

She'd gazed out at her kids playing with their aunt on the beach. Sean had told herself that if anything ever happened to her, Danny and Phoebe would have a good surrogate mother.

She'd phoned Malibu an hour ago, and the nurse had conveyed Dan's concerns: "He wants to know if you're still feeling blue."

"Tell him I miss him, but I'm doing okay," Sean had replied. She'd talked with the kids, then hung up and burst into tears.

Lowering the volume on *The Dukes of Hazard,* she wandered into the bathroom, plucked a tissue from the dispenser, and blew her nose.

A car pulled up outside. She glanced at her door—all the locks securely in place. A moment later, another car pulled up. She heard the car doors opening and closing; a man and woman talking. The voices grew faint. Sean sighed. She wouldn't let herself forget what had happened to Nick Brock.

She also had to keep in mind her mission here.

The Opal phone directory incorporated a score of surrounding towns and cities—along with their Yellow Pages, yet it was no thicker than the average issue of *Time.* The skimpy volume listed four Schneiders; two of them lived in Opal, none with the first name Lauren.

She tried Mr. and Mrs. James Schneider of Birch Lane, and an answering machine picked up. Their toddler read the cutesy announcement and kept screwing up and laughing while they corrected him in the background. Listening to it was sheer torture. Sean hung up before the beep. She dialed T. A. Schneider of Meadow Drive, and a woman answered. "Hello?"

On the desk in front of her, Sean had the list of employees from the lab and fertility clinic. "Yes, my name is Grace Casino," she said. "I'm trying to locate a Lauren Schneider. I wonder if you could help me."

"Well, I know a Laurie Anne Schneider," the woman said. "That's my daughter. But I don't know any Lauren."

"Was your daughter a nurse at the Adler Clinic in Beverly Hills?"

"That's right. But her name is Laurie Anne, not Lauren."

"Is Laurie Anne around thirty years old? And did she used to live on Linden Drive in Los Angeles?"

"Yes," the woman replied. "Who did you say you were again?"

Sean quickly scanned the listing. "Um, I'm Grace Casino. I used to work in the clinic with Laurie Anne. I'm trying to reach her, and I don't have a current address or phone number."

"Why do you need to get in touch with my daughter?" The woman's tone suddenly became edgy. "She doesn't work at that clinic anymore."

"Um, well, the clinic owes Laurie Anne some money." Sean figured this kind of news would make Mrs. Schneider more cooperative. "There was a—a mix-up in accounting, and Laurie Anne has over eleven hundred dollars in back pay owed her. I volunteered to track down her current address. Do you know how I can get a hold of Laurie Anne, Mrs. Schneider? I sure wouldn't want her to miss out on eleven hundred dollars."

"Well, neither would I!" Mrs. Schneider agreed. "But Laurie Anne is moving again next week, so the Los Angeles address I have is only good for a few more days. She's always on the go, that one. I'll tell you what, why don't you have them send the check here?''

"Oh, I'm sorry, I can't do that. But if you gave me Laurie Anne's current address and phone, maybe I can catch her before moving day.''

"Well, all right. Hold on while I get my address book. Don't go away.''

"Oh, I won't, Mrs. Schneider,'' Sean said. "I'll be right here, waiting.''

Sunday morning, Sean decided to go to mass. But according to the Yellow Pages, the closest Catholic church was in another town forty miles away. No Episcopalian, Presbyterian, Lutheran, or Unitarian centers either. And no synagogues. Apparently, there were no Jews in Opal. Come to think of it, in her wanderings around town since yesterday afternoon, she hadn't noticed a single black person, Hispanic, or Asian.

The only house of worship in Opal was the God's Light Christian Faith Church. Sean climbed in her rental and drove by the place—a beautiful, pristine, modern white structure with gold trim, located at the edge of a winding brook. It looked like a smaller-scale Kennedy Center, and probably cost almost as much to build. She watched the congregation pour out at the end of the service. They were gussied up to the nines— the way people used to dress for church. At first glance, there was something very sweet about it.

On her way back to the hotel. Sean stopped by Flappin' Jack's Pancake House. Apparently, the chalet-style restaurant was the Sunday morning hot spot in Opal. The place was already gilded with cheesy Christmas decorations, including a big plastic nativity set by the front entrance. Beneath a red garland and blinking lights on the atrium ceiling, all those churchgoing families waited for tables to open up. But single folks and strangers like Sean found immediate seating at the counter.

Inside Flappin' Jack's Pancake House, she had a closer look at the clean-scrubbed, well-dressed Opal citizens. She heard snippets of dull conversation—mostly about Pastor White-moore's sermon, which maintained that "diversity" meant "perversity." The minister's words must have fallen on welcome ears in this little Aryan township. Sean couldn't help thinking about *The Stepford Wives* as she studied the women. But these robots seemed aware of their own misery. Despite their Sunday dresses, they looked tired and frayed. The husbands perfectly fit the mold of Eisenhower-era Family-Values Dads by saying very little to their spouses and children and drinking way too much. Still, some of the kids seemed happy—at least on the outside. One thing for Opal, it seemed like a good place to raise children—if they were white, the correct religion, and didn't try to be different.

The pigs in blankets at Flappin' Jack's were delicious. Sean returned to The Opal Lakeside Lodge with a full stomach and a copy of *The Quad City Register*—the local newspaper, a thin weekly that came out every Sunday. She hunted through the front section and found a story on page six: CALIFORNIA MAN DIES IN OPAL HOTEL FIRE. The article was brief, focusing more on the damage to Debbie's Paradise View Motor Inn *(still open for business!)* than the thirty-four-year-old guest from California who apparently had been smoking in bed. Nick's identity was withheld *pending notification of next of kin.* Plans for a church raffle and Whitemoore's Special Thanksgiving Services received more coverage.

The telephone rang. Sean almost jumped out of the desk chair. No one knew she was here except her family; and they wouldn't call this early in the day unless it was an emergency. She snatched up the phone. "Hello?"

"Are you out of your goddamn mind?"

"Avery?"

"What the hell do you think you're doing?" he asked.

She sighed. "I came here to work with Dayle's detective, but he's dead."

"I know. Dayle got through to the hotel last night, and they told her he died in a fire—after smoking in bed. Dayle says the guy didn't even smoke. For God's sake, get out of there before some accident happens to you too."

"I'm all right," Sean said. "How did you track me down? Did you call my family? Please tell me you didn't upset them—"

"Yes, we called them, but we didn't let on anything was wrong."

"We?" Sean asked.

"Dayle and I. In fact, your brother-in-law had us say hello to Dan, because he's such a movie nut. He also gave us your the number at the Opal Lodge. Now check out of there and come home. We're sending in the police—"

"No, wait. Not yet. I'm making some headway here, Avery. I found out that nurse's address in Los Angeles, Laurie Anne Schneider on Franklin Avenue, the Ulta Vista Apartments. But we shouldn't move in on her just yet. We can't tip them off that we're on to them. Besides you and Dayle, who else knows I'm here?"

"No one else. Just your family. That's it."

"Don't tell another soul," Sean said. "Give me until Tuesday. If I don't come up with anything else by then, you can send in the troops—"

"Dayle and I already discussed this. It's a matter for the police."

"You'll have to convince Dayle that I need more time."

"Convince her yourself," Avery said. "She's right here."

After a moment, Dayle came on the line: "Sean, are you nuts?"

"Are you guys together? Or is this a conference call?"

"No, Avery's here at my place. What's this about giving you more time? Good God, Sean." Her voice started to crack. "I hate to admit that I actually liked Nick, but I did, damn it. I still can't believe he's dead. I won't go through this with somebody else again—not after Leigh and Hank. You get your ass back here. This is a police matter now."

"The cops are too busy stacking up a case against Avery. Do you think some pie-in-the-sky conspiracy theory will change their minds at this point? They don't want to prove he's innocent. Besides, how can we be sure the police aren't in on this? A cop shot Hank—and Bonny. And I certainly wouldn't trust the police around here."

"All right, then we'll call the FBI," Dayle said.

"Call them on Tuesday. Just give me until then."

"You sound exactly like Nick," Dayle replied. "He wanted more time before I called the police. And look what happened. I'm sorry. I won't make the same mistake twice."

"Then don't tell anyone that I'm here, Dayle. Ask yourself, who else in your camp knew of Nick's whereabouts. Didn't Estelle warn you that they might have gotten to someone close to you? If Avery and you can keep quiet about where I am—and your phone isn't being bugged right now—I shouldn't be in any danger. Just give me until Tuesday, Dayle."

The elevator doors opened, and Avery stepped out to the lobby of Dayle's building. Unfolding his cellular phone, he dialed the Opal Lakeside Lodge and asked for Sean's room number again. "Hello?" she answered.

"Hi, it's me," he said.

"I figured I'd hear back from you."

"Listen, I can't just sit by and allow you to put your life on the line because of me. You might have been able to convince Dayle to give you a couple of more days in that place. But not me. Either you're coming home or I'm flying out there."

"Avery, you're a murder suspect," she said. "If you try to leave the state, a troop of police will be all over you before you even reach the airport check-in. Besides, one reason I'm here is to put some distance between us."

"I understand. But you don't have to endanger yourself to avoid—what happened the other night with me. My God, aren't you scared?"

"Of course I am, but it's okay. I won't take any chances—"

"Bullshit. You're already pushing your luck too far. I'm coming out there—"

"Just—just hold on," she said. "Let's discuss this tomorrow. Whatever you do, please don't come today. It's Sunday. The post office is closed. It's dead time right now. If you arrive here tonight, we won't be able to accomplish anything—except maybe sleeping together. And I wouldn't like either one of us very much if that happened."

"Sean, give me credit for a little self-control, okay?"

"All I'm saying is, if you have to come out here, wait until tomorrow, and we'll talk. It's what I want."

He let out a long sigh. "I'm flying to Spokane tonight. At least I'll be closer—two or three hours away. I'll call you later. Meanwhile, lay low, all right?"

"Avery, it's against my better judgment that you do that. As your lawyer, I advise against it." Her voice dropped to a whisper. "Be careful, okay?" Then she hung up.

As Avery was about to click off, he heard the message tone on his phone beep twice. Heading toward the lobby doors, he dialed his access code. The first message came on: "Yes, Avery Cooper, this is Vic Tolmund of the *Weekly World Inquirer*. . . ."

Avery rolled his eyes. Leave it to a tabloid reporter to dig up the number of his personal cellular.

"I'm calling from the Beverly Hills police station. Do you have any comment about the warrant for your arrest that was just issued? I'll try you again at home, Avery. We want to tell the people your side of the story. . . ."

"What?" Avery said to no one. He stopped dead by the lobby doors.

The second message was from his friend, George: "The cops came by, looking for you, Avery. They even asked to search the house—in case we were hiding you. They have a warrant for your arrest. Sheila and I are by the phone here. Call us. We're worried sick."

Dayle kept thinking about what Sean had said over the phone: *Ask yourself, who else in your camp knew of Nick's where-abouts. . . .*

Only two people knew: Dennis and Ted. Dennis had been her right-hand man for almost four years. She'd come to depend on him. She'd known Ted only four days. Still, she'd entrusted her life to him. He'd spent three of the last four nights sleeping down the hall from her—in her guest room. She hadn't set foot outside of her apartment without Ted at her side. He'd handpicked the two security guards in her building—as well as every one of her temporary chauffeurs.

Then again, he'd caught her at an extremely vulnerable time. And his most impressive reference was Gil Palarmo, who was dead.

Dayle wandered into her study. She shuffled through some papers on her desk until she found Ted's résumé. If Ted Kovak had tolerated Gil and his gay buddies for ten months—and put him down as a reference—it wasn't very likely he'd be connected to some intolerant hate group.

Biting her lip, Dayle reached over and checked her Roladex. One of her acquaintances, Jonathan Brooks, had been close friends with Gil Palarmo. The Rolodex card in front of Jona-than's was a new one, still white and crisp. Dayle had added it to the file less than a week ago. She plucked out the card and stared at the address and phone number for Nick Brock. Last night, she'd burst into tears when she'd heard the news.

She'd grown very fond of that "cool jerk." She returned the
card to her Rolodex. She didn't want to part with it—at least,
not yet.

Dayle moved on and found Jonathan's card. She dialed the
number in Palm Springs, and his machine answered: "Hello,
I'm unable or unwilling to come to the phone right now," he
said in a haughty tone. "But leave word after the irritating
beep, and I might return your call."

Beep. Dayle cleared her throat. "Hello, Jonathan," she said.
"This is Dayle Sutton calling. It's been a long time. Listen.
Do you remember if Gil had a bodyguard named Ted Kovak?
Tall, good-looking, blond hair? I hired this guy recently, and
I'm checking on his résumé. Cart before the horse. Anyway,
he says he worked for Gil nearly a year. If you could call
me back as soon as possible, I'd appreciate it. It's Sunday
afternoon—around one-thirty. And here's my number . . ."

After Dayle hung up, she stared at an old phone message on
her desk. Dennis had scribbled it down for her earlier in the
week. She'd come to know his handwriting quite well. As much
as she hated to think about it, if she couldn't trust Ted Kovak,
she had to question the loyalty of the faithful assistant who
had recommended him.

Avery was third in line, and he couldn't stop sweating.

The agent at the ticket counter had been dealing with a couple
of elderly tourists for ten minutes now. He was a young, East
Indian man with a mustache, and he kept having to repeat
everything to them loudly. Apparently, they wanted special
seats or a special meal—or something.

Avery wiped the perspiration off his forehead. So far, no
one had recognized him—*People* cover boy, movie star, and
fugitive. If he stopped to think about it too much, he'd die
laughing—or just go crazy as Joanne did.

She was sick, and he'd let himself fall in love with someone else. He could try making excuses, blame it on the timing or his vulnerable situation. He might even try blaming Sean a bit—for being so vulnerable herself. But in truth, he'd allowed this to happen. He was responsible. Because of him, Joanne was in an institution—and Sean was risking her life alone in that awful little town. He couldn't do anything for Joanne now. But maybe he could help Sean—before it was too late for her too.

He had to leave town immediately. Turning himself in to the police wasn't an option. He couldn't let himself rot in jail while Sean risked her neck for him in Opal.

He hadn't seen any rental-type cars on his tail. He'd taken a roundabout way to the airport—just in case. He would buy a change of clothes and supplies during his stopover in Portland—if the police hadn't already put a freeze or a trace on his debit card.

A husky, blond woman with airport security sauntered by and scrutinized him with a narrow gaze. He tried to avoid eye contact with her.

The older couple were still talking to the ticket agent, whose name tag read SERGI. He was shaking his head and apologizing to them about something. Perhaps Sergi would be so rushed and haggard after these two customers, he wouldn't notice that he was sending a famous fugitive to Spokane, Washington.

The security guard wandered by again, glancing back at him over her shoulder. She unhooked a walkie-talkie from her belt and whispered something into it as she strolled away.

The man in front of him stepped forward. The old couple shuffled off with their tickets, thank God. Maybe the line would start moving now.

He spied the security guard near the outside doors. She was talking to a cop, and pointing directly at him. Avery's heart seemed to stop. His first instinct was to run, but all he could do was watch the policeman and the security guard descend on him. The cop had something in his hand. "Hey, mister, you're not going anywhere," he said.

Avery started to shake his head. But the policeman passed him by. "Your ticket," the cop said, grinning at a man in the line, four people in back of Avery. "You dropped this when you got off the shuttle bus. Can't go very far without a ticket. I've been trying to track you down. . . ."

Avery felt himself crumble a little inside. He wanted to sit down someplace, but Sergi waved him forward. "Next?"

Approaching the counter, he tried to smile at the ticket agent. "Hi, how are you?" he said. With a shaky hand, he reached for his wallet. "I need to go to Spokane, Washington, today."

Sergi started typing on the computer. "How many people are traveling?"

"Just one, me." He set his credit card on the counter. The card used his full name: Avery O'Reilly Cooper.

"Do you have any bags going to Spokane, Mr.—" he glanced at the credit card. "Mr. Cooper?"

"No, I—I don't." He wiped the perspiration from his forehead again.

"I'll need to see some photo ID, sir."

Avery nodded more than necessary. "Yes, of course." He set his driver's license on the counter.

Sergi studied the license, then handed it back to Avery. "Thank you, Mr. Cooper. Will you be returning from Spokane?"

"Um, I don't know when. So—it's one way—a one-way ticket."

Sergi went back to his keyboard and computer screen. "Hmmm, I can book you on our Portland flight, leaving in thirty-five minutes. You'll have an hour layover for your connection, which arrives in Spokane tonight at eight-eleven. Does that sound good, Mr. Cooper?"

Avery smiled gratefully. "Yes, that's—just fine."

* * *

He hadn't anticipated any problems at the boarding gate. But then he learned his flight would be delayed by forty-five minutes, and one of the biggest attractions at the airport newsstand was *People* magazine—with Joanne and him on the cover. The issue was displayed—one after another—behind a plastic case above the entire length of the periodical section. Avery saw two customers buying the magazine in the shop, and he counted three more people slouched in the boarding area seats reading it.

He ducked into the men's room and hid in a stall. Sitting on the edge of the toilet, he waited out the next forty-five minutes.

They were boarding his row number when Avery emerged from the lavatory. The plane wasn't too crowded. He had a row to himself. For most of the flight—and through the dinner service—he turned his head toward the window and feigned sleep. But he was too wired to nap. He kept wondering if someone had recognized him in the boarding area and called the police. Would a bunch of cops be waiting for him at the gate in Portland?

It seemed like the longest flight he'd ever taken, and he still had to switch planes. When they finally landed in Portland, he was relieved to find no welcoming committee of cops. He got cash from the ATM, bought supplies, then hid out in the men's room again until his Spokane flight was boarding.

Once they'd landed in Spokane, Avery quickly threaded around a barrage of people and carts in the terminal. He followed the signs to the rental car area. He hadn't made reservations, figuring some customer service representative might blow the whistle on the "Beverly Hills Butcher."

Avery caught his breath, and came up to the car rental counter. The attendant was a thin, thirtyish woman in a burgundy jacket with PEGGY on her name tag. She had bright red lipstick and tinted auburn hair that might have been a wig from the cut of her bangs and the way the sides perfectly framed her head, curling in at the shoulders. She greeted him with a professional perkiness. "How can I help you today, sir?"

"Hello." He dug out his driver's license and credit card. "I don't have a reservation. Do you have any cars available?"

"Of course, sir," she said, her fingers poised on the computer's keyboard. "For how many days?"

"Um, just two days, I think."

Peggy started typing. She glanced down at Avery's credit card and license. Her smile seemed to freeze, then immediately wither. She stopped typing, and her eyes met his for a moment.

Either she was starstuck or suddenly very aware that she was face-to-face with a man accused of rape and murder. Avery did his damnedest not to appear rattled. "Is there a problem?" he dared to ask.

She quickly shook her head. "No, not at all." She went back to her typing. But she kept peering up at him nervously. "Um, I think I can upgrade you, Mr.—Cooper," she said. "Could you excuse me for a moment?"

Avery nodded.

Peggy turned and stiffly retreated into an office behind the counter. She glanced over her shoulder at him before closing the door. Avery caught a glimpse of a middle-aged woman seated at the desk in the office. She also wore a burgundy jacket. Now he stared at that closed door. A voice inside him said: *Get the hell out . . . now.*

He peeked over the countertop—to where Peggy had left his credit card and license by her keyboard. He decided to count to ten. If she wasn't out of that office by then, he'd find the nearest exit. *One, two, three . . .*

Avery turned and looked around. He noticed a tall man in a blue uniform, standing by the far baggage carousel. Avery couldn't tell if he was with the Spokane police or airport security, but someone just called him. The guard unhooked his walkie-talkie from his belt, then spoke into it.

Avery glanced back at the closed office door. ... *six, seven ...*

The walkie-talkie to his ear, man in the blue uniform seemed to be searching the crowd, his gaze shifting to the row of car rental booths.

... nine, ten.

Avery quickly reached over the counter and scooped up his credit card and license. He swiveled around and walked as quickly as he could to the nearest exit. He didn't dare look back.

A blast of cold air hit him as he came outside. It chilled the beads of sweat on his forehead. He kept walking—toward a shuttle van for the Red Lion Motor Inn. The sliding passenger door was open while the driver loaded up someone's bags in back. Avery approached the driver. "I didn't call for you, but I have a reservation with the Red Lion," he said, out of breath. His heart was racing. "Can you take me?"

"Sure can. Climb aboard. Sit back and relax."

"Thank you." He ducked into the warm van, then plopped down in the backseat. The only other passengers were a middle-aged couple. Avery wiped his sweaty forehead, and turned to the window. He expected to see the walkie-talkie man out by the curb—or perhaps the car rental woman. But he didn't spot either one. Maybe he'd hear on the local news tonight about someone seeing Avery Cooper in the Spokane airport. Then again, maybe not.

He'd brought enough cash along. He'd take a room at the Red Lion tonight, and try again for a rental car in the morning.

Avery heard the front door shut. The driver settled into his seat, and a moment later, they started moving.

Twenty-two

Riding to the studio in her limo, Dayle had a copy of the shooting script on her lap. But she kept peeking up at the two men in front of her—on the other side of that window divider. Ted sat with the driver—another in a series of strangers acting as her temporary chauffeur.

Now Dayle felt stupid for having such blind trust in him. She'd barely slept last night—uncertain about the man just down the hall from her bedroom. Any tolerance points he'd earned protecting the notoriously gay Gil Palermo laid in the balance. Dayle still hadn't received a call back from Gil's friend, Jonathan Brooks. She'd left him another message this morning.

Dayle stared at Ted and the driver. She closed her script, then pressed the button to lower the divider window. Ted looked over his shoulder as the glass partition descended. "I was just thinking, Ted," she announced. "You don't need to stay with me tonight. I'll be okay with the extra guards in the hall and the lobby."

He shook his head. "You need someone in the apartment with you."

"Well, I'd like some privacy tonight. I'd rather be alone."

"You hired me to guarantee your safety, Dayle," he said, a bit patronizing. "Sometimes that means I have to be a pain in the ass. Let me do my job tonight. I'll make sure you have the breathing space you need."

"Of course you will." Dayle gave him a pale smile, then pressed the switch to raise the partition. "Thanks, Ted."

"You're just nervous, that's all," Hal assured him.

Tom's aim had been miserable for the last half hour. He'd gone through nearly fifty bullets trying to hit ten lousy bottles off the ranch house railing.

"Isn't there some show business saying?" Hal continued. " 'Bad dress rehearsal, great show'? You'll do fine tomorrow."

"Thanks," Tom muttered. He shot at another bottle and missed. "Guess I'm still worried about getting past her bodyguard. Is he good?"

"Oh, yes, and he's an excellent shot too. But quit your worrying, Tom. He's with us—one of our best men, Ted Kovak." He sighed. "Some of the triggermen in SAAMO aren't exactly Rhodes Scholars. Like our late friend Lyle, they're dedicated, but ignorant. Still, we need these bottom-of-the-barrel types for certain jobs. But Ted Kovak is good, top of the heap. He's the one shooting you with blanks tomorrow."

Hal patted Tom on the back, then pointed to his fake mustache. "You need more glue on that lip warmer. It's starting to peel off."

Tom wiped his brow, and pressed on his upper lip to secure the fake mustache. "Will I need to wear this disguise for the plane ride tomorrow?"

"You're probably better off without it." Hal kicked at the dirt. "Have you made a decision where you'd like to go?"

"Yes, Rio de Janeiro." Just saying that made Tom feel better.

"Good choice. You'll be on your way in twenty-four hours. We'll supply you with a passport. We'll take care of everything."

"Won't you need a picture of me for the passport?" Tom asked.

"Right you are. Remind me later, okay? Now, try that target again."

But Tom couldn't get his mind off tomorrow. Hal had gone over the assassination of Dayle Sutton several times—down to the smallest detail. Tom knew what to expect—until the moment his "corpse" was carried into the fake ambulance. Then the plans became vague, and he didn't like that uncertainty.

He aimed at the bottle, carefully squeezed the trigger, and missed.

"Cut!" yelled the assistant director.

Dayle's character, struggling with alcoholism and middle age, sat through her first AA meeting at a "town hall" set. About thirty extras surrounded her. With her gray tweed suit and a matronly makeover, Dayle perched on a folding chair and listened to speeches. Tomorrow, they would film her turn at the podium—a long, very emotional speech, Best Actress Oscar bait.

While they set up another shot, Dayle headed for her trailer. Dennis stood by the door. He gave a long look at her middle-aged makeover. "Here you go, *Mom*," he said, handing her a bottle of Evian.

"Thanks," she muttered, not smiling at his Mom crack.

"You okay, Dayle?" he asked. "All morning long, you've been on edge—"

"I'm not okay," she sighed, pausing on the steps to her trailer. "Nick Brock was killed on Friday."

"What?" Dennis seemed genuinely stunned. "You're kidding."

"Someone set fire to his hotel room. He burned to death."

"My God, Dayle," he murmured.

"I'm trying to figure out how this hate group knew where to find Nick. Did you tell anyone that he was in Opal?"

"No, of course not. Shouldn't you talk to the police about this?"

She shook her head. Dennis seemed so concerned and earnest. Was it just an act?

"I don't want to involve the police yet," she said steadily. "A cop shot Hank and Bonny. They could be part of the conspiracy. I can't trust the police. I can't trust anybody." She opened the trailer door.

Dennis gave her a wary glance. "Even me?"

"Even you," Dayle said.

"You goddamn idiot," Avery muttered to himself. He never should have turned off Highway 95. But on his map, the rural route looked like a quicker way to Opal. But he'd been on this road for an hour now, and still no Opal, just a long, deserted, snaky highway without any markings. For all he knew, he could be driving *away* from Opal. The fuel needle hovered near empty. On the radio, just static. He couldn't get anything on his cellular phone. No surprise, he was outside a roaming zone.

Avery sat at the wheel of a six-year-old Lincoln Town Car. It was like steering the *Titanic,* the thing felt so big. But it had been the only car with snow tires at Merv's E-Z Auto Rentals.

Avery had first noticed the car rental sign last night—half a block from The Spokane Red Lion. Merv's didn't open until 9:30 in the morning, and it looked like a fly-by-night outfit.

But Avery figured they might not be so particular about who he was once the credit card cleared.

They had a room available at the Red Lion Inn. No one at the front desk recognized him. The eleven o'clock news didn't report any sightings of Avery Cooper at the Spokane airport. But the warrant for his arrest was one of the lead stories. He telephoned Sean, and they arranged to meet tomorrow in the lot outside the Opal post office.

In the morning, he called Glenhaven Spa for a progress report on Joanne, but then he remembered his status with the law, and hung up.

At Merv's E-Z Auto Rentals, the puffy, middle-aged man behind the counter didn't seem to recognize him. After climbing inside the Lincoln Town Car, which smelled of stale coffee and cigarettes, Avery glanced at the rental paperwork. The salesman had filled in his name as Andrew O. Cooper.

The snow tires were a good call. Compact snow, slush, and ice covered the road. With white knuckles, Avery clutched the steering wheel and wove through the mountain passes. Along the way, he drove by several abandoned cars that had spun out and stalled in ditches. Finally, the highway dipped to a lower altitude and straightened. No more snow—at least for a while.

Then he'd decided to try this shortcut.

The short cut to hell, was more like it. Except for an occasional farm house in the distance, there was no sign of civilization. Up ahead, he saw more mountains—more snow and ice. He checked the fuel needle again. He'd passed a service station about an hour ago on Highway 95; perhaps this gas-guzzler could make it back. At least he'd know where he was headed.

With a sigh, Avery slowed and made a U-turn. He heard gravel grinding beneath the tires as he swung the Town Car around. After a few minutes, the road beneath him began to feel bumpy. It sounded as if something was dragging along his right front tire. The car listed to one side. "Oh, God," Avery whispered. "Please, don't let it be a flat. Not here. . . ."

He pulled over to the roadside and climbed out of the big car. He could see his breath as he walked around to inspect the tire. It was totally deflated, with the hubcap digging into the gravel. "Shit," Avery growled. He kept spitting out the word—again and again. He went back into the car, threw on his sweater, then checked the trunk for a spare tire. He wasn't sure Merv's E-Z Auto Rentals would have one. But they did.

What they didn't have was a jack. "GODDAMN IT!" he bellowed. He kicked a dent in the car door. He let a few more expletives fly as he searched for the jack: in the trunk, under the seats, in the front hood. He was still searching in vain when he spotted in the distance another car down the road, coming his way.

Avery started waving for help. He caught a better look at the approaching vehicle, a Corsica. Along with the Ford Taurus, it was the automobile of choice for the "rental mentals." He stopped waving for a moment. The Corsica slowed down. Avery saw only one person in the front seat. It looked like a woman. The car crawled to a stop and she rolled down her window. The driver was a brunette in her late twenties. She had a long, thin, pretty face, and wore a red sweater. "Are you okay?" she called.

"I didn't think anyone would come by," Avery said, starting toward the car. "I have a flat. This is a rental, and there's no jack. . . ."

As he stepped closer, she inched her car forward a bit. She looked apprehensive, so he stopped in his tracks. "Um, if you have a jack, I could fix this tire in a few minutes. I'd really appreciate it."

"I'd like to help," she said, wincing in an apologetic way. "But my husband doesn't want me stopping for strangers. . . ."

Nodding, Avery managed to smile at her. "I understand. But—well," he pointed to his car. "I'm kind of stranded here. I really do have a flat. . . ."

He made the mistake of approaching her car again. The

Corsica lurched forward. "Tell you what," the woman nervously called to him. "I have a cellular. I'll phone the police for you. It shouldn't take more than an hour—"

Avery automatically shook his head. "No, not the police. I—I—"

The woman glared at him. She quickly rolled up the window.

"No, wait!" Avery shouted over the Corsica's screeching tires. He watched her speed down the road. At this moment, she was probably describing her would-be attacker to a 9-1-1 operator.

"You goddamn idiot," Avery muttered to himself.

At first, Sean hardly noticed the woman coming out of the video store with her two children. Even when she saw them go into the post office, Sean ruled out the haggard-looking mother as a candidate for PO Box 73.

All morning long, she'd been sitting in her Chevy rental, parked in the minimall lot. With the video store, U-Pay-Less Shoes, Pizza Hut, Sheer Delight Hair Stylists, and the post office as its main attractions, the little mall did a brisk business. Avery still hadn't shown up. Occasionally, Sean started up the car to get the heater going, or she'd step out to stretch her legs. Three times, she'd ducked into the post office to make certain Box 73 hadn't been cleaned out, three false alarms.

The mailboxes in Opal's post office were the old-fashioned kind, brass with numbers on little windows. Box 73 was crammed with several large manila envelopes—along with some bills. Anyone emerging from the post office with a bundle like that was an immediate suspect.

Sean drummed her fingers on the steering wheel. She watched the woman come out again with her kids—a thin, dark-haired, preteen boy, and a chubby little urchin with her blond hair in braids. The kids fought, not just pushing and shoving, but with fists swinging. Their poor mother tried to break it up without getting coldcocked. The sallow-looking blonde wore a pink down vest over her white turtleneck, and a pair of jeans that didn't flatter her pear-shaped figure. She was screaming at her kids, and clutching a big bundle of mail—several manila envelopes and some bills.

Sean climbed out of her rental, and she could hear the woman: "I'll tell Daddy about this when he comes back from California. You'll be sorry. You know how he gets when he's angry. . . ." She prodded them toward a brand-new station wagon, which bore two bumper stickers: MY FAMILY, MY COUNTRY, MY GUN, and JESUS CHRIST: NOW MORE THAN EVER. The woman was still screaming and threatening her kids when Sean ducked into the post office.

Box 73 was empty.

Sean hurried back out the door, across the lot toward her rental. Suddenly, something came at her. Tires screeched. She spun around and almost collided with the front fender of an old-model blue Chrysler LeBaron. She reeled back, momentarily stunned.

Sean couldn't see the driver past the sun's glare on the windshield. But she noticed a pair of fuzzy dice dangling from the rearview mirror. Whoever sat behind the wheel didn't yell or honk. Catching her breath, Sean waved at the driver and stepped aside.

She glanced over her shoulder at the mother. The frumpy blonde stood by her station wagon, staring back at her.

Sean quickly looked away, then walked up to a beige Tempo that wasn't hers. She paused by the driver's door, then pretended to search through her purse for the car keys. After a minute, the woman climbed into her station wagon, pulled out of her space, and started toward the lot exit. Sean ran back to her rental car, jumped inside, and gunned the engine.

She caught up with the station wagon at the stoplight by the mall exit. The woman swiveled around to swat at her kids in the back. When the light changed, she turned left. Sean followed, keeping about three car lengths behind her. They drove by a McDonald's, then past Debbie's Motor Inn, where Sean once again glimpsed the police tape in the parking lot. She checked her rearview mirror. An old lady in a Buick was behind her. Sean didn't notice the next car back. She didn't see the blue Chrysler LeBaron that had almost run into her a few minutes ago.

Somebody was coming, but at this distance, Avery couldn't tell if it was a police car. He'd taken out the spare tire and leaned it against the fender to advertise his predicament. In the past forty minutes, only three people had driven by; and none of them had even slowed down for him.

The approaching vehicle came into view. Avery noticed the police lights on the hood. He stepped in front of his disabled rental and waved. The squad car slowed to a stop about a hundred yards in front of him. Avery couldn't see what the cop inside was doing, but figured he'd better not move. He stood there for at least two or three minutes.

"Raise your hands above your head and turn toward your vehicle," the cop announced over his speaker.

Avery nodded, then did what he was told. He thought about what had happened to Dayle's chauffeur and her stand-in. He heard the car door open, then the patrolman approaching, pebbles crackling underfoot.

"I've been stranded here with a flat for an hour," Avery called. "This is a rental car. They have a spare tire, but no jack." He glanced over his shoulder. "This woman stopped earlier. I must have scared her. She might have called you. Anyway, I'm glad you showed up."

"Oh, really?" the policeman finally replied. He sounded all congested. "This lady told us you didn't want her calling the police."

"I didn't want her *bothering* the police," Avery said. "All I need is a jack to change this tire."

"That sure looks like a flat to me. You can lower your arms, sir."

"Thank you," Avery sighed. Hesitating, he turned and managed to smile at the patrolman. He prayed the guy wouldn't recognize him.

The officer tipped his hat, then pulled a handkerchief out of his pocket and blew his nose. Avery guessed he was around thirty, and with a cold in full bloom. Against his pale complexion, his nose was almost as red as his neatly trimmed hair, and those blue eyes were bloodshot. He stood about six feet tall, and had a solid build. He sneezed loudly.

"God bless you," Avery muttered.

"Thanks." The cop moseyed over to the flat tire. "Where are you from?"

"California," Avery said. "I'm headed for Opal, but I think I took a wrong turn. My aunt lives there. I'm spending Thanksgiving with her."

"That's nice." He blew his nose again, then squinted at Avery. "Say, anyone ever tell you that you look like that movie star, Avery Cooper?"

Avery shrugged. "I don't follow the movies much."

The cop studied his face for another moment, then cleared his throat and spit. "Yeah, well, Opal's about two hours from here. I have a map in my squad car. Sit tight for a second, and I'll show you how to get there."

Avery watched him start back toward the patrol car. "If you have a jack," he called, "I could change this tire in no time. . . ."

The policeman didn't look back at him, but waved, then ducked into the front seat. Avery strained to catch a glimpse of him through the windshield's glare. The guy must have had a hard time finding his road map, because he was in there at least five minutes. Finally, Avery started toward the patrol car. "Um, excuse me?" he called.

The cop climbed out of the front seat. He let out a guttural roar to clear his throat and spit once again. "I can't find the stupid map anywhere."

Avery smiled. "Hey, listen, it's okay. I have a map in my car. If I head back to Highway 95, I should find Opal pretty easily." He glanced over his shoulder at the lopsided Lincoln Town Car. "You know, if you have a jack I could borrow for a few minutes, I'd be on my way."

The policeman took a deep breath that puffed out his chest. "No, I'll tell you what you're gonna do here. You're gonna lean against this vehicle and put your hands behind your back."

Bewildered, Avery stared at him. "What?"

"Do as I say, Mr. Cooper," the patrolman replied, his hand poised by his gun belt. "Lean forward, hands behind you, legs apart."

In a daze, Avery obeyed him. The once-friendly policemen tugged at his arms, then slapped a pair of cuffs around his wrists. At the same time, he felt the cop leaning up against him, and his mouth touched Avery's ear. "You're in a helluva lot of trouble," he whispered. "You know that, mister big shot movie star?"

The following Internet conversation occurred at 1:42 P.M., on Monday, November 18, on the Recipe Hot-line:

HANNAH: The big difference is using beef stock instead of water. That's what makes it so flavorful.

VICKI: Is it really rich? If it's too rich, my husband won't want it. Lyle has a delicate constitution.

PAT: Request private chat with Vicki.

Dialogue from a private mailbox between "Vicki" and "Pat," one minute later:

PATRIOT: What's going on? R-U OK?

VICTORY: I saw A. Cooper's lawyer in the parking lot when I got mail 1/2 hour ago. I'm certain it was her. It was almost like she was looking for me.

PATRIOT: Where are U now? Did she follow U?

VICTORY: I'm home. If she was following me, I didn't see.

PATRIOT: OK, Vicki . . . thanx for reporting . . . This confirms Ray D. thinking he saw her at Flappin Jacks yesterday . . . I'll let Hal know.

VICTORY: Have U heard any more about Lyle? So worried . . .

PATRIOT: I'm sure Lyle OK . . . Maybe Hal has news . . . stay home til U hear back from me . . . God Bless.

It always threw Tom for a loop whenever that newfangled little phone of Hal's rang. They were in the car, diving back to the city after target practice and lunch at a seafood place. Hal sat at the wheel. He didn't flinch at all when the phone went off. He fished the gizmo from the pocket of his fancy jogging suit, then unfolded the thing. "Yeah, Hal here."

Eyes on the road, he frowned. "Okay," he said after a moment. "Call Vicki back. I need a full description of what Cooper's legal whore is wearing and the type of car she's driving. I want her under surveillance within the hour. But no one is to touch her. . . ."

Pressed against the passenger door, Tom watched him. Hal's jaw seemed to clench at the news he was hearing. "So you're telling me that both Avery Cooper and his lawyer are there?" he asked hotly. "What is this? First Dayle Sutton's private detective, and now these two. . . ."

Hal listened for a moment. "We have Cooper in custody? Who's with him?" He grimaced. "Taggert? Shit. Taggert's a loose cannon, he's worse than Lyle Bender. Tell him I don't want anything happening to Cooper until we've come up with a plan. No rough stuff. Have someone relieve Taggert of the prisoner ASAP. We need Cooper alive—for now. I don't trust the stupid, trigger-happy son of a bitch. Only reason Taggert's on the payroll is because he's a cop. . . ." Hal listened for a moment. "I don't care how far away he is. Send somebody out there to take over. And I want this lady lawyer tracked down. I'll expect your call within an hour. All right?"

Hal smiled. "Good boy," he said. "Over and out."

He managed to keep steering while he folded up the little phone and slipped it back into his pocket. The car started to gain speed. He grinned at Tom, very confident, almost smug. "Interesting developments at home," he said. "And on the eve of your eliminating Dayle Sutton. Huh, we just might end up with *two* movie stars dead tomorrow—and one dead bitch-lawyer."

Sean watched the two-story, tan brick house across the street. The place had brown shutters and THE BENDERS wood-burnt on a plaque hanging over the front door. The lawn was littered with a dozen soggy boxes that must have been part of a kids' game a while ago. With the sun starting to set, Sean felt the late autumn chill creep inside the parked car. She'd been staking out the house for close to three hours.

She wondered if Avery was waiting for her in the post office parking lot, or if he'd gone on to the hotel.

"I don't want any fighting!" Mrs. Bender announced from her front door as she let the two children out. The boy ran to one of the boxes and kicked it, while the little girl shrieked. Sean rolled down her car window. Mrs. Bender was yelling: "I have important calls to make, and better not have to come out here for the next hour!" She ducked inside and shut the door.

After a few minutes, the kids calmed down. The boy started building a fort out of the boxes.

Sean watched an Oldsmobile crawl up the tree-lined street, then stop in front of the Benders' house. An old woman stepped out of the car, but left the motor running. "Scotty Bender!" she called angrily. "I saw you in my backyard this morning! That's private property, and not your personal shortcut to school. The same goes for your older brother. I'm sick and tired of it! You tell your mother I said so."

The kid shouted something back at her. Sean didn't catch what he said, but the tone wasn't particularly apologetic.

"Well!" the indignant old woman replied. "Next time I see any of you Bender children in my yard, I'm calling the police. I don't care if your father's friends with them or not!" She jumped back into her car and continued down the road.

Sean watched the Oldsmobile pull into the driveway of a modest white stucco. The garden in front had been covered with plastic tarp to fight frost. Here was a woman who knew the Benders and clearly had some issues with them. And right now, she was in a mood to vent.

Sean hunted through her purse, and found some old business cards rubber-banded together. She plucked one out: JOAN KINSELLA, ATTORNEY, MUNICIPALITY OF EUGENE, OREGON.

The Bender girl let out another shriek, then attacked one of the boxes as if it were a punching bag.

Sean climbed out of the car and started toward the white

stucco house, where the old woman was hoisting a sack of groceries from the passenger side of her Oldsmobile. The overloaded bag ripped along the side, and several items spilled onto her driveway.

"Can I help?" Sean called. The woman barely had time to respond before Sean was on her hands and knees, retrieving a Campbell's soup can that had rolled under the car. "I hate it when they overpack those bags," she said, handing her the soup can.

Bracing the torn bag on the hood of her car, the woman nodded and gave Sean a wary smile. She had close-cropped brown hair that looked like a wig, wire glasses, and lipstick that had been applied with a shaky hand. She wore a wool coat, blue pants, and an ugly floral top.

"I'm from out of town," Sean explained. "Um, could you recommend a good, clean, family-type of hotel in the area?"

The woman shrugged. "There's Debbie's Paradise View off of Main Street. That's nice." Sean could tell she still had her guard up.

"Thanks very much." She nodded politely and started to walk away—for a few seconds. Then she stopped and turned around. "By the way, you don't happen to know the Bender family down the block, do you?"

Frowning, the old woman sighed. "Only too well, I'm afraid."

"Oh, really?" Sean pulled Joan's card out of her purse. "I'm Joan Kinsella, and I'm an attorney from Eugene. I'm conducting an investigation here on behalf of Mrs. Bender's aunt, who . . ." Sean trailed off and quickly shook her head. "Oh, you're too busy. I shouldn't bother you right now."

"It's no bother," the woman piped up. "What are you investigating?"

"Well, it has to do with the children and a discipline problem."

She nodded. "I happen to have had a few 'problems' with

the Bender children myself, believe you me. They're wild little hooligans! The mother can't control them. And Lyle—Mr. Bender—he's never around, always out of town or on one of his hunting trips with the men's club. . . .''

"Men's club," Sean repeated. She glanced back at the children in the yard. "Um, I don't want to impose," she said, turning to the old woman again. "But if you have a few minutes, I'd like to ask you some questions about Lyle and Mrs. Bender—and the children, all in confidence, of course."

"Oh, don't get me started on those kids," the old woman said. "Could you carry in the milk and orange juice for me, dear?" She handed the items to Sean, then hoisted up the torn bag and led the way to her door.

Tom watched Hal's Corsica pull away from the curb. Hal hadn't asked for a photo to use on his passport tomorrow. Passports, vaccinations, converting money—these were basic necessities for international travel, and Hal hadn't addressed them at all.

Tom swallowed hard and glanced at the front entrance of his apartment building. Stepping inside, he checked his mailbox for what would be the last time: only one letter, announcing he was a finalist in the Clearing House Million Dollar Sweepstakes. He lumbered up the stairs, then down the corridor to his apartment. Everything seemed so final.

Wandering around his living room, Tom gazed at the pictures, furniture, antiques, and souvenirs he'd collected through the years. Already he felt homesick. It was sad saying good-bye to everything. He tried to convince himself that tomorrow night he'd be staying at a plush hotel in Rio de Janeiro. But the reward they promised still seemed so vague and unreal.

Tom headed to the kitchen cabinet where he kept the Jack Daniels. He had barely enough in the bottle for a couple of shots. He poured half, then quickly drained his glass. He'd need a lot more to make it through the night.

Since taking that first ride with Hal Buckman, Tom knew Hal's people were watching him. He'd noticed guys standing in the street below his window for hours at a time. Sometimes, they sat in their cars parked out front.

Tom wasn't surprised to find one of them now, smoking a cigarette by the front door. This kid was about thirty, with a handlebar mustache, shaggy blond hair, and a ruddy complexion. He wore jeans and a rugby shirt. Smiling at Tom as if he were an old friend, the kid flicked away his cigarette. "Hey there, Tom. You gotta go back inside."

Tom stopped in the doorway of the building. "What do you mean?"

"Orders from Hal," the kid said, shrugging. "You can't go out tonight. They don't want you to run away or try anything stupid. Didn't you notice in your place? They took out your phone. It's tempting to call up certain people to say good-bye. But no can do, Tom. You can't call the police either. The phone will go back in after you leave tomorrow morning."

"But I just want to get some bourbon," Tom admitted.

"Sorry." He shook his head. "Now, go back inside. Okay?"

Frowning, Tom backed away and closed the door. He retreated up the stairs. The kid didn't understand how important the bourbon was at this time. Without it, Tom couldn't sleep; without it, he would have to face the clear, sober truth that he was doomed.

For a while there, he'd actually bought Hal's sweet talk, and the promise of a hideaway in Rio. It made him more willing to kill Dayle Sutton for them. And for the first time in a long while, he'd felt important.

But the sentry outside his building stood as a reminder that they'd actually trapped him. He had no choice in any of this. What was the term business people used? Cost effective? It wasn't cost effective to hire a phony ambulance and two drivers;

to find a corpse that resembled him; to buy a ticket for Rio, and drop a quarter of a million on someone so expendable.

They had no intention of flying him to Rio tomorrow. He would be killed by that bodyguard seconds after murdering Dayle Sutton for them. He was their fall guy, and he couldn't do a damn thing about it.

The following conversation appeared in a private mailbox on the Internet's Dog-Lover's chat line at 3:55 P.M., on Monday, November 18:

PATRIOT: Subject is staying at Opal Lakeview Lodge, registered as Phoebe Daniels . . . No license plate number . . . but Vicki thinks it's a beige Tempo . . . subject dressed in jeans, black sweater & trench coat, hair pinned up . . . should have her located shortly . . . received call from Ray D. minutes ago, thinks he's spotted her.

AMERICKAN: Have U talked to Taggert about Cooper?

PATRIOT: Yes . . . Taggert enroute to designated spot & will call 4 relief upon arrival . . . so far, Cooper unharmed.

AMERICKAN: B prepared to drive Spokane tonight: 3 cars—1 carrying captives Cooper and lawyer. Arrangements made for staging kinky murder-suicide in Spokane hotel room. Cooper's sperm samples still at our disposal & will B used on lawyer to show evidence intercourse before death . . . Also confirms Cooper's guilt in Stoddard crime. Should nicely close case 4 us. Details 2 follow . . . Notify me as soon as U confirm lawyer's location. SAAMO Lieut. signing off.

The old woman who lived down the block from the Benders was a widow named Mrs. Hildegarde Scott. But after fifteen minutes, she insisted that Sean call her Hildy. Her house smelled a bit like rotten cantaloupe, and the Lipton's tea she served was weak. But once Hildy started talking, Sean couldn't shut her up—which was just fine. Occasionally, Sean had to steer her back to a question: "Um, you were going to tell me about this men's club that Lyle belongs to . . ." But the old woman didn't need much prodding.

Mrs. Bender's name was Vicki. The husband, Lyle, was hardly ever home. A while back, he'd tried to become a state trooper, but had been rejected. He was a part-time security guard for the city, which around these parts meant that they let Lyle direct traffic for parades, graduations, funerals, and weddings—probably with a .45 strapped to his belt, if his bumper sticker were any indication. During the summer, he taught driver education at the high school.

Sean asked how Lyle Bender could support a wife and three kids, manage house payments, and buy a new station wagon— all from two low-paying part-time jobs. Hildy didn't have an answer for that.

Lyle had a group of pals he met regularly for hunting expeditions. Most of the men were married with kids, and none of them held steady full-time jobs. A couple were railroad workers, laid off last year. Yet they all had nice homes, new cars, and enough leisure time for frequent trips out of town with their buddies. Hildy mentioned several of Lyle's friends by name. Sean wanted to take notes, but feared that would make Hildy uncomfortable.

She'd found a spot to sit in the living room that allowed her to view the Benders' front yard. The children continued to play and fight out there for nearly forty minutes. It had become too dark to see them now, and Sean took that as her cue to leave. Besides, Hildy started venting again about the Bender children using her yard as a shortcut to and from school.

Sean asked for Hildy's phone number so they could talk later. Thanking her profusely, she slipped out the door and trotted toward her car. She climbed into the front seat. The Bender kids didn't seem to notice her.

She needed to write down the names of Lyle's friends—before she forgot. Digging a pen and notepad from her purse, Sean glanced out the passenger window, and realized something was new. Another vehicle had parked across the street. It took a moment for her to recognize the Chrysler LeBaron. She squinted at the blue car and the fuzzy dice hanging from the rearview mirror. "What the hell?" she murmured.

All at once, Sean knew she wasn't alone. She glanced in the rearview mirror and saw a pair of eyes fixed on her.

The man in the backseat grinned. "Hey, chickie," he whispered. "Where do you think you're going?"

Twenty-three

The policeman sneezed.

Avery didn't say "God bless you." He'd given up trying to communicate with the creep about three hours ago. That was how long he'd been riding in the back of the squad car with his hands cuffed behind him. The grate partition between him and the front seat made him feel as if he were in a cage. The car was muggy, and smelled of Vicks Vaporub and B.O.

Avery had asked the policeman for his name. He'd asked why he was being arrested, and where he was being taken. The husky cop with the runny nose didn't respond. He sat at the wheel, and occasionally those red-rimmed eyes glanced at his prisoner in the rearview mirror. Mostly, he watched the road ahead, and as the chilly afternoon turned to dusk, he must have sneezed, coughed, blown his nose, and spat out the window about fifty times.

He drove the back roads. His police radio came on from time to time, but he always rolled down his window before grabbing the mike and mumbling into it. The howling wind drowned out his conversation.

Avery leaned forward, moved his cuffed hands, and glanced back at his wristwatch: 6:10. If the lights of a gas station and a neighboring burger joint were any indication, they'd reached some semblance of civilization. But the cop kept driving, and the cluster of sleepy stores and streetlights gave way to darkness again.

Then they slowed down, and the squad car bounced over a set of railroad tracks. Avery saw a deserted train depot and a neglected Tudor station house. Two box cars sat in the depot, so old and ravaged they were mere shells. The policeman pulled up alongside the station house. "The Great Northern used to run through here," he said. "This was a major freight stop. But not anymore. Fuckin' Jews on Wall Street put an end to that."

He stepped out of the squad car, then opened Avery's door. "All right, O-U-T," he said, grabbing Avery's arm and pulling him from the cop car.

Avery finally caught a glimpse of the cop's name tag. "Listen, Officer Taggert, you haven't even told me what I'm being charged with. I think—"

He didn't finish. Without warning, Officer Earl Taggert punched Avery in the stomach, a hard wallop that knocked the wind out of him. Avery doubled over. "That's enough out of you," Taggert said.

He led Avery up some steps to the train platform and station house. The battered door looked painted shut, and cobwebs clung to the top corners. But Taggert unlocked the door and pushed it open. The place had a musty odor. Taggert shoved him, and Avery stumbled across the dusty floor and bumped into a bench. "Sit," the cop said.

In the darkness, Avery plopped down on a bench. He was still bent forward, trying to catch his breath after Taggert's sucker punch. He watched the cop move amid the shadows to an office alcove caged off from the waiting area. Taggert switched on an overhead, and the light spilled into the main room. Avery sat on a long, dusty bench with a curved back. Across from him were doors to the men's and ladies' rooms, and a ticket window with bars.

Sitting on the edge of a beat-up metal desk, Taggert made a call on a beige Touch-Tone phone. Avery stared at the ring of keys he'd casually tossed on the desk. He wondered which one worked his handcuffs. For the last two hours he'd been trying in vain to squeeze his hands free.

"Okay, we'll be here," Taggert said, then he hung up. Grabbing his keys, he swaggered over to the radiator. He gave the knob a twist, and Avery heard the sound of steam building up in the old pipes. "We might as well be warm while we wait for the federal men to come pick you up, *Mr. Avery Cooper.*" He sneezed, then blew his nose. "Murder and rape. If it were up to me, I'd put a bullet through your head right now."

"I didn't kill that woman," Avery said. "I never even touched her."

"Shut your pie-hole," Taggert grumbled. He wandered back to the tiny office and picked up the phone again. "Move one muscle, and it's just the excuse I need to put you down. Okay?"

His hands cuffed behind him, Avery stared at Taggert. Cop or no cop, he obviously worked for the group in Opal. There weren't any "federal men" coming. Taggert was just biding time, waiting for his friends to arrive.

Avery tugged and pulled at the cuffs until his knuckles felt raw. He'd never picked a lock in his life. Still he checked the station house floor for a lost bobby pin or piece of wire.

His only hope was acting dumb and obedient, placating Taggert until he found the right moment for a sudden attack—a head-butt or a kick to the groin. He hadn't slugged it out with anyone since breaking Steve Monda's nose in ninth grade. But recently, the stuntman who trained him for his fight scenes in *Expiration Date,* had said he was a "natural." Avery figured the guy was just yanking his chain. And besides, in these cuffs, he didn't stand much chance of overpowering anyone. Still, he had to try something.

Taggert raised his voice in the next room: "You tell that son of a bitch, Hal, that I'm the one who caught him, I should be able to take him to Spokane and do the job there. . . ." A minute later, he hung up the phone.

Through the barred windows, a beam of headlights swept across the musty waiting room. "What the hell . . ." Taggert stomped over to the window. Avery twisted around to look at him.

"Ah, crap. It's Tonto. Goddamn pain in the ass." He turned and glared at Avery. "Want to get yourself into deeper shit? Go ahead and talk to this guy. But if you're smart, you'll shut up."

Avery watched the headlights go out; then after a moment, a tall figure walked past the dirt-smeared window. Slowly, the door opened. A policeman stood at the threshold, one hand poised at his gun. The cop was a Native American in his late twenties, with neatly trimmed black hair, and almost too brawny a physique. His muscles bulged against his blue and gray uniform. He seemed to recognize Taggert and stepped inside. "Earl?" the young policeman said, cracking a wary smile. "Hey, what's going on?"

"Pete, how's it hanging, buddy?" Taggert gave his shoulder a punch.

"I saw your squad car outside. . . ." He looked at Avery, eyes narrowed.

"I'm hauling this joker to Lewiston," Taggert said, pulling out a handkerchief to blow his nose again. "He raped a teenage girl there on Thursday night. I just stopped here to take a pee."

Pete seemed puzzled. Hands on his hips, he glanced at Avery—and then at Taggert. "I didn't hear anything about a rape in Lewiston on Thursday."

The other cop laughed and scratched his head. "Hell, then you must be slipping, Pete."

He chuckled along. Stepping in front of Avery, he stared at him again. "Wait a minute," he murmured. "My God, you're Avery Cooper. What are you—"

A loud shot rang out.

The young policeman gasped. He seemed paralyzed for a moment, standing there with a dazed look in his brown eyes, Then he twisted around and keeled over, slamming onto the dusty floorboards.

Avery gaped down at the bullet hole in his back, the blood slowly blooming dark crimson on his gray shirt.

Officer Taggert still had the gun in his hand. "Now look what you've done, trying to resist arrest," he said. "You just shot a police officer."

"I asked you a question, doll face."

Sean didn't turn to look at the stranger in the backseat. Gripping the wheel, she studied him in the rearview mirror. "What do you want?"

"I just want to know you better." He brushed her ear with a gun.

"Okay," she said calmly. "Then let's go some place and talk over coffee." She started the car.

"Turn off the goddamn engine," he growled.

Sean obeyed. Leaving the keys in the ignition, she slowly sat back.

"I almost ran you down a few hours ago—outside the post office. You ought to be more careful, honey. Why were you in such a hurry?"

"I had to meet an old friend of my mother's. She lives in that white stucco." Sean nodded toward Hildy's house. She furtively slid her hand toward her purse. There was a pocket-knife inside, within her reach.

"Bullshit. But say something else in that high and mighty tone of yours. Say: 'I'm not supposed to hang up on you, though I'm sorely tempted.' "

Sean stared at him in the rearview mirror.

"We talked on the phone night before last. You're Dayle's lawyer friend, Sean Olson."

Sean swiveled around. The stranger was a handsome guy, despite his unwashed long, black hair. In that leather jacket, the jeans and T-shirt, he had a certain cheap, lounge-lizard sexiness. Beside him on the backseat was a big, black leather satchel. "Are you Nick Brock?" She murmured.

"Pleased to finally meet you, babe," he said with a cocky smile.

She gaped at him. "You're supposed to be dead. That hotel fire—"

"Oh, yeah." He reached inside his bag and took out a wallet. He flipped it open and glanced at something. "The guy toasted in the fire was Charles W. Stample, age forty-nine. I figure, with the police force here, I have another day before Sheriff Andy and Barney Fife figure out the charcoal briquette in their morgue is actually one of Opal's most eligible bachelors. Meanwhile, I'll take advantage of them thinking I'm dead." He slipped the wallet and his gun back inside his bag.

"Charlie," Sean murmured. "Hildy mentioned him. He's one of Lyle's hunting buddies." She scowled at Nick. "Did you kill him? Are you the one who set fire to that hotel room?"

"No, Charlie did. I stepped out for some ice, and the SOB pulled a gun on me by the vending machines. We went back to my room, and he conked me on the head. But what he didn't know is that Nick Brock has one hell of a thick skull. While I was down, he started to torch the place. So I jumped up, punched him in the throat, grabbed his wallet and keys, and got the hell out. The joint was already on fire."

"And you left him there to burn to death?"

Nick rolled his eyes. "Yeah, I feel really bad about it too.

I mean, hell, lady, check out what this bozo did to me.'' He bowed his head and parted a clump of hair to reveal a fresh, ugly scab. "You ought to feel this bump. The guy was trying to ice me, for Pete's sake. Go ahead, feel it.''

"That's okay. I'll take your word.''

"I checked out his apartment. Lots of expensive shit: a big-screen TV, state-of-the-art computer, jacuzzi in the can, the works. Yet the guy lived like a pig. The place was a sty. And old Charlie had a stash of porn tapes and magazines that would curl your hair. Real kinky stuff. I kept only a couple of the videos. The rest, forget about it. Too out there, even for Nick.''

Sean glared at him. "During this *exhausting search for evidence,* did you uncover anything useful?''

He nodded. "With the porn stash, I found some Polaroids he'd taken of naked hookers. And this was among them.'' Nick pulled a photo out of his vest pocket. "I'm not sure I should show you, honey. It's of Charlie Stample—with Tony Katz after they finished with him. It's pretty sickening.''

"Give,'' Sean said, her palm out. But as soon as he handed her the color snapshot, she regretted even glimpsing it. Like a proud hunter, Charlie Stample grinned for the camera and held Tony's head back by the scalp so his face was visible. Tony's eyes were open in a dead stare. The handsome movie star had been stripped naked and tied to a tree. Lacerations covered his limp body, and long streaks of blood ran down his chest, torso, and legs. It looked as if his genitals had been mutilated. Charlie Stample brandished a pistol in his other hand, and aimed it at Tony Katz in a jocular fashion.

"Oh, my God,'' Sean muttered in horror.

"Still feel bad about good ole' Charlie the Crispy Critter?''

Handing the Polaroid back to him, Sean quickly shook her head.

Nick tucked the photo back inside his pocket. "I combed through his place, but couldn't find an address book. I don't know who his buddies are.''

"I have some names from the old woman across the street," Sean said. "She gave me a lot of useful information about her neighbors. Mrs. Bender picks up the mail for this group."

"Mrs. Bender? You mean the heifer with the two brats?" Nick asked.

Sean winced. "You're really offensive, you know that?"

Nick chuckled. "Oh, a tough classy broad, just like Dayle Sutton."

"Dayle's not so tough. In fact, she was pretty broken up over your premature demise. God knows why. But she actually cried."

He smiled. "Really? Well, let's not mend her broken heart just yet. These jokers have somebody working close to Dayle. I'm better off if she thinks I'm toes up." He nodded up ahead at the LeBaron. "Guess that's as good a place as any to ditch his car. I've been driving it around since yesterday morning, scared shitless someone would mistake me for Charlie. I hightailed out of town after the fire. Came back this morning to watch the post office. I had a hunch about you when I saw you hanging around—"

"Heads up," Sean said.

Vicki Bender emerged from the house with the bundle of mail. She said something to the two children, then headed into her station wagon.

"Looks like she's going to make her delivery," Sean murmured, starting up the car. "I can't believe she's leaving those two kids alone."

"Oh, you missed it," Nick said. "About twenty minutes ago, while you were with Grandma, this older kid came home on his bike. Mama met him at the front door, and jumped on his skinny ass about something. From what I could hear, the twerp was supposed to baby-sit for the other two brats."

Nick put a hand on her shoulder. "Listen, let Mama go for half a block, then start to follow. It's how I tailed you."

Sean let out an exasperated sigh, but took his advice. She

watched Vicki Bender back out of the driveway. Then she followed a safe distance behind the station wagon. She wished Avery were with her now—instead of this rude, cheese-ball detective. Wherever he was, Avery had to be worried about her. She hated leaving Dayle in the dark too.

"You know," she said, watching Mrs. Bender's station wagon. "If I don't get in touch with Dayle by tomorrow morning, she's sending in the FBI."

Nick let out a defiant laugh. "Tomorrow morning? Listen, counselor, the shit's going to hit the fan a hell of a lot sooner than tomorrow morning. Let's just try to survive the evening, okay?"

Sean studied him in the rearview mirror for a moment. Then she nodded, because she knew he was right.

Dayle listened to the answering machine in her study while she slipped off her shoes. Leaning over her desk, she lowered the volume on the machine. She didn't want Ted hearing if Sean came on. He was getting comfortable in the guest room down the hall. So far, there were three messages from studio publicity people. Dayle skipped ahead to the next:

Beep. "Hi, Dayle—" It was her agent.

Beep. "Hello, Dayle? This is Jonathan Brooks."

She quickly grabbed a pen. Jonathan's gravelly voice somehow managed to sound unmasculine; on the phone he could have been mistaken for a brash old aunt who smoked too much. "I just flew back into town today and got your message. It's funny too, because I saw you on the E-Channel Friday night, giving a fabulous pro-gay speech, and next to you is one of the biggest homophobic assholes I've ever met. I'm talking about Teddy Kovak. It's true, he worked for Gil, but—well, I'm just surprised you hired him. Anyway, I'm home tonight, so give a buzz. . . ."

Dayle dialed the number on her cordless, then glanced down the hall. Ted's door was open a crack. She heard a toilet flushing.

"Hello?"

"Jonathan?" Dayle whispered. "Hi. It's Dayle Sutton."

"Well, hello there, Dayle. You got my call back?"

"Yes, thanks." She ducked into the study again, and closed the door. "I'm not sure I understood your message. Ted was Gil Palarmo's personal bodyguard for nearly a year, yet you say he's homophobic?"

A robust laugh came over the line. "Did Picasso paint? Of course, it took old Ted a while to figure Gil out. At first, he believed that ladies'-man routine Gil sold to the public. Plus Gil always had these bimbo groupies following him around, and he gave Ted his pick of the harem. If not for those fringe benefits, I think Ted might have quit, because after a spell, like I say, he realized he wasn't in Kansas anymore, Toto. And let me tell you, he didn't try to hide his contempt for Gil and the rest of us."

"Why didn't Gil fire him?" Dayle asked in a hushed tone.

"Oh, we were having way too much fun teasing him. Gil used to flirt with Ted, drove him crazy!" Again, Jonathan bellowed that husky laugh. "I mean, Ted wasn't hard to look at, and we delighted in getting a rise out of him. He was so uptight, so easy to piss off."

"Then Gil just had him around for laughs?" Dayle whispered.

"No, Teddy was good," Jonathan said. "He knew his business. Gil hired him in the first place because he'd had a bad brush with the mob. They wanted Gil to sing in certain clubs, and he wouldn't play ball. Ted knew how they might get past all the security in Gil's penthouse undetected, where they could plant bugging devices or a bomb, how to tap a phone line. He knew everything there was to know about surveillance. I tell you, if Ted was working on the other side, Gil would have been a goner."

A knock came upon the door. It gave her Dayle a start. She hadn't heard any footsteps. "Just a sec," she whispered into the phone. Then she opened the door. Ted had changed into a pair of khakis and a T-shirt. He also sported a shoulder holster and gun. "Sorry to interrupt," he said. "I was going to order Chinese. Do you want some?"

Smiling nervously, Dayle shook her head. "No, thanks," she murmured, a hand over the mouthpiece. "I'll just heat up some soup later. Thanks." She gently closed the door, then whispered into the phone, "You were saying?"

"Well, I was about to say that old Ted has to be pretty full of himself to put Gil down as a reference. Then again, Gil's dead. And like I say, Ted did do a good job. Even I have to admit that much. But . . . well . . ."

"Go on," Dayle urged him.

"I think of that speech you made about fighting homophobia, and I applaud you, Dayle. But I see Teddy Kovak standing with you, and I'm telling you, he's not on our side."

They followed Vicki Bender's station wagon past the post office minimall. Sean stayed two or three cars behind her. She couldn't help looking around at other cars and wondering if Avery was in one of them. Had he even made it to Opal? Certainly, she would have heard something on the radio if he'd been arrested or hurt. It was hard concentrating on her conversation with Nick in the backseat. "I'm sorry, what was I saying?" she asked.

"You were giving me the skinny on this men's club."

"That's right," Sean said, eyes on the road. "According to the neighbor, it's a bunch of hunting buddies, very few of whom hold steady full-time jobs. Yet they all seem financially fit. For example, your late friend, Charlie Stample, owned a gun and tackle store, open three days a week—as long as there wasn't a sign on the door saying GONE HUNTING."

"Other incomes," Nick said, nodding. "It explains all that expensive crap at Charlie's place. This hate group must pay well."

Up ahead, Vicki Bender turned into the parking lot of a bowling alley. On the side of the long building, blinking neon white bowling pins led to a sign: OPAL STRIKE N' SPARE — THE KINGPIN RESTAURANT — GAMES N' FOOD.

Sean parked five rows away from Vicki Bender's station wagon. Clutching the bundle of mail, Vicki headed into the bowling alley.

The glass door was still swinging back and forth when Sean and Nick stepped in after her. Rock and roll oldies were piped over speakers, competing with the echoing din and clamor. The place smelled of cigarettes and shoe leather. Vicki knocked on a door by the vending machines. As the door opened Sean glimpsed five men inside, seated at a round table; it looked like a poker game in progress—except one of the men had a laptop computer in front of him. They seemed normal enough, between the ages of thirty and fifty, dressed casually, but clean. They didn't look like monsters. In fact, all of the men stood up when Vicki walked into the room. Then the door closed.

Sean and Nick strolled over to a rack of bowling balls. She kept glancing back at that closed door. "Well, any ideas?" she asked, over all the noise. Someone had cranked up Del Shannon's "Runaway" on the speakers. "We can't hang around here too long. Someone's bound to recognize us."

Nick feigned interest in a bowling ball. "Just keep cool. I'm thinking."

"Well, don't blow a fuse," she muttered. Sean checked the back room door again. The girl at the shoe-rental booth was staring at them. "Is it too soon to call in the state police or the FBI?" Sean asked. "We could try to explain the situation to them."

"No way," Nick replied. "If what Grandma Hildy says is true, these guys are friendly with the police. Someone would tip off the local authorities about what's coming around the pike, and—chain reaction—these guys would scatter or clean house before anyone got near Opal. No, nice try.''

Sean sighed. Nick was right. And if Avery were here, he'd be the first person they'd arrest—not someone from the group. Outside of the late Charlie Stample's Polaroid, they had no proof implicating these other people in the celebrity murders. ''I have a little recorder in my purse,'' she said, thinking out loud. ''Too bad we can't pry a confession out of one of them.''

''We could always grab the first guy who comes out to use the can,'' Nick said, studying the closed door. ''Then we can take him for a ride to a remote spot, and *scare* a confession out of him.''

''Abduct one of them—right here? Are you nuts? This is their turf. We'll have the whole group on our tail—and the local police too. We'd never make it.'' She took another look toward the shoe-rental booth.

Snapping her gum, the girl leaned on the counter and continued to stare at them. Sean guessed she was twenty-five—with more than her share of hard knocks. She might have been pretty at one time, but now she just appeared tired and burned out. The red STRIKE N' SPARE T-shirt hung on her emaciated frame, and she'd carelessly pinned back her limp brown hair.

''That woman in the booth won't stop looking at us,'' Sean whispered.

Nick glanced over his shoulder. ''Huh, she's checking out my butt.''

''Oh, would you please get over yourself for just five minutes?''

But Nick wasn't listening. He was on his way to talk to the girl, whose face lit up as he approached. Fascinated, Sean watched them. Nick whispered something to her. She giggled and tossed back her head—the official flirt laugh. After a minute, she took a pencil from behind her ear, then scribbled something down on a score sheet. She looked up and caught Sean staring.

Sean turned away—toward the rack of bowling balls. A couple of minutes passed, and then Nick came up to her. "Okay, the wheels are in motion," he said, handing her a piece of paper. In schoolgirl penmanship with little circles over the *I*'s, the young woman had written down seven names. "See if those match with any of the guys Grandma told you about," Nick whispered. "By the way, that's Jill in the booth, and if she asks, you're my sister. Jill says these guys meet here regularly three or four times a week. I asked which one has the nicest house, and is married with kids—in other words, the one with the most to lose."

"What are you talking about?" Sean asked.

"We're going for a ride with Larry Chadwick," Nick whispered. He threw a smile at Jill, raised his eyebrows, and nodded. She winked back.

"What's going on?" Sean said.

"In a minute, Jill's gonna step into that room and tell Larry Chadwick he has an emergency phone call from his wife. Jill thinks it's all part of a practical joke. When he comes out to take the call, I'll walk up, tell him I have a gun, and we'll go to his car—"

"My God, this is insane—"

"You hang by that meeting room door, and make sure Jill doesn't screw up. She's supposed to tell the boys that Larry will call them from home later."

"How could she be dumb enough to cooperate with you in this—this 'practical joke'? You're a total stranger to her—"

"Doll, she's twenty-seven years old, handles smelly shoes all day for minimum wage, and she's hot for me. Believe me, she's dumb enough to cooperate. Once you know these guys have bought Jill's song and dance, head outside. I'll make Larry flash his headlights. Are you following me?"

Sean saw the young woman come out from behind the booth. She started toward the meeting room door.

"We'll drive out of town," Nick went on. "You're the lawyer. Promise Larry a deal, immunity for his confession. We'll get it on that recorder of yours, then call the state police once we're far enough away from Opal."

"And they'll arrest us for kidnapping, you idiot," she said urgently. She watched Jill knock on the door. "My God, she's going through with it. This is crazy. I don't have the power to make any immunity deals—"

"Well, maybe Larry Chadwick won't know that."

One of the men opened the meeting room door. Jill said something to him, and pointed toward her booth. The man nodded, then stepped back inside. The emaciated girl turned and gave Nick a sly smile. Then she scurried toward her workstation.

"Nick, this is a terrible idea," Sean said.

"It's all we got, babe," he replied. "See you in Larry Chadwick's car."

"No—" she started to say, but Nick started toward the shoe-rental booth. Someone emerged from the little conference room, a tall man with wavy, strawberry-blond hair and wholesome good looks. He was about forty, and wore pressed khakis and a crisp white shirt. He looked very familiar.

Nick strolled up to the man—just as he reached for the phone on the shoe-rental counter. Sean moved a bit closer. Nick whispered something to the tall man. Even at this distance, Sean could see him tense up. She kept trying to remember where she'd seen him before. After a moment, he stiffly turned and started toward the exit—with Nick close behind him.

Jill returned to the meeting room and stuck her head in the doorway. "Excuse me?" she announced, loud enough for Sean to hear over all the noise. "Mr. Chadwick had to run home, but he said he'll call you guys later."

Sean heard one the men reply: "Thanks. Can you close the door?"

Sean retreated toward the exit. Jill caught up with her by the shoe-rental booth. She smiled and snapped her gum. "Tell your brother to pick me up here at ten. Okay?"

Sean nodded. "All right. Thanks—for playing along with the gag."

Her stomach in knots, Sean headed for the exit and stepped outside to the cold. "God, please, get me through this night," she whispered.

In the parking lot, a green Honda Accord flashed its headlights twice.

Dear Sirs,
   By the time you get this letter, I will be dead. I will have also killed Dayle Sutton. Much will probably be written about me in the next few days, and I want you to get the story right, why I did it, and who I am.

Tom stopped writing for a moment. He'd never sent a letter to the *Los Angeles Times* before, and he wanted it perfect. He'd thought about typing the letter to make it more official. But if Hal and his gang had planted bugs in Maggie's house, they'd certainly done the same in his place. The clicking of his Underwood's keys would give him away. So Tom had switched on the TV, and started his correspondence in longhand.

The mailbox across the street had a morning pickup at 8:15. If he mailed the letter tonight, it would be posted before Dayle Sutton's death tomorrow. They'd know it wasn't some crackpot. But he still had to slip past Hal's guard outside.

Returning to the apartment after his aborted bourbon run, he'd noticed the telephone was gone—just as the young fellow had said. The phone would be returned once he left in the morning. No doubt, they would also search the place and erase any evidence of their association with him. It had to appear as if he'd acted alone in killing Dayle Sutton.

They might even plant something to confirm that he'd mur-

dered Maggie. Why not? It was true. And they could do anything
they wanted. He wouldn't be around to defend himself. He
wouldn't be in Rio either. He'd be dead.

This letter to the *Times* was his only way of making people
understand. Tom picked up his pen and continued writing:

> *I was forced into killing Dayle Sutton by a group
> who hate her politics. There are several people in this
> organization. I didn't act on my own. I'm the fall guy.
> My contact has been a man who calls himself Hal Buck-
> man. Hal promised to smuggle me out of the country
> when it's all over. But I think they'll kill me after I've
> done what they want.*

> *I have no choice in what will happen tomorrow. But
> if anything comes from all this, at least, people will know
> who Tom Lance was.*

> *I was an actor, a good one too. But I had some unlucky
> breaks, so nowadays, not many people know who I am.
> I suppose all that will change after Dayle Sutton is dead.*

> *People should know that I helped Maggie McGuire
> get her start in movies. I was her fiancé at one time, and
> I've never stopped loving her. I killed Maggie. It was an
> accident. I went to her house, we argued, and I shot her
> with a gun I meant to use on myself later. I wish I could
> take that moment back.*

> *These people were after Maggie the same way they're
> after Dayle Sutton. Maggie's place was wired, and they
> had a recording of me shooting her and used it to get
> my cooperation.*

> *I apologize to Dayle Sutton's family. I also apologize
> to Maggie's children, and her fans. Please know, I loved
> her.*

> *I hope when people talk about Tom Lance, they realize
> that I didn't want to be a murderer. I hope they realize*

that I made some good movies, and I helped Maggie
McGuire become a star.
    Thank you.

Tom signed and printed his name on the bottom. Folding up
the letter, he slipped it into an envelope he'd already addressed.

Moving over to the window, he glanced down at the mailbox
across the street. Only a few car lengths away, Hal's guard
leaned against the hood of a white Taurus. He looked up at the
window, and Tom quickly stepped back.

He turned up the TV, then went to the door. He almost
expected to find another one of Hal's henchmen in the hallway,
but the corridor was vacant. The neighbor he knew best was
an old woman who walked with a cane. He could hardly ask
her to zip down to the mailbox for him. He tried the apartment
across the hall from her. A stocky, young black man had moved
in about two months ago. Knocking on the door, Tom tried to
remember his name.

The door was answered by a huge black woman with big
auburn hair that had to be a wig. She wore a red sequined gown
and brandished a cigarette. "Yes, honey?" she said.

Tom took a step back. "Um, doesn't a young man live
here?"

"You're looking at him," the woman said, a hand on her
hip.

Tom shook his head.

"I'm a performer, I do drag, honey. This is my alter ego,
Catalina Converter. Aren't you from down the hall?"

His mouth open, Tom nodded.

Catalina looked at the envelope in Tom's hand. "Is that
letter for me?"

"Um, no," Tom managed to say. "I have a touch of the
gout, and I need to stay off my feet. I was wondering if you
could mail this for me."

Catalina shrugged. "Sure. I'm about to take off for the club.

I'll drop it in the mailbox outside.'' Opening the door wider, he turned and put out his cigarette, then grabbed a long black feathered boa from the sofa.

Tom saw an apartment even more cluttered with movie memorabilia than his own. On one wall, Catalina had a poster of Marilyn Monroe, and another of Paul Newman. Glamour shots of actresses—mostly Lena Horne and Dorothy Dandridge—adorned the walls. The sofa tables were full of ceramic images of Marilyn, and James Dean, along with framed standing photos of various other stars. Movie books and videos overflowed on the brick and board bookshelves.

Tom had no idea this movie mecca had been down the hall from him. ''I like your film art collection,'' he said to the drag queen, who was checking himself in the mirror by the door. ''Do you have any Maggie McGuire?''

''Oh, the late, Marvelous Maggie,'' Catalina said, turning away from the mirror with a pained expression on his carefully made-up face. ''No, sir. But I cried buckets when I received word she'd passed on. Let me tell you, honey child, I didn't need to see clips from any naughty movie girlfriend made when she must have been starving. No, thank you very much. The lady had class, and she deserves better.''

Tom smiled slightly. ''I agree.''

''On top of that, she has a cute gay son.'' Catalina tossed one end of the boa over his shoulder; a rather melodramatic the-show-must-go-on gesture. Then he plucked the envelope out of Tom's hand. ''Well, I have to get this tired old ass of mine in gear. My public is waiting. I'll mail your letter for you, honey. Stay off your feet.''

Tom thanked him. ''Could I ask you for one more favor? You wouldn't happen to have some bourbon, would you?''

Five minutes later, Tom was back in his apartment with a couple of miniature bottles of Jim Beam. Catalina's last boyfriend had been a flight attendant. Now, at least Tom had something to get him through the night.

He turned off the lights, then crept to the window. Still leaning against the Taurus, Hal's friend puffed on a cigarette and read the *Auto Trader*. He looked up from his magazine— toward the building's front door. After a moment, Catalina came around the corner, sashaying in front of Hal's guard.

Tom could see the letter in Catalina's hand. The huge drag queen in red sequins was hardly an inconspicuous mailman.

''What the fuck?'' Hal's buddy said loudly. Tom could hear through the glass. ''Goddamn faggot! Are you supposed to be a man or a woman?''

Catalina patted his big hair. ''Honey, I'm a *goddess*. And if I weren't in makeup, I'd beat the ever-lovin' shit out of you, and you know I can.''

Hal's friend stood there with his mouth open, looking stupid.

Tom watched Catalina move on, undaunted. He dropped the letter in the mailbox, then sauntered to the bus stop—half a block away. Catalina waved down the bus, then climbed aboard.

The letter had been mailed.

Tom opened the first of the two miniatures. He sat in the dark living room and drank. After a while, he turned on the lamp by the sofa and paged through his photo album. He pried certain photos from the four-corner holders, his favorites: Maggie and him talking with Janet Leigh and Robert Mitchum; Maggie alone; him visiting Lana Turner on a movie set, and a few others. To the pile, he added five movie lobby cards, his best shots from his best movies. Finally, he chose his favorite publicity shot, from 1950: him in a tux, smoking a cigarette, his black hair tousled, pretty damn glamorous. He set the glossy on top of the pile, then pulled out a pen and autographed it: *To Catalina, Thank you for being a good neighbor. Tom Lance.*

He carried these things he'd held so dear down the hallway to his neighbor's door. One by one, he slid the photos and lobby cards under the crack. He knew the drag queen down the hall would take good care of these mementos for him, because like him, he too loved the movies and Maggie.

* * *

Dayle sat at her kitchen table with the *Waiting for the Fall* script, and Fred curled up in her lap. She had her big AA meeting speech tomorrow, and was reviewing her notes. But she couldn't concentrate.

She kept replaying in her head what Jonathan Brooks had told her about Ted's expertise. Ted knew how to break into secured penthouses undetected, where to plant bugging devices, how to tap a phone line. *I tell you, if the guy was working on the other side, Gil would have been a goner.*

She imagined Ted organizing the surveillance on her. She could see him slipping past the guards downstairs and breaking into her apartment while she showered. Was it Ted who had left that note about Cindy on her bed? Was he one of the men up on the roof at twilight a couple of weeks ago?

Dayle told herself not to get carried away. She was basing her fears on the mere fact that Ted didn't like being teased by Gil Palarmo and his gay friends. Besides, even if he was working with this hate group, he wasn't about to try anything tonight. Too many people knew he was supposed to be protecting her.

"Oh, there you are."

Startled, Dayle glanced up at Ted Kovak, standing in the kitchen doorway. "You scared me for a second," she said, straightening in her chair.

"What time do you want the limo tomorrow?" he asked.

"Six-thirty."

"I'll try to stay out of your hair until morning."

She hugged Fred to her chest. "I might take a shower tonight, so if you hear the phone, just let the machine pick it up."

He nodded. "Well, everything's secure here."

"It's comforting to know that—especially while I'm in the shower."

Grinning, he leaned against the door frame. *"Psycho* back-lash?"

"No, more like the other day I told you about—when some-one broke into the apartment."

"Well, don't worry," he replied with a confident wink. "You have some good guys protecting you tonight, and I'm just down the hall. You won't come out of the shower and find any weird notes pinned to your favorite party dress—not while I'm here."

Nodding, Dayle managed to smile back at him. "Thanks, Ted. Um, did the other guys get something to eat?"

"Yes, ma'am. They're taken care of. I'll be in my room if you need anything. Good night."

"G'night, Ted. Thanks again." She watched him retreat down the hall; then her smile waned. He shut the guest room door.

Ted Kovak had slipped. He knew about the break-in; but she'd never told him about finding the message pinned to her dress on the bed. Besides Sean and herself, the only other person who knew about that note was the one who had left it for her.

Twenty-four

Sean approached the Honda Accord. Inside, the blond-haired man stiffly sat at the wheel—with Nick in back. She opened the front passenger door and climbed inside. Larry turned and glared at her. The handsome, strawberry-blond man seemed tense, but not particularly scared.

Sean now remembered where she'd seen him before, The My-T-Comfort Inn. He was The Boy Next Door—or The *Asshole* Next Door: *If I knew you were stocking this place with whores, I never would have booked us here.*

"Honey, meet Larry Chadwick," Nick announced from the backseat. "Larry says he doesn't know Charlie Stample or Lyle Bender." Nick poked the man's shoulder with his gun. "Larry, do you recognize my honey bun here? Here's a hint. She's a real smart lawyer."

Sean frowned. She wanted to slug Nick for involving her in this awful abduction business. Nick handed her Larry's wallet and keys. "Have a look through his wallet," he said. "Lare, take the keys and start the car. We're hitting the road. You still haven't answered my question about our gal here.''

Sean gave Larry Chadwick the car keys. He shook his head at her. ''I don't know you,'' he said. ''But you look like an intelligent woman. Perhaps you can convince your friend here to let me go. You have my wallet. You can take the car. I don't want any trouble.''

Sean glanced at his driver's license. ''We're not here to rob you, Mr. Chadwick. And I don't want any trouble either. So please, start the car.''

He took a long look back at the bowling alley, then turned the key in the ignition. Nick told him to make a left at the lot exit.

As they started down Main Street, Sean flipped through the photos in Larry's wallet: pictures of his wife, two children, a collie, and Larry with a rifle, posed beside a deer carcass. As much as she hated this scheme, she had to go along with it now. ''My colleague's telling the truth, Mr. Chadwick,'' she said, still browsing through the wallet. ''I'm an attorney. I see here you're a hunter—like Charlie Stample and Lyle Bender.''

''I told your friend already, I don't know them.''

''Nevertheless, perhaps I can swing a deal for you.'' Sean looked at the wallet again. ''You have a wife and two very nice-looking children. I can't guarantee anything, but if you cooperate with us, maybe you won't be separated from your loved ones too long. We might work out a reduced sentence for you, maybe even immunity.''

''I don't know what you're talking about,'' Larry said. ''Besides, I'm not the one breaking the law here.''

''Take a left at the light,'' Nick piped up from the backseat.

Sean studied Larry Chadwick for a moment. Something was awry. He didn't seem very scared or intimidated—just miffed at what might be a temporary inconvenience for him. As they turned left, he checked the rearview mirror. Sean glanced back to see a Corsica a short distance behind them.

"A paper trail led us to you," she continued. "This is your chance to cut a deal before—if you'll excuse the expression—the shit hits the fan. We know your group is responsible for several celebrity murders and smears—along with an attempt to frame Avery Cooper for murder. Why not save your family and yourself a lot of grief? Tell us about this local men's club, and your 'hunting' expeditions."

"C'mon, Lare," Nick added. "We'll say you cooperated. . . ."

Silent, he stared at the dark, lonely highway ahead.

They'd reached the outskirts of Opal. Sean checked over her shoulder again. The Corsica was still back there. "Pull over," she said edgily. "Pull over now. I want this damn car behind us to pass."

"I may go over a bump or two," Larry calmly replied, eying Nick in the rearview mirror. "For the safety of all of us, could you please lower that gun for a few seconds? I don't want it going off by accident."

Nick grinned. "Sure, Lare."

Larry slowed the car, steered onto the shoulder of the road, then brought them to a stop. His left hand casually slid off the wheel.

Sean turned and watched the Corsica approaching. She squinted as its headlights illuminated the interior of Larry's car.

"HANDS ON THE GODDAMN WHEEL!" Nick yelled.

"I was just about to open the window—"

"You were just going for the door," Nick said. "Hands on the wheel."

Larry clutched the steering wheel as the Corsica cruised by. The teenage driver and his girlfriend briefly stared at them, then sped away.

Her nerves frayed, Sean took a deep breath and turned to Nick. "Give me that Polaroid, will you?" She switched on the interior overhead light, then showed the photo to Larry, the one from Charlie Stample's secret archives: Charlie the hunter, posing with his kill—the mutilated corpse of Tony Katz. "You were there that night, weren't you?" Sean said.

The tiniest flicker of a smile passed across Larry's face as he studied the picture.

Sean began to tremble with anger. How could he smile at something so brutal and monstrous? Swallowing hard, she tucked the Polaroid into her purse, then pulled out the small tape recorder, and switched it on.

"We can't stay here," Nick said. "Let's get moving, Lare."

Ignoring him, Larry stared at Sean, the tiny smirk still on his face.

"C'mon!" Nick rapped the back of Larry's skull with the gun muzzle.

"Ah, fuck!" he growled, wincing. He pulled onto the highway again. "Son of a bitch," he grumbled, rubbing his head.

"I hope it hurts like hell," Sean said. She adjusted the volume on her recorder. "Though I happen to think you're scum, I'm still willing to cut you a deal, Mr. Chadwick. If you tell us about these friends of yours and your organization, I might get you a reduced sentence."

"Hmmmm," was all he said, as if to ponder whether or not he wanted to cooperate. Sean didn't like it; he seemed too cool under fire.

"I don't think Larry's interested in making any deals," Nick said. "Still, you *want* to tell us about your organization, don't you, Lare? In fact, you're just itching to tell us how powerful and righteous you guys are." Nick nudged his shoulder with the gun muzzle. "C'mon, educate us, Lare."

Larry Chadwick glanced in the rearview mirror and smiled a little. "Neither one of you have heard of SAAMO, have you?"

"Is that an acronym?" Sean asked. "What does it stand for?"

He turned his attention away from the road and gazed at her

for a moment. "It stands for the future. That's something you don't have any more of, *Ms. Olson,* because you're going to die. You, your buddy here, and your other unfortunate friend, Avery Cooper."

Avery sat on the dusty wooden bench with his hands cuffed behind him. He numbly gazed at the young policeman, face-down on the dirty floor, a bullet in his back. Taggert was in the little office, on the phone with one of his cronies. At one point, he raised his voice: "Hey, he identified the prisoner, I had no choice! What was I supposed to do?"

He'd taken the other cop's gun, but hadn't unclasped the keys from his belt. Avery wondered if one of those keys might fit his cuffs. He inched his foot over toward the fallen police-man's belt. With the tip of his shoe he tried to nudge the key ring from its clasp. For a second, it looked as though the dead policeman flinched. Avery hesitated. He checked on Taggert again, then slowly stood. Twisting to one side, he squatted down to reach for the keys.

"Fine," he heard Taggert say on the phone. "So we make it look like he killed the son of a bitch, or you send somebody here to get rid of the body and the squad car." He chuckled. "Yeah, no kidding. Bye."

Avery vainly groped and tugged at the key ring. He heard Taggert hang up the phone. The cop sneezed and blew his nose. Avery almost stumbled backward, but quickly regained his footing and landed on the bench. He was still catching his breath as Taggert ambled around the corner.

Avery reminded himself to act dumb. It was his only chance of throwing this creep off guard. He innocently gazed up at Taggert, who kicked at the young policeman's foot. "Why did you shoot him?" Avery asked, with a meek, obtuse look. "Was he a crooked cop or something?"

The stocky officer gaped at him, not quite sure someone

could be so ingenuously stupid. Finally, he folded his arms and snickered. "Yeah, him heap big crooked lawman. Injun no good. Me fix."

Avery wanted to vomit, but he merely nodded. His eyes downcast, he thought he saw the young cop breathing. Then again, it might have just been air escaping a dead man's lungs. He wondered if Taggert had seen it too. "I hope we can clear all this up once the federal men arrive," he said quietly. "When are they due?"

"In an hour." Taggert blew his nose. "Just hold your water."

"Well, that's why I'm asking," Avery replied timidly. "I almost peed in my pants when you shot this guy. And I've had to go for about an hour now." He nodded toward the men's room door. "Could I? Would it be okay?"

Taggert sighed. "Yeah, sure. Why not?"

Avery stood and stepped around the body on the floor. "Thank you," he said. He pushed the men's room door with his shoulder.

Taggert followed him inside and switched on the light. The bathroom had a sharp rusty odor. It seemed cold and damp after the heated waiting room. A toilet stall occupied the corner, and two tall porcelain urinals lined the graffiti-marred wall. Avery stepped up to one of the urinals, then glanced over his shoulder. "Um, Officer Taggert? Could you—help me out here?"

The cop looked at him as if he were crazy. "Oh, yeah, sure. Fuck that."

Avery shrugged helplessly and wiggled his hands in the cuffs behind him. "I'm sorry. . . ."

Shaking his head, Taggert grabbed Avery's arm and unlocked the cuffs. He left one hand shackled, then stepped aside and drew his gun. "Okay," he said in his congested voice. "I don't have all day."

"Thanks very much," Avery said, unzipping his trousers.

Taggert nodded distractedly. He put the keys back in his

pocket and pulled out a handkerchief. He looked as if he was about to sneeze again. His eyes were closed and he had his mouth open in a sinus-blocked grimace.

Instead of reaching inside his pants, Avery suddenly lunged at Taggert. The cop was in the middle of his sneeze when Avery punched him in the face.

The gun went off, and the shot echoed within the tiled bathroom. Avery felt a sharp burning pain in his left thigh, but it didn't slow him down. He slammed his fist into Taggert's face again. The policeman dropped his gun, then flew back against the toilet stall partition. Avery kept hitting him. He was like a crazy man. He wasn't thinking about escaping. He was pummeling the smarmy son of a bitch who had amused himself with an injun impersonation after shooting that young cop in the back. Avery punched away at Taggert until the crooked cop slid down to the dirty tiles, half dead.

Standing over him, Avery suddenly realized he'd been shot. Blood trickled down his leg and wet the top of his sock.

Taggert stirred a little and reached for the gun on the floor. Avery kicked it away. But he was overwhelmed with fatigue, and his movements were labored as he grabbed Taggert by the front of his shirt and dragged him toward the urinals. "Who killed Libby Stoddard?" he asked. "Who set me up?"

"Fuck you!" Taggert snarled. Blood dripped from his mouth and nose.

Infuriated, Avery let out a crazed yell and swung him against the urinal. Taggert's head hit the porcelain, and he howled in pain.

"Give me a name!" Avery demanded. He pushed the policeman's face toward the bottom of the smelly receptacle.

Officer Taggert started crying. "All right, all right! It was all arranged by higher-ups in the organization. . . ." Blood and saliva dribbled down from his mouth to the rusty drain. "The one who did the job on her is dead now. His name was Lyle Bender. They used your sperm samples from a fertility clinic to make it look like you'd raped her. That's all I know about it, I swear." Taggert started coughing and choking. Avery let go of him. It took a few moments for the cop to recover. He sat up a little, wiped the tears from his eyes, then spat a wad of blood and phlegm into the urinal. "Goddamn prick," he gasped. "You fuckin' broke my nose."

With his last drop of adrenalin, Avery reeled back with his fist and punched Taggert in the face. The policeman flopped over on the tiled floor.

Avery snatched up the gun, then braced himself against the wall.

Almost out of nowhere, a set of handcuffs flew past him and hit the unconscious Taggert in his shoulder. Avery glanced up. The Native American cop had dragged himself to the doorway. "Cuff him to that pipe over there, will you?" he said, nodding toward a corner conduit by the urinals.

"Jesus," Avery murmured, starting toward him.

Officer Pete impatiently pointed to the set of cuffs by Earl Taggert. "Hurry up, okay?"

Avery backed away and grabbed the handcuffs. He managed to drag Taggert over to the corner of the bathroom, then cuffed him to the pipe.

"It was—a—a rewarding experience, watching you—beat the crap out of Earl," Officer Pete said between gasps for air. Sweat covered his forehead. "I've been wanting to do—to do that for three years. Pat him down, take away his keys."

Avery followed his directions. "This guy's with a hate group out of Opal. They're responsible for several celebrity deaths. They tried to set me up for murder and rape. Did you hear any of what he said to me?"

The young cop nodded. "I knew he belonged to some kind of—of good ol' boys' club, but I thought it was just about keeping Opal white."

Pocketing Taggert's keys, Avery hobbled over to Officer Pete and helped him up. He walked him to the bench in the waiting room. His leg started to go numb, and he tried to ignore the burning pain in his thigh. "You need to lie on your side and not move around," he said, lowering him on the bench. "Is there someone I can call? Someone you trust?"

Pete nodded. "Just dial 9-1-1. It'll patch through to my boss, Sheriff Goldschmidt. Tell him Peter Masqua is badly wounded—and so are you. We have someone in custody. We're in the old train station. Tell him I said to move his ass. We're expecting some more trouble here within the hour."

In the last two hours, Dayle hadn't moved from the kitchen table. Now she pushed aside the script, picked up Fred, and tiptoed down the hallway to the guest room door. She checked for a strip of light at the threshold. It was dark and almost too quiet. She didn't hear any snoring. Maybe Ted was lying there with the lights off, listening for her.

With the cat cradled in her arms, Dayle retreated to the foyer. Every creaking floorboard seemed like a loud groan. She checked the front door's peephole. She couldn't see the guard, but her view was limited. Quietly, she unlocked the door and opened it. To her immediate right, the guard sat in a folding chair with a Coke, a box of Archway cookies, and a walkie-talkie on the floor beside him. A husky kid in his late twenties, he had curly brown hair and a baby face. His tie was loosened. He'd been reading *The Fountainhead*. Dropping the book, he jumped up from the chair. "Ms. Sutton? Um, is everything okay?"

She smiled and shifted Fred in her arms. "Oh, hi. Yes, everything's fine." Down by the elevator, she noticed a second guard muttering something into his walkie-talkie.

"I really don't think you should be out here," the husky kid said.

"Oh, I thought I'd go for a walk before bed. I'm kind of keyed up. Maybe it'll help me sleep. I just need some fresh air. In fact, I figured I'd go up to the roof. It's perfectly safe up there. . . ."

"I'm sorry, ma'am. I'll have to clear that with Ted first."

"Oh, now don't be silly—"

"He's right, Dayle."

She spun around.

Ted stood in the foyer with her. He'd thrown on a pair of jeans, a T-shirt, and his shoulder holster. He had a walkie-talkie in his hand. "We've taken all these precautions for your safety," he said. "If you want to step out of the apartment, you need to see me about it."

Dayle frowned at him. "I'm not sure I like that."

"I wouldn't like it either if I were you, but it is necessary." He smiled at her, then set the walkie-talkie on the hallway table. "It's late, Dayle. Why don't you get some sleep?"

Sighing, Dayle retreated back into the apartment. Ted stepped inside after her. She heard him close and lock the door.

Sean's tape recorder picked up everything Larry Chadwick had to say. It wasn't so much a confession as it was an hour's worth of steady gloating. Despite the stranger with a gun in the backseat of his car, Larry seemed to think he had the upper hand. He was still at the wheel, still in control.

Yes, he knew who she was. His friends were quite aware that Avery Cooper's lawyer was in town, and they had a full description of her. They also had Avery Cooper in custody: "Last I heard, he was being held just outside Lewiston, two hours from here. He might still be alive. I'm not sure. My friends were trying to determine his exact whereabouts when you lured me away with that phony phone call."

He explained about his friends, the Soldiers for An American Moral Order, who were going to bring back family values and godliness to the people of this country. He defended the torture and mutilation deaths of Tony Katz and his friend: "Faggots aren't human beings. And right now, those two deviates are burning in hell.''

Larry freely admitted to having participated in the murder of Leigh Simone. They had made it look like a drug overdose: "Leigh Simone got what she deserved. She advocated homosexuality, abortion, and the restriction of our constitutional right to bear arms.''

They didn't set out to kill people. They merely wanted to silence those celebrities who posed a threat to moral order and traditional family values. Often, all it took was a little research into their pasts or intimidation. A good scandal could always discredit a loudmouth liberal celebrity's cause.

"And if you can't dig up dirt on someone, you manufacture it,'' Sean said. "Did SAAMO arrange the murder of Libby Stoddard?''

"Yes.'' Larry studied the dark, winding highway.

In the last hour, they'd encountered only six cars on this road. The most recent was a minivan, which had been keeping a steady, respectable distance behind them for several miles now. They were driving through a forest preserve. The unlit two-lane snaked around clusters of trees.

Sean adjusted the volume on her recorder again. "You had a nurse named Laurie Anne Schneider steal Avery Cooper's sperm samples from the fertility clinic. One of those samples was planted in Libby Stoddard. Is that correct? Yes or no?''

"Yes,'' he said, with a hint of a smile. "And we still have some of those samples, Ms. Olson.''

"You framed Avery Cooper for murder, because he's a threat to your fundamentalist agenda. Is that correct?''

"He's no threat anymore,'' Larry replied.

"Dayle Sutton, she's the next to die, isn't she?''

Larry didn't hesitate to answer. "Yes. But I'm not in on that one. The wheels are already in motion. We have people in L.A. handling it. She'll get hers on the set of her movie. It's slated to happen in the next day or two.''

"Talk about a cold-blooded bastard," Nick whispered from the backseat. "Lare, you must piss ice water."

Unfazed, Larry scratched his chin, then glanced at the tape recorder in Sean's hand. He seemed so blasé. It was almost as if he somehow knew that all the information he was revealing would never make it outside of this car.

Sean looked over her shoulder at the minivan, still trailing several car lengths behind them. Nick caught it too. Frowning, he turned forward and tapped Larry's shoulder with the gun. "Both hands on the wheel, Lare. This is the fourth and last time I'm telling you. See the little trail up ahead? That's where we're going."

With a sigh, Larry pulled off the highway onto a gravel road that dipped into the woods.

"Are they still following us?" Nick asked Sean.

"I can't see," she said, twisting around in the passenger seat to check the rear window. "They might have moved on, I'm not sure."

Engulfed in darkness, they steadied themselves as the car bounced over the rocky trail. Eventually, the gravelly road gave way to a smoother, narrow dirt path.

Sean wondered if perhaps the minivan had switched off its headlights and was now following them. She couldn't see a thing back there. Larry and his hunting buddies probably knew every inch of this forest. No doubt, he and his friends could maneuver these trails blindfolded. Meanwhile, she and Nick were totally out of their element here. The deeper they moved into the bowels of these woods, the more doomed she felt.

Ahead, she could only see as far as their headlights pierced the blackness. The path grew more narrow and hazardous with tree roots and rocks. An occasional branch from above scraped against the roof of the car. Twigs snapped under the tires.

She turned to Nick. "As soon as we can," she whispered. "Let's swing around and head back to the main road."

He nodded distractedly. "In a minute." He tapped Larry's

shoulder with his gun. "Someone in Dayle's camp has been providing you guys with information. It's how you know I was here. Who's the stoolie?"

Larry studied a curve in the path ahead. "It's a guy who works for her, his name's Dennis Walsh."

"Well, well, that fat piece of shit. . . ."

Sean watched Larry casually slide his left hand off the wheel, down to his lap. She wondered why he kept doing that. Nick had already warned him about it four times.

They hit another bump, and she dropped the recorder. It landed between her seat and the car door. She went to reach for it.

"Slow down," Nick barked.

Sean heard Larry laugh a bit. "Sorry." He sounded so damn confident. What did he know that they didn't? Or was he just so self-righteous that he figured no one could hurt him? Why wasn't he scared? It had become so dark in the car, she couldn't quite see his expression. But somehow she knew Larry was smiling.

Sean pried the recorder from under her seat, and an image suddenly hit her. She remembered the first time she'd set eyes on Larry Chadwick—in the parking lot of the My-T-Comfort Inn. He'd pulled up in his car, opened the door, then reached under his car seat, and taken out a gun.

"Nick?" she said. She sat up and stared at Larry. For a moment, her heart stopped. He had only one hand on the wheel, and in the other he held a semiautomatic, pointed at her.

"Oh, God, no," she whispered.

A loud shot rang out. Sean felt as if someone hurled a punch in her shoulder. The force of it took her breath away and sent her slamming against the passenger door. The back of her head hit the window.

Another shot resonated, and the car lurched forward. Sparks exploded from the dashboard. A third blast immediately followed, and Larry let out a howl as the gun flew from his hand.

Sean felt a spray of blood hit her in the face. Dazed, she watched Nick club Larry over the head with the butt of his gun. Larry flopped against the driver's door. A pungent smoke from the singed fuse box began to fill the car as it rolled to a stop.

Sean slouched against the door, not wanting to move. It was as if someone had stuck a hot steel rod into her upper chest— beside her right shoulder. Larry was still half conscious as Nick climbed out and opened the driver's door. He yanked him out of the car. Larry vaguely grumbled in protest, then fell to the ground.

Nick snatched his gun off the car floor, then stared at Sean. "Where are you hit?" he asked, trying to catch his breath.

"My upper chest," she murmured. "By the shoulder . . . can't feel my arm."

"Shit, you're bleeding bad. We have to get you to a hospital, doll."

"Don't call me doll," Sean replied in a shaky voice. "We— we can't go anywhere. The car's dead. The fuse box is shot. . . ."

Nick tried and tried to restart Larry's Honda Accord. The engine made a grinding noise, but refused to turn over. Meanwhile, Larry had managed to sit up on the dirt path. He held on to his bleeding left hand. A trail of blood slid down from the gash on his forehead. Yet he was laughing like a crazy man. "You screwed yourselves!" he called, staggering to his feet. "You're trapped! You're not going anywhere. . . ."

He kept laughing and taunting them, until finally Nick jumped out of the car. Half delirious, Larry didn't even see him coming. Nick coldcocked him. He might as well have been swatting a pesky fly. One expedient, forceful hit, and Larry Chadwick went down.

The last thing Sean heard him say was: "She'll bleed to death. That cunt's going to die out here."

* * *

Earlier, when they'd driven up the dirt path, Sean hadn't noticed all the other forest trails merging into this one. Those few minutes in the car had covered several miles.

They'd been trudging through the woods for close to an hour now—lost, swallowed up in the darkness. Cursing, Nick stumbled over rocks and tree roots while she staggered behind him. With her good hand, Sean clung to his belt at the back of his jeans and faltered along with him.

She tried to ignore the pain in her shoulder. Her arm was in a sling—crudely fashioned by Nick from Larry's khaki trousers. Her arm and her right side down to the hip were sopping wet with blood that had turned cold. Sean could see her breath in the chilly night air, yet she was burning up inside. Drops of sweat trickled from her forehead. She had a fever—an infection from the bullet, or maybe from all the blood she'd lost. Still, she pressed on.

In addition to relieving Larry of his trousers, Nick had also stripped him of his shirt and undershirt. He tore up the shirt and tied Larry's hands in back of him with the shreds. After shooting a couple of breathing holes in the Accord's trunk lid, Nick had dumped the unconscious, underwear-clad Larry inside. Sean weakly protested that he'd freeze to death. Nick said he didn't give "a frog's fat ass." He shut the trunk, then pocketed Larry's keys.

He found a bottle of water in the glove compartment. With that and Larry's T-shirt, he tried to clean the bullet wound by Sean's shoulder. Then he made a sling out of Larry's pants. As they started down the path, Larry must have regained consciousness. They heard him pounding on the trunk lid, the muffled yelling and cursing.

That had been nearly an hour ago. Now, Sean blindly held on to Nick. For all she knew, they could be heading deeper into the forest, away from the highway. She felt herself growing weaker and dizzier with every step. Suddenly, the ground seemed to drop out from under her. She tripped over a tiny rivulet, almost pulling Nick down too. The fall knocked the wind out of her.

"You okay?" Nick asked, hovering over her. "From what I can see, you don't look so hot."

"Flatterer," Sean murmured. She didn't think she could stand up again. "How can you even see *anything?*" For the last hour, she'd been praying for some point of light that might lead them to the highway—some wonderful, bright, artificial light. But there was only darkness.

"Let's rest here for a sec, okay?" Nick said.

Sean nodded again. Shivering and sweating, she listened for the sound of a car, a radio, maybe some people talking at a nearby campsite. Nothing. Yet she and Nick weren't alone. She could hear creatures moving in the shrubs all around, twigs snapping beneath feet—or claws.

"God, listen to that," Nick whispered. "I'm a city boy. Gentle Ben or Bambi, either way, I don't like this shit. . . ."

Sean laughed, but she felt herself slipping away. She didn't think the darkness could become any blacker, yet it was happening. She couldn't move. Nick was still talking to her, but through a fog.

Sean thought of Danny and Phoebe. She remembered them playing on the beach with their aunt a couple of nights ago. And she felt her body shutting down.

Twenty-five

Tom glanced in his rearview mirror at the white Taurus—
his escort to the studio. He wore his blue seersucker—along
with his disguise: glasses and a fake mustache. Beside him in
the front seat, Hal was reviewing details for Dayle Sutton's
execution one last time. When he started to explain about the
"getaway" afterward, Tom told himself not to believe a word.

"In the ambulance," Hal said, consulting a notepad, "you'll
be furnished with a new passport and all the necessary papers.
By the way, your passport photo is just an old picture of you
that we doctored up. Your new name is Robert Allen Bryant.
You'll receive ten thousand dollars' worth of traveler's checks
in the van—"

"Ten thousand?" Tom interrupted. "But you told me—"

"You have reservations tonight at The Best Western Golden
Park in Rio," Hal went on. "Under the name Robert Allen
Bryant. It's not the Hilton, but it's affordable until you find
your retirement villa. Three days from now, you'll receive an
another eighty thousand in traveler's checks. It'll be sent to the

hotel. After that, additional payments will arrive every month You'll end up with a quarter of a million—as promised, Tom.'' Hal grinned and patted his shoulder. "Or should I say 'Robert'?''

Gazing at the traffic ahead, Tom bit his lower lip. Suddenly the whole Rio dream didn't seem like such a lie. He though about last night. He could still see that drag queen dropping his self-incriminating letter to the *Los Angeles Times* in the mail. Had he screwed up his chances for a clean break?

"Um, where will you find a body of someone who looks like me?'' he asked, stopping at a traffic light. "You'll nee a body. . . .''

"I know.'' Hal glanced out the passenger window. "It's a nasty detail we've already taken care of, Tom. The less you know about it, the better.'' His cellular phone rang. He too it out of the zippered pocket of his designer sweatshirt and answered, "Hal speaking.''

The light changed, and Tom pressed on. They weren't fai from the studio. Soon he'd be on his own.

"Well, where's Larry?'' Hal said into the phone. "Hasn' anyone heard from him?''

Tom kept hoping against hope that the call was about cancel ing Dayle Sutton's assassination. He'd done a prison movi years back, in which a last-minute call from the governor hac saved him from the electric chair. Was it too much to ask tha this last-minute call be his salvation?

"I want them tracked down,'' Hal continued. "Have Larry call me right away. . . . Well, then keep paging him. Over and out.'' He pressed a button, and quickly folded up the phone "Damn it,'' he grumbled.

"We're still—doing this?'' Tom asked, feeling his stomach lurch.

"All systems are go,'' Hal said. "Pull over. I'm switching cars.''

Swallowing hard, Tom followed Hal's orders. In the rearview

mirror, he saw the Taurus veer over to the curb and stop behind them.

"Don't forget," Hal said, opening the car door. "At the studio gate, your name's Gordon Swann, and you're an old friend of Dennis Walsh."

Dennis was in a good mood this morning. He'd had a particularly amorous evening with Laura last night, then slept over to help her move today. They'd had another go at it about a half hour ago. Now she was in the shower, and he was dressed, fixing them breakfast.

Someone knocked on her door. "Just a sec!" Dennis called. Threading around storage boxes, he checked the peephole. He didn't recognize the guy; then again, he didn't know Laura's neighbors. "Can I help you?" he called.

"Um, I live upstairs," the man called back from the other side of the door. "Some of Laura's mail was put in my box by mistake."

Dennis opened the door. The neighbor was a small guy, about twenty-five, with athletic good looks, and straight blond hair. He handed Dennis an envelope from Pacific Bell. "Sorry. I wasn't looking when I opened it up. I thought it was mine—until I saw all those calls to Idaho."

Dennis stared at the man, then at the envelope.

"I don't know anybody in Opal, Idaho," the neighbor explained.

Dennis studied the phone bill. One call to Opal after another, and always the same number: 208-555-4266. She'd phoned every day—at all sorts of hours.

Dennis managed to smile at the neighbor, and nodded vaguely. "Um, thank you." Closing the door, he glanced down the hall toward the bathroom. He could hear the shower's torrent. In a stupor, he wandered back into the kitchen, picked up the telephone, then dialed the Opal number.

It rang twice before a man picked up. "Hey, there, Laurie Anne," he said. "How are things with you and fatso?"

Dennis quickly hung up. It took him a moment to realize that the party in Opal had Caller I-D. But who was Laurie Anne?

The phone rang. They were calling her back. Dennis let it ring. Her answering machine came on, and they hung up.

Eyeing the bathroom door, Dennis tried the machine for old messages.

Beep. "Hi, honey—" It was him. He skipped to the next message.

Beep. "This is your mother, Laurie Anne. Pick up. Are you there? Oh, you're not there. Listen, someone from your old job at the clinic called me last night, asking for a *Lauren* Schneider. Anyway, this Grace somebody says they owe you over a thousand dollars from some kind of social security withholding mix-up. I gave her your number. She'll be calling. Maybe now you can pay me back some of that loan, Laurie Anne. Call me, okay? God bless."

"End of Messages," announced the prerecorded mechanical voice.

"Laurie Anne" must have erased all the calls from her Opal cohorts. Dennis didn't want to think it was true. Once again, he picked up the phone and dialed the number in Idaho. It rang once. "Yeah?" the man said warily.

Dennis hesitated. "It's Ted," he grunted.

"Ted? What are you doing at Laurie Anne's? It's execution day, for God's sake. Why aren't you at the studio with the bitch? Ted?"

Dennis hung up on him. In a daze, he wandered down the hall—past all the packed boxes—to the bathroom door. He tried the knob. She hadn't locked it, trusting soul. Quietly, he opened the door. He saw the figure on the other side of the pink-tinted shower curtain. Dennis ripped the curtain aside.

Laurie Anne swiveled around and automatically covered

her breasts. Then she saw him and burst out laughing. "You silly—"

Dennis grabbed her and slammed her against the tiled wall. She struggled helplessly. The shower matted down his hair and drenched his clothes as he held on to her. "I just got off the phone with a friend of yours in Opal, Idaho," he growled. "I know you set me up. I figured out about Ted too. But tell me this, *Laurie Anne*. Who's this Gordon Swann you wanted me to smuggle onto Dayle's film set?"

Tom didn't need to mention this Dennis person at the studio gate. All he said was, "My name's Gordon Swann," and the guard gave him a pass—along with directions to the administration building and visitors' parking.

He felt sickly, and couldn't stop trembling. Within an hour, he would be dead—or riding to the airport in an ambulance.

The thin, pretty Asian girl at the front desk must have seen it in his face. After calling for his escort, she asked if he was feeling all right. She made him sit down, then fetched him a drink of water.

He felt a bit better by the time the studio's young page pulled up to the building in a golf cart. He reminded Tom of himself— about fifty years ago, a good-looking kid with black, wavy hair. Driving down alleyways past the vast soundstages, the kid started in about how big the studio was, the different movies and TV shows shot there—the standard tour-guide spiel. His words were just background noise, like the prayers the prison chaplain reads for a man led to his execution.

Tom felt another wave of dread when Soundstage 8 came into view. The page dropped him off at a side door, where Tom showed his visitor's pass to the security guard. He tried to keep his hand over the bulging pocket of his seersucker jacket. The gun felt heavy and awkward.

The security man led him into the building, down a hallway

to a door with a green light above it. The guard opened the
door for him. Tom was overwhelmed with a million memories
as he stepped onto that movie-making soundstage. The McDonald's ad two years ago had been filmed at a tiny studio. Nothing
major league like this. The cameras and lights were different
from his heyday, but the feel of it was the same: they created
magic here.

He gazed at the movie set: a town hall meeting room. Extras
sat in folding chairs facing a podium on a small stage. Some
folks had cigarettes going—for the scene obviously, since NO
SMOKING signs were plastered on the soundstage walls. Behind
the podium stood Dayle Sutton in an unflattering gray wig. She
looked bored. No one seemed to pay any attention to her.

Tom touched the gun in his pocket.

"Mr. Swann? Hello, I'm Beverly. Is this your first time on
a film set?"

Startled, he managed to smile at the woman with the blond
beehive hairdo. She was around sixty, in great shape, carefully
made up and decked out in a pink suit. "No, I—I've been on
a movie set before," Tom said, carefully taking his hand out
of his jacket pocket. "I used to be an actor."

"Oh, really?"

He shrugged. "Bit parts mostly. That was a long time ago."

"How interesting," she said. "Then you must already know,
sometimes they'll ask for 'quiet on the set . . . ' " Beverly went
into a long, elementary explanation of how to behave on a film
shoot. The only other visitors on the set were three Japanese
businessmen. Beverly paid more attention to them, which was
all right by Tom. He didn't want her watching his every move.

He glanced over at Dayle Sutton, leaning sluggishly against
the podium. "Um, Beverly," he said. "Would it be all right
if I moved a bit further down along the wall? I want to get a
better look at Dayle Sutton."

Beverly grinned. "Certainly, Mr. Swann. But she's Ms. Sutton's stand-in. Dayle's in her trailer right now." Beverly

pointed to the mobile unit against the soundstage wall—past of an array of lights and sound equipment.

Beverly started explaining the various duties of a stand-in. Tom didn't hear a word. He noticed a lean man with thin blond hair standing by the trailer door. He wore a blue suit. Her bodyguard. Was he really with the organization—as Hal had said?

The bodyguard scanned the set. He checked out the group of Japanese businessmen; then those eyes kept moving along the outer wall until his gaze locked onto Tom's. They stared at each other for a moment. The bodyguard gave a single nod, and smiled ever so subtly.

"Quiet please!" someone called.

A dozen spotlights switched on, illuminating the set. Somebody held a light meter to the stand-in's face. Amid all this, Dayle Sutton emerged from her trailer. She looked older and careworn in the dowdy tweed suit, and with her trademark auburn hair hidden beneath a brown-gray wig. She started onto the set, studying her script. The director was talking to her.

Tom felt a little short of breath. He checked his target. He wished the director would move out of the way. Accompanying her up to the podium, he kept stepping into the line of fire. He patted her back and whispered to her.

Tom held on to the semiautomatic in his pocket.

"Quiet on the set!" someone yelled again. The director finally moved away. A mike, hanging from a boom, descended closer to Dayle's head. Both hands on the podium, Dayle took a deep breath. Tom had a clear shot, but then the man with the clapboard stepped in front of her. "Scene eighty-seven. Take four!" He slapped the clapboard together, then stepped aside.

"Roll cameras," the director barked.

She stood alone up there. He had her in range. No one was looking. Tom took the gun out of his pocket and brought it up to his chest, burying it in the folds of his jacket. He glanced up toward the podium.

Dayle Sutton seemed to be staring right at him. She had tears in her eyes. "Hello," she said. "My name is Susan . . . and I—I'm an alcoholic."

Tom took a step back, bumping into the wall.

The congregation applauded her and called back, "Hello, Susan!"

The smile she gave them was heartbreaking. For a moment, the dowdy woman had the face of an angel. "Thank you," she replied in a stage whisper.

Mesmerized, Tom forgot that he was holding a gun—until, out of the corner of his eye, he noticed Dayle's bodyguard coming toward him. The tall, blond man glowered at him and angrily muttered something under his breath.

Tom nodded sheepishly. He raised the gun, and aimed it at Dayle Sutton. *Just another Coke bottle on that front porch railing.*

"Cut!" the director bellowed. "Does everyone in the meeting have to smoke? Looks like a goddamn Turkish bath! I can hardly see Dayle. . . ."

While the director complained, a woman stepped up on the stage to dab powder on Dayle Sutton's chin. She blocked the line of fire. Another woman approached Dayle, pointing to the trailer. Tom couldn't get a clear hit. He watched Dayle retreat back into her trailer, and then he turned to see the bodyguard scowling at him.

Tom looked away. With a shaky hand, he slipped the gun back into his coat pocket.

It would take a while for the fans to blow away the excess smoke. So Dayle headed back toward her trailer to answer an "urgent" phone call from Dennis. She wasn't anxious to talk with him. Having pushed Ted Kovak on her, Dennis didn't sit high on her list of trusted friends right now.

She hadn't slept last night—what with Ted in the next room.

By 5:45 this morning, she'd been dressed and anxious to leave. She and Ted had driven to the studio in her limo together. She'd used studying her script as an excuse for not talking with him.

She would figure out later today what to do about Ted Kovak. For now, she wanted him to think everything was status quo. She felt safe—for the time being. He wasn't about to try anything on a crowded movie set.

On her way to the trailer, Dayle glanced over toward where Beverly corralled the visitors—a handful of Japanese businessmen and an elderly man in a blue seersucker suit. Ignoring Ted, she ducked into her trailer.

She picked up the phone and pressed the blinking red button. "Yes, Dennis?" she said warily.

"Dayle, thank God," he said in a rush. "Listen, I just found out, they set me up. Laura, she's one of them. They've been getting to you through me and my big mouth. I didn't know, I swear—"

"Hold on," Dayle said. "I don't understand."

"Ted Kovak is with that hate group. Laura arranged for me to 'bump into' Ted at this party. She's been making calls to Opal, Idaho, for a couple of weeks now. And that old man I told you about, the one visiting the set today, Laura asked me to arrange it and keep her name out of it. I don't know the guy, Dayle. It's some old fart, but he's a good shot, and he's been hired to kill you. He's probably there already."

"Is he wearing a seersucker suit?" Dayle asked. "Glasses?" She glanced down at the phone. Her other line was blinking.

"I'm not sure what he looks like, but Ted's supposed to waste the guy once you're hit. Listen, Dayle, stay in your trailer, lock the door. I'll call security at the studio and the cops. We'll have a net over these guys within three minutes."

Someone was knocking on her trailer door. "I'm sorry, Ms. Sutton," the studio secretary called. "There's another urgent call for you on line three."

"*What?* Who is it?"

"I don't know. It's collect, from Opal, Idaho."

"Thank you!" She got back on the line: "Dennis? Okay, contact the police. I'll stay put. I have Sean on hold here. I've gotta go. Bye." She clicked off and pressed line three. "Hello, Sean?"

"Yo, don't keel over or anything. You probably figure I'm toes up."

"Nick?" she muttered, stunned.

"Yeah. Are you okay? Has anyone taken a potshot at you today?"

"I can't believe you're actually alive," she murmured. Dayle sank down on the sofa. "What happened?"

"Tell you later. Here's what's important. Either today or tomorrow, they plan to whack you on your movie set—"

"I know," Dayle cut in. "The police are on their way. Listen, did you ever meet up with my lawyer friend out there? Sean Olson?"

"Yeah, she got a full confession from one of them on tape."

"Is she there with you?"

He said nothing for a moment.

"Nick? Where are you anyway?"

"I'm at a police station in Opal. I was arrested. You're my one call."

"I'll have somebody get you out of there. Is Sean with you?"

"Um, no," he said soberly. "I don't think she's going to make it, Dayle."

"What do you mean?"

"The guy whose confession we taped, he was hiding a gun. He shot her. It was hours before the cops picked us up. They took Sean to the hospital just a while ago. She lost a lot of blood. The paramedic said she didn't have much of a chance." He sighed. "I'm sorry, Dayle."

"Oh, God, no. . . ." Tears came to her eyes, and she started to tremble. Dayle took a couple of breaths. "Okay. Find out what you can about Sean and—and let me know. I—I'll have someone get you out of there, Nick.''

Dayle hung up the phone, and wiped her tears. As if in a trance, she moved to the vanity, pulled off her wig and hair net, then shed the jacket. She went to the trailer door. She was supposed to lock it, stay inside until the police showed up. Instead, she opened the door and came down the trailer steps. The police and studio security hadn't arrived yet.

Ted Kovak stood beyond the sound equipment—near where Beverly had assembled the visitors. Dayle started toward him. He was scowling at the old man in the seersucker suit. Ted didn't see Dayle until she was right on him.

''You son of a bitch!'' She slapped him hard across the face.

Everyone on the set stopped to gape at them. Ted reeled back, startled. ''What the hell—''

She slapped him again. ''Murderer . . .''

He took another step back and put up his hands to defend himself. But she swatted at his arm, then connected again across his face with another forceful slap. ''Goddamn you and your hypocrite friends! How many good people have you killed? Tony Katz and Leigh, Maggie, my friend, Sean . . .''

Ted grew more furious with her every slap. He glared at Tom, who retreated back with the other stunned bystanders on the set. Ted seemed ready to shoot Dayle himself. She clawed at his face, drawing scratch marks above his left eye and down his cheek. Finally, he pushed her away. ''You crazy bitch!'' he snarled.

''It wasn't enough for you to kill these people,'' she hissed. ''You had to shit on their memory too. You made Leigh look like a drug addict, and you dug up those stag films Maggie McGuire did back when she was struggling. Think about their families. . . .''

She lunged at him again, swinging her fist. But Ted dodged her and reached for his gun. He glared at Tom. ''Kill her,

goddamn it!'' he growled. Only a few people might have heard
him over the noise and chaos.

Tom was one of those few. Yet the words still echoing in
his head had been spoken a moment ago by Dayle Sutton: *You
dug up those stag films Maggie McGuire did back when she
was struggling.* Tom wondered how he could have blinded
himself to that fact. The group he was working for had—as
Dayle put it—*shit on the memory* of Maggie McGuire.

"What are you going to do, Ted?'' Dayle said, gasping for
breath. She clinched her fist. "Are you going to shoot me in
front of all these people?''

His face bleeding and nearly purple, Ted glared at his
employer. He aimed the gun at her heart. Someone screamed.

Dayle Sutton spit in his face. "Go ahead and shoot, you
lowlife, sorry son of a—''

She did not get the last word out. The loud gunshot silenced
her.

Tom Lance had raised his semiautomatic, aimed carefully,
and squeezed the trigger. He put a bullet through Ted Kovak's
right eye.

Twenty-six

The police and studio security had a lot of questions for the old man who had wandered onto Soundstage 8 with a concealed gun. But after saving Dayle Sutton's life, Tom had some leverage. He was a hero, and people wanted to believe him. His story didn't stray far from the truth. He was recruited against his will to assassinate Dayle Sutton by an extremist group. They threatened to kill him if he didn't cooperate. He gave a not entirely accurate description of Hal Buckman, hoping his SAAMO contact could elude authorities for a while. As long as Hal was on the run, Tom figured his story was safe. In his telling, Tom had never intended to kill Dayle; he'd shown up on that movie set to protect her. When asked why this group had singled him out as their assassin, Tom explained: "I was very close to Maggie McGuire once. These people were going to pin her murder on me."

No fake ambulance ever arrived. Tom knew he'd done the right thing. His picture would be on the front page of the evening edition—sans the glasses and fake mustache. Blinding

camera flashes went off inside the soundstage while Dayle
Sutton thanked him. She didn't seem to recognize Tom from
the failed audition. She shook his hand, and hugged him. The
photographers would use that shot for the news story, he knew.

Leaving the soundstage with a police escort, Tom watched
members of the press shoving one another to get closer to him.
"Tom, over this way, please! Tom, just one picture! Over here,
Tom!" He smiled as the shutters clicked. At last they wanted
him.

Dennis Walsh arrived at Soundstage 8 in time to see two
attendants carrying out the draped corpse of Ted Kovak. He
also caught a glimpse of the hero of the hour, Tom Lance, as
they escorted him to a police car.

Back in his fraternity days, Dennis had learned how to trap
a frat brother in his room by squeezing a penny between his
door and the hinge near the latch. The pressure against the
latch made it impossible to pull the door open. He employed
the same trick on Laurie Anne, incarcerating her in the bathroom—only he raised the ante by tossing out her clothes, the
towels, and that ugly pink shower curtain. She was trapped in
there, wet and naked. Dennis phoned the police about her
involvement in a conspiracy to commit murder, then left the
apartment unlocked for them.

Laurie Anne was violent, hysterical, and still quite naked by
the time the police were reading her her rights and offering her
a robe.

At that same moment, Dennis struggled through the crowd
outside Dayle's trailer. Dayle stood on the steps by her door
with reporters firing questions at her. Dennis had only one
question for his boss. He wanted to know if he still had a job.

Though still dressed in her "old lady" tweed suit, Dayle
must have had someone perform a quick touch-up on her face
and hair, because she looked every bit the movie star, standing

by her trailer. She saw Dennis in the crowd and waved at him. "Dennis, please, I need you!" she called.

He worked his way up to the steps. She grabbed his arm, then pulled him into her trailer. "Thank God you're here," she sighed. "You have to get rid of these reporters for me. I'll talk to the police, but that's it."

Dennis gave her a wary look. "So I'm not fired?"

"God, no." Dayle said, her voice quivering. "I'm not dumping you just because you made a mistake. You're my friend, Dennis." She gave him a quick hug. "Listen, more than anything, we have to track down Sean Olson. She's in a hospital somewhere around Opal. I need to know if she's still alive."

After making his one call, Nick Brock was cuffed to a desk in the Opal police station. He was covered with scratches, dried sweat, and dirt.

He and Sean had been lost in those dark woods for nearly three hours. Her strength and determination amazed him. In the second hour, Nick held her up. The only peep out of her was when she mumbled incoherently to someone named Dan. Limp as a rag doll, she pressed on. But she began falling so many times, he had to carry her the last couple miles.

They stumbled upon the highway at around three-thirty in the morning. Nick covered her with his jacket, then sat by the road and waited for a car. In two hours, he counted only six cars—each one speeding by. He tried flagging them down. But who would be dumb enough to stop at this hour—in the middle of nowhere—for a crazy man covered in blood? It became light out. Sean's face had a blue tinge, and her every gasp for air was a death rattle.

Somebody in one of those automobiles must have called the cops, because two patrol cars came up the timberland road at seven in the morning. The policemen were from Opal: a gaunt,

old sheriff, and his deputy, a tall, big-boned kid who seeme
like a pretty dim bulb.

Nick told them his girlfriend had been shot by someone i
the woods, and their car had broken down. The sheriff took
look at Sean and radioed paramedics. Nick helped him mov
Sean into the warm police car. They covered her with a blanke
She didn't regain consciousness.

It was another forty minutes before the paramedics arrive(
Once they'd loaded Sean in back of the ambulance, Nick pulle
one of them aside, and asked about her chances. The medi
frowned. "She's in bad shape, and the hospital's fifty mile
away in Lewiston. Doesn't look good."

Once the ambulance sped away, the old sheriff asked hii
for more details about the shooting. Nick reluctantly forfeite
his gun, showed him his private detective credentials, an
explained that he wasn't answering any questions without hi
attorney present. However, he did volunteer to lead them bac
to where he'd left the car.

They found the original trail and, eventually, Larry's Hond
Accord. The backseat had been kicked through from the trunk
and Larry was gone. The sheriff sent his deputy to look fo
him.

When he finally hauled Nick into the Opal police statior
the sheriff was greeted by a chorus of ringing telephones. Onc
a line cleared, Nick was allowed his one call to Dayle. Th
phones kept the old sheriff busy, while Nick remained cuffe
to the desk. Over the police radio, the deputy reported that he'
located Larry Chadwick, staggering along a forest trail in hi
undershorts. With a bullet wound to his left hand and a gasl
on his forehead, Larry explained that he'd been kidnapped an(
assaulted.

Two hours later, he marched into the police station as if h
owned the place. The dim-witted deputy was on his heels
Cleaned up, and with his wounds bandaged, Larry now wor
an aviator jacket, an Izod sport shirt, and pressed blue jeans

'There's the scumbag!'' he declared, stabbing a finger in the air at Nick. "He's the one! Asshole. . . .''

With his free hand, Nick snuck Sean's tape recorder from the pocket of his jacket. He let the tape rewind for a moment, while Larry continued his tirade. "You're gonna get yours, prick. . . .''

The sheriff and his deputy restrained Larry. They gently guided him to the other desk, then sat him down.

Nick pressed play on the recorder, then slowly increased the volume to compete with Larry's diatribe. " . . . close-knit group," Sean was saying. "You and your hunting buddies had a real time of it in those woods outside Portland back in September, didn't you?''

"Yes, it felt good," Larry answered on the recording.

Larry stopped yelling as he listened to the sound of his own voice.

"It felt good murdering Tony Katz and his friend? It felt good torturing two fellow human beings?''

"Faggots aren't human beings. And right now, those two deviates are burning in hell. . . .''

"Turn that off!" Larry barked. "You can't use that, you son of a bitch. You had a gun to my head the whole time. . . .''
Red-faced, he glared at Nick. He didn't seem to notice that the sheriff was pulling out another set of cuffs. The old man locked one cuff around the desk drawer handle, then slapped the other around Larry's wrist. "What is this?" Larry let out a stunned laugh. He yanked at the handcuffs, and the heavy desk moved a bit. "Hey, what gives?''

The tired-looking sheriff shook his head. "Sorry, Larry,'' he said. "The feds are on their way. Within the hour, they're gonna have a net over this whole town. You and the guys are finished.''

"Goddamn it!" Larry shouted. "Let me go! You can't do this! What the hell is happening here anyway? Son of a bitch, LET ME GO!''

Nick Brock shut off the recorder. He sat back and smiled a him. "Hey, Lare. You know, you have the right to remain silent."

One of the nurses at Lewiston General Hospital showe Avery the bullet they'd extracted from his thigh. Stored in small glass jar, the tiny, dark-gray projectile couldn't be kep as a souvenir just yet. It was part of the state's evidence agains Officer Earl Taggert, now charged with two counts of attempte murder and a growing list of misdemeanors.

Avery and Deputy Peter Masqua had shared an ambulanc to Lewiston General. Earl Taggert had ridden behind them i a police car. After doctors had treated his broken nose, spli lip, and other bruises, the soon-to-be-ex-cop had been escorte to jail. His cohort, an unemployed timber-mill worker name Don Sheckler, had pulled up to the old train depot in his nev Cadillac to find three state troopers waiting for him in th station house.

Officer Peter Masqua was in stable condition. Confined t a wheelchair, Avery kept trying Sean's cellular. No answei He called her hotel, but she wasn't in her room. He knev something had to be wrong.

After all of Taggert's talk about the impending arrival of th "federal guys," the real FBI had shown up at the hospital earl in the morning. Both Avery and Officer Pete had given then enough information to expose the Opal Chapter of SAAMO The FBI clamped a tight lid on the hospital to keep the informa tion contained and the press oblivious about what was happen ing. No more outside calls for Avery. Rumors spread amon the Lewiston General staff about a gag quarantine of hospita personnel for the next twenty-four hours.

"You're the biggest thing to hit this little hospital since th Chichester quadruplets were delivered here in 1987," said Judy the nurse who had shown Avery his bullet. A petite redhead

she had freckles and a cute face that belied the fact that she
had a son in college. She was pushing Avery in his wheelchair
down the corridor after a visit with Pete Masqua.

Avery liked Judy. On her morning break, she'd dashed out
and bought him pajamas and a flannel robe. "K-Mart's best,"
she'd joked. But it was a big improvement over his skimpy
hospital gown. He made a point of telling Judy how grateful
he was.

"Well, as an Idaho native and a Christian, I'm on a mission
here," she said, steering him down the hall. "I want to prove
to you that we aren't all hate-mongers. A tiny fraction of nutcases have given this beautiful state a bad rep. And most *real*
Christians are very tolerant, good people."

"I know that," Avery assured her.

Judy patted his shoulder. "Okay then, end of sermon. Did
you hear? The FBI is now monitoring all calls going in and out
of here. Visiting privileges are temporarily suspended. There's
even talk that none of us on staff will be able to leave today."

"I've really screwed things up for everybody, haven't I?"
Avery said.

"Oh, I think it's kind of exciting," she said. "But maybe
you could use your influence with the warden to release me in
time for Thanksgiving."

Avery managed to smile at her over his shoulder. "I can't
promise anything but an autographed eight-by-ten glossy."

"Just the same, maybe you can offer me some inside information. I seem to be the only one around here who sees a connection with you and Pete Masqua—and this third gunshot case
who came in this morning."

Avery shook his head. "I don't understand."

"Neither do I, that's my point. The paramedics brought in
a woman at eight o'clock. She's upstairs in intensive care,
practically in a coma. She has an infection, and her temperature's a hundred and five. Apparently, she was wandering
around with a bullet in her shoulder for seven hours. I heard

it was a hunting accident in a forest outside Opal. But snoop
that I am, I checked her admission chart and she's a lawyer
from Los Angeles. . . .''

Tom watched *Entertainment Tonight* in his hotel suite.
Bracket, McCourt & Associates had put him up for the night
at the Beverly Hills Hilton, hoping to sign him with their talent
agency. He'd agreed to meet them for breakfast downstairs in
the morning.

Tom sat on the bed, wearing one of the hotel's terrycloth
bathrobes, sipping champagne and snacking on some foreign
crackers from the honor bar. The night final of the *Los Angeles
Times* was at the foot of his bed. The photo of Dayle hugging
him had made the front page, with the headline: ASSASSINATION
ATTEMPT ON DAYLE SUTTON FAILS, CONSPIRACY EXPOSED.

By the time the evening news came on, several arrests had
been made, including seven of Opal's most solid citizens. But
Howard Buchanan—a.k.a. Hal Buckman—had eluded authorities, and so far, Tom's story still had no detractors.

Everyone wanted to quote him, and take his picture. Suddenly
Tom Lance *mattered*. Several video companies were now vying
for the rights to his old films. At last he'd be in video stores.
There were job offers too: playing Tom Hanks's guardian angel
in a comedy-fantasy and as an aging mob boss in a Harrison
Ford movie. His dreams were coming true.

"Continuing with our top story," the handsome, sporty *E.T.*
anchorman announced. "The man who saved Dayle Sutton's
life and blew the lid off an extremist conspiracy is a seventy-
six-year-old film-acting veteran named Tom Lance. According
to Lance, an organized hate group used extortion and intimidation to get his cooperation. . . ." Tom watched the same clip
of himself from all the other evening newscasts. It was taped
outside the police station. The seersucker suit didn't photograph

well, and he looked a bit tired. Still, he relished seeing himself on TV.

The telephone rang. It was the hotel operator. She'd been screening his calls. He'd taken only a handful since checking into the hotel: a couple of talent agents, someone from *People* magazine, and somebody at *The Today Show*. With the remote, Tom muted the TV, then picked up the phone. "Yes?"

"Hello, Mr. Lance. Do you want to take a call from an Adam Blanchard?"

Tom frowned. "Who's he with?"

"No, I'm sorry, Mr. Lance. He didn't say."

He sighed. "Well, I don't know this Blanchard fella. Take a message and . . ." He trailed off. *Blanchard.* Maggie's first husband. Adam was the son.

"Mr. Lance?"

"Um, yes. On second thought, put him through. Please."

He heard a click, then: "Hello, Tom Lance?"

"Yes?"

"Tom, you don't know me, but I'm Maggie McGuire's son, Adam."

"Oh, well, hello," Tom replied, feeling awkward.

"I want to thank you for helping put a stop to this hate group. They killed a lot of good people—including my mother. If it weren't for you, they'd have gone on killing. Anyway, I'm very grateful to you."

"Well, I don't know what to say. I don't deserve any gratitude, son."

"Just the same, thank you, Tom. I've always wanted to meet you. I've seen *Hour of Deceit* several times. I know you helped my mom get her start in films, she told me."

"She did?"

"Oh, yeah. Anyway, you're probably swamped with calls. I don't want to keep you."

"How's your health?" Tom suddenly asked, remembering his HIV status.

"Good, thanks. I'm taking a new drug. It's supposed to help."

"Son, I wish more than anything your mom was still alive." Tom struggled to say the right words. "I—I wrote a letter to the *L.A. Times,* and they'll probably print it in tomorrow's night edition. You should know, I meant what I said in that letter."

There was a dubious chuckle on the other end of the line. "Well, I'm sorry, but I really don't understand."

"You will tomorrow night," Tom said. "I'm glad you called, son. Thanks."

"Thank you, Tom," he said. "Take care."

Tom hung up. He didn't want to think about tomorrow. In the past few hours, he'd basked in the knowledge that they wanted him again. He was important, a hero to millions of people. But by tomorrow afternoon, his letter—with its full confession—would reach someone at the *Los Angeles Times.* That letter was supposed to be read after his death.

Tom tossed back his glass of champagne, then poured another. Grabbing the remote, he channel-surfed for more news coverage of the assassination attempt, another story about Tom Lance. He had only tonight to savor the glory—before it turned bad.

On one of the movie channels, he paused to watch Robert Duvall walking with another man around a chain-link fence. Tom turned up the volume. It took him only a moment to identify the older, raspy-voiced actor as Michael V. Gazzo from The Actors Studio. The movie was *The Godfather, Part II.* Duvall was explaining to his old Mafia chum how in Roman times, some generals, accused of plotting against the emperor, chose to die with dignity. They'd draw a warm bath, then slash their wrists and bleed to death.

Frowning, Tom switched channels. One of the news shows had a clip of him with Maggie in *Hour of Deceit.* With a sad smile, he watched and drank his champagne. Only two weeks ago, he'd been a forgotten film actor, ready to shoot himself by the Hollywood sign. His death would have gone unnoticed. But by tomorrow, his suicide would make headlines.

Another movie scene came to mind: George C. Scott's speech in *Patton,* about how—again, in Roman times—during a victory parade, the general would have an aide-de-camp whispering in his ear: "All glory is fleeting."

Tom had the speech in a book of movie monologues. He'd read it aloud a few times. But he'd never fully understood what it meant until now.

"All glory is fleeting."

He went into the bathroom and found a disposable razor in the complimentary kit from the hotel. Tom broke off the plastic and took out the blade. Then he ran the hot water in the bath.

Stepping back into the bedroom, he called the hotel operator and asked her to hold all his calls. He poured himself another glass of champagne, and toasted Maggie.

Then Tom Lance went into the bathroom with his glass, a razor blade, and his dignity.

"Hello, I'm Mrs. Russell Marshall."

"Hi, Elsie!"

Elsie Marshall sat behind her desk, surrounded by copies of her book, *A Little More Common Sense.* In the guest chair today sat a balding, pasty-faced man of fifty with a sparse, thin mustache that failed to draw attention from his small eyes and double chin. He wore a pinstriped dark-gray suit.

"If you're just tuning in," Elsie chirped. "You don't want to touch that dial, because we're talking some *Common Sense* with Mr. Roger Crayton, who decided enough is enough, and got certain filthy books banned from public libraries in his home state of North Carolina. Stay tuned!"

The studio audience applauded. Elsie glanced up at the sound booth and made a slashing gesture at her throat, indicating they should turn off the mikes. Then she turned to her guest. "Mr.

Crayton, I hope you won't mention how you tried to ban *The Color Purple* and *A Catcher in the Rye* from the libraries. I for one say *bravo*. But there are just too many bleeding-heart liberals out there who think that—well, if you pardon me—such *crap* has literary significance. Let's stick to the books you actually had pulled from the shelves—like *Heather Has Two Mommies,* and that other horrible one—''

Mr. Crayton seemed distracted by something going on behind her. Elsie turned to see an Asian woman in a beige suit shaking her head at the production assistant, who was trying to keep her from coming onto the set.

Elsie glared at the intruder, then looked around at all her production people. ''What's going on here?'' she demanded to know. ''I'm taping a show, for pity's sake. Somebody get this Oriental woman off my set!''

The audience became restless. A rumbling of whispers rose from Elsie's subjects. She bristled at the disruption this trespasser was causing. ''Who do you think you are?'' Elsie said indignantly.

The ''Oriental woman'' pulled out a wallet and flashed a badge at her. ''I'm Lieutenant Susan Linn, LAPD, homicide division,'' she said. Then her quiet little smile widened. ''Hi, Elsie.''

Judy had invited Avery to share Thanksgiving dinner with her family, but he preferred to stick around the hospital's intensive care unit. He was still confined to the wheelchair. The press had been allowed to interview him and Officer Pete for an hour yesterday. Now the state patrol worked overtime—with holiday pay—to keep out the reporters. All visitors had to be screened.

A few thousand miles away, the Beverly Hills police had dropped Avery as a suspect in the murder-rape of Libby Stoddard. Their manhunt for Howard ''Hal'' Buchanan had ended late last night with the discovery of his body inside a rented Ford Taurus in the underground parking garage at a San Diego Ramada Inn. He'd shot himself in the mouth.

Elsie and Drew Marshall denied any knowledge of an organization known as SAAMO. As federal investigations progressed, the Marshalls lost several of their more lucrative *Common Sense* sponsors—but none of their audience. In fact, there was even a small boost in ratings of the syndicated show.

Still, they were now a target of ridicule, and an embarrassment to most conservative politicians who had once backed them. In newspapers and magazines, editorial cartoons showed Elsie and Drew behind bars in prison garb—and made references to Drew's Best Dressed Man credentials and *The Family That Slays Together*. . . .

"The sexiest man headed for San Quentin," one TV talk show host called him. "Drew Marshall's a ten, all right. That's how many years he'll have to serve. . . ."

Like Tony Katz, Leigh Simone, and Maggie McGuire before them, Elsie and Drew Marshall became the tainted stars of tabloid headlines. Even if they avoided prison, their reputations had been poisoned by scandal.

The strangest development of all was the suicide of Tom Lance. He'd locked himself in the bathroom of his suite at the Beverly Hills Hilton, and slashed his wrists. A hotel maid found him at ten o'clock Wednesday morning. He'd left no suicide note in the suite, but the *Los Angeles Times* published a letter from Tom Lance, confessing to the murder of Maggie McGuire.

From the hospital in Lewiston, Idaho, Avery phoned Glenhaven for updates on Joanne. She was still letting the same nurse feed her, and seemed aware of people addressing her. But she'd yet to say a word to anyone.

Avery's brother, parents, and George and Sheila had all volunteered to fly out to see him. But he'd told them to stay put. He would be released from the hospital Friday anyway.

He didn't mention his plans to remain in Lewiston—close to the hospital—until his lawyer was off the critical list.

Sean's infection had developed into pneumonia. Her temperature was still dangerously high. She needed an oxygen mask to breathe. Perspiration from the fever had left her hair in limp, wet tangles. She drifted in and out of consciousness. When not sleeping, her thoughts were muddled. At one point this morning, she'd squinted at Avery in the wheelchair by the foot of her bed. "Dan? Honey?" she'd said weakly. "Phoebe's school clothes are dirty. . . ."

Avery had become a liaison for her family and the doctors at the hospital. For the last couple of days, they routinely paged him at the intensive care unit desk. One of her brothers was due to arrive later this afternoon. He telephoned from the Boise Airport.

Avery took the call on one of the phones in the small visitors' lounge outside the ICU. A fresh box of Kleenex adorned every end table, the sofas were beige, and a TV—on mute—was fixed to a bracket on the wall.

"Tell me what I should expect," her brother said warily. His name was Jack, and he was younger than Sean. In the background, Avery could hear a lot of people talking—along with flight announcements on a loudspeaker.

"It's like I explained to you yesterday," he said. "The doctors aren't very optimistic about her chances. I'm sticking around, hoping she'll prove them wrong. Has anyone told the husband how serious it is?"

"Yeah," her brother replied. "Dan wants to come here, but the doctors won't let him. And if the medical experts won't allow him to fly, neither will the airlines—what with all the equipment he needs. He's not doing too hot lately." Jack's voice become shaky. "God, if those two little kids lose both parents so close together, I don't know what." He sighed. "So listen, are you okay? I heard you were shot in the leg."

"I'm fine," Avery said. "I'll be hobbling around for a little while, but I should be okay."

"Well, I'll be there in a few hours. Where can I reach you later on?"

"I'm not going anywhere," Avery said. "I'll be right here."

After he hung up the phone, Avery maneuvered the wheelchair around. He started back down the hall to Sean's room. He would stay with her until after visiting hours were over.

Epilogue

Fans and paparazzi gathered by the cemetery gates. They had been standing in the rain for two hours just to see Dayle Sutton and Avery Cooper among the mourners.

The showers had ceased, leaving a mist above the wet grass and shiny, dark headstones. The clouds still looked ominous, so people clung to their umbrellas as they assembled at the graveside. A priest recited prayers over the casket. All the surrounding flowers seemed so vivid and colorful under the gray skies—and amid the congregation in their traditionally dark attire.

Dayle spotted Avery Cooper in back of several people on the other side of the grave. He caught her eye, nodded and gave a her a shy smile.

Citing "family obligations," Avery had bowed out of their film project, now slated to start principal photography in February. The producers—along with Dayle—had begged him to reconsider. They'd even offered to push back the film's starting date, but Avery couldn't be swayed. Sniffing Oscar bait, a dozen big-name actors now vied for his role of the gay-bashed man on trial.

Everyone knew his wife was still in a mental hospital. The tabloids really cashed in on *Avery's Anguish*. He looked lonely and uncomfortable, poised behind so many couples and families at the cemetery plot.

Dayle had already met most of Sean's family during the wake. The in-laws, Doug and Anne, solemnly clung to each other by the graveside. In back of them stood a couple of Sean's brothers with their wives. Dan Olson's favorite nurse, Julie, was there. Dry-eyed and looking rather lost were Sean's two children, Danny and Phoebe. They stood on either side of their mother. Danny was too old to hold on to her hand in public, but Phoebe had no such qualms. Her little fist clutched at Sean's black skirt. Dayle had loaned Sean the charcoal brocade jacket she wore.

Sean still looked a bit pale and thin from her hospital stay. She'd been released from Lewiston General the first week of December. She'd had only six days with Dan before his condition had taken a drastic turn. He'd died at home on December eleventh.

Danny and Phoebe Olson each placed a flower on their father's casket, then were led to a waiting limo by their uncle and aunt. Sean hugged and shook hands with people as they started to wander back toward their cars. A few starstruck mourners approached Dayle to say hello or ask how she knew Dan Olson.

Finally, Sean came up to Dayle and embraced her. "Thanks for use of the jacket," she said. "And thanks for coming. It means so much to me that you're here. We're having a buffet back at the house. Can you come?"

Dayle touched her arm. "Oh, Sean, I'm sorry. I'd like to, but I have a publicity thing in an hour, a magazine cover story. I can't get out of it."

Sean smiled graciously. "I understand."

"Did Dennis call you about the meeting next week? We need our technical advisor there. After all, the movie's about you."

"I wouldn't miss it," Sean replied. She glanced down the rolling hill of the cemetery, where reporters and dozens of stargazers waited outside the gate. "Dan really would have been pleased at this," she said, with a sad laugh. "You didn't know my husband. He was such a film buff. And here it's his funeral and there are reporters, fans, and two movie stars in attendance."

Dayle spotted Avery Cooper across the way. "Have you— talked to Avery yet?" she asked quietly.

Sean shook her head.

"Maybe you should at least say hi. You know, back when he found out that you'd gone to Opal, he went crazy. I was with him, and I could tell there was something—special between you two. I—" Dayle saw the pained look on Sean's face, and she sighed. "It's none of my damn business. I'm sorry."

"Nothing ever happened," Sean explained. "But the feelings were there just the same." She smiled. "I'm glad you said something, Dayle. I didn't like carrying around that secret all alone, especially today."

Dayle gave her hand a squeeze. "Go talk to him."

Sean nodded, then turned and started down the hill toward Avery.

The other movie star at Dan Olson's burial was now retreating toward his car. Sean's young nephew, Brendan, had stopped Avery to ask for an autograph. Avery scribbled his name on Brendan's church program, then shook his hand. As the boy moved on, Avery glanced back and saw her.

Sean stepped toward him. The wind suddenly kicked up, and

she swept back her hair. For a moment, she was once again on that ocean-view bluff, snuggled in his jacket, wanting so much to kiss him. She put aside those feelings now—just as she'd tried to ignore them back then. Crossing her arms to keep warm, Sean managed to smile at him. "Thanks for coming, Avery."

He nodded. "How are—you holding up?"

She shrugged. "Okay, I guess. I miss him. I miss the sound of his respirator. I—"

"Sean?" a woman interrupted, passing behind her. "We'll see you at the house. All right, dear?"

She glanced over her shoulder and nodded. "You bet, Lisa. Thanks." Sean waited until her friend moved on; then she turned to Avery again. "How's your wife? How's Joanne?"

"She's doing much better. In fact, I'm on my way to see her now."

"That's nice," was all Sean could think to say. "Um, since you quit the movie, I guess I won't be seeing you for a while." She took another step toward him. "Avery, I don't mean to pry. But if Joanne's showing signs of improvement, and they're shooting most of the picture around here, why did you quit? All these actors are fighting for that part now. Why would you give that up?"

He glanced down at the ground and sighed. "You know why."

"Because of me?"

"We'd be working together—sometimes very closely. I couldn't handle that, Sean. You know how I feel about you. But I still love my wife too. I can't leave her—no more than you could have left Dan while he was sick. I wouldn't like myself very much if I did that. I don't think you'd like me very much either."

Sean let out a tiny, grateful laugh. She took hold of his hand. "Thank you, Avery Cooper."

He shook her hand and smiled. "Take care, Sean."

She forced herself to turn away from him. Walking toward her car, Sean imagined him tonight in that place—at his wife's bedside.

From a couple of weeks ago, when she'd been so sick and feverish in the intensive care unit, she remembered Avery in the room with her, a constant, comforting presence. He would be there for his wife tonight—and for as long as she needed him.

Glancing over her shoulder, Sean saw him walking alone down a grassy slope toward his car. He was still hobbling a bit.

Sean figured it was all right to cry. She wouldn't have to explain her tears to anyone right now.

She turned and spotted Dayle, waiting for her. Dayle pulled a Kleenex from her purse and offered it to her. Sean blew her nose with the tissue. "Thanks," she muttered, her voice a little raspy. "Aren't you going to be late for your publicity thing?"

"The hell with it," Dayle said. "I think you need me around today. And that's more important than some lousy magazine cover story."

Sean wiped the tears from her eyes. She hadn't expected Dayle to come to her rescue. Yet nobody else really understood what she was dealing with today—except for Dayle. At a time when she felt all alone with her pain, she had Dayle Sutton coming through for her. "You're giving up a shot at some major publicity?" Sean said. "That doesn't sound like a movie star to me. Sounds more like a true friend."

"I hope that's what I am," Dayle said. She took her hand and squeezed it. "Your kids are going back with your in-laws, right?"

Sean nodded. "I thought I'd want to go back alone, but—not anymore."

"Well, then I'll send my driver home, and ride with you." Dayle glanced down toward where the cars were parked. She nudged Sean. "Only first we have to make it down this damn hill in our high heels."

Sean smiled and put her arm around her friend's waist. "We'll make it, Dayle," she said. "We'll just lean on each other."

BOOK YOUR PLACE ON OUR WEBSITE AND MAKE THE READING CONNECTION!

We've created a customized website just for our very special readers, where you can get the inside scoop on everything that's going on with Zebra, Pinnacle and Kensington books.

When you come online, you'll have the exciting opportunity to:

- View covers of upcoming books
- Read sample chapters
- Learn about our future publishing schedule (listed by publication month *and author*)
- Find out when your favorite authors will be visiting a city near you
- Search for and order backlist books from our online catalog
- Check out author bios and background information
- Send e-mail to your favorite authors
- Meet the Kensington staff online
- Join us in weekly chats with authors, readers and other guests
- Get writing guidelines
- AND MUCH MORE!

**Visit our website at
http://www.pinnaclebooks.com**

A World of Eerie Suspense
Awaits in Novels by Noel Hynd

"Book 'em!"
Legal Thrillers from Kensington